Anonymous

The Paris Law Courts

sketches of men and manners

Anonymous

The Paris Law Courts
sketches of men and manners

ISBN/EAN: 9783337096373

Printed in Europe, USA, Canada, Australia, Japan

Cover: Foto ©Andreas Hilbeck / pixelio.de

More available books at **www.hansebooks.com**

THE
PARIS LAW COURTS

SKETCHES OF MEN AND MANNERS

TRANSLATED FROM THE FRENCH BY

GERALD P. MORIARTY, B.A.

Balliol College, Oxford

LONDON
SEELEY AND CO., LIMITED
ESSEX STREET, STRAND
1894

TRANSLATOR'S PREFACE

THE French work entitled *Le Palais de Justice de Paris* was written in collaboration by certain members of the " Association de la Presse Judiciaire," or Association of Journalists attached to the Paris Law Courts. Their object was to describe, for the general as opposed to the purely legal inquirer, the organisation and procedure of the Paris Law Courts, the history and customs of the Paris Bar, and the psychological aspect of that varied world whom interest or necessity attracts, day by day, to the Parisian Palace of Justice.

The greater part of the work is here translated. In place of the detailed account of the old French legal system and the archæology of the Palais de Justice with which the French work begins, I have given a short explanatory sketch of the whole French judicial system as it now is.

The differences between French and English law are so numerous and fundamental that it has been difficult to adopt a uniform rule in the translation of French technical terms. Where a French institution occurs to which England contains no parallel, it has been thought best to retain the original term. Occasionally, *e.g.* in certain special cases of procedure, a paraphrase has been given. Wherever possible, however, I have, at the risk of being styled a purist, rendered the French technical terms by English technical equivalents. My thanks are due to Mr. Joseph Turrell, M.A., B.C.L., Barrister-at-law, of the Inner Temple, and to Mr. Arthur Abrahams, Solicitor, of 8 Old Jewry, London, and 23 Rue Taitbout, Paris, for much valuable assistance in this, the hardest part of my task.

GERALD MORIARTY.

BALLIOL COLLEGE, OXFORD.
October, 1893.

CONTENTS

CONTENTS

THE PARIS LAW COURTS

INTRODUCTORY—THE FRENCH JUDICIAL SYSTEM

THE French judicial system is in many respects entirely different from the English.

The English law courts can trace their descent, without a break from the Curia Regis of Henry the Second ; those of France date only from the legislation of the Constituent Assembly in 1791. English judicial reformers have never done more than occasionally modify existing institutions to meet the needs of a growing community ; the French revolutionary reformers completely swept away a system built up by centuries of custom and tradition, in favour of one based solely on reason and convenience. The English judicial system exhibits an agglomeration of antiquity and newness in the development of which legal fiction, equity, and legislation have all played their part; the French system, springing as a whole from one single enactment, is uniform, harmonious, and exact. One of the marked features of English polity is the separation between the law courts and the executive government ; in France, no civil or criminal action can take place save under the direct supervision of a state official. In England, high judicial office is only given to barristers of long standing and approved success ; and removal from an inferior to a higher grade is infrequent. In France, an advocate while merely a probationer is appointed to an inferior judicial office, and gradually rises to the higher courts by successive promotions. In England, cases to which a government official is a party are tried in the ordinary courts and by the ordinary rules; in France, these actions are tried in special administrative courts and by special administrative rules.

The French Government maintains a constant and regular supervision over the administration of justice by means of the *ministère public*. This is a state department, members of which sit in every court throughout France "to represent there the cause of public order and the interests of society in general."[1] Members of the *ministère public* who sit in the courts of first instance are known as *procureurs*. In the courts of appeal they are styled *procureurs-généraux*. They have deputies (*substituts*); certain agents of the *procureurs-généraux* being, however, styled *avocats-généraux*. Collectively, the members of the *ministère public* are also known as the *magistrature debout* in distinction to the ordinary judges, or *magistrature assise*. In criminal actions the members of the *ministère public* act as public prosecutors. In civil cases they either side with the plaintiff or defendant, as they think fit, being then known as *partie principale;* or they merely make a general comment on the matters before the court, in which case they appear as *partie jointe*. The body of public advocates attached to any one court is known as the *parquet*. The *procureurs-généraux*, of whom there is one attached to every high court in France, have a right of supervision over their several *parquets;* but the whole *ministère public* is strictly subordinate to the minister of justice. He is entitled to give its members instructions on every point connected with their duties. They are appointed and can be dismissed at will by the chief of the State, who, however, always acts on the advice of the minister of justice in this particular.[2]

---

[1] See *Dictionnaire d'Administration;* article "*Ministère public.*"

[2] It is impossible to find good English equivalents for the French terms *procureur-général* and *procureur*. "Public advocate" expresses their duties generally; "public prosecutor" their duty on the criminal side. Both these terms have accordingly been used in the ensuing translation. Occasionally, however, as, for instance, when the *procureur-général* appears in a ceremonial character, I have thought it best to use the French word. *Procureur-général* cannot be translated "attorney-general," owing to the difference in the special meaning attached to each word in France and England. The *procureur-général* is a permanent official; he is only one of a group of equals; he acts at the suggestion of the Government, which when it needs legal advice applies to the Council of State. The "attorney-general" in England changes with the Ministry; stands alone; and is the chief legal adviser of the Crown. There is, however, a faint resemblance between the *ministère public* and the department presided over by the solicitor to the Treasury.

The ordinary judicial system of France may be summarised as follows :—

I. *Tribunaux de paix.*—In each canton[1] is a *tribunal de paix* (magistrate's court), presided over by a *juge de paix* (justice of the peace, or, more properly, stipendiary magistrate). He is assisted by a *greffier* (registrar or magistrate's clerk) ; and he has two *suppléants* (deputies) to take his place in case of absence or indisposition. His jurisdiction extends to all cases of *contravention* (petty offences) specified by the penal code. He can impose, without appeal, a fine of fifteen francs or a sentence of imprisonment for five days. Fine or imprisonment beyond these amounts can be appealed against to the *tribunal correctionnel* (criminal court of first instance) of the arrondissement. In criminal cases the State is represented in the magistrate's court by a commissary of police, by the mayor of the commune in which the court is located, or by a *suppléant* of the magistrate himself.

In civil matters the *juge de paix* has summary jurisdiction in all actions in which the property in dispute, or sum claimed, does not exceed 100 francs in value. He can also judge actions up to 200 francs, but an appeal here lies to the *tribunal civil* (civil court of first instance) of the arrondissement. He is also entitled to try certain special actions up to 1500 francs value, as, *e.g.* disputes between hotel-keepers and their guests ; and certain special actions for indefinite amounts, as, *e.g.* claims for damage to standing crops or underwood laid by farmers resident in his locality. In both of these cases appeal lies to the *tribunal civil.* His chief civil duty however, is that of an arbitrator. He is bound, by law, to try and effect, in a friendly way and without charging any fee, a reconciliation between all persons wishing to go to law. In theory, no plaintiff in a civil suit can issue a writ till he puts in a statement to the effect that the *juge de paix* has failed to reconcile him to the defendant. In practice, however, exemption from this attempt at conciliation (*préliminaire de conciliation*) can invariably be obtained by application to the president of the *tribunal civil.* There are also certain special cases in which the *préliminaire de conciliation* may be dispensed with of right, *e.g.* cases to which the State or a municipality is a party ; cases in which the rights of infants are concerned ; and cases in which there is more than one defendant.[2]

---

[1] France is divided into eighty-seven departments, 362 arrondissements, and about 36,000 communes. The latter correspond to the English township.

[2] The *juges de paix* are called on to arbitrate in about two and a quarter million

The *ministère public* is not represented in the magistrate's court in civil cases.

II. *Tribunaux de première instance.*—In every arrondissement sits a court of first instance.[1] It is usually known simply as *le tribunal;* it takes both criminal actions, when it is called *tribunal correctionnel* (translated in the text " correctional court "), and civil actions, under the name of *tribunal civil* (civil court of first instance.) The *tribunaux* vary in size. That of Paris contains no less than seventy-four judges and fifteen *suppléants*. Every tribunal is divided into different chambers, among which the work is distributed, the Paris tribunal, for instance, comprising eleven chambers. The *ministère public* is represented in all the courts of first instance, both civil and criminal, by a *procureur* and his *substituts.*

The correctional court hears appeals from the magistrates' courts, its judgment in these cases being final. It also tries, but in first instance only, all offences specified as *délits* (misdemeanours) by the penal code. Appeal in these cases lies to the Court of Appeal.

Certain members of the correctional court are deputed to act as *juges d'instruction* (examining magistrates). The latter are empowered to examine all accused persons. If they think there is no ground for the charge they issue an *ordonnance de non lieu*, and the accused is set at liberty. If they consider it their duty to commit the accused, they give directions for his trial before a magistrate if the offence amount only to a *contravention*, and before a correctional court if the offence amount to a *délit*. If the accused is charged on good grounds with *crime* (felony) the examining magistrate passes him on to a *chambre des mises en accusations* (chamber of indictments), which formally draws up the charge and sends the accused before the court of assize. It should be noted that an examining magistrate questions the accused personally and in private. He can remand him into solitary confinement for an indefinite number of times, no limit being placed on the time allotted to examination. The system thus readily lends itself to abuse ; and there are said to be cases of prisoners wrong-

civil cases every year. On an average, one case out of every three is satisfactorily settled in this way.

[1] But there is only one court of first instance for the department of the Seine. It sits at Paris. The arrondissement of Puget-Theniers (Alpes-Maritimes) is grouped with that of Nice for judicial purposes.

fully confessing to a charge in order to put an end to the worrying torture of private examination.

The civil court of first instance hears appeals from the magistrate's court. It has a summary jurisdiction in all claims up to 1500 francs value. It can also try any actions beyond this amount; but, in the latter case, an appeal lies to the court of appeal.

III. Cours d'appel.—For purposes of appeal jurisdiction, France is divided into twenty-six districts, in each of which sits a *cour d'appel* (court of appeal) with authority over several departments.[1]

The courts of appeal, like the courts of first instance, vary in size; that of Paris contains seventy-two judges. In the provinces the number of judges varies from twenty to thirty-one. Every court of appeal is divided into three chambers. Its judges are divided into a first president of the whole court, a president for each chamber, and a number of puisne judges, known as "counsellors of appeal." The three chambers are:

1. *La chambre civile* (the civil chamber), which hears appeals from the civil courts of first instance on questions of fact; and, rather singularly, acts as a criminal court in case of misdemeanours committed by great officials, judges and knight commanders of the Legion of Honour. Seven judges form a quorum.

2. *La chambre des appels correctionnels* (chamber of criminal appeals), which hears appeals from the correctional courts. The appeal can be made either by a convicted prisoner, or by the public prosecutor on the ground that the defendant was wrongfully acquitted or received too slight a sentence. The latter is called an appeal *a minimâ*. The court of appeal has power to increase sentences of the correctional court. Five judges form a quorum.

3. *La chambre des mises en accusations* (chamber of indictments), entrusted with the duty of examining into charges of felony and with power to order commitment or discharge.

A judge of the court of appeal also presides over the *jurés d'expropriation* (juries of ten appointed to assess compensation in case where property is taken for public purposes). This is the only instance of a jury in civil cases.

---

[1] Except the court of appeal at Bastia, whose authority is confined to the department of Corsica.

The *ministère public* is represented in the appeal courts by a *procureur-général*, *avocats-généraux*, and the usual *substituts*.

IV. Cours d'assises.—The French assize courts resemble the English in the fact that their members go on circuit. They are held in the chief town of each department every three months, and have cognizance of offences specified as crimes by the penal code.

An assize court consists of three judges taken either from the court of appeal in whose district the department lies ; or, in some cases, of one member of the court of appeal and two members of the neighbouring correctional court. The charge is laid by the chamber of indictments and the prosecution conducted by a *procureur-général* or one of his *substituts*. The question of guilt or innocence is left to the decision of a jury of twelve. The verdict of the majority is always taken. Equal division is regarded as tantamount to an acquittal.

V. La cour de cassation.—The court of cassation, which sits at Paris, is the supreme court of appeal for all France. Application may be made to it from any decision of any court. An appeal to the court of cassation, which is specially called, not *appel*, but *pourvoi en cassation*, can only be made on a point of law, *e.g.* an error in an indictment, or a misinterpretation of an article of the code, or an excess of powers committed by a court. The court of cassation is thus a school of jurisprudence. Arguments brought before it must show a minute knowledge of the letter of the law ; and it has a special bar, the members of which do not plead in the other courts. The court of cassation also exercises a disciplinary power over the whole French judiciary. Thus it is always open to receive complaints of corruption or denial of justice against any judge or magistrate. In these cases the whole court of cassation sits *en audience solennelle*, the minister of justice acting as its president. The delinquent judge is allowed counsel. The court of cassation consists of a first president, three presidents of chambers, and forty-five puisne judges, styled counsellors. It is divided into three chambers :—

1. *La chambre des requêtes* (chamber of requests), which merely examines civil appeals to see if they are justifiable.

2. *La chambre civile* (the civil chamber), which finally hears the civil appeals remitted to it by the above.

3. *La chambre correctionnelle* (the criminal chamber), which hears criminal appeals direct.

After careful examination of the pleas put forward by the appellant, the court of cassation either declares that no error of law having been committed the judgment must be upheld, or, in the opposite case, quashes the judgment, and orders a new trial.

The above courts comprise the *ordinary jurisdiction*, with which the ensuing work is mainly concerned. There are, however, two other systems of jurisdiction which, as they are also referred to later on, may be described very briefly. They are :—

VI. La juridiction commerciale, consisting of (*a*) the *conseils de prudhommes* (arbitration boards) established in the chief industrial centres, to decide disputes between workmen and employers ; and (*b*) the *tribunaux de commerce* (commercial courts), established in the chief commercial centres for the settlement of commercial disagreements. Where no arbitration boards or commercial courts exist, industrial and commercial disputes come before the ordinary civil courts. And,

VII. La juridiction administrative, to judge all charges brought against servants of the State in their official capacity. It comprises (*a*) the *conseil de préfecture*, which sits in every department as an administrative court of first instance ; (*b*) the *cour des comptes*, established to check the management and disbursal of the revenue ; and (*c*) the *conseil d'état* (council of state), which hears appeals from both these courts, but is chiefly occupied in giving legal assistance to the executive government. The two latter courts sit at Paris. The administrative courts act under a special procedure, they have a strong official bias, and actions laid by private individuals against State officials rarely succeed. Questions occasionally arising as to whether a case comes under the ordinary or administrative jurisdiction are decided by a special court known as the *tribunal des conflits* (court for questions of conflicting jurisdiction).

All the French judges are appointed by the chief of the State. They are all irremovable except for misconduct, saving the *juges de paix*, who are dismissable at will.

French judicial salaries are very low when judged by the English standard. The president of the court of cassation, the head of the French judiciary, receives 30,000 francs (£1200 a year), the remuneration of other members of the court varying according to their rank from 25,000 francs (£1000) to 18,000 francs (£720). The first president of the court of appeal at Paris receives 25,000 francs a year. The salaries of other members of that court range from 13,750 francs (£550) to 11,000 francs (£440). The salaries of appeal judges in the provinces range from 20,000 francs (£800) to 5000 francs (£200). The president of the Paris court of first instance receives 20,000 francs (£800) a year. The vice-presidents of the eleven chambers 10,000 francs (£400) a year each. In the provinces, judges of first instance receive from 10,000 francs (£400) to 2,400 francs (£96) a year. *Juges de paix* in Paris receive 8000 francs (£320). In the provinces their maximum salary is 5000 francs (£200), and the minimum 1800 francs (£72) a year. Members of the *ministère public* are paid salaries proportioned to those received by the judges in whose courts they appear.

The following work deals with the law courts which have their home in the Palace of Justice in Paris. Of these, the court of cassation alone has a sovereign authority over the whole of France.[1] The others have a purely local jurisdiction, and in organisation and procedure are identical with any of the other corresponding local courts. The Palace of Justice, if we count with it the Prefecture of Police and the Tribunal of Commerce, occupies about half of the islet in the river Seine known as the *cité*. The *cité* is the most ancient part of Paris. The Palais de Justice itself was originally a residence of the kings of France. It so remained till 1431, when it was made over to the chief French law court, then known as the " Parliament of Paris," by Charles VI. Like most public buildings in Paris, the Palace of Justice has suffered greatly from the effects of political revolution ; especially during the Communist movement of 1871, when a great portion of it was burnt down. Little of the ancient palace thus remains, except the incomparable Sainte-Chapelle, which has stood through the vicissitudes of six centuries of political turmoil, as a monument to the saintly genius of Louis IX. But owing to the care and liberality of the French government, the modern Palace of Justice, an irregular but stately pile of buildings, bounded on two of its sides by the Seine, and on the other two by the Place Dauphine and the Boulevard du Palais, is well worthy of its duties.

---

[1] The three other sovereign courts, the *conseil d'état*, the *cour des comptes*, and the *tribunal des conflits* sit in the Palais Royal.

The principal entrance is from the Boulevard du Palais, by the Cour de Mai. A grand flight of steps leads to the Galerie Marchande; on the right of which is the celebrated Salle des Pas-Perdus, the great meeting place for all whose business brings them to the Paris law courts. From here the way to the different courts lies open ; the reader will find their appearance, their inhabitants, and their every-day life fully described to him in the ensuing pages.[1]

---

[1] Since the above was written, certain laws have been in process of enactment with the object of effecting a reduction in the number both of the courts and the staff of judges.

CHAPTER II

A MODERN LAW-SUIT

" Justice is merely the observance of forms."

A LEARNED judge placed this aphorism at the head of one of his works. Did he intend to pass a criticism on justice, or a panegyric on procedure? Those who knew him will incline to the latter hypothesis. In either case what this author said was true. It is not enough for a man to know his rights; he must know the way to assert them. This the code of procedure teaches, but in a manner so subtle that only officers of the revenue and men of law can thread the maze. Far be it from us, therefore, to attempt here a detailed explanation of the mystery. Space would fail us, even if the reader's patience did not. A modern brief still bears too close a resemblance to the lawyer's bag spoken of by Rabelais, which was swelled every day by a new document, and took to itself beak, paunch, legs, arms, and talons, while, in the meantime, the poor suitor's purse grew gradually leaner.[1]

[1] See Rabelais: *Pantagruel*, Book iii., c. 42. Judge Bridlegoose speaks as follows: " A suit in law at its first birth seemeth to me shapeless and imperfect. As a bear, at its birth, hath neither feet nor hands, skin, hair nor head : it is merely a rude and shapeless lump of flesh. The dam, by much licking, puts its limbs into proper shape ; *ut not. Doct. ad l. Aquil, l. 2, in fin.* Just so do I see suits of law at their first bringing forth, to be without shape and without limbs. They have nothing but a piece or two ; they are ugly creatures. But when they are piled up, packed, and put in bags, we may term them duly provided with limbs and shape. In such way lawyers. . . . by sucking very much, and continually, the purses of the pleading parties, engender to their law-suits head, feet, claws beak, teeth, hands, veins, arteries, nerves, muscles, humours."

But let us take an example of an actual law-suit, which will give the reader some idea of the thing known as *procedure*.

Pierre, at the first breath of spring, had rented a country house not far from the banks of the Seine. He takes possession ; and lo and behold, the summer heat makes the building uninhabitable, It had been flooded during the winter, and dried and repaired in haste. The walls had been soaked with water, which now began to ooze through all the joints ; spoiling the curtains, covering the wood-work with mould, and filtering through the ceilings.

Our friend's one idea was to be quit of his bargain. The landlord, having got a substantial tenant for three years, swore at floods, architects, and mankind in general ; and would not hear a word. There was nothing for it but to go to law.

Pierre put the matter into the hands of his friend, Maître Renard. "We shall put the facts in evidence," said the solicitor, "and you must tell your architect to assist the officer of the court in framing his summons. Then we will make application to the judge in chambers." This application in chambers is a summary process, which consists in asking the president of the court to direct urgent measures to be taken without prejudice to any rights or proceedings.

A summons then is issued against the landlord. The latter, in his turn, hurries to his solicitor, Maître Leveau. Both parties attend in the judge's chambers. Maître Renard puts in his evidence. Maître Leveau maintains that if the house is damp, it is because the tenant has a horror of sunlight, and keeps the shutters closed. To settle this dispute, the judge makes an order appointing [1] a competent surveyor to inspect the premises.

Up to now things have gone on swimmingly. But the surveyor is an important person, with heaps of clients and heaps of commissions from the courts, and he takes everything in its regular turn. Autumn comes, and matters have not moved an inch. Pierre has had to leave the house, which was melting away ; but he has duly to pay his landlord's rent, his solicitor's charges, and the surveyor's fees. At last the surveyor finds his way to the place and prescribes extensive repairs, which cannot be executed till the spring. The landlord sees himself ruined already, and yet is only half in the wrong.

Already the expenses incurred on one side and the other are

---

[1] *Nommé par ordonnance un expert.*

so heavy that an amicable settlement has become impossible. The
surveyor sends in his report, bears testimony to the landlord's good
faith, and allows that the Seine made too long a stay in his house.
The law-suit proper is only just going to begin.

The code of procedure prescribes an *attempt at reconciliation*[1]
before a justice of the peace. But at Paris a petition is presented
to the president praying that a writ be issued at once, on the

AN OFFICIAL SURVEY.

ground of urgency ; the petition is always allowed, or, it would be
better to say, granted as a matter of course. This practice is
peculiar to Paris, and does not work badly.

The landlord then is served with a writ claiming the annulment
of the lease and damages. He must, in accordance with the writ,
appear within three clear days. But his lawyer tells him what

---

[1] *Préliminaire de conciliation.*

this means. He must be represented by a solicitor, whose services cannot be dispensed with. Maître Leveau notifies his friend that he is retained for the defence.

From this day to the service of the judgment [1] all papers in the action will be exchanged between the two solicitors ; in the shape, be it understood, of documents stamped and registered, and through the agency of an officer of the court. Maître Renard, solicitor of our friend Pierre, then deposits at the office of the court a sheet of paper on which the claims mentioned in the writ are word for word repeated. This document is called the *placet ;* it will be taken some day from the pigeon-holes of the office to lie for a while on the bar of the court ; it will come under the judge's eye when the case is argued, and will finally end its days amidst the dust of the archives. But it has not reached this stage yet.

Mark what follows. The registrar has entered the case on the general cause list of the tribunal. The landlord's solicitor Leveau, now puts in a special plea requiring discovery of documents.[2] No answer is given ; the solicitor does not press the point, and, at the end of three or four weeks, he pleads to the merits of the case [3] denying liability.

These pleadings could be comprised in two lines, but they will have to be engrossed on a number of folios (sheets of paper written on both sides) proportional to the importance of the suit. A law book will furnish the subject-matter ; but the clerk might quite safely introduce newspaper articles or comic literature. Nobody reads this trash, the sole purpose of which is to increase the income of the court officials. The abuse is provided for and legalised in the authorised scale of charges. In summary affairs, that is those in which no appeal is allowed, there are no engrossed pleadings.

The landlord's statement of defence has now been delivered. His solicitor has explained to him that it is purposely meaningless. Later on, when the counsel have shown their briefs to each other, both parties will proceed with a thorough knowledge of the matter,

From this time forward issue is joined. If the defendant had not instructed a solicitor to appear for him after receiving the writ of summons, there would have been judgment for default (of

---

[1] *Signification du jugement.*

[2] *Prend des conclusions exceptionnelles, tendant à la communication des pièces.*

[3] *Prend des conclusions au fond.*

appearance) against the party.[1] The court would have given the case in Pierre's favour, reserving, however, to the landlord the right of being heard after service of the judgment, even after execution. If the defendant had instructed a solicitor to appear for him, but had not formally pleaded to the merits of the case, there would have been judgment for default (of pleading) against the solicitor;[2] and the claim to be heard after service of the judgment would have had to be made within eight days' time.

The cause has been assigned to the sixth chamber of the civil tribunal, and entered in the particular list of that chamber. It is an urgent affair: for Pierre, who goes on paying his rent ; for the landlord, whose house, repaired under the direction of the official surveyor, remains shut up. But this is not the only urgent cause on the list ; the sixth chamber has heavy arrears ; and the president, beset by applications from solicitors, counsel, suitors, and the friends of suitors, entrenches himself behind the strictest rules of order. Thanks to the united efforts of the opposing parties, the suit at last comes up for trial at the end of thirteen months.

"At last," says Pierre, " I am going to have my case tried." On which his solicitor, Maître Renard, remarks: " I take the needful steps ; some one else argues the case. I have sent your brief to counsel." Pierre begins to have doubts about the famous principle of the division of labour : the officer of the court, the architect, the solicitor, the advocate. What a number of wheels ! and all have to be greased !

Our suitor makes a virtue of resignation. He sees his counsel, explains the matter, pays with the best grace he can command the customary fee, and keeps up his spirits. For the case will be taken on an appointed day of the week, though sixty others which were ripe for hearing before it have to be tried first. Happily the two parties are equally anxious to get it over, and their counsel are eager for the fray.

They communicate their documents to each other. This is a practice little known and still less appreciated by the world at large. Even upright men would rather like to confound their opponents by not unmasking their batteries till the hearing. The less scrupulous would be glad to profit by the uncertainty which the previous examination of documents renders impossible. The bar is very punctilious on this point ; and thus it comes about

---

[1] *Défaut contre partie*   [2] *Défaut contre avoué.*

that there is light and comparative security in law-suits. After exchange of documents and the final close of the pleadings, the proceedings are completed, and leave is obtained from the president to have the case marked ready for trial. During the last three months, every time the list of cases was called on Thursday this case has been called from week to week. It will continue to be called, but henceforth as one of a privileged class. At last the counsel get their chance. The court gives judgment ; and Pierre wins his case.

It is true that the lease has nearly expired, and Pierre has reckoned without his host. The landlord, who has already been compelled to repair his house under the most onerous conditions, is horror-struck at the united cost of the proceeding in chambers, the survey, and the action, which last also includes surveyor's fees. Every judgment in an action for unliquidated damages or for an amount exceeding 1500 francs, is subject to appeal. Pierre's rent was 1800 francs a year, and the term of the lease which he claimed to have cancelled was three years. The landlord therefore determines to appeal.

Pierre then has to pay the full three years' rent of a house in which he has lived for two months; for the appeal suspends the operation of the judgment. He believes, however, that he will not have to employ fresh persons to represent him. Maître Renard undeceives him : " I only practise in the Court of First Instance, so I will pass you on to my friend, Maître Prudent, who is a solicitor of the Court of Appeal." Needless to say that Maître Prudent's services, like those of Maître Renard, cannot be dispensed with, and are not more gratuitous. Pierre is something of a logician, and wonders why his solicitor, like his advocate, should not be able to follow him through all the stages of jurisdiction. He has to buy a new experience.

His visit to Maître Prudent cheers him up. He thought that the case would last another two years and a half, as it had done before the lower court. "Set your mind at rest," answers Maître Prudent, "you will get judgment in nine months." Maître Prudent spoke the truth. Suits take so long in the courts of first instance that the suitor's courage and purse are often exhausted in the earliest stage of jurisdiction. Pierre, moreover, is charmed with the simplicity of the procedure. The appellant sets forth the grounds of his appeal in a formal statement. The respondent, relying on the reasons given by the first judges, contents himself with asking that the decree of the court below may be affirmed.

After nine months' waiting, the appeal comes up for hearing. A month later it was decided, and this time Pierre has lost his cause! The court held that when he took the house in question he knew that the Seine had inundated it. The injury caused by damp was not serious enough to render the house uninhabitable; and, besides, the landlord has executed all the repairs ordered by the official surveyor.

" I shall go to the Court of Cassation!" cries Pierre.

" Don't think of such a thing," remonstrates his advocate. "You may know all about the condition of the place, and the seriousness of the damage caused by damp ; but these are questions of *fact* which the Court of Cassation does not decide." "What does it do, then ? " " It begins by ascertaining the facts recognised as authentic in the judgment appealed from. Then it inquires if the *law* has been properly applied. Now, it is the correctness of the facts that you dispute, not the legal deductions drawn from them by the Court of Appeal."

Pierre would not give in, and he asked his advocate if he would appear for him in the Court of Cassation. "Nay, I cannot," answered the latter. "At the Court of Cassation there are special functionaries whom you must retain. They are called advocates like ourselves, but they perform the duties of solicitors as well."

Pierre was once more filled with admiration for the principle of the division of labour. He again explained his case, and he again paid a fee. The advocate at the Court of Cassation was of opinion that there was nothing in the case. But Pierre persisted ; and, eventually, it was discovered that there had been a failure to decide on a minor point of the claim. The advocate drew up first an application to this Supreme Court, and then a long statement of the grounds on which it was based. The whole was deposited at the office of the Chamber of Requests. This is an examining board by which an appeal must be sanctioned before it can be submitted to the Civil Chamber—the real Court of Cassation, properly speaking. Thus the opposite party is not represented in this first stage of the proceedings. But it would be absurd for fifteen counsellors to meet together simply to see whether a notice of appeal is serious ; and the Chamber of Requests really looks into the grounds of the petition so thoroughly that the unhappy appellant has to pass two courts, and to bear the cost of two trials.

Pierre did not enjoy this pleasure. Both the counsellor appointed to examine and report on his application and the advocate-general were of opinion that the court below had, by implication, decided the point which the appellant alleged had been passed over; and leave to appeal was refused in spite of the advocate's rhetoric.

The proceedings before the Chamber of Requests had lasted a year. They would have lasted eighteen months more before the Civil Chamber. And, if the judgment of the Paris Court of Appeal had been quashed, it would have been necessary to begin over again before that court, as the Court of Cassation restores everything to the state it was in before the irregular judgment was given.

When Pierre, who had some philosophy as well as something to lose, thought of this, he felt consoled. The case had lasted five years. It had cost about 2000 francs in the first instance (including 700 francs paid as fees to the surveyor), 1000 francs in the Court of Appeal, and the same amount before the Chamber of Requests. Yet we are only speaking of the taxed costs; counsel's fees, be it understood, do not come under this heading. All this has not gone to the lawyers. The public treasury has had the lion's share, more than half in fact, in the shape of fees for registration and stamps. The landlord has been not less thoroughly fleeced, for the surveyor had directed the repairs to be carried out with due respect to the rules of art.

Good people! if you will go to law, see that you have time, money, and resignation.

Time!

There is hardly a law-suit at Paris, even among those classed as summary proceedings, which does not last a year. For ordinary cases a much longer space of time must be allowed. To fix precisely the interval which separates the issue of the writ from the judgment, it would be necessary to take into account many factors; the nature of the suit, the court to which it is assigned (for justice is not equally halting in all), the diligence of the solicitors in bringing the case on for trial, the readiness of the counsel to argue it. . . . But I know of few which have not lasted for two or three years. In the first chamber of the tribunal, one must no longer count by years but by lustres.

Money!

Here again any exact calculation is out of the question Everything depends upon the nature of the suit and on the side issues which may arise out of the original claim. Generally speaking, we may say that the costs bear no relation to the importance of the matters in dispute, and that they are thus disproportionately heavy in actions of lesser importance. The registration fees payable on all documents of procedure are uniform. There is, however, an *ad valorem* duty on the amount recovered, the rate of which varies, according as the action is one for debt or damages. Of course, if the judgment is reversed on appeal, the registration office pays back nothing. This is a fundamental maxim of our fiscal legislation. Shall we give a few examples? It is reckoned that a summary proceeding costs from 100 to 200 francs. A divorce with judgment by default rarely runs to less than 500 francs. If the action is defended, the costs may be reckoned at 1000 or 1500 francs. If there are collateral questions as to alimony and custody of children, if commissions have to be sent to other tribunals to examine witnesses who live far from Paris, the figures may be easily doubled.

A suit for judicial separation, going by default (to take the most ordinary case), costs more than 500 francs, from the expense of having to advertise the judgment in different newspapers.

It is impossible to escape from an ordinary civil action for less than 300 francs, exclusive of the dues payable on the amount for which judgment is given. These dues are at the rate of $\frac{1}{2}$ per cent. in case of debts, and 2 per cent. in case of damages.

All this is neither moderate nor just. But the abuse becomes flagrant when the suitor is in poor circumstances. It is true that judicial assistance is liberally afforded to persons suing *in formâ pauperis*. This makes it possible for any man to go to law ; but it does not help him to bear the law's delay. Take the case of a workman who has been run over at a crossing by a clumsy driver. The wheels of the vehicle have passed over his body. He leaves the hospital a cripple. He obtains judicial assistance, and claims compensation from the company employing the man who caused the accident. His case will remain on the files of the court for twelve or fourteen months. It will not be decided in less than two years, and yet the plaintiff is a poor fellow who, more often than not, has a family to support. How will he be able to wait for the decision of the court?

One of two things must happen. Either he will compound on disastrous terms with the insurance company which is the real defendant, or he will throw up judicial assistance, and fall into the hands of some speculative agent who will make a private bargain

with him and sue in his name. Accident cases ought to be treated
as urgent, and taken on specially assigned days, without having to
wait their turn on the list. It is true that all accident cases could
not be decided immediately ; they would have to be taken in order
according to the date at which the writ was issued. But it would
be a matter of months instead of years.

As regards other cases, the crowded state of the cause list is no
sufficient explanation of the delay they undergo. If the courts opened
at the stated hours ; if the sittings were not indefinitely suspended ; if
leave to have a case deferred were not so readily granted; if, in one
word, judges and advocates did their duty, urgent cases would
come on in a reasonable time. The only person who profits by
this general system of indifference is the pettifogging agent.
Access to his office is so easy, that the advances he demands seem
unimportant or prudent ; the client does not inquire whether this
man who styles himself " ex-notary," " ex-solicitor," "jurisconsult,"
or " advocate," is not an ignoramus or a rascal.

To cut down the expense of litigation, to quicken the progress
of law-suits, to simplify procedure, and in consequence to substitute
for monopoly some guarantees of learning and uprightness, this is
an ideal which the necessities of the public revenue and respect for
vested interests place hopelessly beyond our reach. The evils
from which French justice suffers are indeed more keenly felt at
Paris than anywhere else. It would be no small reform to establish
a more vigilant and rigorous supervision over all persons and
matters in the law courts, and to make costs bear some proportion
to the interests involved.

CHAPTER III

LIFE AT THE COURTS

THE world of the law courts has not merely a building to itself. The life with which it inspires its home has also an individuality ; it is original in both senses of the word. A calm life, in which the excitement of Parisian existence shows itself only in a faint reflection. Just as moats filled with water used to guard the feudal castle against hostile attacks, so the Seine, in surrounding the Palace of Justice with its two arms, seems to protect it from the outside world.

It is not any personal peculiarity that marks off the *justiciards*, as they used to be called, from their fellow-men. In Paris, when they have put off their lawyer's caps, plain or ornamented, advocates and solicitors, counsellors and judges, lose themselves in the crowd with which they mingle. Most of them are men of the time; they affect current theories ; they share in prevailing prejudices, and they follow the fashion of the day. They go to the Variétés, to the Théâtre-Libre, or to the Chat-Noir, neither more nor less than ordinary mortals who have never donned the lawyer's garb. But the moment they cross the gate opening off the boulevard, or mount the steps which lead from the Place Dauphine, they undergo a change which renders them morally unrecognisable. The savant,

CRYPT OF THE SAINTE-CHAPELLE.

the stock-broker, the actor, carry with them everywhere the signs that betoken their connection with science, finance, or the theatre. The lawyer is only a lawyer at the law courts. We are going to study him on the spot, under all his aspects, in all his varieties; magistrate, advocate, solicitor, usher, registrar; while moving round all we shall see the throng of litigants. But it will not be enough to lead our readers through the corridors and halls of the Palace of Justice like common visitors; we shall penetrate farther into the world there. For we ourselves[1] form a humble part of that world, and know all its secrets; we have questioned members of the profession; we have lived their life; and we have pushed our way with them into the inner chambers, far from the public eye, which are reserved for them alone.

THE PALACE ASLEEP

From August to the end of October, the Palace of Justice takes its rest. Unlike the dormouse, it sleeps during the summer, and its courts only open when the leaves are falling. Up to that time silent and still, the vast building would seem dead, did not certain vacation sittings indicate that the life of the place, though suspended, is not quite extinct. During these three months nothing can be more mournful than the long empty corridors, all the more resounding for the silence around. The Salle des Pas-Perdus is a desert; the galleries, usually filled with the buzz of conversation, are silent; in the robing-rooms, five or six hats, at the most, occupy the shelves where during the rest of the year there is not an inch of vacant space; no civil actions are tried, no consultations take place. Sometimes, however, a rare frequenter of the place invades the solitude; and, as he passes along, echo repeats in a deep tone the clang of the doors as they close behind him. Through the lofty windows, the sun, striking the white flagstones, glares upon this judicial Sahara. The few ill-fated advocates who cross it walk with an air of irritation, gloom, and weariness; they think of their absent brethren whom bad fortune does not keep at Paris like themselves, of those who scour the fields or plunge in the sea-waves; and irate at being stifled within walls, raging, perspiring, sick at heart, they hurry towards the court where they are expected. Often a caravan

---

[1] The members of the *Association de la Presse judiciaire*, to whom this book is due.

of tourists, Baedeker in hand, starts up before one of them. " Look ! an advocate in his robes," says their guide, in some European language or other. " Really !" they cry. They repeat the explanation to one another, stare with curiosity at the poor representative of the Parisian bar, and then continue their stroll through the Palace. Then again, for an hour, everything is quiet. The robing-room attendants, on duty at their posts, though unoccupied and listless, knit as if their senses were dulled by the heavy silence. A general depression weighs upon them; they yawn with all the weariness produced by lying awake in a dormitory where every one else is asleep. And the same sadness, the same gloom, seizes on all those who come to the Palace of Justice in the long vacation ; for nothing is so deplorable as a place of meeting without the people for whom it is intended ; a theatre without spectators, a museum without visitors, and our Palace without its familiar crowd might serve as a symbol of melancholy.

We have said that in this huge sleeping body a remnant of activity is still manifest. Business is transacted in the Judges' Chambers ; there are sittings on flagrant offenders ; and the sessions of the Court of Assize are not interrupted. But even there every one feels that it is the long vacation. In the sweltering heat there is apathy on the bench, languor at the bar, indifference even in the dock. Proceedings on the criminal side are devoid of interest ; embezzlements by clerks, petty thefts, fraudulent bankruptcies, misdemeanours, indecent assaults—such is the uninteresting list of offences that come up for trial. Cases which might make a noise in the world have been adjourned, by tacit consent, to the next sessions, on the pretext of a petition to the Court of Cassation against an order for a new trial, or a reference to the examining magistrate for further information. What is the use of an argument well conducted, or a defence well managed in the presence of empty benches ? The accused can easily wait till the courts reopen. Besides to wait is for his benefit ; he is better off in a house of detention than he will be when confined to the central prison, which expects him, or on the convict ship, sailing for New Caledonia. Let him be patient then as advocates are patient whose cases have been deferred till after the vacation. People have not the heart to trouble themselves about him with the thermometer at thirty degrees centigrade.

THE BOULEVARD DU PALAIS.

THE AWAKENING

But here is autumn ; coming, like the king's son in the old fairy tale, to awaken the sleeping beauty of law, and the dormant Palace of Justice. For some days past faces, lost to view since the end of July, have been seen again. For some days past the life-blood has again begun to flow through the arteries of the reviving edifice. From all sides people are coming back, with cheerful faces and outstretched hands. For a whole week the rush of arrivals will go on increasing in volume ; and on every hand there will be cordial greetings and affectionate words spoken by men sincerely glad to see each other again. Rest has been pleasant, and the collar of work is galling, but at the moment of taking to it again, men feel a real pleasure at rejoining their comrades in past labours. At sight of them, the hours of toil they have spent together come back to memory ; the recollection brings a smile to the lips and effaces for a moment the unfriendly feelings and jealousies of the by-gone year.

But in this Temple of Formality work cannot be resumed without some preliminary ceremonies. A certain amount of pomp and speech-making is indispensable ; and, before settling down to their task, certain customary rites must be gone through, to wit, the Red Mass [1] and the Solemn Sitting.[2]

THE RED MASS

Saint-Esprit des lois ! descendez en nous !

Our lawyers are sceptics nowadays ; and they make us think of those peasants who, though unbelievers, would not for anything in the world cut their bread without first having made a rapid sign of the cross over the loaf with the end of the knife. Counsellors, judges, attorneys-general and their assistants, advocates, every one who bears a name known to the bench or the bar, attends the Red Mass at the opening of the legal year. Yet it may be taken for granted that it is not faith which brings together the greater part of these worshippers beneath the vaulted roof of the church of

---

[1] *La messe rouge.*   [2] *L'audience solennelle.*

Saint-Louis.   Still if religion is not the cherished object of their
affections, it is none the less the oldest of their prejudices.   The
majority go there just as people go to many a place in Paris,
partly to see, but really because it is a first representation, the
grand first representation of the judicial year.   And thus the Red
Mass is in no danger of being abolished.   And, putting philosophy
aside, we say so much the better, for it is an interesting spectacle
and most picturesque.   It removes the thoughts far away from the
world that rumbles outside the door, carries them back to far

THE RED MASS.   THE PROCESSION.

distant times, and revives, for an hour, something of the old
ceremonial of the courts, and the stately pageantry of days gone by.

The scene is superb : the wonderful Sainte-Chapelle, usually
so cold and dead, on this one day of the year comes back for a few
moments to life.

It is noon : the old glass of the windows, set in lace-like tracery
of stone, allows the mellow rays of the autumn sun to struggle
through, flecking with tints of violet, red, yellow, and blue the
slender columns, the pointed arches, and the gold-starred walls.

THE SAINTE-CHAPELLE.

The patches of colour on the walls might be taken for fantastic offerings, fastened up by a mischievous chorister. The nave is crowded with worshippers, half of them robed in red. It is an astonishing blaze of scarlet, tempered here and there by the white gleam of ermine. Red is the robe of the Cardinal-Archbishop of Paris as he stands by his golden chair in front of the illuminated high altar ; red are the gowns of the counsellors of the Supreme Court on the right ; red the members of the Court of Appeal on the left ; red the attorney-general who stands behind ; red the advocates-general, and red their deputies—all is one blaze of red.

The effect is gorgeous ; to complete it and give it a true air of antiquity, one is almost sorry not to see behind these magistrates in full dress, one of those appalling headsmen of old time, so grand and grim in their purple doublets, as we knew them in the pictures of our childish story books.

As if to make the colouring of this foreground stand out more boldly, the back of the chapel is packed with rows of magistrates all clad in black.

Judges of the Civil Tribunal and of the Tribunal of Commerce, the Procureur of the Republic, the members of the Council of the Order of Advocates, solicitors, ushers of the courts, and others ; lastly, perched in a little gallery, are a few privileged spectators of both sexes. The spectacle, as we see, is no ordinary one. But it is not the eyes alone that are gratified. The choir of Notre Dame lend their gracious aid to the celebration ; and sometimes it is hard to keep from applauding the superb voices which intone the *Veni Creator*, the *Domine Salvam*, &c., accompanied by harp and organ.

The mass ended, there begins a procession more curious still. With the strictest regard to precedence, the worshippers traverse the terrace, the walls of which are for this occasion hung with Gobelins tapestry, and pass slowly into the Galerie Mercière. Nothing can be more amusing for an observer than to study the attitudes and the countenances of the magistrates as they pass. It is like the judicial history of half a century unfolding itself in a panorama. At the head come the veterans of old time, phantoms of ancient judges, who make an effort to remain majestic beneath the weight of years. Their cheeks are hairless and pinched, their small eyes sunk deep in the orbits. A few white hairs straggle from beneath their cap, under which one can picture the polished white crown.

Their character, their worship of tradition and form, may be read in the stock which supports their necks ; rising high above the collar of the coat, and stiffening the rugged and wrinkled head. After them comes the next generation ; the figure is stout, gray whiskers fringe the pale cheeks, the lips are set, close-shaved, crafty, and have a look of weariness ; the cravat is less voluminous, the step firmer. With the judges of the Civil Tribunal appears the modern face ; the head erect, the eye bright ; the sceptical mouth wears a slight smile. They step out, thinking of the gallery as much as of the regularity of the procession ; they find that those in front of them take a long time to cover the ground, and, little by little, they show annoyance at having to move so slowly. Meanwhile, kept back by the municipal guards presenting arms, the onlookers form a hedge on either side and press forward to get a glimpse of the men in red as they pass.

THE SOLEMN SITTING

The worshippers at the Red Mass make their way straight to the first chamber of the Court of Appeal where the Solemn Sitting, which might also be called the Red Sitting, is about to be opened. The judges of the Court of Appeal and the functionaries of the public ministry appear there in the same costume as in the Sainte-Chapelle ; and, still in their scarlet robes, they leave the council chamber and place themselves on the benches ranged on either side of the pretorium. The judges take up their position on the right, the law officers on the left. The first president of the Court of Appeal takes his seat surrounded by his colleagues ; the benches allotted to advocates are filled by the members of the council of the order and by a few fair visitors who, on the pretext that they too wear the gown, have insinuated themselves before any one else into these reserved places. At the back, there is a standing crowd made up of the junior bar, the probationers and a few idlers.

" The Solemn Sitting is open," proclaims the first president of the Court of Appeal, after a moment's pause. " We call on the Procureur-Général." The Procureur-Général, who is seated first on the bench allotted to the law officers, rises and says, " With the permission of the first president, I will give way to the advocate-general, X or Y.

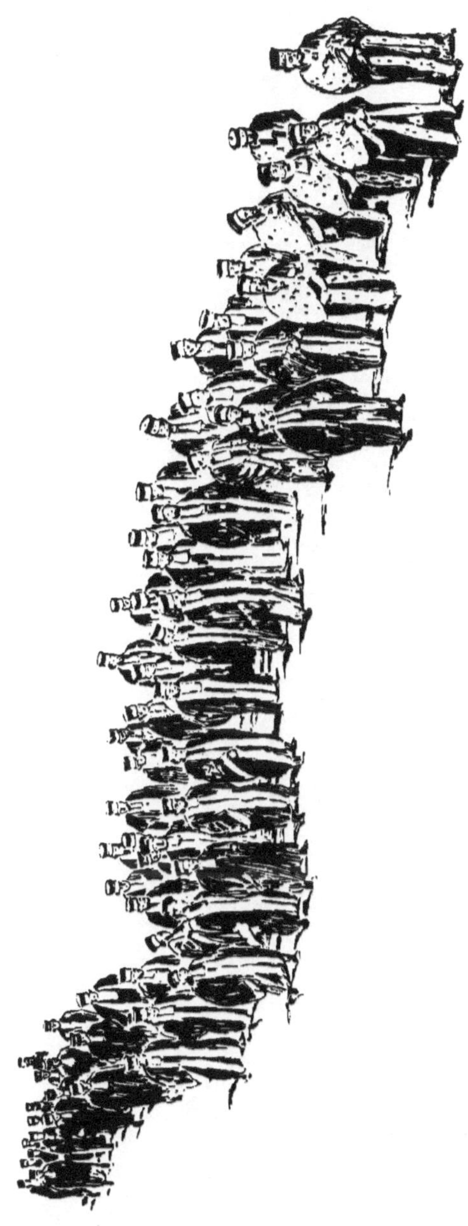

D

The first president inclines his head in token of approval, and Mr. Advocate-General X or Y, who is on the left of the Procureur-Général, rises with a sheaf of papers in his hand, while his superior, the Procureur-Général, resumes his seat. Then, in the midst of a rather cold, almost hostile silence, he begins reading a thesis on some point of law. The young and bold usually take for their subject some question which has been a little in dispute: the proof of paternity, divorce, the paternal authority, and the right of correction. Sometimes, even, they take up criminal subjects: transportation, the solitary system, tickets of leave. Two essayists have recently been rash enough to enter upon politics. The older hands, those who are really versed in legal traditions, choose, on the contrary, as dry a subject as possible—marine insurance, the law of mortgage, the contract of carriage for hire, and so on.

What is the connection between these questions and the reopening of the law courts? What is gained by turning the Court of Appeal into a students' debating society? These are inquiries which indiscreet persons may take upon themselves to make, and they are not easy to answer. On this point, however, we may venture to display a little—a very little—erudition, which will perhaps put investigators on the road to truth. The custom of reading an essay at the reopening of the courts would seem to have had its origin in a fancy which one day, in the sixteenth century, seized on Duménil, the king's advocate, to quote in full parliament the commentaries of the grammarian Asconius Pedanius on the orations of Cicero, in order to show the difference which existed, at Rome, between the advocate and the law officer of the government.

This dissertation, like those of the present time, had some congruity with the solemnity of the day, but in succeeding years the strange spectacle was witnessed of magistrates discussing in connection with the reopening of the parliaments all kinds of subjects, theological, metaphysical, and scientific. Omer Talon talked about time and sun-dials, colours, angels, fire, and the birth of Minerva; which later on led his son, Denis Talon, to apologize for not being able to examine into the question whether the stars are fastened to the sky, or are formed from vortices of particles like the dust of our earth, whether the sun is placed in the centre of the universe, whether one ought to admire the division into four elements, the substantive forms of Aristotle, Plato's doctrine of reminiscence, the conflict of bodily humours, and the circulation of the blood. And all this on the occasion of the reopening of the law courts!

In our own day, the opening address always ends badly. It concludes, that is to say, with an obituary notice of all the magistrates who have died during the past year. Most of them belong to the illustrious unknown; but for the time being they are raised to the rank of great men. Must it be said? This little general interment, coming after the consideration of some point of law, this funeral oration after a juridical harangue, would seem somewhat grotesque and almost comic to any one who was unprepared for it.

A few compliments to the advocates and solicitors of the court usually serve as a postscript to the discourse; and after this the president of the order and the senior advocates present renew their oaths. And if the Procureur-Général has no requisitions to make, the Solemn Sitting concludes. The judicial year has begun.

CHAPTER IV

BEFORE COURT OPENS:
THE ROBING ROOMS

As a general rule, it is only towards eleven o'clock that the Law Courts begin to show signs of life. One step at a time, a few magistrates who are due at morning sittings toil up one of the great staircases of the Palace. Advocates who have to argue at these sittings run up in hot haste, afraid of being late; but they stop to take breath when they catch sight of a magistrate, knowing that it is not worth while hurrying any longer; and the usual forms of polite greeting follow, accompanied by a ceremonious bow or brief shake of the hand. The magistrate reaches his private room; the advocate dons his gown, ties his bands round his neck, puts on his cap and disappears in his turn. Silence again, broken by arrivals that become gradually more frequent; clatter of banging doors; sound of last words of conversations in the street below which can be heard distinctly in the stone galleries. The arrivals now follow each other quite closely, so closely that acquaintances bound for the same destination are constantly meeting outside and enter in groups. The omnibuses, especially those on the line from the St. Lazare Railway Station to the Boulevard St. Michel, bring regular loads of advocates, magistrates, registrars, and ushers—enough to make up a whole courtful of themselves. For it is not every advocate or magistrate who can afford the luxury of stepping out gallantly from his own private carriage, or of coming in a cab and paying the fare without even turning his head, as a man does when in a hurry. Towards half-past twelve or one o'clock the rush diminishes ; the lawyers, who send their clerks on beforehand, arrive at their ease, some who are late come running ; while idlers saunter in to take a look round. The robing rooms, which for three-quarters of an hour have been thronged, grow empty.

The advocates have three robing rooms. In the gallery facing the Boulevard du Palais there is a partition—its upper half consisting of ground glass—which leaves a narrow passage between itself and the wall. This is the robing room known as the *Vestiaire*

THE AQUARIUM.

Bosc. There are three recesses in the wall so as to give more space ; and at the other end of the gallery, looking out on the Cour de Mai, stands a little glass-house—called by humourists the aquarium—which forms a useful addition to the robing room. Through two wickets in the partition can be seen a couple of damsels who take charge of the coats and hats ; and, standing in the recesses, one can behold with admiration through the robing room doors the great luminaries of the Bar in their shirt sleeves and without neckties, performing their toilet in front of the looking glass. Their different habits are well known. Maitre F—— always takes off his coat, even in winter, and puts on a jersey or a pair of lutestring sleeves; Maître W—— never takes off his necktie; Maître D—— always does and. . . . sometimes forgets to put it on again; Maître Lachaud used to bring a flannel waistcoat in his brief-bag; Maître V—— has a store of little cakes to fall back on in case of need; Maître M—— some sandwiches; Maître Lenté used to have a flask of ether and a crust of bread. Time may be well spent in studying the different modes in which the bands are put on.

THE FONTAINE ROBING ROOM.

Some fasten the strings behind; others tie them in front, holding meanwhile the tip of the bands between their teeth; others pass the bands under their collar button; others fasten the top part between the necktie and the shirt without taking any precaution to prevent the bands from working up to their very chin. As increasing numbers put by their hats, rows of bandboxes begin to line the rack of the partition.

On the staircase leading to the Court of Appeal is a private door, which leads under gloomy archways to two little rooms lined with cupboards. These form the dressing room taken charge of by the court porter. The interior has a homelike look; a woman and a young girl sit sewing at the window.

The dressing room known as the *Vestiaire Fontaine* is at the other entrance, on the side of the Place Dauphine, an official-looking, comfortable place with well-polished tables and a lavatory attached to it. Please note an ingenious little stick with which to take down, as in a tilt-yard, the band boxes on the shelves above. Those who use the *Vestiaire Fontaine* have also their little peculiarities. Maître La—— possesses a gown sewn in a particular way, with buttons on the collar and button-holes in his bands so as to fasten them on tightly; Maître Ma——, an ex-president of the Council of the Order, wears beneath his gown an old coat, the skirts of which have been cut off, so that it resembles the jacket of a waiter at a café. Maître Bé——, another ex-president, pushes his necktie round to the back of his neck and keeps it on underneath his gown, fastening it in place by a pin.

There is a wonderful variety in the legal costume. The official dress is always the same, a black gown with two buttons on the shoulder to which is attached the *épitoge* or hood. The latter is shaped like a macaroon, with two loose flaps falling the longer one in front, the shorter behind. For solemn sittings, great ceremonies, and the Court of Assize the flaps are trimmed with ermine. Besides these, there are the bands more or less plaited, and the flat cap like that of a parish priest. But there are differences in the material of the gown and in the style of wearing it; as a rule it is worn with the skirt somewhat raised; sometimes it sweeps the ground, thus giving the wearer the appearance of a tall black sugar-loaf. The caps also have their degrees of cost, and get out of shape in different ways according to the different handling of the wearer. The stylish kind is worn by Maître B.-D——, rigidly cylindrical, lined with white silk, on which are printed the owner's initials. Maître M.-J—— prefers one more elastic; Maître W.-R—— never wears one at all.

THE ORDER OF ADVOCATES

The advocates whom we have just seen in the hurry of arrival and the undress of preparation, whom we shall find again walking up and down the corridors, gossiping in the Pas-Perdus and addressing the courts, form a strong corporation, proud of its past and jealous of its privileges.

As one would expect, certain parts of the Palace are set apart for it, where the members work and talk scandal ; where they elect representatives of the Council, where the Council of Discipline sits, and the *bâtonnier*, the grand master of the institution, has his throne ; where the business affairs of the Order are administered ;

DUFAURE.
After the portrait by Mlle. Nelly Jacquemart.

and where penniless defendants come to seek counsel who will undertake their cases out of charity.

At Paris, advocates only have the right to plead for clients, but power is reserved to solicitors to apply to the court in any difficulties of procedure and on any incidental points which are capable of summary decision. In civil cases, a party interested cannot even appear in person with the assistance of his solicitor, unless he obtains leave from the tribunal. A person indicted before the Couit of Assize has the right of choosing as his advocate any of his relatives or friends, but only with the sanction of the presiding judge. The Order of Advocates, with its exclusive right of pleading, takes great pride in an origin which goes back to the year 518 of our era ; and it glories in a founder who was no less a personage than the uncle of that Emperor Justinian, whom M. Victorien Sardou has lately brought before us on the stage of the Porte-St.-Martin theatre.

The Bar has passed through many changes of fortune. At one time lost to sight, then reappearing, thanks to Charlemagne, and preserving its continuity under the varied names of *causidici*, of *avantparliers*, of *plaidoux*, and of *chevaliers de la loi*, finally in the reign of St. Louis forming itself into the " Order of Advocates," so as to be distinguished from the guilds of artisans established at that time. By turns losing and regaining some of their privileges, the advocates maintained their organisation till the date of the Constituent Assembly, which on the 2nd September, 1790, decreed that " the men of law heretofore called advocates, being no longer permitted to form an order or corporation, shall wear no particular costume in the exercise of their calling." The Revolution proved only an eclipse for the profession. The ex-advocates entered themselves on a list to which they admitted only men of their own choice, and thus formed a small voluntary society in the midst of the unorganised mass of people who were allowed to practise as " men of law." This list acquired a legal character, and the Order of Advocates was reconstituted by a law of the 22nd Ventôse, year XII. which also reorganised the Schools of Law.

Since that time the monopoly of the " Order of Advocates," has been untouched. There are, it is true, certain privileges which it has not recovered and doubtless never will recover : for example, the right once enjoyed by advocates of removing from their neighbourhood all artisans likely to annoy them during their work, the right of wearing a red robe or a silk sash and wearing gloves while pleading in court, and the right to the rank of nobles. But the law relieves them from the danger of outside competition ; while in return the Bar offers incontestable guarantees of good faith and provides all in distressed circumstances with unpaid defenders.

Successive ordinances and decrees have been passed to regulate the profession of advocate, the mode of keeping the Table of the

Order, the elections to the Council of Discipline and the choice of the President. The Table of the Order, for each Bar, is the list on which are written, in order of seniority, the names of those advocates who have passed the period of probation and been duly admitted either by the Council of Discipline or by the tribunal entrusted with this duty. The whole body of admitted advocates in any one place constitutes the Bar. For every Bar comprising more than twenty advocates (at Paris, for example, where there are 962 on the Table), the discipline and the interests of the Order in general are entrusted to a Council, called " Council of Discipline" or " Council of the Order." It is elected every year by the body of advocates on the Table, and presided over by a *bâtonnier* who is the head or, rather, the representative of the Order.

In days gone by the dean, that is the oldest advocate on the roll, was head of the Order. His chief duty was to ask the Parliament for a holiday for the " Lendit" and the " day of St. Nicholas," patron saint of advocates. As there was always the risk of having a dean broken down by weight of years, the custom arose of choosing, at the same election, another representative of the Order, known as the *bâtonnier*. He is thus styled because one of his duties is to carry, at all solemn processions, the staff of the banner of St. Nicholas, the patron saint of advocates. Under the old Monarchy the *bâtonnier* was chosen by the assembly of advocates. After the Revolution, he was nominated by the attorney-general. From 1822 to 1830, and from 1852 to 1870, his election was in the hands of the Council of the Order. During the years 1830 to 1852, and from the beginning of the third Republic, the *bâtonnier* has been chosen by the votes of the whole Bar.

The *bâtonnier* has to speak in the name of the Bar on solemn occasions such as funeral ceremonies ; undertakes the details of administrative work, appoints advocates for the defence of poor prisoners, listens to all complaints, gives advice to young advocates, settles disputes, sees that due respect is shown to his brethren at the Bar, and, whenever necessary, admonishes those who have committed some slight breach of political etiquette.

The Council of Discipline looks after the pecuniary interests of the Bar ; for the Order has a treasury of its own kept up by a compulsory subscription of thirty francs a year from each of its members ; the Council distributes help among advocates, or the families of old advocates, who are in distress ; and has power to impose fines when incurred, a paternal warning to be administered by the *bâtonnier* to the delinquent, a warning to be formally notified to the offender, a reprimand, suspension or erasure from the Table of Advocates. The Council of Discipline, lastly, admits candidates to the rank of probationers,[1] and revises the Table of Advocates every year.

To be entitled to plead in court, a man must have first obtained the rank of licentiate in law, and taken an oath before one of the Courts of Appeal. This only gives him the bare title of Advocate. He must, in addition, have his name inscribed on a table of advocates, and be formally admited probationer by a Council of Discipline, after an investigation into his moral character and private means. He then becomes a member of the Bar, practising at such and such a court or tribunal.

A man who has been admitted to one Bar can plead at any other. The advocates of Paris appear in the provinces, and the Parisian judges are addressed by more than one provincial advocate.

The probationer has the same rights as regards pleading in court as an advocate who is fully qualified; but, at Paris at least, his name does not appear on any official table. A man ambitious of passing his probationership at Paris (the formalities are not so severe in the provinces) must be provided with his diploma of licentiate in law, be able to show that he really lives in Paris, has furniture, and is of good morals—for which purpose his *concierge* should have nothing but good to say about him—and, lastly, he must have no interest in any commercial business, and he must not practise any other profession than that of advocate, not even the giving of French lessons to eke out the fees which perchance will never come. Before 1870 he was, besides this, compelled to shave his moustache.

When our candidate has taken all these precautions and resolutions, he will carry his diploma to a very worthy gentleman at the Procureur-Général's office ; then, after making some calls and leaving cards with the *concierges*, he will bring his papers to the office of the secretary to the Council of the Order.

This is the beginning of his career.

Budding advocates about to blossom in the beer-houses of the Quartier Latin, fathers who dream of the lawyer's gown for your sons, turn your eyes to the end of the Palace, near the Place

---

[1] *Stagiaires.*

Dauphine, and there at the extremity of the new buildings of the Court of Appeal, you will see a staircase and a wooden gallery which like a Venetian bridge spans the court below. This is the path which leads to the Bar.

The neophyte, favoured of the gods, who crosses the bridge for the first time, will perhaps hear the sound of children's voices, ascending in shrill discordant cadences from a small garden.

By standing on tiptoe till he reaches the glass of the gallery, he will see below him the charming garden, closely walled in on three sides, and filled with troops of imprisoned children.

Even though the sound of voices should not arouse his curiosity, the future defender of orphans should none the less hoist himself up to see what lies below. In a sanded court, prettily enlivened here and there by evergreens, he will notice the figure of a sister of mercy, a harmony in blue, white and black, possibly with a companion, while through the open door at the end of the garden the light shines in on a flight of steps, and a nuns' refectory. It is the only part of the Palace which possesses any mystical charm, and is known to few.

On the other side of the gallery there are no windows. Were there any, they would afford a view of a prison yard swarming with women prisoners engaged in having their lunch ; this yard is only separated by a corridor from the building allotted to the sisters of mercy.

We now come to a square on which opens out the library, a robing room door, a large and gloomy corridor lighted by gas, and a private door which leads to the office of the secretary to the Order.

At the end of a dark narrow passage (by pushing a glass door one is in full daylight) we come to a flight of steps, with a balustrade, and handsome but somewhat steep, descending to the cheerful apartment occupied by the apparitor of the Order of Advocates. It is impossible to think of the apparitor as otherwise than immortal. As he is to-day, so he will always be, grave and polite, by name Léon, with the manners of a majordomo who has made his fortune and would be on good terms with all. His blonde whiskers have grown gray, his shoulders have slightly rounded ; but we do not notice it, and to us Léon will always be the eternal apparitor of the Order, just as Delaunay used to be the eternal stage lover, and his successor will only be a new incarnation of himself.

With what a kind yet lofty grace does he guide the first steps of the candidate for forensic honours, initiate him in the ceremonies to be observed, and teach him the traditions of the oath! He provides the agenda papers, distributes the printed Tables of the Order, and is, in short, the *bâtonnier's* factotum. Imbued with reverence for the place, he must find it hard to take his plumed cocked hat and silver chain with the pendant medal, which are the insignia of his office, from their case without deep emotion. The day to see him is Tuesday, when the Council meets. He is more majestic than usual then, though quite unassuming, and salutes with a shade of respect the *ex-bâtonniers* as they pass by. A little after two o'clock on Tuesday, the members of the Council may be seen descending the stairs with heavy tread towards the apparitor's room. The procession is curious. The straight steep staircase is well suited to stately members who are still strong and not short-sighted; and they take the steps slowly and regularly. But the feeble take some time, and make the descent slowly, and walking sideways; the excited run down as briskly as they can, catching at the useless rail with hurried movements of the left hand, whilst others come down delicately, feeling the way at every step with their foot before they set it down. All promptly disappear to the left, at the end of a corridor, with a rapid noise of doors opening and shutting. We are now at the Council Hall, a lofty, well-lighted apartment, occupied by a table with a green cloth, around which the elect of the Order deliberate beneath the protecting presence of the elder Berryer, a fine pastel; of a portrait of Dufaure, painted by Mdlle. Nelly Jacquemart; of one of Chaix d'Est-Ange, after Hippolyte Flandrin, and of photographs and medallions of other eminent counsel departed.

It will be a lucky chance for the probationer candidate if he comes with his diploma to the secretary's office on the day when the Council have summoned before them a member who has committed some fault through awkwardness or inadvertence. He will have a foretaste of the vexations of the profession at the very moment when he is just beginning to relish its first joys. He will see the culprit pacing up and down with nervous but rather haughty gait; he will note the side glances which advocates come for some other purpose cast at one another, each suspecting his neighbour to be the person cited before the Council, and he will observe Léon trying to put every one at his ease, and seemingly unconscious of the coming storm.

As a rule the only people who pass by Léon's table or sit in the window-sill from which one can see the dark tree-tops of the Place Dauphine are solicitors timidly looking for an advocate, solicitors' clerks with papers, youthful members of the Bar come to obtain some special information, or learned counsel waiting for the time when the *bâtonnier* is open to visitors in his private room. This is a typical lawyer's study, plainly furnished, its only ornaments being a bust of Gerbier by Houdon, a portrait of Dupin by Court, a plaster medallion of Chaix d'Est-Ange taken from the portrait by Flandrin, and the sole existing bust of Tronchet. The room also contains a cabinet of medals which were found under the ruins of the former council chamber, burnt in 1871, and a few engravings of the old law courts.

In the summer the scene from the secretary's ante-chamber is much more lively ; the eye is dazzled by the vivid green of the trees, the white glint of the houses opposite, and the glare of sunlight. In the stone gallery at the head of the stairs all along the balustrade one can see advocates, looking like the figures in a monochrome of the marriage at Cana ; walking up and down indefatigably, rustling their black robes with violent gestures or draping them in statuesque folds. From midday till four there is a continual procession of advocates coming to take a drink from the cask of fresh liquorice water, provided for them by the Council. And Léon watches to see that only members of the Paris Bar refresh themselves there ; if any intruder pushes in, he warns him off with a severe reprimand or a stately wave of the hand ; in serious cases he informs the Council.

The apartments allotted to the Bar include, lastly, a private office for the secretary and one for the treasurer. To the latter place the future probationer goes with timid steps to pay his admission fees ; here, also, he will come later on to be inscribed on the list of those ready to plead gratis for poor prisoners ;[1] here, lastly, if he goes on with his career during his whole life at the Bar, is the place for paying the annual subscription, with which, it is not at all improbable, he will be generally behindhand.

The last duty of a candidate for the probationership is to submit to an investigation into his private affairs, and receive the visit of an inspector nominated by the Council of the Order. As a rule the inspector is satisfied with a talk with your porter just to

---

[1] A barrister who pleads for nothing is called an *avocat d'office.*

see that you have not given a false address, that your apartment does credit to the corporation which is going to take you to its bosom, and that you do not scandalise the neighbours by your mode of life. Conscientious inspectors—those who love youth and think of the possible votes of future electors—will climb five

COCOA FOR THE ADVOCATES.

stories, if need be, and enter into a familiar conversation with the amazed future voter. Have no fear even though a petticoat be hanging on the back of the sofa ; the inspector will be discreet and place himself so as not to see it. As a matter of fact the investigation is not severe. Complaints are made that it constitutes an invasion of private life. But it was much worse in old days. It was then the fashion to exclude from the Bar those who had failed to show respect to their parents, had declined public office, had been seen in dubious resorts, or had squandered their patrimony in riotous living. The Bar was also closed to those who were not Catholics, and to those who happened to be blind or deaf. At the law courts to-day one has a choice of all religions; the deaf are numerous, and the one-eyed, if not the blind, are legion. After the inspector's visit comes the candidate's formal admission by the Council, and, the same night, a delightful letter from the inspector informing you of the fact and addressing you as " our dear colleague."

A few days afterwards the candidate, conducted by Léon and presented by the *bâtonnier*, takes the oath before the chief president of the Court of Appeal. All is now finished. The probationer will then enter on his duties; during the ensuing three or five years he will assist at a certain number of conferences held every Monday, signing his name on a slip of paper in the office in front of the public auction room ;[1] twice a year he will be present at the assembly of the sections into which the Bar is divided ; at the end of this period he will be entitled to have his name entered on the Table of the Bar.

If, by the conclusion of the fifth year, he does not ask to be entered, from fear of the patent fees, the treasurer of the Council will send for him and, after a short address in praise of the profession, will place before him the alternative of having his name entered or bidding good-bye to the gown.

We shall again see the probationer being sworn in, and taking part in the Monday conferences. Let us now describe his experiences at an assembly of the sections.[2]

THE ASSEMBLY OF THE SECTIONS

In the early morning, at half-past nine or ten o'clock, our probationer makes his way to the Council Chamber or to one of the rooms which go to form the library. Other probationers are there in legal costume, grouped round a table at which is sitting

---

[1] *Salle des criées.*

[2] Or meeting of the Columns. The French is *réunion de colonnes.*

a member of the Council.   With him, as secretary, is a probationer who has been classed among the first twelve at the last conference. The member of the committee expatiates at length on the subjects mentioned in the programme, and puts some difficult questions to the probationers present.   These young men, who a moment ago were displaying their new feathers in the galleries of the Palace, suddenly fall back into the nervousness of the candidate, and give answers at random which they fancy may suit the examiner's taste, while the secretary smiles with an expression of ominous sarcasm. From time to time an orator appears ; a probationer crammed with facts, who gets to the root of the controversy, and *corners* the president of the section.

The gravest questions of the profession are discussed in these debates.

Questions of incompatibility.

Can an advocate be a teacher of the deaf and dumb ? No.

Can he be an actor ? Yes, but only if he accepts no salary.

Can he be a doctor ? No, for he cannot be at the law courts and with his patients at the same time ; an advocate owes all his time to his clients.

The advocate, however, can be a deputy or a senator. Is this because a representative of the people is supposed never to attend in his seat in Parliament ?

The question of fees forms a subject by itself ; it comprises a chapter full of interest for members of the junior Bar who, having never pleaded otherwise than gratis, are delighted when they hear mention of that rare bird, *the client who pays*.

The theory laid down for their instruction is simple. " Fees must be offered by the client of his own free will ; the advocate cannot claim them."

The mere statement of this theory immediately strikes the probationer dumb.   He asks himself how the president of his section, in ordinary matters a business-like man, comfortably off and free from all chimeras, has been able to remain so long in such a profession. Some presidents of sections, either too sceptical or over sincere, will, it is true, state this theory, prove its wisdom, and point out that it is based on disinterestedness and devotion, the foundation of the true advocate's character. They will show, moreover, that its aim is to check demands which under the circumstances would naturally tend to become excessive. But, all the same, they have no hesitation in enumerating the methods by which practice has been able to effect a compromise with principle.

Either the solicitor, on whom there are no restrictions, undertakes to ask for counsel's fees, or the barrister, at the second visit—for it would not be proper on the first occasion—after a certain amount of circumlocution mentions the amount of his fees to the client ; if the latter turns a deaf ear, it is usual to send him a letter to the effect that another interview is urgently needed, " for final instructions "—so the formula runs—and in the recesses of the consulting room the barrister asks for what he wants : one must earn one's living. Demands by letter, however, are strictly forbidden : so long as the demand is made by word of mouth, any method may be used, at any rate before the suit is tried.

The trial once ended, the advocate has no resource against an obstinate debtor ; and, if he clamours for his due, the debtor will complain to the Council.

" Wherefore, my young friends, let those of you who do not disdain pecuniary considerations remember to ask for your fees beforehand, and by word of mouth." We have had the theory ; this is the practice.

The probationer is a little reassured ; but his brow will soon again grow cloudy. After the chapter dealing with fees, comes the lesson *on seeking for clients*. How are clients to discover unknown talent ? What means are there of attracting their attention ? None whatever. To canvass for clients is forbidden. The advocate must await the hoped-for client in his own chambers, at certain fixed hours, which he is not even allowed to print at the head of his writing paper. Unless the young advocate possess zealous patrons who will keep him before the public, family influence, or the interest of some important man of business, clients will not come to him.

There is a well-worn legend of the advocate who made himself known by a brilliant argument in some suit without remuneration ; but do not believe it, my young friends ; do not believe that real clients will come to you because your name has been five or six times in the newspapers, and because you have won a great success in some sensational case. In eight days, unless you happen to be a regular pleader at the assizes, nobody will think any more about you ; and during your consultation hours you will wait in vain for a ring at the bell. Unless you have laid in a large stock of patience,

unless you can stand all kinds of disappointment, if you cannot
help envying blockheads who are luckier than yourself, if the joy
of pleading once in a way does not console you for all the rest, or
if you do not feel any aptitude for making advances in the right
quarter or for forming advantageous friendships, then hang up
your gown in the robing room, lock up your cap, and try a more
remunerative career.   Amen.

THE LIBRARY

The " lessons" above described are usually given in the library.
It is open for advocates at eleven o'clock. Let us pay it a visit,
although it is closed to laymen, with the exception that they may
stand on the threshold to summon some legal friend within, and
may enter if they wish to speak to the amiable librarian, M.
Boucher. But perhaps you would like to hear its history? Know
then that the advocates' library dates from 1708. It was founded
out of the money left by Étienne Gabriau de Riparfonds, advocate
in the Parliament of Paris. This worthy loved his profession more
than anything in the world; he thought also that "an advocate who
can speak is worth nothing unless he has gone through solid studies
which ripen the mind, and render forensic controversy clear and
full of instruction for the listeners." And therefore he bequeathed
to the Bar of Paris an annuity of 800 francs a year and the
library, composed partly of the law books given him by his god-
father, partly of the additions made thereto by himself "on all
and every occasion that the state of his fortune or his family had
allowed them."

After four years had been spent in looking for premises, the
library was first established in 1708, rather far from the law courts,
in a gallery rented from the Archbishop of Paris. It was situated
on the third floor of a pavilion in the outer court of the episcopal
palace, between Notre-Dame and the Seine.

The books numbered 10,000 altogether, and there were few
readers; in 1725 the library was in the care of an old woman
assisted by a young girl of seventeen ; and they were not troubled
much by intruders. But on this spot were held the meetings of
the Council of the Order, the sittings of the committee for free
consultations, and the *conferences*, assemblies where the seniors
came to hear essays read by the junior bar.

An engraving by Saint-Aubin, minutely described and commented upon by M. Herbet in *The Annual Transactions of the Conference of Advocates for* 1889, represents a conference at the library in 1776.

At the Revolution the Order of Advocates was suppressed, and their books confiscated by the State. They eventually fell to the Court of Cassation ; and, at the library of the Supreme Tribunal, books may still be found stamped with the words " *Bibliothèque des avocats*, 1762." Even before the re-establishment of the Order, the library had been re-formed ; an old advocate, named Nicolas Férey, bequeathed his library in 1806 to the Order of Advocates, " under whatever name it might please his Majesty to re-establish it " : and the Order, on its reconstruction in 1810, was authorised to accept the legacy.

From this date, the advocates' library remained fixed in a narrow, dark corner in the midst of the buildings occupied by the Court of Appeal, near the present Chamber of Indictments,[1] at the end of the gloomy corridor allotted to the ushers of this court. It grew gradually wealthier from gifts made by retiring barristers, till in 1870 it contained 25,613 volumes.

Then came another catastrophe ; one of the rooms of which the library was formed was burnt during the last days of the Commune, many precious books being destroyed, in spite of the devotion of the *bâtonnier*, Maitre Rousse, and of the librarian, M. Boucher, father of the present librarian. At the present day, the losses have been made good, and the younger M. Boucher has 38,000 volumes under his care.

The dark, narrow library of old has been transformed into a comfortable establishment. But the change has only been effected recently. The library at first consisted of a corridor overlooking the exquisite court where the nuns of the prison ply their task ; the corridor opened into two narrow chambers where the books stood in piles upon piles. The present installation was soon finished by opening a large hall in communication with the corridor, which was turned into a gallery ; it only remained to unpack the judicial records heaped up in this place. This work lasted eleven years, and it was not till the beginning of the October sittings in 1890 that, thanks to the persistence of the *Bâtonnier*, Maitre Cresson, energetically seconded by those advo-

---

[1] *Chambre des mises en accusation.*

cates who were members of the Municipal Council, the actual rearrangement of the books could be completed.

The Bar have now got a library to be proud of. A vast reading room, with the gallery as an annexe, two stories of book-cases protected by wire gauze, the upper part being rendered accessible by a light iron foot-bridge ; a long table, as if intended for conferences, some smaller ones that might do for supper parties, and writing materials everywhere. The decoration is of the approved kind. There are two pieces of Gobelins tapestry between the windows, representing Bonaparte surrounded by diplomatists and soldiers ; above one of the windows is a memorial plate :

"CETTE BIBLIOTHÈQUE A ÉTÉ
OUVERTE LE 16 OCTOBRE 1890
SOUS LE BÂTONNAT DE ME. CRESSON.

Scattered about, and forming a collection useful to biographers, are the busts of old *bâtonniers :* an enormous one of Jules Favre, by Barrias ; one of Paillet, beautifully carved by Pradier ; a graceful one of Marie with the hair curled, the cheeks creased, the lips set ; one of Nicolet, by his wife, delicious in its charm and ironical elegance. There is another one which merits particular mention ; at the foot of the staircase leading from the great hall to the foot-bridge is a bust of Gerbier, an exquisite face, with an expression of raillery softened by abundant good humour. While the fire of 1871 was at its height, Maître Rousse might have been seen "carrying this bust into safety, through a maze of staircases, beams and ropes, like pious Æneas on the last night of Ilium, with old Anchises and his household gods on his shoulders."

A deep recess shows us the office of the librarian. As already stated, he is M. Boucher, son of a librarian, and, one may hope, father of a librarian, for his son is already employed in the place. His politeness is proverbial, and, with a charming grace, he has placed his memoirs and papers at our disposal. Of the two other apartments which in times gone by formed the whole library, one, called the *newspaper-room,* has, over the looking-glass, a portrait of Riparfonds, in red robes, the chin bordered with a white beard that looks like mould ; this apartment is still the favourite working place of those who feel the cold and are enamoured of the past. The other, the *parlotte*, is a dark corner which does not answer to the name prematurely bestowed upon it, for few persons go there, and none talk in it.[1]

To make up for this, the conversation in the reading room is overpowering. Advocates engaged in research appear at an early hour and settle down to work comfortably. Nothing disturbs them save the passing by of a learned friend, who, having come down to the court too soon, reads a brief through absently or goes to have a chat with the librarian. But readers begin to increase, running in hurriedly to copy a decree or find an answer in some out-of-the-way authority. There are long promenades from shelf to shelf in search of the right volume, and the librarian comes and goes, accompanied by his assistant, as polite as himself. Then come the idlers, still in official or already in ordinary costume ; they say goodday to one, shake hands with one another, sit down by a learned friend's side and begin to talk. If there be a worker in front of them, he fidgets, goes feverishly to look through a volume on the shelves, returns to take his place, and sits down to the table, with his head between his hands and his fingers on his ears ; at last, tired out, he goes to do some talking on his own account farther off. Books and papers are left behind in picturesque profusion, and new-comers, not venturing to disturb this grand collection, have great difficulty in finding a place. There are some terrible talkers at the library, and these are not always those whose voices are most heard in court. They speak in high tones and with the air of great authority, give opinions on difficulties stated by their neighbours, and tell professional stories of interminable length. They are especially dangerous just after the vacation ; and when they encounter old campaigners as voluble as themselves, there is no resource but flight. The leaders of the Bar are rarely seen in the library; Maître Cresson comes sometimes to smile upon his work ; and the member of the Council specially charged with supervision of the library occasionally passes through with correct and official bearing. Only three or four seniors are in the habit of coming to work at the library with their secretaries ; on these occasions they choose the little tables, with seats for two, which stand in the gallery. One may be seen giving his instructions in monologue ; another dictating something to a young man of talent ; another from his place directs

---

[1] Two other rooms are about to be opened, a smoking room and a lavatory.

some research into the mysteries of jurisprudence; another who prefers the *newspaper-room* distributes papers to be copied out and works his way through a pile of books. Less regular visitors run in, write some letters, consult a guide book or a directory, and disappear.

In the winter, at three o'clock, when work is at its height and every one engrossed in his subject, the three attendants begin to put the books together. So much the worse for the student who has left his place for a minute; he returns to find the volumes which he had carefully picked out, and opened at the right place, put back on their shelves; this is a bitter pill, for at four o'clock the library closes. Vainly does the student turn a deaf ear to the representations of the attendant or librarian, he must leave his copying unfinished. When will the library have the electric light? In summer, closing time is at five o'clock. But there are still some people who complain when they are turned out, and who have only been there about twenty minutes.

THE ELECTIONS OF THE ORDER

For two or three days in July, decks are cleared, and work put a stop to at the library on account of the elections, that is, the elections of the *bâtonnier* and of the members of the Council. During these days little groups gather all about the place, with scouts going from one to another; some youthful canvassers in the doorway silently, or with a cautious word and a friendly gesture, remind members that So-and-so is a candidate; the bolder ones seize on every arrival, and follow him to the voting table with a vigorous and animated flow of words.

In old days a long table used to be set out in the corridor. It was divided by little partitions, like those on the counter of some telegraph offices, into separate compartments where the elector could fill in his ballot paper, sheltered from prying eyes; and much amusement was to be had from the game of standing behind a writer so as to see over his shoulder.

It is still amusing to note the different styles of writing, the vague promises, the encouraging pressure of the hand, the familiar comedy of the procession of voters past the ballot-box, and the formal counting of the votes. In a word, these elections are like other elections, but more secret.

On the day for the renewal of the Council the crowd is particularly noisy, for there are many ambitious of election. There is no occasion to call for scrutineers, parties of volunteers undertake the work, and when it comes to casting up the votes, the old hands show their skill at the game. The leader of each party calls out his figure, and there is a competition among the bystanders who shall be the first to add the figures up. There are specialists in calculation who are never seen at the library except on this day.

The election of *bâtonnier* is simpler. There is only one place to be filled, and the counting of the votes goes on while the spectators are still passing through the excitement of the ballot. The successful candidate's name is rarely known at an early stage of the proceedings. At first, strokes of luck alternate with almost equal regularity for each candidate, or if one of them gets markedly ahead, and his partisans begin to reckon on victory, the other regains the advantage by an unexpected run of good fortune.

IN THE LIBRARY.

The scene resembles a fine game of billiards where careful aim is taken before every stroke, and where the stake is the highest honour to which the perfect advocate aspires.

An absolute majority being at last obtained, the victor's friends run to him with the good news.

There are cases on record of friends being too hasty, and telling a candidate that he is successful before the votes have been all recorded. In these cases the anecdote gets much discussed in the corridors, and ensures the candidate's success at a second trial. Meanwhile the expectant *bâtonnier* is waiting with an air of indifference in the *Salle des Pas-Perdus*, or one of nervousness in the Council Chamber, where the result is officially reported by our friend Léon. Then, stirred by the news, and without having had time to compose himself, we may see him in the library before the voting table, face to face with the retiring *bâtonnier*. The latter with perfect calmness congratulates him in a speech so worded that, with a few trifling variations, it could just as well have been addressed to the other candidate had he been successful.

Equally studied is the speech made by the incoming president— for every candidate prepares his speech, hard though it may be to swallow it again in case of defeat; but it is always a little disordered by the speaker's agitation. This in fact gives the speech its charm. Thus the happy man inevitably talks of his modest youth, of the first step in his career, of the folly of any one who should then have prophesied such an honour for him, and of the efforts he will make to prove worthy of it; and he sheds tears while his supporters cheer him and sceptics smile.

In the October following the *bâtonnier* may again be seen in the same place, doing the honours of the house, and engaged in reading, with an independence born of success, a long discourse on the duties of the profession, followed by a series of obituary notices which custom requires to be given with some literary grace.

The election of the *bâtonnier* only presents amusing features once in two years, for it is customary to reappoint the same *bâtonnier* twice running.

IN THE CORRIDORS

The advocate is at home in every part of the Palace ; it is he who takes up most room, it is he who predominates everywhere by force of noise and numbers. From the robing rooms to the library, he flows into every corner. In old days the chief abode of his sovereignty was the *buvette*, a little restaurant inside the Palace. This had at first been situated in the *Galerie Marchande*; it was then moved to the residence occupied by the Prefect of Police, while from 1879 it was set up in the corridors reserved for the prefect's staff, above the advocates' library, and close to the lost property office. This was the favourite place for conversation, the room being under the care of the Council of the Order. In 1863 it was redecorated, Jules Favre being *bâtonnier*. At present jurymen engaged in criminal and compensation cases, and persons employed in the Prefecture of Police have an equal right with the barristers to use the place. This, added to its gloomy aspect (a paltry hall lighted from a little court where building operations are always going on), has caused the *buvette* to lose some of its old renown.

The *buvette* still numbers some faithful friends who drop in for a cup of coffee at the first moment of rest, or who come there to wait during an adjournment of the court. There are regular customers, and counsel pressed for time who, to save the trouble of taking off their gown between two cases, come there for lunch. Poor Maître Lejoindre, the most brilliant story-teller in the law courts, was at his best here, as was Maître Oscar Falateuf, in the waiting times before the sittings of the first chamber of the court. His cap at the back of his head, with a genial smile, bright, good-tempered, and very clever, he would reel off story after story till his auditors forgot all about their lunch.

Why does not the Council of the Order, in the spirit of Jules Favre, restore the glories of the *buvette*?

In this age of syndicates, co-operative societies and clubs, why does not the Bar, reserving the library for its original purpose as a place of study, start a club-room in proximity to it, where members could lunch pleasantly on moderate terms, talk at their ease, read the daily papers, and, if need be, prepare their arguments and receive their clients. This, it seems to us, would be quite *fin de siècle;* so they should lose no time over it.

Meanwhile, let us return to the everyday life of the Palace. The day's work is at its height.

Nothing can be seen but a cloud of black gowns through which are passing bewildered citizens, insinuating men of business, and a few fair dames in search of adventures.

In the Galerie Marchande, in front of the Bosc robing room,

there is a crush of advocates who are having a talk before they take off their gowns, or are waiting to get away. A stir runs through the groups when a lady of alluring air, and crowned with a most effective hat, passes through in search of her counsel or some friend who has promised to show her round.

In the *aquarium*, advocates in full dress are engaged in smoking and speaking well of their comrades. On a green bench, in the full glare of the light, clients of both sexes are waiting for their counsel to pass by, when they seize hold of him and get a consultation on the spot. Every five minutes " lines of English lady tourists, moving as if by clock-work, come out from the balcony of the Sainte-Chapelle, pass along the gallery and disappear in the direction of the Salle des Pas-Perdus."

The Salle des Pas-Perdus makes a fine show, with its broad bay windows looking out on the Boulevard du Palais, its massive pillars, the beauty and simplicity of its proportions ; and when crowded with the legal world it is full of life and movement. The noise one hears does not resemble the confused clamour of the Stock Exchange, nor the humming of a hive of bees at their work ; followers of the law do not put on the busy manner of financiers, and have nothing in common with bees except the sting. No, the noise is so like that of low and sustained conversation, that a superficial and malicious observer might christen the place " *Salle du Temps Perdu.*"

The appearance of the Salle des Pas-Perdus is constantly varying. It is as changeable as the heavens, as woman, as the law.

On election or other important days, crowds form round prominent persons, voices are raised, and the once gentle murmur of conversation increases in pitch till it equals the din of a public meeting On Monday, which is the probationer's day, ordinary clients leave the place to these young gentlemen. Wednesday and Saturday are auction days for movables. On Thursday, the day for forced sales of land and houses, the spectator will see the lawyers in stronger force than usual, engaged with a special class of clients, the investors in real property. These are well-set-up gentlemen, walking up and down as if they were at the Stock Exchange, pillars of society, with good banking accounts, who come to ask a solicitor to bid for them ; with these come shop-keepers or yeomen bewildered by their new excitement, who hesitate at the very last moment, and in turn ask advice or make suggestions to their man of business ; there are married couples who thought to share the struggle of bidding, and who end by quarrelling ; and little groups in mourning who follow the solicitor as if he were a good shepherd. Occasionally a well-dressed woman ventures in.

On Wednesday ladies involved in some divorce case move quickly through the crowd, and disappear behind a staircase on their way to a hall where we shall again meet them.

On Tuesdays and Saturdays the groups, not so lively as usual, and made up in most part of laymen, collect in front of the door, underneath the clock, leading to judges' chambers ; and knots of men, not remarkable for cleanliness, consult a large placard at the side which contains the list of applications to be made in judges' chambers.[1]

On Friday, as there is nothing special doing, and as solicitors rarely come to court on that day, advocates are fewer than ever. The sound of talking is less continuous, and strikes the ear with a slighter rumbling ; and the building soon resumes its early morning stillness, only broken by two or three pairs of laggard talkers walking up and down.

The majority of the regular frequenters who give the Salle des Pas-Perdus its peculiar character are men of law, whether counsel or solicitors. They use it as a meeting place for the discussion of their common concerns. They talk, sometimes passing one in front of the other, as if they were playing a complicated game of *four corners* with words ; they talk, standing quite still, in little groups ; and they talk, as they do the hundred paces which measure the length of the hall in bands of four or five. You will note the different bearing of people while waiting till the man they want has finished his conversation.

Some give him a touch on the shoulder, and then plant themselves two steps off ; others, talking all the time on some indifferent matter with some one else, watch his gestures, and keep pace with his every movement.

In this crowd of figures, all wearing the same costume, it is an arduous task to find the man one wants. Often one does not know him, and the inquirer's first step is to question some acquaintances, who are beginning their solitary promenade, as to his whereabouts. As often as not he is dark with a pointed beard, or a young man

---

[1] *Rôle des référés.*

—one is not certain about his complexion—with a small moustache which information throws little light on the object in view. In the case of a barrister, one can bethink one's self of his characteristics, the way he carries his brief bag, or what corner of the hall he prefers.

For instance he may be always found with a large, worn, and bulky brief-bag, with rents so broad that the books inside nearly slip through them ; or he may be one of those who come to the law courts in a fashionable coat, like amateurs, with their bag neatly doubled up, the list of engagements fastened to the outside ; another has a way of holding his bag at arm's length by a band or leather strap ; if you are looking for an *ex-bâtonnier*, who is counsel for the Rothschilds, you will recognise him by his broad shoulders, by his wonderful eye-glass, his snub nose and the mass of papers held nonchalantly against his hip; or possibly you will be told that the man you are looking for carries his briefs, with the title upper-most against his left breast, as a nurse does her baby.

· Out of a thousand figures you will mark that of the tall advocate with an eye-glass and stooping shoulders, an *ex-bâtonnier*, who stands with his arm thrown like a black mantle round his charmed and bewildered client.

Maître Allou might have been always found on a corner of the bench which stands near the first chamber of the Court of Appeal, listening gravely, with his proud weary air, to any learned friends who came to pay their court. He has had no successor. Other advocates may still be seen sitting in this same corner, but they have no mark to distinguish them from the crowd. The bench in front has its regular patrons of different kind ; but they do not stay there long. On the other benches are advocates of every class, resting for a moment to look at their briefs, worn out with work, or sick of clients whom they do not care to show round the building.

A solicitor is much harder to find than an advocate ; a solicitor in his gown can be distinguished at once as he wears no hood ; in place of the large macaroon-shaped boss with two hanging flaps, he only has two buttons, sometimes not even that, on his left shoulder. But solicitors have few individual characteris-tics, and very often they do not wear a gown. To be sure of finding them, the best thing to do is to make for the part of the building reserved for them, which lies at the right end of the Salle des Pas-Perdus, towards the Boulevard du Palais, a modest apartment containing a little partition, round the grating in which hover solicitors' clerks with documents. Instead, however, of entering there the seeker should mount the stairs, knock at the door of a bare dressing room, ask if the solicitor required is at the law courts, and lie in wait for him.

Conversation is difficult in the Salle des Pas-Perdus even with a friend, if he happens to be an advocate with much practice. You think you have got him, you fix him with your eye ; then, a moment's inattention, and there is nobody there ! He has disappeared behind a pillar ; and you run through the hall to find him flown. So you, in your turn, join one of the bands of strollers who are discussing some legal or other point, while the bell for auctions or judges' chambers rings incessantly. Many look on it as a duty to frequent the Salle des Pas-Perdus, especially when they have nothing to do. Only a few of the foremost advocates can afford not to appear there, and solicitors advise junior men to come and show themselves with a heavy brief-bag, stuffed with the first thing that comes handy, with a melon if they are hard up. For many, barring the melon, it is a pleasant task. It is there that a man will meet the comrades and friends whom a long brotherhood in arms makes more welcome or dearer every day ; it is a place for learning in friendly talk all the news both within and without ; and thither come legislators to put off party bitterness and sharpen their reason on the daring humour of their colleagues.

In that case, it will be said, it is a place for losing a great deal of time. Many people would think it wiser to go straight to the robing room the moment court is closed. To these wiseacres a few points may be suggested for consideration.

Let them remember that there is no existence so wearing as that of an advocate in large practice, that for him the physical fatigue of the Bar is doubled by the work he has do in chambers, and that the time spent on this daily promenade between a speech in court and an interview with a client is a necessary relaxation for his mind. Let them also remember that this constant friction with men of his own profession, not only in court but outside as well, can only benefit him, and that this time lost for practical work has special value in developing his critical ability.

Let them remember, lastly, that to lose time is a necessity of the profession.   Better lose it in the Salle des Pas-Perdus than waiting one's turn to address the judge in the stifling atmosphere of court.   Is it not, moreover, the place for meeting solicitors, for making appointments, for settling plans of campaign, for showing letters ? The gentlemen of the long robe are all peripatetic philosophers.

However, it must be owned that the glories of the Salle des Pas-Perdus are on the wane. Men of wit do not spend so much time there as of yore. The reason is they no longer find the same charm there. The judicial family is becoming too numerous,competition too keen ; and those who have abandoned law for politics, without obtaining either the honour or success they hoped for, have imported into the legal profession an element of discord which it needs much philosophy, disinterestedness and mutual indulgence to extinguish. Despite these ominous shadows, there is no spot in the Palace so loved by the lawyers, or so interesting, and so accessible to the general public as the Salle des Pas-Perdus.

There visitors wander at their leisure, a little bewildered, but amused ; they gaze at the marble statue of Berryer carved by Chapu, who gave him as companions two graceful figures, Fidelity and Eloquence ; they fall into raptures before the ponderous monument of Malesherbes, the decoration of which is generally completed by two or three advocates in the flesh, leaning elegantly against the pedestal : the English tourists read in their Baedeker that it is by Dumont, the bas-relief being by Cortot, and the statues on the side by Bosio. These statues represent, it seems, France and Fidelity, which has called forth the sarcastic remark that poor Malesherbes has no claim to Eloquence.

THE OLD "PARLOTTE."

There is an annexe to the Salle des Pas-Perdus which is interesting to notice. It is a little room, entered from beneath the inside double staircase of the Salle, and communicating with the sixth chamber. In old days it was called the Parlotte. But this name being from recent years restricted to a part of the library, the old Parlotte is now only a private writing room for advocates. The last of its frequenters in the days of its greatness was Maître

Malapert, a veteran freelance who could never help being inspired with a real passion in his clients' affairs. It has a good fire in the winter which makes it look comfortable. When writing materials run short, please address the usher of the sixth chamber. Facing the door of the Parlotte is another little door, painted brown. A push will reveal a winding staircase set in open ironwork, through the bars of which can be seen an immense empty hall with graceful columns, like a crypt of the Mont-Saint-Michel forgotten beneath the Salle des Pas-Perdus; it is the Salle de St. Louis, also called the guard hall of Philip the Fair. It is attached to the Conciergerie and is closed to the public. It can only be seen properly in all its splendour from this little staircase, which few know of. Let us go down it, but do not tell.

CHAPTER V

DURING our wanderings round the Salle des Pas-Perdus, the
courts have been in full swing. They are mostly furnished in a
uniform style. In the fore-part of the hall are rows of oak
benches with backs, one of them having also well-stuffed cushions
for counsel, a long shelf—*the bar*—being placed in front to hold
their papers. In the middle is a gangway leading to the pretorium,
as it is called, a narrow open space which separates the counsel
from the judges. In former times it was ironically called the
Park; it is now occupied by the usher on duty. At the end of
the hall is the judges' bench, a long oak table with armchairs
for three or four persons; on the side, between the windows, is
the daïs reserved for the honourable representative of the public
ministry, and close to this is the registrar's desk. The walls are
panelled in oak, and papered in dark blue with a pattern of some
sort or other. The ceiling is white with gilt cornices. A clock
stands in a recess carved with oak-leaves. There is a plaster bust
of the Republic identical with that to be seen in every mayor's
office; and, facing the public, hangs a picture of the crucifixion, the
usual faded figure on a bluish-grey background.

The doors open late; at noon, sometimes at a quarter-past
twelve, sometimes not till half-past. How different from the days
when the bar had to be at the châtelet at sunrise, allowing only
for the short time needed to hear a low mass! The first movement begins in the corridors behind the courts leading to the
vice-presidents' private rooms. There is only one president for each
tribunal, and he sits in the first chamber; in each of the other
chambers the presiding judge is a vice-president or the senior judge
present. In the cramped waiting-rooms counsel are growing

impatient; they are waiting for the vice-president to ask him for some ticklish postponement, requiring explanations which the petitioner would rather give in a little casual chit-chat than in a formal application when the cause list is called over. This learned gentleman is witness at a marriage ceremony, and has only just time to keep his appointment ; another will be detained all day by "family business," a wide phrase covering all kinds of excuses, from the sickness of a near relative to an assignation with a pretty woman; another is not ready, his case is not yet prepared, he has not yet received from his client the indispensable documents (in plain terms his fees) ; another is holding a brief for a learned friend who is ill or gone into the country. Here comes a youthful clerk whose master has merely said to him : " Go and see the president ; I can't be in court to-day." And he is thinking of the stereotyped phrase he is to use, rather nervously, mumbling the words to himself beforehand. Several gentlemen, who in a moment will be transformed into magistrates in full costume, glide towards the council chamber, a place which serves as robing-room and meeting place for the magistrates of each court.

Suddenly there is a stir among the advocates in the waiting room ; the officer, surly or obsequious as the case may be, clears the way, and opens the door for a busy-looking man in civilian dress ; it is the president. Quick follows the stream of applicants. Advocates follow advocates, pushing against one another as they pass the door. The president, with his nose in his wardrobe, listens to the requests for postponements, which, one after another, are poured into his ear ; he listens to the last as he turns round with his waistcoat, sometimes with his shirt uncovered, and one arm in the air as it is being thrust into the flowing sleeve of his gown. Now he is ready. Nobody else can be received. Every one must be in court. And the stream, not a very broad one after all, makes for the bar and into the pretorium. This is the time for good stories and traditional anecdotes, for the careless talk of advocates who lead each other on. Groups of standing listeners gather round the seniors, who seat themselves comfortably on the cushioned benches, and repartees, to which long practice has given keenness, flash through the air. Men try their epigrams here just as fencers try their foils against a wall. There are a few younger talkers, bold juniors or sons of advocates or solicitors, who follow their fathers' profession ; but they stand aloof from the crowd, engaged in some

grave debate among themselves, or dreaming of the pleasant
excursion they might be making to St. Cloud, with a fair friend,
on one of the river steamboats.

A door now opens at the back, a voice announces the entry
of the court, and the judges, in black robes with ermine collars,
and caps bordered with silver lace, enter and take their seats on the
bench, which is not far removed from and not
much raised above the bar. They are of every
age, of every appearance, and of every character. With few exceptions the magistrate is
no longer, as heretofore, of a fixed type. He
is manifold, different from what one would
expect, always changing, like humanity itself.
You may see, issuing from the door at the
back, now a judge with heavy beard, cap over
one ear, and robe unbrushed ; now one who
resembles a spick-and-span wax doll, or a
lackadaisical æsthete ; now an old gentleman,
so broken down that he needs support and
seems on the verge of a paralytic stroke, accompanied by a stately individual with long
grey whiskers, and a nervous man who is constantly scratching himself; at another time

A BARRISTER.

From a sketch by P. Renouard.

appears a sleepy judge, who rolls about as he walks ; then one so
short-sighted that he has to feel his way ; then a young man, with
pale austere features, or a big fat fellow, the picture of good temper.
The three or four judges have taken their seats, the deputy who
represents the Procureur has ensconced himself in the shade
between the two windows, and the registrar holds his pen ready
for use.

CALLING THE CAUSE LIST

" Usher of the court, call the cause list."

The usher, to whom these words of the presiding judge are
addressed, is not an usher in knee breeches and a silver chain ; he
is a very respectable gentleman, perhaps a doctor of laws ; he wears
a plain gown, like that of the solicitor whose managing clerk he
was, until he got tired of waiting to step into his employer's
business. Instead of a doctor of laws, an ordinary manservant

with strong lungs and able to read would do the work much better ; for it only consists in calling out in a loud voice the names of the parties on the cause list, and in crying "Silence" every now and then. Now it is possible to be a doctor of laws and yet have a weak voice, and be ill-fitted to read out a list of names. As for the issuing of writs, the ushers could perform that duty quite as well without being compelled to spend their weary days in court.

But let us avoid polemics.

In high falsetto, in deep bass, or in dumb show, the usher of the court begins reading.

Trichet *v.* Trichet!

Poteau *v.* Duparquet!

THE PRESIDENT.—No answer ? I must warn the solicitors that unless they appear this day week, the case will be struck out.

Caffin *v.* Lamouche!

A BOY'S SHRILL VOICE.—To stand for hearing, if the court pleases.

THE PRESIDENT (*in a matter-of-fact tone*).—Stands.

Chamoin *v.* Pingouin!

VOICE OF AN ADVOCATE (*who has just come in*).—To stand first, Mr. President.

THE PRESIDENT (*with a sweet smile*).—First—after the others.

Durand *v.* Pichard!

A DEEP VOICE.—I appear for M. Durand, but I don't see my opponent. I cannot go on in his absence.

THE PRESIDENT (*in his judicial tone*).—We will hear you all the same ; your opponent will be heard next week.

THE DEEP VOICE.—But, Mr. President, I shall have to state my case all over again next week.

THE PRESIDENT (*softening*).—I will see if there are other cases enough to occupy the sitting. Usher, go on calling the paper.

Labat *v.* her husband.

COUNSEL (*with a bald head, smiling*).—Mr. President, my learned friend writes to say that he is to be married to-day.

THE PRESIDENT (*in a rage*).—Then if everybody was getting married, it would be impossible to try a single case ; the court would have to rise at one o'clock. This must remain on the paper. It was set down for hearing three years ago. Your learned friend has not been on the point of getting married all that time.

The advocate makes a frightful grimace and a gesture of despair; in reality, he is delighted at the prospect of arguing without his learned friend.

Boulanger *v.* Dupont!

A WHINING VOICE.—Mr. President, my client is very ill. I have been unable to see him, and was told that he was dying.

THE PRESIDENT (*calming down*).—Dying! You had better lose no time in getting on with the case, so as to avoid the risk of having to revive proceedings.

Navet *v.* Canard!

A SECRETARY'S VOICE.—Mr. President, my principal is detained in another court.

THE PRESIDENT (*beside himself*).—Very well, you shall argue it in his place.

THE SECRETARY.—Mr. President, I haven't got the brief; I know nothing about the case.

THE PRESIDENT (*obdurate*).—I say that you shall argue in his place. Your principal must hand over some of his business to you, if he has too much!

Barreau *v.* Lachaize!

A LOUD COARSE VOICE.—The case is not ready.

THE PRESIDENT (*with his eyes starting out of his head*).—So much the worse.

Chicot *v.* Mouton!

TWO VOICES TOGETHER.—In course of being settled.

THE PRESIDENT (*wounded*).—Oh!

Labbé *v.* Léglise!

TWO OTHER VOICES (*equally together*).—We wait the pleasure of the court.

THE PRESIDENT.—Will the case take long?

THE TWO VOICES.—Oh! the whole sitting, Mr. President.

THE PRESIDENT (*brightening up*).—All the other cases will stand over till this day week, unless the parties interested apply for special days to be fixed. Then several counsel ask that their suits may be declared ready for hearing, which is begging a favour of the court.

We have given a short specimen of what goes on at the reading of the cause list. It varies in every possible way, according to the temperament of the president and the excuses made by the counsel. But we have hardly exaggerated. The coincidences of ridiculous

names are more frequent than would be believed, and the rage of
certain presidents at seeing their business slip away from them by
one adjourment after another rises to frenzy.   There are some
who would gladly try the lookers-on rather than leave before the
proper hour.

On the other hand, there are some who smile gratefully on
counsel who ask for causes to stand over, and close the sitting at
the first chance.   Others enliven
the reading of the cause list by
facetious remarks, never refuse a
request for a postponement when
it is drolly made; they love to
get a laugh out of the spectators,
and generally are the delight of
the idlers in court.   The cause
list ended, the president reads
the judgments on cases the
decision of which has been reserved ; another function for the
performance of which there

From a sketch by P. Renouard.

ought to be a good reader attached to the court.   Sometimes
the ¡president has no voice, sometimes he is troubled with some
defect of pronunciation, sometimes he cannot read the writing of
the judge who drew up the judgment, or perhaps his own.   The
counsel concerned, who have come to hear the result, lean over the
bar with their ears outstretched and bodies hoisted, throwing disturbed glances at each other.   The president mumbles through his
reading, or interrupts it to ask some explanation of his neighbour.
And when it is finished, bets are opened as to the result of the
litigation.   Towards a quarter to one, or at one, pleading begins,
unless the Procureur's representative comes forward to make a
neat and concise statement regarding a suit taken at the previous
sitting.

THE JUDGES

The time spent in court is a time of repose, at any rate for
judges to whom sleep comes at pleasure.   But how hard it is to
acquire the art of sleeping gracefully on the bench !   To slumber
undisguisedly, with half open mouth, thick breathing, nodding

head, is unworthy of a magistrate even in our levelling age. The point is to find proper attitudes to sleep in while assuming the appearance of being melancholy, or buried in thought, or wrapt in attention. The forehead supported by the hand is a good posture ; it denotes the lofty soul of a thinker. The head between the two hands with the eyes fixed is not bad either ; the speaker is at liberty to believe that he has hypnotised his subject. But to sleep with the eyes open demands a certain amount of practice. One plan which may be strongly recommended is to rest the neck firmly against the the chair-back and to wear spectacles; this is simple, natural, and makes it impossible for any one to tell whether you are asleep or awake. There is one possible danger—that the sleeper's body may slide over the edge of his chair, and the judge disappear under the table, which would not be regular; but fortunately the leather chairs are the reverse of slippery, and hitherto accidents have been rare. Certain meditative attitudes also deserve recommendation, as, for instance, the chin resting on the hand ; but in this case please sit well in the centre of the chair, with your back supported throughout its whole length by the cushion. There is yet the plan of sleeping openly, with the arms crossed behind the head ; this excess of cynicism disconcerts the spectator, who cannot believe that you would sleep for so long ; in this case, remember to preserve your posture in case you wake ; this is an essential point. In short, any attitude will do, provided that it is steady, and that sleep does not produce an unseemly movement of the body. There is always at least one judge who listens, the president. Sometimes the three relieve one another by turns. And the modes of listening are as various as those of sleeping.

One president stolidly takes notes without even raising his eyes, as if he were doing dictation ; another watches counsel's lips with unfaltering attention, and makes such desperate efforts to follow the speaker that his face turns purple, and his veins swell to bursting ; another with restless eye explores every corner of the hall, and catches here and there in an absent manner some shred of an argument ; another smiles benignantly at the speaker without listening to a word of his speech ; another seems to follow with interest and makes signs of assent, though he hears nothing, but merely wags his head from habit. Another is impressed by the least word, turns sharply round to his neighbour on the right to

give him the benefit of his remarks, flings himself back to his
neighbour on the left, discusses the case in a loud voice while the
arguments are still going on, scribbles down ten contradictory
judgments on the same matter, asks the counsel for explanations,
shakes himself, bounces about, jerks round on his chair as if it were
a gridiron, and leaves the court without having any opinion at all.
Another sits shrivelled up on his seat, listens immovably to the
opening of a case, forms his opinion quite unaided before even the
opening is finished, and calmly writes out his judgment while the
defendant's counsel is still pleading ; another lazily struggles
against sleep, till some rule of law strikes him, when he starts like
a wild animal struck by a shot, and sets to work conscientiously.
Another writes letters or signs papers, looking all the time as
if he were drawing up his judgment. Another keeps interrupting
a barrister from the first word he utters, so as to put a little
liveliness into the case, and transforms counsel's argument into a
comic dialogue ; another interrupts to an equal degree, but
feverishly, wanting to know everything at once, and not giving
the unhappy counsel time to make their explanations in full.
This judge is a tartar. From the moment he grasps the plaintiff's
case, he is unable to rest till the defendant has said yes or no to
the question raised. Counsel also are liable to lose their temper,
and have peculiarities which are not always a source of amusement to the bench. Taking everything into account, the judge is
most defenceless.

When the judge wants to talk to his neighbour, a susceptible
counsel stops short, and the judge blushes, unless he follows the
example of a certain president, who every time counsel came to
an abrupt pause in order to reduce him to silence, used to
mutter " The case is finished." He then trotted out of court with
his colleagues, or delivered an oral judgment on the spot. When
a judge interrupts too often, the advocate heaps up fine phrases
about the liberty of defence, or leaves the bar with a majestic air,
to the great annoyance of the judge, who has no wish to make
enemies. Judges who are light sleepers meet with some terrible
counsel who roar like men stone deaf, stamp on the floor, and
thump the table till the windows rattle. In ancient Greece,
advocates who stamped were punished with a fine. Quite right
too ! In those days they knew how to protect judges ! To listen to
harsh voices arguing for four or five hours at a stretch ; to watch

ugly faces grimacing, hands shaking and bodies undergoing every kind of contortion—such a mode of spending time is not always amusing.

THE ADVOCATE'S COMPLETE GUIDE

Judges must regret the time when the speeches of counsel were confined within certain limits of duration, and when the advocate before the old Parliament was a worthy representative of the type sketched by Dubreuil:—

I. An advocate should be of stately deportment and well-proportioned figure, so as to make a good impression on the eyes of judges and spectators.

II. His countenance should be open, frank, courteous, and well-bred, and should afford at the outset a testimonial in his favour.

III. In his bearing he should show no trace of presumptuous assurance; on the contrary, he should win the favour and interest of those whom he addresses by an air of modesty and reserve.

IV. There should be nothing fierce or reckless in the expression of his eyes.

V. His attitude before the bench should be seemly and respectful; and his dress should exhibit neither foppery nor negligence.

VI. In speaking he should refrain from distorting his features by any twisting of the mouth or lips.

VII. He should avoid bursting out in a loud strident voice.

VIII. He should know how to regulate his intonations so as to keep them at an equal distance from the gruff and the shrill; his voice should be full, clear, and preserve the character of a perfectly medium quality.

IX. In declamation he should be careful to retain an exact pronunciation.

X. He must see that he neither raises nor lowers his tone too much.

XI. He must be careful to keep his style in harmony with the subject he is treating of, and he must avoid the absurdity of putting rhetorical emphasis on insignificant matters.

XII. He must be on his guard against moving his head or his feet too much.

XIII. Lastly, his action should be harmonious and appropriate to his discourse, nor should it be spoilt by exaggerated or feeble gesticulation.

If those who speak in court had to unite all these qualities, there would not be many advocates in Paris or anywhere else. A charming woman who visited the Law Courts said that she had never seen so many deformed bodies or bandy legs before ; and she declared that the Salle des Pas-Perdus, to judge from the robe-clad figures to be seen there, reminded her of the Cour des Miracles. A few years ago there was actually a barrister who was such a dwarf that a presiding judge seeing him address the court called to him in perfect good faith : "Rise, sir ; it is not usual to speak seated." Some barristers argue with their hands in their pockets ; others walk up and down in the empty space before the bar ; others in the course of their speech, moving up little by little, lean over the judge's table and drop into conversation ; others make pathetic appeals to the ceiling till the loose sleeves of their gown fall back from their upturned arms ; some shed tears and beat their breast till it sounds again. Others scatter their papers in all directions, and send the ushers running on all fours after the flying leaves. Some bellow till they are black in the face. Others hum and haw painfully, and, in an anxious voice, spin out interminably observations that ought not to occupy more than five minutes. Some have a way of repeating fifty times, "This is my last word." Others identify themselves with their clients, crying out : "No, gentlemen, we have not deceived our husband ; we are an honest woman." Some

HEADS OF ADVOCATES.
From a sketch by P. Renouard.

stammer ; others lisp ; others scream. Some have always one brief formula on their lips : "My opponent's reasoning is absurd." Some are as rapid as postboys in their speech ; others are short-winded. Some stop to spit, perhaps decorously in their pocket-handkerchiefs, perhaps with noise and to a distance, it may be on the floor or on their shoes, after a sniffling and drawing up their collars. None of these would have found favour with Dubreuil.

Another thing also which would not have pleased him, and which is of frequent occurrence, is the scene which takes place as to the production of documents.

An advocate is bound to show to his opponent all documents he intends to make use of. There is hardly a case in which one of the counsel engaged does not vociferate like a peacock because some document is read by the other side which has not been communicated to him ; he appeals to the court, and enlarges on the duties of the profession. The judges listen sardonically, for the same scene is certain to be acted over again in five minutes on the opposite side, as soon as the objector's turn comes to speak. And the two advocates say many bitter and personal things to each other, though as a matter of fact they are the best friends in the world, and on leaving court will call one another by their Christian names ; but as a general rule there is only one of them who laughs.

As the counsel follow one after another, from one o'clock to four—with a half-hour's interval for rest—loungers look into the court for a time and pass out again. Solicitors' clerks come and hand in papers to the registrar, who grunts in acknowledgment ; barristers look at the *placets* that lie on the bar close to the registrar before mentioned, whom it is dangerous to trouble ; others exert themselves to carry on a brief parley with the government official at the other end while they are putting the papers in order again on the bar. They have to apply to him for briefs to attend [1] and to glean from the *placets* whether the case in which they are engaged is likely to come on soon. The placets are rectangular strips of paper, setting forth the matters at issue between the parties, and to these the advocates sign their names. There are several bundles of placets, one relating to cases which follow the ordinary course, another to motions, another to demurrers, another to cases specially set down for immediate hearing. One should be suspicious of the latter: if a counsel in one of these cases is not present in court, the president reprimands the solicitors, and threatens to decide the case on the pleadings. For some years past an order for immediate hearing has meant little ; orders of this kind being so numerous. In certain chambers of the civil court of first instance, the titles of cases which have reached this stage are posted up on a green notice board outside the door. There is a special cause list for each day in the week, and cases not disposed of are adjourned from week to week.

But it should be added that with all this abundance of precautions, it is impossible to say when a case will really come on ; and

---

[1] *Les dossiers d'assistance.*

STAIRCASE OF THE FOURTH CHAMBER.

it usually happens that advocates have to take the cases to which they attach the most importance on the days when they least expect them.

A case is fixed for a particular day. But it is preceded by another which was begun the week before, and which is bound to last another hour. One must be patient. When a barrister talks of an hour that means two or three. Towards half-past two, when the sitting is suspended, the part-heard case is not yet finished, and the interval often exceeds the regulation half-hour.

This over-long pause in the middle of a too short sitting is unnecessary and annoying. It is true that the judges spend it in deliberation, and not, as malicious persons declare, in playing cards or sipping coffee. But they could easily deliberate after court was over ; this would be so much gained for the cause of justice and the convenience of the bar. Counsel spends the time till half-past three in impatiently walking up and down the half-empty court ; the judges then return, and the president tells him that his case will not be taken till that day week. The whole day is lost !

THE CHAMBERS

The scene described above as taking place in one court is being acted in all. The character of the causes and the aspect of the audience alone differ. There are cases which are assigned indiscriminately to all courts ; and in the same way there is a well-known public which appears everywhere, and which goes from court to court, according as it finds the doors open or shut. This consists of people who come to hear anything that happens to be going on and want to look in everywhere ; and of the ragged crew who go to the trials to sleep, in winter because they find it warmer there than outside, and in summer because they find it cooler. But there are certain courts in which chance visitors like to linger and settle down more than in others, owing to the nature of the cases which are tried or the reputation of the barristers to be heard there. The roving idlers also have their preferences, which are determined not only by the convenience of the place, but also by the nature of the proceedings.

We will begin with the First Chamber.

THE FIRST CHAMBER

This is the largest and handsomest of all. The arrangements
are like those of the typical law court described above, but its
decoration is exceptionally rich. The windows are lofty, set in
rectangular stone frames, and surmounted, inside, by carved
mouldings picked out with gold ; they open out on a square
court-yard, that of the Conciergerie, and are flanked by other
lofty windows, where people, waiting for cases referred to the
judge in chambers, may be seen moving to and fro ; while, down
below, there is a view of iron gratings, vaulted arches, and a
gaoler's lodge embowered in creepers. The ceiling is gilt and the
panelling of the walls blue, with designs in gold ; round the
Chamber runs a frieze in the same colouring, with allegorical
figures in high relief. There are medallions of children above
the doors. The part railed off from the public is spacious, the
daïs and its adjuncts sumptuously appointed in keeping with the
chamber, with side benches for the judges' friends. Loungers have a
special fondness for the place, partly because it is the First Chamber,
partly because of its architectural pretensions ; and they stroll up
and down at their pleasure, or rest with their elbows on the iron
backs fixed in the last row of benches. Elderly idlers prefer this
Chamber as a sleeping place to any other, partly because the seats
are more comfortable, partly because it is more airy, partly because
the very majesty of the place tends to make people walk lightly
and speak in subdued tones. Certain old stagers use it as a
regular reading room. They may be seen to the number of five
or six, very respectable in appearance, with rather seedy clothes
and ill-brushed hair ; they come early with a book wrapped round
with a newspaper, and sleep stolidly, their nose between the pages.
What suits them best is some administrative difficulty, the great
question of cognisance,[1] which, attracting no hearers, and exciting
no interest, even in the counsel engaged, is discussed in subdued
tones and at prodigious length. They are fond also of cases of
a rather heavy kind, for which it is usual to bring out of their
retirement certain senior members of the profession who are rarely
to be heard ; other interests having withdrawn them from the bar.

---

[1] *Compétence.*

With happy air, their eyes shut and their ears fast closed, these
visitors attend to witness the last flickerings of expiring genius.
They have a weakness for cases which go by default; and they
like to listen to suits *in formâ pauperis*, and the scarcely audible
remarks of some young probationer. They love judges who never
interrupt, and government counsel who dislike speech-making.

The diversion provided by typical *Parisian* cases rarely gives
them satisfaction ; many of them curse the practice of bringing to
the First Chamber of the tribunal, and before their turn, cases
which concern well-known writers, members of the dramatic
profession, or people whose doings are chronicled in the press.
A case of this sort attracts a crowd of ladies, usually good-looking,
but who fidget and chatter, take up all the room, spread their
skirts over the knees of the regular comers, or contemptuously
push them aside with sharp little thrusts, so that a quiet nap
becomes impossible. There comes a posse of noisy probationers,
the other courts send their own regular contingents, and passers-by
flock in ; our friends no longer feel at home. It is true that
occasions like these are field days for popular counsel, regular
professors of eloquence, who speak in harmonious phrases ; men
who sparkle with jest, tell broad stories, or utter blunt home
truths ; but the regular frequenter of the First Chamber only likes
eloquence, irony, or invective in small doses ; these things prevent
him from going to sleep over his book.

When a great financial case comes on they are quite swamped
by the inrush of persons interested. In ordinary actions the client
is rarely present in court to hear his counsel speak, to encourage
him with approving gestures, or to suggest, by quick signs, some
crushing reply, during the opponent's address. Suppose, however,
that an action has been brought against the directors of a company
(cases of this kind, when the company is not commercial, come
before the civil court) ; then the shareholders pour into court in
crowds, they get possession of all the good places, they relate their
woes to uninterested neighbours, and they show indignation or fall
a-laughing when counsel for one of the wretched promoters asks
pity for his client, a poor victim, who has only acted out of love for
his country and the public good. On those days it is impossible to
enjoy a quiet sleep !

How many eminent advocates have conducted famous cases in
this First Chamber ! The faithful sleeper has no recollection of

them. Sometimes, when he has some difficulty in getting to sleep, or when a counsel speaks with special force, he asks some member of the bar, "Who is that speaking there?" And in a week's time he has forgotten all about him.

It is among the counsel that one meets the old gentleman with an inexhaustible store of anecdotes, who has seen everything, heard everything, and never misses being present at a great case—one wonders when his own cases come off. He knew Berryer, Marie, Paillet, the great Liouville, Chaix d'Est-Ange, Dufaure ; he knew Grévy when *bâtonnier*, and he saw our present political leaders make their *début* at the Palace; he has by heart the whole collection of Léon Duval's witticisms; he repeats good sayings of Nicolet ; his picture gallery of the illustrious dead includes the stately form of Allou and the delicate and subtle features of Durier ; he recalls the powerful argument of Lenté on the will of Ben-Aïad ; and he draws portraits of all the celebrated litigants who have appeared in the First Chamber. He waxes most amusing over that of Sardou, who stuck close to his advocate, Maître Cléry, throughout the *Fiammina* case; he grows tender over the Duchesse de Chaulnes, who looked so bewitching, during the midday interval, when standing up, with her back turned to the bar, looking down on the barristers seated on their benches, she chatted with her counsel, and gazed absently on the crowd. Lastly, whenever a case of any importance comes before the First Chamber, not only the whole band of students but the whole clan of dilettante advocates become wild with excitement ; they crowd the space reserved for the bar, and climb up on to the judge's daïs. The latter are mostly juniors of from thirty to forty, whom solicitors never trouble, but who from pure love of their profession delude themselves into the notion of doing business by watching others do it. Those of them who do not drop out of the chase after briefs will in ten years time be able to play the part of an old stager of the profession.

THE SECOND CHAMBER

In the Second Chamber there are no gala-days. Neither clients, nor loungers, nor fashionable beauties, nor old stagers, nor make-believes ever appear there ; it has never been able to muster a body of regular frequenters; and even the poorest avoid it. It has a gloomy look. Yet there is nothing remarkable in its furniture. The picture of the crucifixion it contains is no worse than that in other Chambers. There is the usual government functionary hidden between the windows ; and these windows open out, like those of the First Chamber, on to the quadrangle of the Conciergerie. Nor are its judges specially chosen because of their ugliness. Whence comes the sadness which prevails ? a dulness so profound, that a lounger who chances to look into this solitude is frightened by the sound of his own footsteps, and lets the door fall to again with a bang. Whence, we repeat, comes this air of sadness ?

MAÎTRE POUILLET.

It is because, in this Chamber, are settled cases connected with the stamp duties, suits for separate maintenance, and actions relating to the public taxes.

THE THIRD CHAMBER

The Third Chamber decides all cases connected with patents, infringements of trade-marks, and literary disputes which are not important enough for the First Chamber.

It has an audience of many types. Often the clients are present along with their family, their friends, and the representatives of the industry interested in the annulling of the patent or the throwing open to the public of the trade-mark claimed.

The speeches, instead of turning on sentimental commonplaces or articles of the civil code, deal with technical matters, with machines and processes ; and their novelty has an occasional attraction for chance hearers who having looked in for a minute, end by staying there. They do not venture to sit down, but crowd together under the bust of the Republic.

The general public is amused by the necessary display of little models of machines, sometimes full-sized machines—heavy machines for making cigarettes, enormous bellows for forges, looms, telephonic installations are sometimes exhibited,—and by the rows of trade samples, blacking-bottles, pots of preserves, bottles of different liqueurs, &c., which line the table of the court, and form a kind of frame for the judges' faces.

Sometimes the bench is blocked in with a collection of statues, by which the judges' heads are almost concealed. On some days are to be seen toys, mechanical fish with movable tails, jumping frogs, gymnastic figures that do tricks on the trapeze ; and while the president smiles on the counsel engaged, the other judges wind up the springs, the animals dance, and the puppets go through their performances. Sometimes the speeches are accompanied by tunes from musical boxes ; there are occasions even when people give an air on the trombone. Or the judicial table is transformed into a dressmaker s show-room ; the furniture being covered with false busts, corsets, and crinolines. Or even there may be a lavish display of fans and perfumes, which gives the court the air of a lady's boudoir.

The counsel also help to charm and retain the spectators. Here practise the two great authorities on fraudulent imitation, both of them specialists in matters connected with manufacture and commerce.

The first, majestic and statuesque, speaks with all the weight of his powerful form. At one time pouring the whitewashing flood of his eloquence on the heads of wrongdoers, whom his words comfort and reassure ; at another time annihilating poor wretches with his contempt, and drowning their arguments under a stream of words that flows on like the waves of the North Sea.

The other is quick, nervous, and seductive. He begins on the sly by carefully explaining some most complicated piece of mechanism with a subdued grace of style. This done, he gives way to his natural fervour, and with vigorous gesticulation makes the persons and objects before the court glow with life. He discusses the evidence with a freedom, which, however, never oversteps the plan he has marked out for himself, and with a wealth of fancy which veils the hardness of the outline. As he disentangles the point at issue he grows excited, strikes at the other side, unnerves his opponent, and marches straight to the conquest of the judge. Finally, with the nimbleness of a Parisian street boy, his glasses fixed on the tip of his nose, his hair floating behind him, a satirical but kindly expression on his shaven upper lip, and an aggressive short gray beard showing from beneath his chin, he sounds the assault in strident tones, and sums up in a triumphant flourish, with a dazzling rush of speech rich in many a picturesque expression and luminous flash of thought.

When one of these two is speaking the other is not less amusing to watch. The calmer of the pair grows frantic beneath the storm of words that descends upon him. At each period he leaps up in a new fit of indignation, utters cries of protest, or raises his eyes and shoulders towards the white and gold ceiling and draws a long breath. The more nervous calms down during his opponent's address, restrains himself from making abrupt movements, adjusts his glasses, makes notes in minute handwriting on slips of paper, and smiles with close-set lips.

Besides these two regular opponents, there are several other specialists who deserve mention. One, unpretending, spruce, and bald-headed, is interesting because of the simplicity of his style and the clearness of his explanations. Another, a taller man, with high shoulders, a smiling but rather bitter mouth, an elegant though formal way of speaking, looks like a Roman of the decadence or a diplomatist from the Vatican. A visitor will hear many others, but not exactly specialists, and for that very reason envied by the specialists proper ; because the latter are invariably looked upon as skilled only in one department, though their greatest pleasure is to emerge from it and show that they have enough general talent for any branch of practice.

THE FOURTH CHAMBER

The specialists of the Fourth Chamber are the counsel of the omnibus companies, the cab proprietors, and the accident insurance companies. Many divorce cases are also tried there, but the advocate employed in such cases is not a specialist properly so called. Parties suing for a divorce find their counsel among retired magistrates and past *bâtonniers*. Respondents choose theirs from the ranks of the criminal bar and professed humourists.

If a cabman has run over some luckless foot passenger you have a chance of hearing a barrister, still young—youth lasts long at

the law courts—just beginning to grow stout, always stroking a
pair of soft gray whiskers, possessed of charming manners, and
cheeks on which beads of moisture readily appear, or an old
gentleman, with whiskers also, though they are white ; and with

THE "PONT" OF THE FOURTH CHAMBER.

smooth yellow hair that sets off a florid complexion ; who, with
eyes looking very fierce behind their glasses, will express himself
in severe terms respecting people who are mean enough to get
themselves run over by cabs.

If the defendant is an omnibus driver, his counsel is pretty certain to be a charming man with a brown moustache, who will talk nicely for ten minutes in perfect good temper, rolling his r's with a strong Touraine accent. On certain occasions, however, you will hear a professed humourist, largely employed in divorce cases and a performer much in vogue; he is now rather sobered down, but is still recognisable by his bushy eyebrows, his clear metallic voice, and his fascinating blue eyes. If the accident has taken place in a house in process of construction, it will be the turn of a learned gentleman whose speciality has won him the name of "the building machine," and while he is speaking you will see his eyes swell with tears and hear the stifled sobs in his throat. For other accidents the counsel most in request is a stout, jovial-looking fellow, whose gown looks a tight fit, always busy and always running about; he has countless briefs to read, and speaks in a loud voice.

The Fourth Chamber has a crowd of regular frequenters, even worse dressed than those of the first; they are, however, far more attentive. They seem to have chosen the place not for its convenience—for the space is confined, the only place to sleep on is a wooden bench fixed to the wall, and a very unpleasant smell arises from the wretched creatures who occupy it—but for the kind of cases to be heard there, for its reputation as the divorce court.

Spicy cases are, however, becoming rarer and rarer; the most sensational divorces are decided upon statements previously laid before the president, and the public only hear a few short and veiled allusions; but the reputation of the court has survived, and people flock to it in crowds. Visitors who are taken over the law courts by a relation or friend always begin by asking for the divorce court; and they are quite disappointed, on their arrival, to hear a trial about a labourer who has had his hand caught in some machinery, or a gentleman who has been thrown from his horse, nothing, in fact, in the slightest way suggestive. The only charm of the court lies in the gray-blue landscape, gray or blue predominating at different times, which can be seen from its windows, stretching from the Quai aux Fleurs to the roof of the Hôtel de Ville with its sculptured figures of men-at-arms.

The three last Chambers that we have inspected are on the same bridge-shaped landing which is reached by a double staircase

leading from the Salle des Pas-Perdus.   The stair-head is full of
life.   It has two benches for those who have to wait.   One of them,
which is close to the Fourth Chamber, is often honoured by some
fair party to a divorce suit, sitting close by her counsel's side ; the
other is usually occupied by garrulous advocates waiting their turn
in the Second Chamber.   Others lean their elbows on the parapets
of the bridge leading to the Third Chamber, their briefs fully displayed ; behind them clerks pass hurriedly, and down below they
can see, in the hall leading to the Sixth Chamber and the president's private room, other members of the bar pacing to and fro ;
while on Wednesday this hall is thronged with male and female
applicants for divorce, wrathful husbands still burning to chastise
their wives, and fainting women whom Dr. Floquet delicately
unlaces, and whose charms are disclosed to eyes looking down
from above.

From the landing one can go down the stairs leading to the
Salle des Pas-Perdus ; on wet days clouds of mist float about ; in the
summer the air is thick with dust ; and, ever and again, the little
black groups collect on the white pavement, break up into parallel
lines, which march up and down in military fashion, till they re-form
and dissolve again in a confused murmur beneath the interlacing
rays of light that fall from the diamond-paned windows.

FIFTH, SIXTH, AND SEVENTH CHAMBERS

By taking the staircase on the left, the visitor will arrive in the
Salle des Pas-Perdus at the threshold of the Fifth Chamber, which is
placed exactly beneath the Fourth.   The counsel here are of every
type, the public is miscellaneous ; there is no distinctive mark.
Stay a moment : nowhere is the picture of the crucifixion so
atrociously bad.

Under the arch at the back of the hall is concealed the entrance
to the Sixth Chamber.   This again is a court with nothing to distinguish it, where cases that present no special feature are disposed
of indiscriminately.   It has a fine view over the Seine and the
outlet of a sewer ; beyond and above lies the Place du Châtelet,
pleasant in the summer time from its verdure, out of which rises
a gilded statue of Victory.   In winter, the view is calculated to
draw unfortunate suitors to the river.

Lastly, the Seventh Chamber lies in an angle of the Salle des Pas-Perdus, by the side of the first. This is the domain of the junior bar, their field of exercise, a narrow little place, badly lighted, where trumpery cases are dispatched in the most summary manner. It looks like the court of a justice of peace ; there are three judges and no public. No one goes there save the counsel engaged, who quickly run through their little statement, listen absently to their opponent, mark their brief and depart. When the president is a man of business and not over technical, the proceedings resemble a familiar conversation rather than a regular argument. But there are certain counsel of such ardour and conscientiousness that neither years nor presidents have any effect on them.

Court of the Sainte-Chapelle.

CHAPTER VI

ADJUNCTS TO THE CIVIL COURT

THE OFFICE

AN important case is about to be heard. You have obtained
admission to the court, have settled yourself in a front place, and
are waiting to be thrilled by the eloquence of some leading counsel.
Have you, at this moment, ever felt any curiosity as to the preliminary trial undergone by the mass of legal documents that swell
his brief? I fear not.

De minimis non curat praetor.

And, like the prætor of old, you do not trouble your head about
such trifles.

All the same, these trifles have their interest. For there is not
a single bit of stamped paper in the brief which has not given rise
to journeys without number in what may be called the ante-
chambers of the Palace of Justice.

In order to learn something about these preliminary stages, let
us follow this sharp-looking little fellow of fourteen or fifteen who,
with a bag on his arm, has just arrived at the courts at about
eleven o'clock, in company with a crowd of little fellows as brisk
as himself.

This is the junior clerk, nicknamed, from time immemorial, the
saute-ruisseau. He lunched in the office, before the other clerks, in
a rough-and-ready fashion, off stewed mutton and potatoes, with a
pennyworth of cheese, bought at the cook-shop over the way,
bread and wine being kindly furnished gratis by his employer. He
then sets out for the courts, with a song on his lips and gaiety in
his heart.

All junior clerks, however, are not young. Some of them, who
have done nothing but run up and down the courts for twenty-five

years, may be seen with hair and whiskers turning white. For these the "holy places" of the Temple of Themis have no mystery; they know its most secret windings, its most hidden corners. If pressed, they could tell you from what part of the building comes any grain of dust which chances to fall upon their hats. Sometimes, in fact, a glorious veteran, his breast glittering with stars, may be seen fulfilling this duty in spite of an amputated arm. Sometimes the real junior clerk is replaced by an amateur, dressed up to the eyes; and thus, in that part of the law courts where junior clerks reign supreme, one may notice many different types in the jostling crowd.

But let us follow our junior clerk. Here he is in the Salle des Pas-Perdus. His first step is to go and deposit in the hands of the clerk at the office of the First Chamber a petition for leave to issue a writ at once,[1] asking the judge to relieve the plaintiff from the obligation of going before a justice of peace for an attempt at conciliation, and to give him leave to summon the defendant to appear at the end of three days' notice. At four o'clock, this petition, answered or not by the judge as the case may be, will be returned to him along with the papers on the case from his office, through the Chamber of Solicitors practising before the Court.

He then ascends the little double staircase leading from the Salle des Pas-Perdus to the Second and Fourth Chambers, crosses the landing, turns to the left, mounts another flight of steps and deposits all his papers, writ of summons, pleadings, notice of trial,[3] service of judgment on the solicitor, &c., at the ushers' office,[4] on the first floor. These documents will be returned to him in two days' time, duly registered and served, at office No. 17, which is situated on the second floor. To this the junior clerk is now making his way.

At office No. 1 he takes away the ticket assigning an action and copies of judgments.[5] On reaching office No. 2 he perceives two women dressed in mourning, seated in a corner. They are waiting for him to sign, perhaps a formal acceptance, perhaps a formal renunciation of some deceased's succession, or of the community of goods between husband and wife.[6] At office No. 3

---

[1] *Requête à bref délai.*

[2] *Chambre des avoués.*

[3] *Avenir à l'audience.*

[4] *Bureau des huissiers.*

[5] *Il retire le bulletin de distribution et les expéditions de jugements.*

[6] *Soit une acceptation, soit une renonciation à succession ou à communauté.*

he lodges a writ of execution ; at No. 4 he looks in to ascertain whether a will has been deposited. Going on, he receives from the official at No. 5, sheltered, like all his colleagues, behind a grating, a certificate that no opposition has been entered.[1]

He passes by Nos. 8 and 9, which deal with the formal inquiries held before the civil chambers, and by No. 9A, where papers relating to civil rights are examined. Then he enters No. 10, where the archives are kept, and sits down for a minute. There are arranged, chamber by chamber, the judgments delivered in the seven civil chambers during the last ten years. Those of the years before this date are kept in the reserve, in an immense hall annexed to the Record Office, and extending right above the Salle des Pas-Perdus.

After having inspected the judgment he requires our clerk lodges at office No. 11 the minutes from which the judgment will be drawn up.[2] Proofs of debt, in the distribution of the proceeds of real and personal estate sold under execution,[3] are lodged at office No. 13 ; lastly, at No. 16 are deposited the records of all the cases tried in the law courts, so that they may be put on the general list and be distributed among the different chambers of the courts.

Such then are the principal rounds which every junior office clerk has to make every day ; such the process which all legal documents must go through before they are finally inserted in the brief.

PROCEEDINGS IN JUDGES' CHAMBERS

Half-past twelve has just struck from the clock placed in the Salle des Pas-Perdus, above the old first chamber of the civil court, which is nowadays a room where applications not made in open court are heard.

The junior clerk has come down stairs to wait for the opening of certain departments. He meets a fellow-clerk from his own office, better skilled than himself in the mysteries of legal procedure, a student or a future solicitor, who has already acquired the look of an official of the Public Ministry. This

[1] *Certificat de non-opposition.*
[2] *La minute des qualités sur lesquelles se fera l'expédition du jugement rendu.*
[3] *Productions à ordre, et productions à contribution*

clerk, a managing clerk or second clerk, has two applications in chambers to support, one on a report, the other on an originating summons.[1]

Suddenly the door of the room where the cases are heard is thrown open. A crowd of petty tradesmen, wine-sellers, grocers, fruiterers, dressmakers, &c., push their way in at the same time as the general agents and the clerks sent to support applications. In the corners are little groups busy talking; some look resigned, others gesticulate furiously. A few more patient people stand at the window, and gaze stolidly at the gray paved court and postern gate of the Conciergerie. Poor tenants, whose ejectment is demanded, consult a shady-looking general agent about the seriousness of their case, timidly slipping three francs into his hand.

The judge appears, accompanied by his registrar; quiet is restored, and the applicants begin to file past him one by one.

First sitting. Applications on reports, claims for the ejectment of backward tenants, requests for time on the part of the latter, applications to discontinue actions [2] for removal of seals,[3] &c., cross

IN JUDGES' CHAMBERS.
From a sketch by P. Renouard.

and recross one another. In three-quarters of an hour, with a whispering that recalls a sick-room—for here no one speaks up, the parties or their representatives state their case in an undertone —more than forty applications are disposed of.

A rather long interval follows. Some fresh interested parties come on the scene; the lawyers have gone off on other business. The managing clerk, to whom we were conducted by our first little friend, has lost his first application. The judge has given time to the tenant whose immediate expulsion he demanded. Being conscientious as times go, the clerk sits down on an unoccupied bench in the Salle des Pas-Perdus, and works away at his second batch of papers.

---

[1] *Un référé sur procès-verbal, et un référé sur placet.*
[2] *Discontinuation de poursuites.*
[3] *Levée de scellés.*

Two o'clock strikes, and the doors are again thrown open. A fresh judge appears; sometimes it is the president of the court, attended of course by the registrar.

The second sitting now begins. Applications on originating summonses for official inspections, for replevin,[1] for reduction of the amount of distress,[2] for appointment of receivers,[3] &c.

Many solicitors in their gowns are in attendance to support the interest of their clients.

And now it is our clerk's turn; he argues, explains, replies, and, if it is his first appearance, awaits, with beating heart, the decision of the judge. Let us say that he wins. One lost, one gained. This sounds well in a story, and will satisfy the equitable instincts of our reader.

Nearly all our modern orators have commenced their career by mumbling applications in chambers. Presidents have sometimes been so much struck by the intelligent air of the clerk, who in his nervousness was passing by the decisive argument, that they have encouraged him and gradually brought him back to the right path. An *ex-bâtonnier* perhaps remembers that during his early years of clerkship, he had to make an application in chambers before President de Belleyme. Though he had a good case, his whole face showed terror at the thought of losing it, and he went on a completely wrong track in his statement.

"Ah!" said M. de Belleyme, "you want to win your application? Why then do you not lay stress upon the arguments in your favour?"

"Because, Mr. President. . . . . ."

"Come now, another time, when you have an application like this to make, I will tell you what you should say."

And to the astonishment of the future advocate, M. de Belleyme set forth in order all the arguments bearing on the case then before him.

"There now, I tell you again, that is what you will say another time, and then the president, in his turn, will tell the registrar as I tell him to day: 'Registrar, order as asked.'"

Maitre——went away very well satisfied. Thanks to the judge's arguments, he had gained his application.

---

[1] *Mainlevée de saisie-arrêt.*　　　　[2] *Réduction du montant de la saisie.*
[3] *Nomination de séquestres.*

DIVORCE CASES

It is 2 P.M. on Wednesday. The glass-roofed hall—the *atrium* our architect calls it—which connects the Salle des Pas-Perdus with the Sixth Chamber of the Civil Court and the rooms annexed to the First begin to fill with women. Some wear hats, some bonnets, others are bare-headed ; some are smiling, others sit down without saying a word. Some of them shed tears, but these are very few. Then come the men, some grave, others cheerful. The men and women are husbands and wives engaged in suits for divorce or judicial separation, who must first appear before the president for an attempt at reconciliation. From time to time, in the middle of this crowd of common people, there appears, followed by her solicitor, an elegant young lady, dressed in black silk with dark *suède* gloves. In deference to the occasion she wears no jewellery, excepting a pair of costly ear-rings. These she cannot leave off even for a minute, because they light up her whole face. While waiting her turn, this very modest suitor will seat herself without shame on the corner of a bench close to a bare-headed woman, perhaps her dependant ; and the latter watches her

DIVORÇONS !

From a sketch by P. Renouard.

neighbour curiously, thinking, no doubt, that fortune, in this respect, like the guard which in old days used to keep watch at the gates of the Louvre, does not protect the rich any more than the poor from conjugal troubles.

Each couple then passes into the private room of the judge who is charged with the duty of trying to effect a reconciliation. And there, performing the office of a physician of souls, the magistrate occasionally succeeds in effecting a reconciliation. But more often than not he fails.

After a while the hall grows empty; several months, sometimes several years after this preliminary attendance, the couple or their solicitors reappear with the witnesses, to stifle in the low-roofed ante-chambers of the examining judges ; every one, when he has the chance, going to breathe at one of the square windows which enable those in the hall of the divorce court to see the figures of people walking in the square below. As a general rule, the witnesses and the solicitors come without their clients for this little ceremony, which takes place, according to the law, in the judge's plainly furnished private room. Assisted by the inevitable registrar, and seated before a small mahogany desk, the examining judge takes down the depositions of the witnesses brought forward by each party to justify his or her statement of facts. The witnesses or the actual parties interested grow animated and warm. The examining judge, surfeited with experience of human failings, wears a mask of serious impassibility. The registrar, like his superior, scribbles away at his notes. But, when the examination is finished and the two inquisitors are left alone, a curious observer would see them unbutton their waistcoats—so as to have a laugh at their ease !

THE PRESIDENT OF THE COURT OF FIRST INSTANCE

The hall, where we have just seen the applicants for divorce, leads to the private room of the president of the Court. The best time for a visit is half-past four : the solicitors form a line in a little corridor, in the middle of a crowd of young clerks ; ladies, and as a rule ladies only, are seated immovably on leather chairs, in the little waiting room, with a sort of hope that the green velvet-covered door of the president's room will soon open ; their sole consolation being a few words from a polite, fair-haired gentleman, the president's secretary. Those who have the good luck to enter will find themselves in a spacious, well-lighted room, with President Aubépin seated at a large writing table, his features refined, serious, and a little worn by fatigue. After being a Deputy Procureur of note, M. Aubépin was, in 1872, appointed president of the Court of First Instance of the Seine, which he has ever since filled with a tact and firmness acknowledged by every one. Around him, on the wall, are the portraits of his predecessors.

To the right of the corridor leading from the president's private room, is a way to the postern gate of the Conciergerie. On the left is the Council Chamber, lighted, like a studio, by the tripartite pointed window that can be seen from the Place du Châtelet, between the two towers of the Conciergerie. At the extreme end is a little enclosed courtyard, and in this courtyard is the base of a tower which contains the records connected with the office of the First Chamber.

SUING IN FORMÂ PAUPERIS

Everybody finds the expenses of litigation serious ; to some they are crushing. The heavy sums that have to be paid out in fees to court officials, solicitors, and counsel form an insurmountable obstacle to the poor. The free dispensation of justice is an ideal which financial necessities have relegated to the kingdom of Utopia; but, in the meantime, those who, being without resources, have legal rights to assert, can bring them before the courts, thanks to the *poor suitors' aid department.*[1]

This department, established with the view of enabling poor people to commence an action at law, or to obtain legal defence when sued, ends indirectly in the curious result that the very rich and the very poor are equally relieved from any anxiety as to law costs. Only those persons of slender means, who live in straits, though not in poverty, and who find it very difficult to make both ends meet, are deterred from seeking justice through fear of the heavy expenses it entails; it is this class of people who are too often compelled, in dread of a costly law-suit, to forego their rights or to accept the ruinous terms imposed on them by some rich adversary.

How must people proceed in order to obtain help from the poor suitors' aid department? and in what way are they to apply for it? Few advocates or regular frequenters of the law courts have not been called on to answer this question, put to them in a humble voice by some poor fellow they meet wandering about in the Salle des Pas-Perdus or its side corridors.

The applicant's first step must be to provide himself with two indispensable documents. First, a copy of his tax-paper or a certificate from the collector of his district to show that he is not assuming a false position. Secondly, a declaration of poverty,

---

[1] *L'assistance judiciaire.*

setting forth that he has no means, and is unable to assert his rights at law. This declaration must show in detail the applicant's means of livelihood; and it must be taken to the mayor of his parish, who at the foot of the document authenticates its execution and appends his signature.

Furnished with these two documents, the applicant indites a letter addressed to the Procureur, making in formal terms his request for public aid. This letter can be written on ordinary paper, but it must contain precise information regarding the actual suit in respect of which the applicant prays for help. Attached to this letter are the two documents before mentioned. The whole is then put in an envelope and posted, or, what is better, personally delivered at the procureur's office. This done, nothing remains but to wait. This is just what it is difficult to impress on the petitioner, who fidgets and wonders what has become of his letter. What happens is this: the procureur forwards the petition to the staff of the poor suitors' aid department, who will examine it, determine on its merits, and decide whether it shall be granted or refused. The staff of this department for the Tribunal of the Seine is divided into three sections, each section being composed of five members: a delegate of the director of the Registration Office, an advocate, a solicitor nominated by the solicitors' chamber,[1] and a retired magistrate, advocate or solicitor, nominated by the Tribunal. Its sittings are not public.

When a request for aid has been forwarded to the staff, it is assigned to one of the three sections. The latter appoints some one to report on the petition, and the parties to the suit in question are then summoned by letter, and heard, not only as to the petitioner's plea of want of means and inability to bear the expense of going to law, but also on the subject of the case itself and the rights in dispute. The opposite side is at liberty to call in question the poverty of the petitioner as well as his grounds of action in the suit. The official reporter advises the department to adopt or reject the petition, and the department give their decision without assigning any reason for it; they merely state the facts and give a brief summary of the suit in question. This decision is final and without appeal. A petitioner, moreover, must not forget to present himself on the date fixed by the official reporter,

---

[1] *Chambre des avoués.*

for, even though the department decide in ignorance of some special plea or argument which might have been put forward to materially strengthen the petition, they cannot, on this pretext, reverse their decision.   At Paris, in case of the petitioner's non-attendance, it is customary to send a second notice ; but, if the petitioner fails to appear at the second summons, his application is finally struck off the list.   If the claim to public assistance is allowed, a copy of the decision is sent, through the procureur, to the President of the Civil Court.   To this copy are added the papers in the case.   The president then writes letters to the *bâtonnier* of the Order of Advocates, to the Chamber of Solicitors, and to the Chamber of Ushers, who will have to appoint an usher to serve proceedings, a solicitor to take them, and an advocate to appear—in each case without payment on the suitor's behalf.

The benefits of public aid are liable to be withdrawn while the action is pending if the person assisted acquire new resources, or if it is found out that he has deceived the department by a fraudulent declaration.   In the latter case, criminal proceedings can be taken against the person who has been guilty of deceit.

CHAPTER VII

THE AUCTION ROOM

CROSSING the little courtyard of the First Chamber, we find ourselves back again in the Salle des Pas-Perdus at its western end. There, on the very spot where once stood the marble table,[1] two large doors open, giving access to a spacious rectangular apartment, down the middle of which is raised a kind of long platform, the parts of the room near the wall being furnished with tiers of benches arranged to form the segment of a circle. Here sales by auction of land and houses take place. At two o'clock on Wednesdays, Thursdays, and Saturdays, the loud ringing of a bell announces the commencement of proceedings. The crowd rush in, the hall is filled with the mass of people we have seen waiting at the door; solicitors representing clients, men, women, general agents; tall hats are seen mingled with workmen's caps, and the stuff gowns of solicitors with ladies' silk dresses. All distinctions of occupation, ambition, and class are lost in one and the same pursuit of gain, each one, according to his resources, feeling the same intensity of interest and the same passion, whether the property in question be a plot of ground worth a thousand francs or an estate valued at two millions.

The seats on the tiers of benches are quickly taken, and in every part of the room, from centre to corners, the people crowd in till they are packed so tightly that they cannot move. The doors

---

[1] A vast table on which mysteries are said to have been played in the Middle Ages.

bang, people enter and leave; there is a constant coming and going, and the place is as full of bustle as a fair. The only things wanting are the cattle, the sheep, and the little flesh-coloured grunting pigs for sale. The judge—there is only one—arrives, and takes his place at the desk in the middle of the daïs. On the extreme right, by his side, sits the registrar; on the extreme left, an official appointed to take charge of the lights—the auction lights.[1]

The auction lights are an old custom. On a huge silver candlestick, like the chandeliers to be seen in churches, is placed a sort of iron box, above which is an upright needle. To this needle is fixed a diminutive taper, like a wax caterpillar, which burns for a few seconds, and is replaced, as soon as it is out, by another, lighted at a candle close by.

The lots put up for sale include properties held in undivided shares as to the value of which the owners have not been able to agree, or forming part of the estate of some deceased person in which minors or persons under disability are interested, and which in such a case the law directs to be sold by order of the court; the lots also include property sold by mortgagees; in one word, everything that is put up for sale by process of law and disposed of to the last and best bidder. The persons present frequently consult a sheet of paper, which contains the particulars of the lots offered for competition. Every time that a new number is called out there are movements on the benches. The solicitor goes and sits by his client, or the latter goes down to his solicitor, who stands in front of the rostrum and who alone has the right to bid. Every would-be purchaser more or less openly pesters his man of business, to whom he has already given long instructions in the Salle des Pas-Perdus. "Let me alone," he answers. "Don't stop me! I will give the other bidders no respite. Tell me your maximum price, and I will so take their breath away that they won't dare follow." Another preaches opposite tactics. "Keep quiet! Pretend at first that you don't want anything. Let them begin, and, then, at the right time we will step in and win."

At the summons of the usher on duty, the solicitor having the conduct of the sale uncovers, and asks to see that the proceedings are in form. Then as soon as the upset price is announced the bidding begins. Two tapers are lighted. Before the third, the

<hr>

[1] *Les feux des enchères.*

officer in charge calls out in a clear voice: "Last light!" But higher bids keep coming in, and as three lights must burn through on each bid, as soon as a new price is offered, the following light, which was announced as the last, becomes the first of the three required by law. In this way, when a large property is for sale, it happens that the uninitiated, to their astonishment, hear the warning of "last light" twenty times over without knowing why there are so many last lights. There are few things so amusing as to mingle with the public, identify one's self with some purchaser and

"LAST LIGHT!"

follow his tricks and stratagems. All assume an air of indifference; they affect an uninterested tone of voice and attitudes of lofty disdain. "Ten thousand francs!" cries the usher. "Eleven thousand," answers a distant voice. "Twelve thousand!" shouts some one at the other end of the hall. "Thirteen thousand!" rejoins the first bidder. "Any one fourteen . . . . ?" asks the usher, with a glance at the opponent's solicitor; but the latter shakes his head. No more for him. It is too dear. His rival carries off the prize.

Suddenly the silence is broken by the sacramental words "Last light!" The situation grows exciting. The reluctant solicitor wakes up, urged on, spurred on when he is not forestalled in his bidding by his client, who gasps out, "Take care, sir, or I shall lose this! Bid away, can't you?" "Don't be afraid, I know what I am about." And, calmly, the auctioneer puts down his list. "Fifty?" "Thirteen thousand and fifty francs, by Maître X——" repeats the crier. His opponent retorts, and the "last lights" follow on one another in quick succession. At last, after alternate advances managed with more or less address, the victory is decided in favour of one of the bidders. He is always delighted at his triumph, although often he has made a bad bargain, carried farther than he intended to go by the fascination of the contest, and by the infatuation which is produced by the running up of the bidding, giving it all the illusion of high play.

There are also the puffers, pretending purchasers, who fight "for a good motive," and who often become its victims. Their sole aim in raising the bids is that the property, in which they have a share, may fetch a higher price. They urge on the bidders, reckoning on a demand, the strength of which they have miscalculated, and the force of which is spent but all too soon. The property remains on their hands. Often they have not the means of paying for it. They will have to put it up for sale again and pay the costs of the resale ; enormous costs which will swallow up all their share. How often, too, purchasers deceive themselves ! How many in their dreams had redecorated the house, made new plans, furnished the apartments in exquisite style, given a house-warming, and then, after all, their dreams have been scattered by the excessive prices they have paid. Another source of disappointment is to be found in the practice of uniting lots. There are, for instance, three different lots in one inheritance. Each of these lots is sold separately, but with power for the vendors to unite the three into one, after the separate biddings, to see if a higher aggregate price can be obtained for the whole together. The property includes a charming little house. A pretty woman—she is always pretty in these cases—comes to the auction room with beating heart. She has paid a visit to the house ; she wants it, she must have it. Her solicitor sends up the bidding. The little house is knocked down to him. So great is her joy that the fair client can hardly help embracing him. But now the whole three lots are put up as one. The total sum realised up to now is announced ; the whole is put up at this price, and a horrid lawyer, abominably ugly—he is always abominably ugly in this case—offers an advance on the aggregate sum and takes all. Farewell to the little nest! Perrette often comes to the auction room to have her jugs of milk broken. The judge, who calmly declares the property knocked down to Maître L——, seems not to have even a suspicion of these emotions and woes that quiver around him. From time to time, on a fixed day of the week, advocates appear amidst this throng to argue points that arise in connection with forced sales.

CHAPTER VIII

THE ADVOCATES' CONFERENCE

EVERY Monday, from the beginning of November to the end of June, a change comes over the character of the auction room. The judge is replaced by the *bâtonnier* of the Order of Advocates, who looks quite magisterial in this position. In place of the man who lights the auction tapers, a young probationer, conscious of his glory, reads a paper on some point of law, which, with the consent of the *bâtonnier*, he proposes as a subject for discussion in the ensuing week—a discussion which the orators will not fail to conduct with their usual skill, showing once more that, when necessary, knowledge and style can be combined together.

In the registrar's place another rising young probationer is preparing to resume the discussion set down for the day. To the right and left of the president, in the shade where the light coming from over their heads leaves them, is a crowd of other probationers, forming, with the two before mentioned, the body of secretaries to the advocates' conference. A space has been cleared in the middle of the room. At the bar are four aspirants, who each deliver their little speech in the hope of being admitted to the honours of secretaryship. On the tiers of benches is a mixed crowd of probationers. The general public are not allowed to enter. If they did, they would hardly understand the bearing of these exercises, these callow variations on well-worn themes, nor would they realise the magic that the title of " Secretary to the Advocates' Conference " can have for young ambition.

The advocates' conference is an institution resembling the École Polytechnique and has on its side the prestige of a long past. It seems that it leads to everything, and that the title alone is equivalent to the pledge of a happy future. Towards it tend the dreams of every young probationer who is regarded, in the bosom of his family, as possessed of some rhetorical talent; and if he be son to a gentleman of the long robe, whether judge, solicitor, or advocate, his father impresses upon him that he will never do anything in the world unless he gets appointed a secretary to the advocates' conference. The legend has had its effect. All our great orators have been secretaries to the conference. Allou was third secretary in 1842 and delivered the panegyric on Fercy, at the commencement of the legal year in 1843. Nicolet held the same office in 1844. M. Buffet was second secretary in 1843. Ernest Picard was fifth in 1848, the year when Maître Cresson was second; Maître Bétolaud was third in 1852, while M. Kæmpfen, director of the National Museums, was first and Durier fourth; in 1860, Maître Barboux had the number one and the Bethmont Prize; the number three of 1863 was Léon Gambetta, whilst the number one was M. Decrais, our ambassador at Vienna,[1] and the number two was Maître Albert Martin.

It is at the barristers' conference that all our most famous politicians have made their *début*.

M. Jules Grévy was the thirteenth secretary of 1838 and the sixth of 1839 (at this time a man could be chosen several years running) ; M. Floquet was the sixth of 1853, M. Jules Ferry the seventh of 1854, M. Léon Renault the second of 1861 (the first was Maître Pouillet, the third M. Guillot, the present examining magistrate, the last but one M. Camescasse), M. Méline was the second of 1864, M. Ribot the first in 1865 ; again, among the first, are M. Jamais in 1879, M. Poincarré in 1882 ; M. Develle, equally first in 1868, before M. Laferrière, vice-president of the Council of State ; M. Laguerre is the ninth of 1881, M. Millerand the seventh of 1882, M. Barthou the sixth of 1886, M. Joseph Reinach was nominated in 1879 to replace one who had resigned.

The advocates' conference has supplied recruits, especially during the last ten years, for the Parisian bench, and it has provided the cream of the official representatives chosen by the Minister of Justice. An association of former secretaries to the advocates' conference was founded in 1878 in order to raise the prestige of the title of secretary, and to renew the bonds of good fellowship among those

---

[1] Recently appointed ambassador at London.

ex-laureates who have become scattered in different professions. It counts on its roll two members of the French Academy, Maître Rousse and Count D'Haussonville, eight professors of law, one ambassador, several prefects, many cabinet ministers, and some men of letters; it has even produced an iron-master. Every year, in the month of July, the Council of the Order select, from a list of the young men who have spoken in the course of the judicial year, the twelve of highest merit. These will form the body of secretaries for the ensuing year. A man can only be secretary once. As a matter of fact, the choice is made by the *bâtonnier*, who alone is present at the conferences, and the council content themselves with ratifying his choice; but the *bâtonnier* asks the opinion of the twelve acting secretaries and makes them draw up a list, to which he pays more or less attention according as he is less or more positive in his opinions.

These functions of consulting jurymen which are assigned to the secretaries of the conference, their place on the daïs by the *bâtonnier's* side, and the consciousness of talent which has received official recognition give them a mingled expression of discreet reserve and patronising benevolence that would become a young professor just elevated to the bench. Each annual promotion forms a little clan, the members of which are in duty bound to live on intimate terms with one another and to dine together once a month; they all have nearly the same manner, and seem to possess a slight family resemblance. Their common mannerism is that which was in vogue during their year of office. It is not always that of the *bâtonnier* who then filled the chair, for there are some men who cannot allow in another the little peculiarities they have themselves, of which they are perhaps quite unconscious. In order to become secretary to the conference a man must win favour with the *bâtonnier;* he must not make enemies of the outgoing secretaries; and, if he hopes for one of the first places, his legal essay must be a little masterpiece. Here is the recipe. Take two or three very simple arguments which bear on the subject set for discussion, develop them on paper in elegant phraseology ornamented with conceits, add a few telling and, above all, brand-new anecdotes, learn the whole by heart, and recite it, with serious conviction, magisterial dignity or wild volubility, according to your temperament, and the trick is done! Such, then, is the pursuit to which our young geniuses devote themselves every Monday!

The desired goal once attained, the proud secretary will soon lose the illusions he cherished when a candidate ; the old ideal of happiness will now seem vain, the annual list which once seemed a roll of victors becomes a catalogue of failures, and the name of Barrême, prefect of the Eure, will stand out quite brightly in this book of martyrs ; they will learn by experience that briefs do not necessarily come to the heroes of the Conference. And yet, those who ought to know have told us that it is a good institution that should be faithfully preserved. People make fun of it, look down on it, but it has given to many the joy of a first and perhaps a last success, and now that speaking in court is becoming more and more practical and commonplace, the Conference remains the last refuge of the delightful art of saying empty nothings in a graceful style.

But the Conference, in its turn, is sure to see some changes. It has already passed through many a transmigration. In 1710, in deference to the wish of M. de Riparfonds, the founder of the library, it was a meeting of all the advocates in the Parliament of Paris who had been more than ten years at the bar. The chairman proposed for discussion some question suggested by the *bâtonnier* a few days before, he touched on its chief difficulties, and each person then gave his opinion in due order, beginning with the youngest. From 1775, a young advocate, who had given some proof of ability, used to be chosen every year to deliver a panegyric on some eminent judge or advocate lately deceased ; on the 13th January, 1775, Henrion de Pansey pronounced the eulogy of Mathieu Molé ; on the 14th December, 1776, Mathieu delivered the eulogy of Guy Coquille. Besides this, charitable conferences used to be held to advise poor people on their legal rights. This was a kind of board for giving free consultations. From the year 1818 the advocates' Conference assumed its modern character of a school for probationers; ten secretaries to the Conference were named each year, and two of them were chosen to deliver addresses at the beginning of the legal year. A man could be chosen for several years in succession. In 1835 the number was raised to twelve.

The Conferences used, in old days, to be held in the library but as the number of probationers increased and the library grew more and more inconvenient, it became necessary to find a more comfortable apartment, and the auction room was fixed on. From that time the sittings at the reopening of the courts have taken place in the same room. There the *bâtonnier* delivered his inaugural address, and the next two leading members of the Bar read a panegyric on the late *bâtonnier* or some literary study, usually of a juridico-historical character. But this traditional ceremony now takes place in the new library.

On Conference Mondays a change comes over, not only the auction room, but over the whole law courts, the Salle des Pas-Perdus, the robing rooms, and the corridors. For, on this day, the probationers must come and put in an appearance, and the law

PROBATIONERS SIGNING THEIR CARDS.

courts are given up to them. Down to 1884 Monday was a legal holiday, and the tradition has left its mark on the practice followed by legal gentlemen of keeping away from the courts on this day unless they have business there. The probationers can then be seen in all their splendour. This year there were 942 of them, almost as many as the barristers enrolled.

At midday one of the watchmen attached to the law courts, places before each door of the auction room two wooden machines, which from a distance look like mill wheels set up horizontally on a pivot. If a spectator, rendered curious by these strange preparations, approaches the wheels in question, he will find that they have openings down the side, and that the right wheel bears a little flag marked A. H., the left wheel a little flag marked I. Z.

Next, a table covered with green cloth is brought in; on this table is laid an enormous blotting pad; in front of the pad is placed a box with two compartments; lastly, the installation is completed by the appearance of two or three inkstands, a dozen pen-holders and some bowls full of sawdust. At this moment, Léon, apparitor of the Bar, of whom we have already spoken, comes on the scene with an air of paternal solemnity.

From the large box, which now lies open, he draws a number of small wooden cases containing square cards. Each of these cases will be put into an opening of one of the wheels described above. And if, in defiance of the pass-word, we can manage to get a look at one of the cards, we will find it is printed as follows :—

Year 1891-2	........th Section.
Admitted probationer	
2 Nov. 1891	4 Jan. 1892
9 Nov. 1891	11 Jan. 1892
16 Nov. 1891	18 Jan. 1892
23 Nov. 1891	25 Jan. 1892
30 Nov. 1891	1 Feb. 1892
7 Dec. 1891	8 Feb. 1892
14 Dec. 1891	15 Feb. 1892
21 Dec. 1891	22 Feb. 1892
28 Dec. 1891	29 Feb. 1892

This is a probationer's certificate; each card is destined to receive a signature attesting that the young barrister has come regularly. . . as far as the door of the conference room. Léon meanwhile fastens to the door of the auction room a slip of paper on which is written the subject for debate and the names of the speakers.

As late as one and half-past one the probationers continue to arrive. Resplendent in hired gowns they take two or three turns round the hall: some, stiff as old-fashioned magistrates; others,

with the cap at the back of the head, a glass in the eye and a
jaunty air.   Then they turn their back on the auction-room and take
their departure.   Only the minority remain behind; but these in
spite of the eccentricities developed by the academic tournament of
the Conference are always workers, and, in many cases, are on the
road to becoming leading counsel.   The robing rooms are filled
with a noisy crowd; every corner, every table is heaped up with
gowns, and every gown will in the course of the day appear on quite
a dozen backs; by their side are picturesque mountains of caps,
and, pell-mell with it all, a male or female attendant may be seen
impartially handing out gowns that are always too short or too long,
and caps which either won't stick on or else fall right over the eyes.

By the side of the robing rooms and towards the Salle des Pas-
Perdus some gay ladies may be seen.   They come on Monday with
the probationer who has not yet given up Bohemian ways, and whose
study can easily be transformed into a place of assignation, all
the rooms in the Quartier Latin being furnished with alcoves.   But
the student does not feel at his ease.   He is afraid of the *bâtonnier*,
of the member of the council who reported on his case when he
was admitted probationer; but, perhaps, he is most afraid of Léon.
So Mdlle. Pâquerette seats herself demurely on a bench, while her
companion signs his name and takes a turn in the law courts with
his comrades.

CHAPTER IX

TAKING PROPERTY FOR PUBLIC PURPOSES

Down below, at the end of a corridor lighted by gas, beyond the office of the secretaries to the advocates' Conference, in the middle of the rooms allotted to the police department, is the Court of Expropriation, a low, gloomy room, blocked up in the middle by an enormous stove.

At one end is the court table with the regular green cloth cover. This time it is shaped like a horse-shoe, and by an unusual arrangement the magistrate who directs the jury sits next to the registrar, at the right point of the horse-shoe, the ten jurymen occupying the semicircle. The jurymen are chosen by lot and have to decide on the compensation to be given to those whose property is taken; the judge is only there to superintend the proceeding, to guide the jurymen, and to set them going; he is their school-master. The representatives of the State, of the City of Paris, or of some public department, according as the property is taken by one administrative body or another, have brought heaps of documents, plans, and briefs. They form a regular phalanx round the solicitor or advocate who commands them. They take up their position on the left, an army in battle array, with compact squadrons.

On the right are the battalions of those whose property is to be taken. They are of all ages and of all conditions, and are commanded by those special agents to whom their interests have been entrusted. All mount with fury to the assault on the money-box ; and terrible are the combats waged between the champion of the public despoiler, terrible as the angel who with flaming sword barred the gates of Paradise, and the counsel for the owners and tenants—advocates insinuating, tenacious, and strong in the manifold resources of a persuasive exordium and a honeyed peroration.

Oh, those jurymen! Those noble, good, honest jurymen! Both sides flatter them, tell them stories, try to make them laugh, arouse their pity, envelope them in the toils of subtle and caressing eloquence. Nothing is spared which is likely to please—or delude—them. They are overwhelmed with wrong valuations, fictitious leases, and rentals thrice as large as the reality.

" Yes, gentlemen of the jury," says the counsel for the undertaking, " look upon this good old woman, who now stands before you, with her child! Certainly she is worthy of respect, she is honest. Her life has been one long record of work and courage. Never has she tried to rob her neighbour of a farthing! But one day she was told that she was to be driven from her home. Some one told her that, in consideration of being evicted from the den where she lives from hand to mouth, without even a lease, she will be entitled to recover a great sum of money. Dreams are coming true ; good fortune is at hand ; there is to be a shower of gold over the whole district. And then, boundless claims crowd upon us, exaggerations without limit. You say that no one is being robbed. But it is the taxpayers who will have to pay ; that is everybody. This poor old woman has two rooms under the tiles ; she pays a rent of 150 francs a year ; she is offered the liberal sum of 50 francs as compensation for her enforced removal. But this is far from being enough. Come now, she must have 2,000 francs! The jury, this generous jury, the providence of dispossessed persons, will surely not grant her less than this. And they now come before you, gentlemen, and tell you some ridiculous tale, as you will presently hear. . . . . . You are expected to pave with gold the two ruinous and unwholesome garrets, which, fortunately for her health and life, this poor woman is obliged to quit. There, gentlemen, is the whole matter."

" But, no, gentlemen of the jury, you do not know," retorts the opposing counsel, " what this unhappy woman will lose by being turned out of her home. For forty years she has occupied this dwelling, poor and miserable, it is true ; but bound up with her dearest associations, her very life. All her recollections are connected with the place. Her husband died there. Where can she go, without finding herself in a strange land, in exile ? It is true these garrets are high up, but there is a magnificent view from them, a splendid panorama. . . . . ."

OPPOSING COUNSEL (*with a sneer*).—" The view is of course a separate item ! "

THE CLAIMANT'S COUNSEL.—" My learned friend laughs. Everything, however insignificant, has an interest for one who is descending into the vale of years. Habits have become fixed in every detail, have passed into eccentricities if you like ; but in their little circle they include the last remaining pleasures of old age. Respect them, then, and think not that in paying for them, even at a high rate, you have given their real value. You inflict an injury by interfering with them, and it is this damage that the jury, always an equitable, always a good judge, is bound to estimate and compensate. Again, you are destroying old quarters of the town out of regard for the beauty of the whole, and the health of the greatest number. Let the greatest number then, in return for these advantages, pay those on whom the change brings suffering. The cheap lodgings of former times are disappearing from the central part of the city ; the poor must seek them farther out ; and when found they cost more. Lastly, the mere process of removal, which my client obviously never contemplated, is also costly. Is 2,000 francs too much for all that. . . . . . ? "

The jury decide to go the next morning to the places in question and inspect every house and every apartment ; for they have obtained a very poor idea of them through the contradictory and fantastic descriptions of the rival orators ; and they have been unable to gather much from the plans, which, as a rule, are quite beyond their comprehension.

They make their little expedition, they deliberate, and, at the next sitting, they award the old woman 100 francs compensation.

Thus, during sittings which last from a fortnight to whole months, figures dance, millions slip away, and Paris is transformed. Some landlords are made wealthy at a stroke by an unexpected donation from the jury ; others do not even get the fair value of their property. Some lessees rejoice ; others lament. Compensations are scattered broadcast by pure haphazard, according to the weather, the temper of the juries, or the caprices of fortune.

After all, the best plan would be to settle everything by a cast of the dice, in the fashion of good Judge Bridlegoose.

In the Corridors.

CHAPTER X

THE COURT OF APPEAL

THE Court of Appeal will soon enter its new home. With the appearance of this volume, the First President will take his seat in the hall, resplendent with new gilding, the decoration of which he has superintended so that it may be worthy of the First Chamber of the Court.

But let us say a last farewell to what will so soon be a thing of the past.

At the top of the staircase leading to the middle of the Galerie Marchande, there stands the statue of a woman holding an open book, on a page of which are inscribed the words—*In legibus salus.* Here we find ourselves in a spacious vestibule. It once served as a chapel to the law courts, and is embellished with seeming porticoes and statues, painted so as to deceive the eye. This vestibule, by means of inconvenient lobbies, affords entrance to the Second and Third Chambers. If the visitor, instead of entering the vestibule, will skirt the balustrade, till he comes to a few steps, he will be able to descend straight into the First Chamber of the Court. It is here that on the 16th October the inaugural address on the reopening of the law courts is delivered.

All the magistrates of the Court of Appeal meet there at other times, in accordance with the ceremonial described above, for the formal reception of a new member of the Court or the Procureur-General's staff. Two acting judges introduce the new member. At the request of the Procureur-General the chief registrar reads aloud the decree of nomination ; then, at the invitation of the First President, he pronounces the form of the oath and the new magistrate swears to it.

Under Louis Philippe the form ran as follows :

"I swear fidelity to the King of the French, and obedience to the Constitutional Charta and the laws of the realm."

A STAIRCASE OF THE COURT OF APPEAL.

In 1849 a decree of October 22nd prescribed a different form

" Before God and men, I swear and promise, with my soul and conscience, to perform my duties faithfully and well, to observe strict secrecy regarding the deliberations of the Court, and to conduct myself in all things as becomes an upright and loyal magistrate."

Napoleon III. suppressed "God and men," "soul and conscience"; he replaced them by the Constitution and by his own person :—

"I swear obedience to the Constitution and fidelity to the President; I swear also and promise to perform my duties faithfully and well," &c.

The "President" then gave place to the "Emperor"; next, "obedience to the Constitution" and "fidelity to the Emperor" disappeared in 1870.

The different chambers of the Court of Appeal also meet together in solemn sitting for the installation of the chief registrar.

All judges of first instance from whom an appeal lies to the Court take the same oath as the magistrates of the Court of Appeal, but before the First Appeal Chamber only, and in black gowns, without the least ceremony. Judges of the Tribunal of Commerce and all advocates before their admission also take an oath before the First Chamber. The advocates present themselves in full dress, with white bands and ermine-trimmed hood ; they pass before the bar as their names are called, and, under the direction of the *bâtonnier*, they pronounce the words "*Je le jure*" and make their bow.

They have sworn the oath administered by the registrar.

"I swear to neither say nor publish anything, in my character of counsel, that may be contrary to law, regulation, good morals, the safety of the State and the public peace, and never to forget the respect due to the courts of justice and the public authorities."

The judges of all Chambers of the Court of Appeal meet together with closed doors, and dressed in black gowns, to hear appeals brought by advocates against sentences passed on them by their Council of Discipline.

The following persons have a right to have their cases brought before the Court of Appeal when they are charged with breaches of the penal code: magistrates, generals, archbishops, prefects, bishops, and grand officers of the Legion of Honour.

The Court is also charged with the ratification of letters of grace by which the President of the Republic commutes the penalty of persons condemned to death on appeal ; and it is a curious sight

to see the con-
demned, alas, how
fallen in his prison
dress from the
splendid appear-
ance he made at
the Court of
Assize, listening,
with bewildered
air, to this con-
fused medley of
legal forms. The
judges do not put
on their red robes
for his sake. These
are displayed, but
only those of the
First Chamber of
the Court, and
those of one other
of its chambers
appointed in ro-
tation to form
a complement to
the First Cham-
ber, at sittings
which are styled
solemn, though
they must not be
confounded with
the opening sit-
tings before de-
scribed ; the sit-
tings now spoken
of are sittings for
business at which
the judges present
must number at

M. PÉRIVIER, FIRST PRESIDENT OF THE COURT OF APPEAL.

least fourteen, and where the matters decided are disputes about
the civil status of citizens, actions for false imprisonment, and cases

sent back for rehearing after a judgment has been quashed by the Court of Cassation. On ordinary days the First Chamber of the Court of Appeal busies itself with a little of everything. On Tuesdays, Wednesdays, and Thursdays it meets under the presidency of *M. le Premier*—this is the regular, though rather familiar name given to the First President of the Court. On Fridays it sits under the auspices of the President of the Chamber.

To *M. le Premier* belongs the duty of apportioning the business among the seven civil Chambers of the Court. He naturally keeps for his own Chamber all the important cases which demand extraordinary labour or are likely to create interest outside. To him are assigned by right the following cases : questions affecting the government, the municipalities and the public departments, disputes relative to the authority of parents, to the custody of the goods of absent persons, to applications made by married women for power to act without their husbands' consent, and to the naturalisation of aliens. The First Chamber also regulates adoptions, and receives the oaths of experts, interpreters, &c. The sittings of the Court of Appeal are distinguished from those of the Court of First Instance only by the greater number of the judges, who must be not less than five and not more than nine ; and the only difference in costume is that the robes of the appeal judges have gold instead of silver braiding.

The First Chamber of the Court of Appeal has the honour of possessing the celebrated picture of the Crucifixion which belonged to the Parliament of Paris. It is a marvellous work which cannot be rightly seen during a sitting of the Court ; a picture where one may faintly see around the Calvary, on a background of charming though inappropriate landscape, a figure of Saint John, frail and slightly clad, carrying a lamb ; an ascetic monarch in crown and robe bedecked with lilies ; Saint Denis in the act of his martyrdom ; a sumptuous Charlemagne ; and, among other figures to be noted, a trusty spaniel with a dirty coat. Below this picture sits the First President. The First Chamber of the Court is also remarkable for a registrar who is a power in himself, and a benevolent power too, M. Piogey. The presidents are glad to have his opinion, and he gives advice to the bar.

The moments of waiting before the sittings begin have here a peculiar charm ; brilliant talkers are common at this bar, the registrar is happy in repartee, and they have as much time as they

want to run through their list of anecdotes ; for the members of
the bench, in the ardour of private deliberation, often keep the
court waiting till three in the afternoon.   The calling of the cause
list is besides a more lively proceeding here than elsewhere ; but
the credit of this must at present be given to M. Périvier, the
First President.

He is quite a modern president.   His speech is high toned and
concise ; his gestures are familiar ; his expression is mobile and
always alert ; with a constant attitude of easy good humour,
checked now and then by an access of dignity, there is in him
none of the stiffness customary in times gone by.   When necessary,
he puts an inquirer at his ease, and does not deny himself the
pleasure of a witty repartee.   The *Gazette des Tribunaux* might
publish every day flashes of wit thrown off by him during the last
sitting, as it used to publish those of First President Séguier—but
he knows how to keep all to their proper level.   In spite of his
unfailing geniality, he never forgets that he is the head of the
court ; he is skilled in the arts of management, and knows better
than any one how to quicken the pace of an advocate and get his
argument out of him.   With a quick intelligence and indefatigable
powers of work, he never shrinks from his task, and his judgments,
written if need be in a single night, are models of vigour and
lucidity.   It is curious to compare him with his predecessor, M.
Larombière, who was also a judge of the first rank, but in a
very different style.   In proportion as M. Périvier is lively and
impulsive, M. Larombière was calm and reserved, though without
stiffness, having no more vivacity than befits a learned professor
of law.   In proportion as M. Périvier holds by the small rules of
etiquette, merely modifying their rigour by his amiability, so much
did M. Larombière disdain them, though at the same time he made
all around feel their chilling effect.

M. Larombière, on working days, sat at a little table below the
bench, and he looked very imposing, though a stout little man
with spectacles.

M. Périvier has had the table removed and never quits his
elevated position.

Both are characteristic types which will not be soon forgotten
by legal anecdotists.

SOME OF THE COUNSEL

It is in the First Chamber more than anywhere else that the great leaders of the Bar are commonly to be heard. There it was that Maître Lenté argued in the Premsel case. There also have been discussed the great financial cases of which the last few years have been so prodigal, such as that of the Peruvian Guano Company, and the Annuity Company; the case of the corner in copper bars; and the suit against the Stock-brokers' Syndicate.

MAÎTRE ALLOU.
After Jules Jacquemard.

The last few years have been fatal to the most eminent speakers of the First Chamber; and several ex-*bâtonniers* have fallen victims,.among them being Le Berquier, Allou and Durier. Le Berquier died six years ago.

But he is not forgotten, and the reason why we write so few lines in his praise is that his son is with us now. His was a cynical but kindly nature, and a loyal soul; he was an elegant writer, his book on *The Modern Bar* being justly celebrated, and judges liked to listen to his subtle statement and breadth of argument.

In the speeches of Maître Allou, it was the flow of the language, the music of the diction, that held the ear of the court. In every outburst of his eloquence, his style retained its purity. In the most impassioned moment his voice never lost its perfect modulation; and his wealth of metaphor and resounding fluency covered the dry severity of his reasoning. Most of the writers who

have taken part in the production of this book only knew Maître
Allou at a time when his power, though still imposing, was a little
on the decline and its majesty somewhat impaired. It is only by
reading aloud his speeches, above all that for Trochu, and by listening to the recollections of his contemporaries, that they have been
able to call up the image of the great orator as he was. Durier is
more present to all of us ; no one would be astonished at seeing
him reappear, and it would be a rare treat to hear once more, as of
old, in the First Chamber of the Court, his fluent speech, at once
so sparkling and so pregnant with conclusive reasoning. Maître
Lenté never held the office of *bâtonnier;* but, none the less, he has
his place among the great ones who have passed away, and the
bar will always count him among the most glorious of its bygone
heroes. He was at once a brilliant orator and a first rate man of
business. He excelled in clearing up financial mystifications, in
the manipulation of figures, and in finding a way out of the most
hopeless difficulties. He could analyse illusory balance sheets, and
confused accounts with such ease, that, for the moment, the whole
medley seemed the simplest thing in the world, and people asked
one another how anyone could venture to attack financiers of such
scrupulous probity. When he waxed indignant, his indignation
convinced the most sceptical. How could they refuse to believe
the solemn declarations of this hearty straightforward man, who
appeals to your experience, gives you such lucid explanations, and
addresses you with such good humour—a man who, if he had
a mind, could knock you down with a blow of his fist? His
athletic figure, his powerful voice, his way of looking the judges
straight in the face, impressed them from the first ; his clear
style of speech completed their conquest. He never sought after
refinements of expression ; he merely used the words needed to
make himself understood. Though he had taken his degree and
passed through the *École Normale* with About, Prévost-Paradol and
Weiss, he spoke as incorrectly as Berryer himself. But there was
in his voice, as it were, the clink of gold pieces ; the sheets of his
brief, as his hand strayed among them, rustled like bank-notes ;
and they seemed to shake in the very quiver of his sleeve. On
great occasions, when it was his task to restore the credit of some
institution which had been the subject of calumny, like the Bank,
or to excite pity for some misfortune, his talent took a higher
flight, his style became more flowing, his action more pathetic, his

emotion more contagious, till, overcome in his turn by the nervous excitement he raised about him, his eyes streamed with tears, and he fell back half fainting on his seat, in the atmosphere of ether which enveloped him.[1]

A scene like this took place in the First Chamber of the Court, at the conclusion of his speech on behalf of the heirs of M. Premsel, when the First President was compelled to check the storm of applause, saying, "Gentlemen, let everybody admire the orator from the bottom of his heart ; but do not forget that silence must be kept in the presence of Justice."

Another great occasion was the trial of M. Wilson, before the Correctional Court, when Maître Allou, invoking the bust of the ex-President of the Republic, cried out :—

" You have before you a mournful and historic spectacle in this grand old man. But two months ago, he was the equal of the sovereigns of Europe, who rightly prized his patriotism and his uprightness. He was France, he was the fatherland! And now in this hall, so familiar to the sweepings of our gaols, I stand before you struggling to save the name of his daughter and his grand-child from dishonour ! "

The task of maintaining these great traditions now falls on the surviving ex-*bâtonniers*, Maître Rousse, Maître Bétolaud, Maître Barboux, Maître Oscar Falateuf, Maître Martini, and Maître Cresson.

Maître Rousse is one of the brightest glories of the bar. He is neither a faultless extempore speaker, nor an impassioned orator. His voice is sharp, his gesticulation angular. But he is a stylist, steeped in Greek and Latin scholarship, who loves to adorn our modern speech with classic beauty. His professional life has been above criticism. His practice has been, comparatively speaking, limited, and his talent is not of the kind which wins its reward from the admiration of great financiers. He has been able to remain, without becoming old-fashioned, the typical advocate of a past age. The French Academy has chosen him as representative of the bar ; he has been honoured by the friendship of illustrious men ; but his best title to the admiration and respect of all is to be found in his undaunted demeanour as *bâtonnier*, during the troubles of the Commune ; while the speech he wrote for the opening of the conferences in 1871 was a masterpiece.

<hr>

[1] See p. 39 *ante.*

As to Maître Bétolaud, he is an advocate pure and simple. He is, one might say, the advocate, stiff as the Procureur-General of popular tradition, careful to bring no slur on a spotless character, and scrupulously careful in the briefs he accepts and the arguments he uses. When pleading, he thinks of nothing but how to place the case fully before the judge. He has no outbursts of passion, except when carried away by the feeling that there is an injustice to be redressed. He avoids flourishes, except for an occasional grave witticism. His strength comes from the accuracy of his expressions and the logical character of his ideas; his self-respect is the source of the authority which belongs to him.

Maître Barboux is not indifferent to the graces of style or the charm of apt expressions. His speeches are prepared with elegance and care, and they sparkle with happy phrases and subtle aphorisms. He has a weakness for definition, but he defines as no one else can. It is he who defined legal technicality as "an ingenious absurdity of which we must have a thorough knowledge before we can appreciate its merit." His taste for Latin quotations is perhaps excessive, but he enlivens what he quotes by his incisive voice and by the connection in which he always uses it. He has been called a word artist in dry point; the criticism is just; it should be added that his finest periods are touched in with aqua-tinta.

MAÎTRE BARBOUX.

Maître Oscar Falateuf is an enchanter; he has grace, fervour, constant sincerity, and a real emotion which no one, not even he himself, can resist; he has the kindest of hearts and the most tender of voices; he is the tenor, the poet, a tenor in the Italian style, and a poet after Adolphe Musset, always fastidious, always full of feeling, a man far more inclined towards poetry than prose. He will sing of the attractions of love, of the woes of the forsaken mistress, of the soothing influences of religion, and the sublime madness of patriotism; no one equals him in the art of dressing up an obituary notice of some second-rate person, as happened on one delicate occasion, when, coming forward on the public platform in the name of the Paris Bar, he rose to his task, and gave his hearers an unexpected display of forensic eloquence.

Maître Martini has won the reputation of a wit, and thoroughly deserves it. But this would astonish people who had only heard him in court. He sticks close to his argument, almost harshly with the tenacity of a mollusc that refuses to let go its hold; at the risk of seeming dry, he takes special pains to keep his natural vivacity within bounds, so as not to let slip a word likely to distract attention from the point he is handling. Is this disdain for his judges? Is it an economy of wit? Is it discretion or timidity? It is none of these. It is simply cold calculation. He reserves his fireworks for conversations with his friends, for chats in the Salle des Pas-Perdus, and for professional dinner parties. These are curious functions which advocates, in evening dress, attend, a dozen at a time, to enjoy the hospitality of a member of the council or some candidate for a seat on that body, and form a gloomy funereal party round the hostess, the only lady present.

Maître Martini is the lion of these little feasts. It is then that, a perfect *bâtonnier*, he shows his marvellous power of conversation and his incomparable wit, reeling out legal anecdotes and stories of the day with a fluency that none can hope to rival. Of Maître Cresson, Maurice Joly wrote, in 1862, that to the labours of his profession he brought a capacity and zeal which had won for him precocious successes. To these same qualities are due the honours of his declining years. He no longer has the youthful and some-what unruly vigour which his admirers marked as his chief charac-teristic, but he has remained an administrator; he was the most practical of all the *bâtonniers*, and he has bequeathed his name to the library of the order.

The *bâtonnier* now in office is Maître Du Buit, a tall, spare man, very stiff, with the pale, drawn face of a doctrinaire. He pleads with a pitiless rigour and a sovereign contempt for any one who differs from him in opinion; he has a domineering tone and brings a moral pressure to bear on any judge who seems disinclined to agree with him. Modest, in spite of his haughty exterior, he has been able to win the esteem of his brethren without flattering them. This is the highest compliment that could be paid him. By the side of the *bâtonniers* we could mention many other names : the ex-ministers Waldeck-Rousseau, Martin-Feuillée, and Thévenet ; senators Léon Renault, and Bérenger ; and Maître Clausel de Coussergues, the deputy. Maître Devin has taken part in most of the great financial cases ; the presence of Maître Cléry, or Maître Carraby is indispensable to give a case the true Parisian stamp. Maître Pouillet and Maître Huard appeared in the First Chamber of the Court of Appeal in the Aciers-Martin suit, and in the great telephone case. Maître Ployer. . . . . But, stay ! if we go on any longer with this list, our book will end in being a mere enumeration or panegyric, and will lose the character of impartiality which should mark a work written in collaboration.

Of the other Chambers of the Court of Appeal besides the First nothing need be said. They have the same number of magistrates, but are more confined in space. From eleven o'clock in the morning the different Chambers are thrown open, one after another, at intervals of ten minutes, beginning with the Seventh Chamber. They have a regular programme for each day in the week, but in accordance with the system introduced by First President Périvier, cases are often deferred from one day to the day following, and, whatever engagements the counsel may have made elsewhere, they must be in their place, for the Court of Appeal never waits for any one.

CHAPTER XI

ADJUNCTS TO THE COURT OF APPEAL

THE PROCUREUR-GENERAL

To find the Procureur-Général, the best plan is to ask the way of one of the court keepers on duty. After a pleasant walk a building is reached which has quite the look of a government department. Pass through the glass doors, which shut again without a sound, and here you are in the ante-chamber. On the left is an inner door pierced with a little glass window like that which leads to a green-room ; on the right, an usher, duly adorned with the chain of office, sits slumbering in an upright attitude.

The chief law officer of the government has been sometimes accused of a too great readiness to relieve the cares of office by indulging in the pleasures of lighter literature. This legend can certainly not have arisen from the appearance of his private room. Everything there betokens that we are in the presence of justice. The whole place has an air of plainness and learned severity. The most humble dentist makes a greater display of gilding. The apartment is large, longer one way than the other ; the light enters by three enormous windows, the glare but slightly softened by dark blue curtains. In the Procureur-Général's private room there are only two colours, black and blue. Blue predominates in the curtains, the carpet, the walls, and the wall paper, black in the furniture.

By a handsome mantel-piece, surmounted by a deep unoccupied niche, which waits for the bust of some celebrated man, possibly the present Procureur-Général himself, stand four arm-chairs, straight in shape and black in colour, arranged in symmetrical order. Between the two windows is a large sofa, of such severe aspect that no one would have courage to sit down upon it. The visitor instinctively recoils from fear of committing an indecorum. The middle of the room is occupied by a table, so large that the whole Penal Code might be printed on it ; at present, however, it has nothing on it but a Sèvres vase in harmony with the rest of the room —a graceful little attention to M. Périvier from the Chief of the State. Add to the above two funereal-looking presses, with a clock which has wandered from the Cluny Museum, and is always too slow, and you will have a catalogue of the whole array of judicial magnificence.

At the extreme end of the apartment, the Procureur-Général may be seen seated at a little table, beneath the portrait

M. QUESNAY DE BEAUREPAIRE, PROCUREUR-GÉNÉRAL.

of a venerable sage in red robes (the only gay note of colour in the room), who from his frame sadly watches his successor signing papers. All this has a depressing effect, and fills visitors with a presentiment of evil. But the Procureur-Général is accustomed to it, and is unmoved by these mournful surroundings. With an air of unvarying calmness he listens gravely to grievances and complaints, to prayers and supplications ; occasionally a faint smile glimmers on his clean-shaved lips when some office-hunter mistakes the door, and comes in to ask for a recommendation to aid him in obtaining a tobacco shop. But it is not here, in the midst of his administrative work, that we intend to draw the Procureur-Général's portrait ; we shall see him at his best in the full light of the Court of Assize.

We are now arrived at the office of the Court of Appeal. Before mounting the stairs, let us take a glance on our left. All these doors opening on a long corridor, so strangely built that it looks like the gangway of a passenger steamer, are those of the private rooms allotted to the three Advocates-General and to the numerous secretaries employed by the Ministry of Justice. There is nothing very interesting to be seen, and we can pass on. In all these rooms men are engaged all day in carefully sifting papers, which are brought to the Procureur-Général for signature every evening.

THE RECORD OFFICE OF THE COURT OF APPEAL

This office is situated at the top of a staircase, the walls of which are enlivened by the notice : " Civil Record Office to the right, Criminal Record Office to the left." Let us, following this guide, first enter the Civil Office.

We find ourselves in a very long room, where a number of clerks are seated at little desks, writing away under the stern eye of a deputy registrar, whose raised seat gives him a view over the whole room. It looks like a school-room where the scholars are engaged in doing their impositions. Nor, as a matter of fact, are these scribes amusing themselves ; they are making engrossments. An engrossment is an authentic judicial decision, judgment, or decree, put into legal language by the registrar. The word aptly expresses the thing ; a large roll of paper on which is stated in great detail the opinion of the judges who have given the decision.

An engrossment may be recognised by several distinctive peculiarities. In the first place, the paper which receives it and preserves its legal beauties is yellow in colour, very stiff in texture, extremely ugly, and showing traces of hair. It is generally known to the public as *stamped paper*; but the persons employed in the office have christened it "our high-class illustrated paper." The style is generally incomprehensible, and in a well-drawn engrossment at least four words out of five ought to be quite superfluous. All engrossments end with the words: " For which the fee is. . . ." The engrossment, in short, costs a great deal of money, this being one of the peculiarities above referred to. Once completed, engrossments are carefully arranged on special shelves, where they remain indefinitely, till some day an inquisitive litigant comes and asks the registry clerk the question: "May I examine the judgment or decree which has condemned me to pay such-and-such a sum to Mr. So-and-so?" Then this judicial record is hunted up, and the victim can consult it at his ease, but always in return for the payment of one franc. Why this one franc? you ask me. My dear sir, I know nothing at all about it. People who want to consult engrossments have to pay a franc; that is all I can tell you.

This office is not a lively place.

The office for criminal matters, which lies on the right, is a receptacle for papers relating to cases tried at the assizes. It consists of two rooms; one for the inevitable clerks, the other reserved for advocates who wish to study the set of papers. Every set of papers respecting a person accused of crime pays two visits to the office of the Court of Appeal: one before the trial, the other, which is final, after the trial. It is born in the office, and it dies in the office.

Here every one is affable: the clerks are polite, and constant familiarity with criminal procedure has given them a marked urbanity. An advocate must apply to them if he wants any information connected with his case, and it must be confessed that this information is always given with the promptest courtesy, After having searched through ponderous registers and hunted through many files of paper, the counsel for the defence receives the document he requires, and goes to read it in the second apartment. This is a little room, very bare, very gloomy, looking out

on a high dead wall ; its sole furniture is a table and chairs. What
countless histories have been read through in this room, feverishly
ransacked by advocates getting up their defence ; and in these sheets
of paper, scanned hurriedly, one after another, how many a tale of
shame has been made known, how base the sins, how heartrending
the sorrows that have seen the light !

CHAPTER XII

THE COURT OF CASSATION

LET us leave the Salle des Pas-Perdus in the middle of some afternoon, while our ears are dizzy with the incessant buzz of conversation that fills the place for three hours daily, and half deafened by the shrill tinkle of the bell that summons solicitors before the judge who is sitting in chambers, or into the Auction Room. Let us then follow the long *Prisoners' Gallery*, and make our way into the corridors of the Court of Cassation. We shall be astonished at the extraordinary contrast that exists between two parts of the Palace so near to each other in situation. Down below, the noise and tumult of the crowd of advocates, suitors, and spectators ; here, the gloomy silence of a deserted dwelling. One might say that jurisprudence, an enchantress armed with a spell to produce sleep, had plunged her fervent admirers into a profound slumber. Old counsellors, ranged on stately chairs, wag their venerable heads, crowned with the black velvet cap whose peculiar shape has procured for its wearers the irreverent and flippant name of *Lancers;* a few clerks pass silently through the long corridors. A solitary municipal guard, seated at his post on a bench in the Galerie Saint Louis, looks half frightened by the solemnity of the place. Such are the sombre shades which guard the sanctuary of the Supreme Court.

The sittings of the Court complete the impression of utter dreariness given by the building itself. Here are none of the glowing or brilliant orations, none of the impassioned or mirth-moving debates which engage the attention of counsellors and judges in the Court of Appeal and the Court of First Instance. Matters of fact, with their endless complications, their human interests, their infinite variety are rigidly excluded. In the Court of Cassation law takes its full revenge ; the only things mentioned there are the driest rules of law, profound decisions of the Supreme Court, or interminable arguments cited from authors who have discoursed learnedly on some infinitesimal point of jurisprudence. Here may be seen the triumph of the old classic disputation; for the speakers in the Supreme Court still argue *pro* and *con*, ending with a conclusion in *baralipton*, as they used to do at the old Sorbonne; Latin alone is lacking at the banquet. Thus oratory holds but an unimportant place at the Court of Cassation; the main dish in every suit is the Case, drawn up carefully and at great length by the advocate; this contains a detailed statement of the whole matter, and a minute discussion of every legal problem involved in it, with endless divisions and subdivisions. When the counsellor appointed to report on the suit has brought his monotonous lecture to a close, the advocate develops his Case, and the Advocate-General states his conclusions. Then, if the question has only a slight technical importance, the counsellors form a circle in the centre of the Court itself to discuss, adopt, or reject the judgment prepared beforehand by the reporter. This is called *faire le rondeau*. And there, in the cold light of the hall, beneath the gilded oak ceiling of the Civil Chamber, the gray or white heads may be seen to shake, and passion—a passion inspired by pure law—revives once more. The apathy, the somnolence of a moment ago disappear, and, for an instant, these hoary sages are again inspired with an ardour which seemed for ever extinguished.

The principal court where these sittings are held may be called handsome; it is that for criminal cases, since the new chamber for civil cases has for the last twenty years been in process of construction. It would be more pleasing were it free from the perpetual allegories of justice which painters and architects scatter in such profusion over all the tribunals of France. At the side, the Galerie Saint Louis, with its Romanesque architecture, its columns and its red-coloured arches, interposes an original note, the only one, unhappily, in this chill and classic pile. The reserved gallery of the Court, with its row of marble busts, that of the Procureur-Général, with its portraits of judges in red robes, have a fitting official austerity. L'Hospital and d'Aguesseau, Cujas and Patru, Chancellor Séguier and President Henrion de Pansey, seem from their gilded frames to regard with satisfaction the stiffness and solemnity of their resting-place, and the melancholy painted profile of the Procureur-Général Ronjat opposite them.

The silence, a silence which is rarely broken by the cautious steps of an occasional visitor, and an icy coldness are the unvarying characteristics of the precinct where sits the Supreme Court of France.   Let us respect it, let us imitate those who pass through it out of curiosity or in fulfilment of their daily task, and leave these lonely galleries, with hushed voice and finger on our lips, lest we disturb the repose of its inhabitants.   The First President of the Supreme Court is however a man of wit and lively character— M. Mazeau, once an advocate there, who has been a Senator and a Minister of State.   He must find life dull at the Supreme Court.

M. MAZEAU.

CHAPTER XIII

THE COURTS AT NIGHT

FOUR o'clock strikes, then half-past four. The whole Palace of Justice will soon become as gloomy as the Court of Cassation itself.

LEAVING THE COURTS.

There are a few more chats in the robing-rooms, some items of the latest gossip pass to and fró, as the counsel resume their ordinary dress, and there is a rustling of umbrellas taken haphazard from the heap. Then advocates and judges drop off into the corridors, under the seductive glance cast on them by ladies of a particular class, who come to seek their fortune at the breaking up of the Courts. If you notice the lights of the robing-room glimmering in the darkness at a late hour, it is because some trial in the Assize Court is dragging its slow length along. As a general rule everything is finished by six o'clock.

But in winter time, when nine o'clock strikes, there is a faint return of animation. In the black corridors, in the Salle des Pas-Perdus, looming larger in the darkness, and echoing beneath the resounding tread of a solitary night-watchman, the noise of closing doors is heard from a distance, and shadowy forms move rapidly towards the Auction Room or one of the Civil Chambers. Have Malesherbes and Berryer descended from their marble pedestals? And does their impassioned eloquence gather round them at night the busts of the illustrious judges and famous advocates whom one sees in the daytime ranged along the corridors of the Supreme Court or the Advocates' Library? Not so. More humble are these shades, and less fanciful the object of their zeal. These are young probationers, or simple law students, come to prepare themselves by means of evening conferences for the contests of the bar. Each of these conferences—miniatures of the advocates' conference—has its day, its hour, and its local habitation. Each has its constitution. Each elects its governing body. At all of them legal questions are discussed, and the orators, wearing their robes, occupy the seats reserved for the judges, the government representative, and the bar. The practice is at once diverting and useful. It ends by eleven o'clock, and now the numerous officials who lodge at the law courts can sleep at their ease, and the sentries also. They will not be troubled again till the next morning.

CHAPTER XIV

CRIMINAL COURTS—THE ACCUSED

BESIDES advocates, judges, and others who are at home in the Palace, besides the litigants who are attracted thither by their interests, there is the host of unfortunates whom justice drags thither against their will. This long array of persons coming up for trial is now to pass in review before us. Among them we shall see the professional thief, educated at the house of

correction, and taught there to handle no tools save the crowbar and the picklock ; we shall also find the honest citizen, arrested in the eddy of some surging mob, and standing, dazed with terror, in the dock as the accomplice of anarchists. Perhaps we shall also find there the popular poet or the fashionable pamphleteer. We are certain to come across the heroines of love idylls and maidens of nihilistic fame, jealous lovers and husbands who have taken the law into their own hands, besmirched damsels and guilty women, charlatans and procurers, sharpers in broadcloth, and bullies in blue cotton jackets, unskilful Shylocks and speculators who have been a little too clever. The most various classes will pass by in our kaleidoscope.

For it is not true that everything ends with a song. The simpleton who said so knew well that the bench of justice is the final goal. Misery, vice, love, politics, finance, sometimes literature, all come to the law courts for their closing scene, and extremes are ever meeting in this chamber of moral horrors. Society is going to reveal itself to us with its monsters and its victims, laying bare its blemishes and its ulcers; we shall see it naked in its ugliness and its deformity, often odious, but more often humorous. Crime has its grotesque as well as its tragic side, and no great drama is without its comic relief.

CHAPTER XV

OUR review must begin with the least important on the list ; the humble folk charged with petty delinquencies who are to be found at the Police Court.

To reach it we have not to make a long journey. When by the boulevard gate we enter the Great Court of the Palace of Justice, we find ourselves face to face with a broad staircase, on the right of which is the old entry to the Conciergerie, and on the left the Police Court.

Pass through a side door, go down a few steps, and cross a little court which lies before you. Enter a large gloomy ante-chamber, and here you are. The Court itself is right in front.

It is lighted by two lofty windows ; but the daylight they let in never reaches as far as the back of the Court, which nearly always remains in shadow. Its general aspect is cold and cheerless, and beneath these stone arches, which date from Saint Louis, the atmosphere is always damp.

It is well known that the justices of peace, besides their civil functions, are charged with the duty of sitting on contraventions,[1] those peccadilloes of the Penal Code, which usually cost the offender the modest sum of one franc, sometimes more (the maximum fine being fifteen francs), with the alternative of five days' imprisonment, and of which no record is kept.

At Paris there is only one Police Court for the twenty *arrondisse-*

---

[1] The French law divides offences into contraventions, misdemeanours, and crimes. The first class are within the competency of the justice of peace ; the second belong to the police or correctional chambers of the Tribunals of First Instance ; the third come under the cognisance of the Courts of Assize.

ments. Every justice of peace sits there in turn for one week. Sittings are held every day in the week except Mondays, and, of course, Sundays. Besides the justice of peace, the Court comprises three commissaries of police appointed by the Procureur-Général to represent the Ministry of Justice, one acting as chief, the two others being his deputies; lastly comes a chief registrar and four registrar's clerks. The Police Court is by far the busiest tribunal in France. In 1890 it issued summonses against 43,528 defendants, including publicans, shop-keepers, drivers of public vehicles, porters, house-owners, &c. Leaving the pavement before one's house ill-swept, shaking carpets out of the window, watering the flowers on the window-sills too copiously, not putting up the shutters of a shop soon enough, letting a dog stray without a collar or muzzle, such are the delinquencies which bring before this indulgent Court hundreds of worthy men who have unwittingly broken some police regulation.

The number of summonses issued in 1890 was, as stated above, 43,528 ; which, after all, is not so very large for a city of 2,500,000 inhabitants.

But the Court of Simple Police, a deduction being made for Sundays, Mondays, fête days, and the vacation (during which it only sits three times a week), only holds about 240 sittings in the year. If you divide the 43,528 delinquents by 240, you will have nearly 200 cases for every sitting. Each sitting lasts, according to the expedition of the presiding magistrate, from an hour and a half to three hours. This only gives about one minute for each case !

How do they manage to get through the business at such miraculous speed ?

Listen, and we shall be able to satisfy ourselves by actual observation.

The representative of the Ministry of Justice begins. He has put each delinquency into a particular class according to its nature.

He then proceeds as follows : " Summoned for a breach of the police regulations as to wheeled carriages, Pierre, Paul, Jacques, &c."

From time to time, at the calling out of each name, the word " Present !" comes from the back of the hall.

As soon as the roll-call is ended, the sitting magistrate who has put a mark on his list against the names of the absentees, reads these names over again, passes sentence on them in default, and inflicts on each delinquent the maximum fine incurred.

The names of those charged who are present in Court are then read out a second time.

"Which of the persons named have anything to say?" asks the official prosecutor.

Two or three defendants step forward, and mutter some kind of excuse which receives little attention ; and the whole of this second batch are condemned in the same penalty, smaller however than that inflicted on the absent.

For certain offences there is a fixed price, just as if they were patties ; but an offence of this kind costs more and brings less return than the pastrycook's productions. Thus, every one breaking the police regulations as to wheeled carriages is fined five francs, if absent; three francs, if present. But, in the majority of cases, delinquents prefer to suffer judgment by default.

The time spent in coming to court causes them a total loss greater than the penalty inflicted in case of non-attendance, even though this be on the highest scale allowed by law.

Sometimes the magistrate gives reasons for his sentence in a solemn preamble, "Whereas, &c.," worthy of the Court of Cassation. At certain times, moreover, the Police Court assumes a kind of political character. As for instance on the day following a public demonstration, when it is crowded with loafers and spectators arrested in the confusion for making a disturbance, who are lucky to have escaped being brought before the Correctional Police Court for resisting the officers of the law.

On these days, according to some, the peace-maker on the bench becomes "an accomplice in the infamous tyranny of the police"; according to others, he helps in saving social order from the attacks of anarchy.

In cases of this kind, professional men frequently, and sometimes advocates, may be seen at the bar, but as a rule the Court of Simple Police decides cases summarily without listening to any defence.

Astonishment has been sometimes expressed at the rapidity with which magistrates of correctional police get through the cases that come before them. What should be said of the Simple Police Court? If one acts by steam, the other must work by electricity!

CHAPTER XVI

THE COURT OF CORRECTIONAL POLICE

LET us leave the Court of Simple Police, pass under the arch which we find on our right, and make our way round the Sainte-Chapelle ; we find ourselves in front of folding doors over which are printed the words : *Tribunal Correctionnel.*

We have just seen those humble folk who count for nothing in the hierarchy of crime ; we shall here meet the middle class, or as one may say the burgesses of vice and misery.

We mount to the first floor, and find ourselves at the eighth and ninth Chambers. At the door we are stopped by a municipal guard, who says, in the tone of an omnibus conductor, " Full up!" So it is ; within, the people are crowding in a closely packed throng, attracted by the widely spread belief that there is nothing so amusing as a sitting of the Correctional Court. Very often, however, the idler who has turned in there with the hope of spending a good lively afternoon comes out with moist eyes, as much taken by surprise as the stranger who forgot that serious dramas are sometimes performed at the Vaudeville Theatre.

As a matter of fact, a visitor to the Correctional Court will laugh or cry according to his temperament. I have met one of its regular frequenters who used to say that nothing saddened him so much as a case of adultery. The desolated hearth, the deserted husband, the dark shadow cast over the future of the children, all these thoughts rose up before him, and forced themselves upon his mind whenever one of those gross cases came up for hearing which the general public greets with roars of laughter. But it is to be feared that the majority belong to the class who share the opinion of *Ma Cousine*, and at the

ONE.

From a sketch by
P. Renouard.

sight of the injured husband say with the dramatist Meilhac : " It is useless to conceal the fact ; every time we meet a case of that sort it gives us pleasure."

We, who wish to see the Correctional Court under its two aspects, shall take two guides in our visit : the first will be a disciple of Democritus, the second a pupil of Heraclitus of Ephesus.

Following these two leaders, John who laughs and John who cries, we shall be able, in spite of the orders of the guard, to slip through the barrier, and make our way into the Court in a few moments.

ANOTHER.

From a sketch by
P. Renouard.

But let us first of all take a look round at the approaches. We see an immense staircase, opening on to the Court of the Sainte-Chapelle, and leading to the four Chambers appropriated to this jurisdiction ; the eighth and ninth Chambers are on the first floor ; the tenth and eleventh on the second ; on each landing is a miniature Salle des Pas-Perdus.

Unlike the Chambers of the Civil Court, these are not confined to special kinds of cases. However, during the second period of the Boulanger crisis, when the movement was on the decline, political cases came before the ninth Chamber, at that date under

L.

the presidency of a judge whose severity for some time was a matter of constant talk. During the first period, press offences and cases of riot came before the judges of the eighth Chamber, who were rather inclined to clemency.

Eleven o'clock! A crowd of people are hurrying up the stairs—witnesses, interested parties, and spectators. The advocates arrive by the corridors : some enter the Courts where their cases call them ; others who, on the contrary, are in quest of cases, remain outside, with a busy air, their brief bags empty, or, more often, stuffed full of old newspapers. These are the canvassing advocates ; a distinct type, hitherto undescribed, we believe, at any rate little known to the general public. It is our duty therefore, in a work dealing with the legal side of life, to devote a few pages to them. The trouble will not be thrown away, for to point out an evil is always a step towards its removal.

SOLICITING BRIEFS

The despised profession of a canvassing advocate is carried on, either here or in the prison corridors, by certain individuals widely differing in age, whose notions on the meaning of the word dignity are, to say the least of it, incomplete.

The canvassers at prisons content themselves with greasing the palms of warders who are willing to recommend them to the prisoners during the hour for exercise. The advocate does not in this way obtain clients who pay high fees, but he may sometimes get hold of a sensational case. His name will be printed in the newspapers, and they will be a good advertisement for him. These canvassers for briefs *extra muros*, these dwellers in the suburbs, are not very interesting, owing to the extreme simplicity of the methods they employ.

The canvassing advocate of the Correctional Court is, on the contrary, very amusing to follow in his scientific poaching manœuvres—seeking whom he may devour. His plan of operations is complex ; he has at one and the same time to drive the game into his snares, and to keep a look out for the keepers, in his case represented by the *bâtonnier* and the members of the Council of the Order.

The Paris Bar is rather poor in individuals of this type ; it however possesses a few specimens of the species, who are known throughout the law courts. Any barrister or judge will easily point them out to you, and they take care, for the matter of that, to make themselves conspicuous by passing their whole day in the chambers or ante-chambers of the Correctional Court.

Round the heads of the profession, members of the pioneer corps, as they say in the army, gravitate a number of timid satellites—apprentices who do their utmost to imitate the great stars, but want the qualification of boldness indispensable for success. The appearance of an honest member of the bar makes them nervous. Let a member of the Council happen to pass by, and they are seized with a panic. If the *bâtonnier* shows his face, they are off like a shot. . . .

But, by the side of these lesser men, it is interesting to watch the evolutions of the leaders of this special bar. These latter do not hide; they display themselves. They are perfectly conscious of the contempt they inspire ; but this causes them no uneasiness. Their canvassing is stamped with a certain grandeur. There is arrogance in their solicitation, magnificence in their humiliation, and pride in the way they bear the disdain of their brethren.

They seem to have taken as their device the saying of Danton : " Audacity, and then again audacity ! " At the first stroke of eleven they are on the look out, moving about through the midst of the crowd of defendants, witnesses, and spectators who are waiting for the opening of the Correctional Chambers. Weeping women, brought thither for shop-lifting at the Magasin du Louvre, or caught in open adultery, are the first victims, their very air pointing them out to the canvassers. The latter cast the net, or rather the line, a little at a venture, and with the risk of meeting a contemptuous rebuff. The client once hooked, they play him for his money, proving to him, to use their own words, that it is " much better to pay forty sous more and have a good advocate."

One of these freebooters practises his profession with a superb *maestria*, with an activity and zeal positively astounding. The type of his class, he canvasses in the corridors, he canvasses in the Courts, even in the dock itself. He canvasses sitting, he canvasses standing, he is canvassing now, and always will be ; and his dreams, if he has any, ought to bring before his view a delusive mirage of wonderful successes in his art, of marvellous anglings for briefs, of extraordinary clients who let themselves be caught—everything is possible—up to a louis d'or. How magnificent he looks while engaged in his daily rounds, moving about like the busiest of mankind, his head high, his eye wide open, with a noble bearing like that of a horse suddenly reined in; turning his face incessantly from side to side, like a cabman on the look out, exploring the streets with piercing glance, in eager quest for the slightest sign of a client. This is not *a* canvassing advocate ; he is *the* canvasser, the leading genius, the emperor of his kind.

In a few moments we shall see his disciples in Court, and there let us do them one justice—to make up for that which they get done to their clients—they are by no means niggardly of their rhetoric. One of them, Maître Y——, is celebrated for his zeal in trying to win hopeless cases. He is gifted with a skill in the art of speaking which is amply proved by his flow of language, and with an astonishing wealth of argument, or rather with a power of dressing up the same argument in different ways, so as to present it three or four times. Never stopping at an interruption, he goes straight on, in the hope of wresting the welcome words " We are with you " from the very weariness of the Court. This advocate is the terror of the judges, and they can scarce retain their equanimity when they see him appear at the bar.

With Maître Z—— it is the same thing. Only, when he is speaking, a listener can indulge in forty winks, or more if he wishes. In any case, both these gentlemen make people yawn.

There is also a third who, as a rule, talks rodomontade, and never fails to excite shouts of laughter. Unfortunately for French gaiety, he rarely appears at the bar ; and, unfortunately also for law reporters, he buttonholes them in the corridors, in order to tell them, with an ineffable smile, about the occasional cases in which he is retained.

The canvassing advocate's career is of brief duration, and the members of this order are constantly changing . . . . One after another, in his turn, ends in being caught some day, while engaged in open poaching, by the officers of the Council of the real Order. The poacher then betakes himself to the dubious profession of a general agent, which is his proper field, unless he prefers, as many of them have already done, to take refuge in politics. *Sic transit gloria mundi.* Our readers have now heard enough about these prowlers dressed in advocates' gowns, so let us cross the threshold and enter the Court itself. With the exception of the dock in which the prisoners are placed as they come from the Souricière or the

ADVOCATES OF THE CORRECTIONAL COURT.

Dépôt, it is practically identical with the Civil Courts described above. Note however that here the registrar sits immediately below the judicial bench.

But there is a great difference in the character of the spectators.

In the Civil Court, excepting the advocates and the parties to the cause, we saw no one but unfortunates come for warmth or for shelter from the rain.

Here there are real loungers besides the witnesses; good stout mothers of families, people living on small independent incomes, law students, clerks with a spare hour to waste, little family parties in search of amusements that cost nothing. By their side are wenches without any covering for their heads, come to see their lovers tried; street roughs come to encourage a mistress or a "pal"; mothers come to hear how much "time" their scapegrace sons will have to do. On certain days, numbers of loose women, summoned to the Palace for being without the certificates required by the police, come in a crowd to spend the day at *la correctionnelle*.

From this dense throng there rises a strong frouzy smell of seething humanity; add to this perfume that of the boots of the municipal guards; season it with the stench of filthy rags; mix the whole with steam arising from the perspiration of advocates, ushers, and judges, and you will have a full explanation of the little flasks of vinegar that stand, near the Codes, before the three judges who form the Court, and before the public prosecutor's deputy sitting silent on his chair. This little flask is a privilege of the magistrates.

THE VINEGAR BOTTLE.

The advocates have none at the bar, and the registrars possess them only when, like M. Liévin, they have occupied their office so long that they are almost become actual presidents of the Chamber to which they act as secretaries.

THE AMUSING SIDE OF THE CORRECTIONAL COURT

Even for those most inclined to derive amusement from petty correctional cases, there are days when even Gwynplaine[1] could

—————
[1] The hero of Victor Hugo's romance, *L'homme qui rit.*

not laugh ; for instance, those when a financial case or a charge of fraudulent imitation comes up for hearing.

But even when the case contains food for laughter, everything depends on the president. The amusing points in the hearing are brought out or passed over according as the judges like or dislike their functions at the Correctional Court. Some time ago there was a curious example of the latter. The first day he was called on to preside, this Solon, who had only entered Court at twelve, had by half-past two disposed of no less than seventy-four cases ! There is an instance of another president from whom it was hopeless to try and get a laugh. One day a prisoner attracted the attention of the whole Court by his extraordinary apparel. From the moment he appeared in the dock, the people pointed him out to one another with suppressed fits of laughter, every one's attention being fixed on the amusing trial they expected to hear. The culprit, a tall strapping fellow, was dressed in woman's clothes ! Such an attempt at deception had never been seen. This man was a

M. LIÉVIN.

vagabond. But in less than two minutes after his name had been called he was judged, convicted, and taken away by the guards. The president had not even asked him the reason for his disguise.

Other judges like to give a humorous turn to the trials. On one occasion there appeared a lady, no longer young, but coquettish in air and highly rouged. The judge asked her some personal questions, at which she hesitated, simpered, smiled, and replied, " I do not tell my age any longer." " Very well, madam," said he, " tell us any age you like." Sometimes it is the presidents themselves who provide the public with something to laugh at. Such was the worthy judge whom cases of procuring young girls for immoral purposes used to throw into an extraordinary state of excitement.   At the end of a long trial, he once recalled one of the girls who had been procured by her assumed name, crying out, " Blanchette, come here ! "

Some austere presidents enjoin silence at the first sign of mirth, adding that no one should ever laugh in a court of justice.   But they themselves used to excite laughter by the famous phrase " Go and sit down ! " addressed to witnesses.   This saying, which in the conversation of persons unused to good society is equivalent to " Shut up ! " or " Hold your noise ! " has now in Court been replaced by the words " You can now retire."   This is so much gained for the majesty of justice.

Offences tried before the Correctional Court are numerous and varied : thefts, acts of swindling, frauds, breaches of trust, wrongful conversion of goods seized, assaults, abusive language, &c. Quarrels between house-porters and disputes between neighbours are those in which the public takes most pleasure, especially when old gossips relate with many blushes the invectives they have hurled in one another's faces.

" Sir," says one, "this woman has covered me with insults."

THE PRESIDENT.—State the insults.

THE WITNESS.—Oh, sir, I dare not.

THE PRESIDENT.—But you must dare.

THE WITNESS.—Well, sir, she called me a . . . *hetaira*, but she did not use that exact word.

On which the whole Court roars with laughter.

On entering the Court we find the box occupied by a witness— one of those who love the sound of their own voices.

It is an open-air huckstress, a well-set-up dame who has been attacked and robbed by a strolling vagabond.

THE PRESIDENT.—You swear to tell the whole truth and nothing but the truth ?

" Yes, sir," answers the buxom female.

THE PRESIDENT (*in formal tones*).—Very well, then.   Say " I swear."

The witness makes no sign.

THE PRESIDENT (*losing his temper*).—I tell you to raise your hand and to take the oath.   Are you deaf?

THE WITNESS (*starting off at a gallop*).—Oh, sir, nothing of the kind, I am glad to say.   I take the oath, as I hope for salvation. By this crucifix, sir, I swear to tell the whole truth, and nothing but the truth. But that, sir, I shall do of course ; for in the first place I never told a lie. (Laughter.)

THE PRESIDENT.—Very well ; make your deposition.

THE WITNESS.—With pleasure, sir. I am afraid of nothing. This is how it all happened. First, sir, you must know that in the morning I go to Batignolles to sell cabbages, leeks, carrots, &c. . . . a poor living I get out of it, too. Well, the other day, towards nine o'clock in the morning, this rascal, who is now in the dock,

IN THE CORRECTIONAL COURT.

came sidling round my market cart with a comical look in his eye. At first I never thought that he wanted to rob me ; on the contrary, there was a business-like air about him.

THE PRESIDENT.—But come to the point. Never mind his business-like manner. Let us hear how he tried to rob you. How did the prisoner at the bar steal your goods ?

THE WITNESS.—I am just come to that, sir ; but you must first of all let me explain.

The president, in despair at her prolixity, after a few more attempts to bring her to the point, sends the witness back to her place, and reads out the declaration she made to the commissary of police. The public meanwhile receive with peals of laughter the unhappy huckstress, who is heart-broken at not having been able to tell her story.

Other prisoners now come up for trial. Most of them are professional beggars, idle scamps, to whom begging is a regular trade, by which they earn, on an average, from six to ten francs a day; *i.e.* more than is earned by many artisans and workmen with a family to maintain.

All these people are soon disposed of. A few answers, however, deserve note.

One of those charged with begging, a dirty-looking man of forty, who shams blindness, energetically denies that he asked alms of the passers by.

THE PRESIDENT.—But you were caught holding your hand out to a lady.

THE PRISONER. — It was because I thought I felt a few drops of water, and I was stretching out my hand to see if it rained.

To another the president says, "The policeman caught you holding out your cap to a lady."

POCHARDS.

THE PRISONER.—It was a lady from whom I asked the way; so, naturally, I took off my hat out of politeness.

The judges are hard on these regular delinquents. But they show a little more indulgence to prisoners with no previous convictions against them, and there are plenty of these. A man once turned up who did not know what this meant.

THE PRESIDENT.—Have you any antecedents?

THE PRISONER.—No, sir; I have only a sister.

The most remarkable thing at the Correctional Court is the absence of any moral sense in so many of the prisoners and witnesses. This is specially shown in cases in which adulterous women and kept mistresses are concerned. Many in this world of ours are blind, and many are deaf, but they are far inferior in number to the people who are incapable of appreciating the habits of civilised life. Zola has represented Coupeau as inviting his wife's old lover to his house. The Correctional Court shows us many happy homes of this kind, and far more lively and amusing ones than that of the three heroes of *L'Assommoir*.

Here is a case in point,

THE PRESIDENT (*after having set forth the whole case against the prisoner*).—What have you to say in answer to this?

THE PRISONER.—Simply that my wife is a b———.

THE PRESIDENT.—What has this to do with the case?

THE PRISONER.—Everything, Mr. President. This gentleman, who complains that I landed him one, has been making love to my wife, whenever I was away.

THE COMPLAINANT.—The prisoner's wife used to be my wife, so I was only renewing old acquaintance.

THE PRESIDENT (*to the prisoner*).—Your wife used to be the complainant's wife?

ACCOMPLICES.
By P. Renouard.

THE PRISONER.—Yes, but she has been divorced from him, and married to me; so she is my wife now.

THE PRESIDENT.—And you actually receive into your home your wife's divorced husband?

THE PRISONER.—It is he who arranged the marriage. "Look here," says he, "you want a wife; I've the very thing that will suit you, a regular beauty, as you shall see; and I know what I'm saying, because I've been married to her myself." So I married her, as she was warranted good by the gentleman, who was my best man at the wedding.

THE COMPLAINANT.—Well, I told you she was a beauty; is she?

THE PRISONER.—Yes, but she is a beast for all that.

The lady who has been wife to both these friends is condemned to pay a heavy fine. After which the comic sitting comes to an end.

THE SAD SIDE OF THE COURT

The comic sitting is over, but here comes our second guide, who will take us to another Chamber, where we shall see the Correctional Court under its distressing aspects.

The burlesque characters are gone, and we shall now have before us the lepers of society in all their foulness. Let us take note of the creatures as they pass by, and we shall have no lack of food for thought.

To-day it is a body of young men whom the guards are bringing in. They are sixteen, seventeen, and eighteen years old, not more. Unlike to one another in face and figure, they have two traits in common: a pale, livid complexion, as if it had been washed in dirty water; and thin lips without colour, like razor blades. Morally, they are all of the same stamp; they live on the earnings of their mistress, a wretched girl who tramps the outer boulevards; and when her infamy fails to support them, they go and steal.

They are now called upon to answer for various thefts. They avow them without the least compunction, nay, with effrontery. They have never worked. All labour, all discipline, all rule is hateful to them.

"Left at an early age to live by my wits," wrote one of this set in a memoir which the director of the Mazas Prison asked for, "it ought not to be a matter of surprise if I do not like work. I have given way to my father's worst weakness, absinthe drinking. When I had money, I always drank two or three tumblers of it every day. Hating work, to seek it was the last thing that could have occurred to me. The worse my clothes and the bigger blackguards my friends, the prouder I felt."

The offspring of morally diseased parents, and brought up amidst bad surroundings, they have nothing but scorn for virtue, for the law, for society itself. Knowing nothing but their appetites, they make it their aim to satisfy these at any cost. Provided they can escape the clutches of the police, they care for little else. Incapable of remorse, they sleep soundly every night, whatever crimes they may happen to have committed during the day. A doctor would call them men whose moral sense is blinded.

While the president of the Court is examining them, they exchange signs of intelligence with comrades in the body of the hall. The Court condemns them. They go out with a shrug of the shoulders. Prison life will complete their ruin, and in three or four years we shall meet them again at the assizes.

The brain of these precocious wretches is already in a confused sort of way a home for thoughts of assassination.

M. Joly has said of them, "they are in a permanent state of readiness to commit a murder for a word, for a fancy, for a wager."

They will sometimes do it to satisfy a pure wild beast curiosity. As an instance of this take the conversation overheard by Dr. Laurent at the Prison de la Santé between a vagabond and a youth under twenty, who had tried to strangle his father.

"Look here," asked the first, "you might as well tell me why you wanted to strangle the old man."

"I don't know."

"Did you want to get at his savings?"

"I've told you he hadn't a farthing in the world."

"Then what did you want to screw his gizzard for?"

"Well, *just to see what sort of a face he'd make.*"

MAÎTRE ROLLET,
Member of the Society for the Protection of Children.

Allorto, Sellier, Catelin, Ribot were well known at the Correctional Court. Kaps had just left gaol when he murdered the old man Vinçard.

But let us return to Court.

Another set of thieves, still younger, is now occupying the dock.

The first, eleven years old, François D——, with a sweet expression, large wondering eyes, very small for his age, has taken a pair of cheap shoes from a stall in the Temple market.

His father and mother are dead. An aunt had taken him to her home ; but, being old, infirm, and earning very little, she could only give him a bit of bread every day. She cannot trouble about his clothes or shoes. He had to go about bare-foot in the winter.

"Why did you steal these shoes ?" asks the president.

"To wear them, sir," answers he, in a child's clear tones ; "I saw them, I stooped down, took them, and ran away."

"But you know very well that it is wicked to steal."

"Yes, sir," murmurs the child blushing, and he adds a remark, the import of which is deep for those who care to understand it :

"But I did not think of it, at the moment."

Luckily, a member of the Society for the Protection of Children[1] is present. He comes forward to the bar, and asks that the child be entrusted to him, a request readily granted. In old days a judge would have had no option but to send the child to gaol.

The next, who is fourteen and a half, Jules C——, with a bad expression, has stolen a box of sardines and a bottle of liqueur from a grocer's shop in the Rue Saint-Honoré.

This is his third appearance before the judges for similar acts of larceny. The son of honest working people whose hearts he is breaking, he refuses to stay in any situation they get for him, and insists on running about the streets in company with other scamps of his own age.

When the case is called on, a man of forty, well-built, with a frank and energetic expression, goes into the witness-box.

"You are the prisoner's father ?" asks the president.

"Yes, sir," answers the witness, ashamed and looking down. "Sir," he goes on, in a tone he tries to make harsh, though in spite of his anger a strain of deep grief runs through it, "I have already taken him back twice ; I can do nothing with him ; he won't work. . . . This time I will not take him back ; send him to prison."

While he is speaking, his son's features relax ; they lose their bad expression ; there comes over them a look of the deepest anguish.

"Father ! father !" he cries in accents of despair, "I promise to behave better."

<hr>

[1] *La Société protectrice de l'enfance.*

"No! I have done with you."

"Father! father!"

"No! no!"

"Father!" stammers the child, his whole frame shaking with sobs.

"No!"

But the man's voice grows weaker. His last "No" is scarcely heard. He is silent for two, for three seconds. At last, giving way, he murmurs:

"Well, then, I will take you back again, but it will be for the last time."

And he quickly passes his sleeve before his eyes, whilst the women seated in the Court shed tears silently.

After an interval, the scene changes.

A FINANCIER.

Gentlemen of a high rank now come before the Court. Faultless in dress, in manner and in speech, but a little time ago they passed everywhere as perfect gentlemen. Somewhere behind the Stock Exchange they had opened a bank which offered enormous dividends. Money flowed into their coffers. Clerks, cooks, domestic servants, officers on half pay, flocked to their counters. All were graciously received. No sum was too small for acceptance. One morning, the game being up, they levanted, and the police commissary on being summoned to the place only found in their safe the sum of forty-eight sous in copper.

In the end they are brought back from the frontier between two gendarmes.

To the president's questions they answer politely. Not a word is out of tune. They talk figures in long, calm phrases. They explain their carriages, their mistresses, their sumptuous dinners, their magnificent style of living by "the necessities of their position." Their victims have been stripped to the very bone; yet some of them who appear at the bar as witnesses—such is the stupidity of mankind—nod their heads approvingly, and retain confidence in their plunderers.

These gentlemen are condemned to two or three years of prison. In less than six months they will be pardoned, and swagger along the boulevards, saluting the world in general with a flourish of their hats, silk hats, quite new and of the latest fashion.

To the swindlers succeed some portly middle-aged women, horrible to look upon with their rolls of flesh, their painted cheeks, their oily hands.

Keepers of infamous *brasseries*, they are accused of procuring girls under the age for purposes of debauchery. And ten or twelve girls of sixteen or seventeen, scarcely developed, but already steeped in vice, come forward, all of them telling the same tale, quite carelessly, without shame, without grief, like passive instruments of pleasure.

The wretched creatures give details. From their young lips the filthiest words come quite naturally. Among the audience a few law students burst out laughing, but thinking men shudder. As for the girls, they do not trouble themselves about it, and go on with their story almost unconsciously.

Another change—mothers who have tortured their children. One has exposed a little boy of five under a spout of ice-cold water, yelling out to him, as he shivered, " You shiver; die then!" Another has burned her little girl's limbs with a red-hot iron. Another has hung up her child by the wrists till, under the frightful suffering, the quivering flesh turned white.

One after another, when the president reproaches them with their cruelty, remarks drily:

" I only used my right of correction " !

They are indignant because the Court inflicts a penalty upon them. They do not understand. These human females make one think of certain female animals who devour their own offspring the moment they are born.

Then come convicts who have broken their ticket of leave.

The majority of them could not tell the exact number of times they have been apprehended for having returned to Paris in spite of the decree which forbids them to enter it. The list is too long; one has been arrested ten times, another fifteen, another twenty or more.

Listen to this stereotyped dialogue.

THE PRESIDENT.—Your name is Louis Chaussin; you are thirty-four years old; Paris is prohibited to you; yet you have re-entered it?

THE PRISONER.—Yes; but what would you have me do? Can a man in my position live in the provinces? An employer, knowing nothing about you, gives you a good post. In three or four days he finds out who you are, and off you go; he kicks you out of the house. Look here; I was once a soldier. While out on leave I stole 42 francs; it was my first offence. I got five years' imprisonment and prohibition to come to Paris for ten years. The imprisonment I don't care about, though five years for 42 francs is rather stiff; but the prohibition to enter Paris. . . !

THE PRESIDENT.—Besides your first sentence of imprisonment you have had six others?

THE PRISONER.—For breaking my ticket of leave as now, but not anything else. It is always the same story. I come to a town, I can't find work, it is only at Paris that I could find it because here people don't ask you about your antecedents. What would you have me do?

Does not this man speak the truth? Nevertheless the Court sentences him to a month's imprisonment. It is the law.

Then several ladies appear, fashionably dressed, but ashamed and trembling. An inspector from the Magasin du Louvre tells how he surprised them in the act of slipping into their pockets either bottles of smelling salts, lace, or embroidered handkerchiefs.

They shed tears, deny nothing, stammer a few indistinct words: they saw these articles before their eyes—within their reach—the temptation came upon them—with an irresistible force—they yielded to it—they do not know how it was. . .

While they speak their limbs shake, their faces grow pale as death. One of them, twenty-four years old, only just married, on hearing the president pronounce the words " Three months," sinks in a heap on the floor, seized with convulsions so violent that four guards, with all their united efforts, can scarcely carry her away.

By the door, which has been left open, may be heard this piercing cry, which she utters without ceasing: "No! no! I will not go to prison; I will die first!" She grows delirious, and in her frenzy seems to see the portals of Saint-Lazare prison opening before her.

The doctor attached to the law courts on being summoned reports the case as one of "hysterical epilepsy." Her mother and husband pass her in the corridor; the one in tears, the other stunned, with livid face.

A SHOP-LIFTER.

In the Court opposite persons caught *flagrante delicto* come up for judgment. Between noon and five o'clock the Court passes sentence on a herd of 108 wretches arrested by the police the preceding night, some in one place, some in another; in the Bois de Boulogne, in the Bois de Vincennes, under the bridges, in the trenches below the ramparts, on the benches that line the boulevards, among the rubbish of houses in process of demolition. The rabble comprises men and women of all ages. Old men with white hair and bent backs; decrepit old women with toothless and receding mouths. Male and female companions of about forty; beardless youths; girls in their teens. For garments they have nothing but a few shapeless rags probably alive with vermin; patched up peticoats, torn vests, pantaloons made up out of twenty different pieces, old coats full of holes. Young, middle-aged or tottering on the verge of the grave, in the full light shed on them by the lofty windows, they offer to the spectators a succession of cadaverous faces, emaciated features, hopeless eyes. They are beings without hearth or home. Like street dogs, they sleep where they find themselves and eat when they can. Society calls them vagabonds and declares them guilty of misery.

A VAGABOND.
By P. Renouard.

Arrested pell-mell, they are brought into the dock in batches of ten, taken at random. The registrar puts down their names, the president sentences them, and they disappear.

No advocate has appeared in their defence ; the president has listened absently to their answers, his colleagues thought of other things as they signified their assent [1] while condemnations somewhat at random were rained down upon them. The public prosecutor has spent the time in drawing pictures of flowery arbours on his blotting-pad, or in preparing a charge for some ensuing case which has excited great interest in the public press. Once or twice the president has asked him if he has any comments to offer. But he has merely half raised himself from his chair, and bowed without saying a word—a pantomime, which means "I am in agreement with the Court."

In this way the judge, who has a host of charges to hear in a single day, hurries through the roll of crime and misery. He knows well that he is sometimes mistaken, that several of those before him are condemned unjustly. But he soothes his conscience with the reflection : " Never mind ! those who are innocent will be sure to appeal."

Few of those who come before the Court, however, avail themselves of this resource. Old offenders, who are sentenced to a short term of imprisonment and would not be able to find bail, think, in fact, with terror of the long weeks they would have to wait—possibly without any result—before their trial in the Court of Appeal. So those who can get bail and persons with an unstained record are the only ones who care to risk a " return visit " to Court, as the prison phrase is.

Let us follow them to the other end of the Palace of Justice, where stands the Court of Criminal Appeal.

---

[1] The French is "*en opinant du bonnet.*" When the presiding judge delivers judgment, the puisne judges raise their caps (*bonnets*) in token of assent.

CHAPTER XVII

THE justice of jurymen and the justice of lawyers differ from one another in theory and in practice. But these two varieties have their homes side by side in two courts, which occupy the part of the Palace of Justice overlooking the Place Dauphine. A narrow corridor forms the only separation between them.

The Chamber of Correctional Appeals is spacious, chilly, and filled with rows of benches. In its complete absence of decoration and its dull gray ceiling, it reminds the spectator of a Protestant meeting-house. The law would seem to reign within these walls in all its rigour. And yet the atmosphere of the Court has, on the moment of entry, nothing to cause disquiet.

A visitor feels himself in the Chamber of Justice, it might be said of justice in repose. The faces of the judges are stamped with an expression of haughty unconcern. There is in them no trace of the passion which so readily enlivens the features of some judges of first instance while they are engaged upon a trial. In the Appeal Court, not only do the judges hear the case at a greater distance from the events which give rise to it, but also without the presence of the witnesses, whose depositions, now committed to writing, have lost in the registrar's notes all power of exciting emotion. The prisoner, who is still bewildered by the expeditious and sometimes brutal style in which his trial was conducted at the former hearing, begins to dream of an acquittal when he contemplates the comforting solemnity which pervades the Court, and above all its punctilious observance of legal formalities. The poor man, surprised at the scrupulous attitude of his new judges, anxiously drinks in with eyes and ears every detail of the scene in which he figures.

It is his case they are trying, and yet he has scarcely any part in its discussion. The president, in a tone courteous in its formality, asks him a few brief questions respecting his antecedents. Then he adds politely, turning to one of his colleagues, "The reporting counsellor will now make his statement." A sharp voice, rising from somewhere among the seven counsellors, at once recapitulates the different phases of the case, and sets forth minutely the proceedings, the arguments, and the judgment in the Court below. This report is completely devoid of any literary graces ; it is merely a formal statement stuffed full of facts, and bearing the stamp of real impartiality. No personal observation finds its way into it.

From the commencement of the reporting counsellor's address, the prisoner's whole thoughts have been concentrated on the task of finding out whence comes the hard voice which strike his ears. His eyes range up and down the line of seven judges, seated on his left, round a table in the shape of a horse-shoe, with a green cloth, loaded with papers and bulky legal tomes. He examines them one after another, in their carelessly varied attitudes, all engaged, not in listening, but in reading or writing. The lips of one of the judges move, and his hands change their position from the necessity of selecting papers from the heap before him ; by these signs the accused distinguishes the reporting counsellor. From that moment he never takes his looks off him ; his ears are as it were closed, and all his powers of attention are concentrated in his eyes.

At the end of ten or twenty minutes the reporting counsellor's voice comes to a full stop. The president, recalled from the extra-judicial occupation on which he was engaged, raises his head, and says in a cold tone :

"Prisoner at the bar, stand up."

The examination of the prisoner now takes place ; a summary proceeding in which the president, without a shadow of acrimony, in the style, as one might say, of Suetonius, quietly runs through the chief counts of the indictment, and asks the prisoner what he has to say in answer. The counsellors then for the first time turn their eyes towards the accused ; they listen to some of his explanations, and, like men whose scruples are readily satisfied, they return to the tasks they had for a moment interrupted. The president then says "Counsel for the defence." Thereupon the advocate of the accused begins a long address. After a second statement of the case, a statement made from his own point of view, he goes carefully to work to break down each of the grounds stated in the judgment against his client ; and contends, both for reasons of fact and for reasons of law, that the decision of the Court below should be annulled or at any rate modified. Then when at last the confirmation of the sentence appealed against

begins to look in danger, the Advocate-General, in his turn, offers a few brief observations. In his conclusions, as they are called, he does his best to demolish the arguments for the defence, and to show with a logical power equal to his opponent's that the Tribunal of Correctional Police has made a correct application of the law. Sometimes, but only in very exceptional cases, the representative of the Public Ministry asks the Court of Appeal to increase the sentence. In legal language, this is called an appeal *à minimâ*.

During this oratorical duel, of which he knows well he will be the

THE ADVOCATE-GENERAL.

only victim, the accused keeps changing his attitude mechanically. For the first-half hour he follows the arguments of his counsel ; his expression is animated, and he looks fondly on the speaker with admiring eyes. But, little by little, his attention flags ; it ends by becoming completely wrecked in this sea of legal quibbles. His blinking looks now wander from one side to the other, turning always principally on the row of counsellors. Should one of them at any time raise his head, and seem to listen to a passage of the speech for the defence, the unhappy man makes desperate efforts to read on his countenance the impression made by the words. And his heart sinks when he sees the judge after this fit of distraction return to his interrupted task.

Growing anxious, he looks round for a friendly face, and with this object he explores every corner and recess of the hall of justice. But nowhere does he find what he is in search of. The registrar and usher have their regular expression of professional apathy. Seated in front of him, before long tables in tiers, where the juries of the Seine Assize Court sometimes sit when there is a double Assize Session, the members of the bar, with wearied air, wait for their cases to come on. They have no eyes for anything except the clock, which, with mechanical movements of the head, they consult every five minutes.   The audience and the policemen with their set faces are too far off for him to make

a guess at their sentiments.   Affrighted by this absence of sympathy, oppressed by the isolation in which he finds himself, he returns as a last resource to watching his own counsel.   The latter, having finished   his   speech,   is   now relaxing his mind by drawing a caricature of the Advocate-General   on   a   corner   of   his brief.   The accused feels himself gradually yielding to the atmosphere   of   indifference which surrounds him.   Rather than pay attention to the contemptuous address of the Advocate-General,   he   examines abstractedly   the   architecture of   the   Court,   stares   at   the ceiling, then, turning his head, gazes   with   attention   at   the bust of the Republic, below which is inscribed in golden letters this couplet in post-classical Latin :—

" Hic pœnæ scelerum ultrices posuere tribunal,
Sontibus unde tremor, civibus unde salus."

But the president's voice is heard once more saying : " The Court will now deliberate. . . ."

The judges rise heavily from their seats; and after a few moments' discussion in a circle behind the president's chair, they file out in line to the Council Chamber.   This means that some question of law has cropped up.   Had it not been for this, judgment would have been immediately delivered on the spot.   The accused catches at every straw.   Is this solemn deliberation in his favour ?   Alas, no.   The Court of Appeal rarely withdraws to the Council Chamber except to patch up a somewhat hasty judgment delivered by the Court of First Instance ; a judgment which, excellent so far as the condemnation goes, has some trifling defect of form, which could not bear the scrutiny of the Supreme

Court. The spirit of jurisprudence, always stirring in the breasts of the counsellors, gives itself full play. The decision appealed from receives the touch of juridical varnish needed to make it perfect. Vying with one another, they display their skill in supporting it by the most subtle arguments. With a marvellous refinement of logic, the legal text referred to in the original charge is made to include the case against the prisoner. There is not even a semblance of opposition.

Accompanied by the six smiling counsellors, the president, with the documents of the case under his arm, makes a triumphant return into Court. With lively notes of joy in his voice, he reads the decree, setting forth that, though the grounds given for the original judgment are invalid, the operative part must nevertheless be confirmed.

The condemned man listens with stupefied air as the hopes he had built up on the solemn judicial debates in which he was not badly treated are dashed to the ground. Are we to gather from this that the Chamber of Correctional Appeals, irreverently designated by Henri Rochefort the "Chamber of Bishops," always confirms the judgments of the Court below? Not so. It has given celebrated decisions in which it has manifested its high judicial tone, and has proved both its independence and its disdain for the verdicts of the multitude. To it in fact was due the acquittal of M. Wilson, who, during the arguments in his case, while nervously stroking a long russet beard, kept a confident gaze on the Latin couplet inscribed under the bust of the Republic ; a couplet in which the pentameter

" Sontibus unde tremor, civibus unde salus "

seemed to stand out with an unusual brightness.

CHAPTER XVIII

THE CHAMBER OF INDICTMENTS

BEFORE proceeding to the Court of Assize, the great stage on which the chief criminal dramas run their course, we must make a little detour, and, under the guidance of some Asmodeus, try and visit the scaled Chamber of Indictments, the ante-chamber where for several weeks the most important criminal cases sent for trial undergo a preliminary preparation. After having mounted the steps of the grand staircase, the visitor will hear the first hum of counsel and litigants in the robing-room corridor. Here he will find a little low door. It leads by a dark stairway to a series of gloomy apartments, on the level of the ground, with no other horizon but the walls of the Sainte-Chapelle. It is here that the Chamber of Indictments still holds its sittings. Very soon it will migrate with the Court of Appeal into new buildings, which will be lofty and well lighted. And yet this old-fashioned accommodation forms a very suitable frame for the Chamber which labours within closed doors at the work of despatching defendants to take their trial before the Assize Court. At the foot of the little staircase is a room occupied by the registrar, M. Horoch, whose courteous address forms a singular contrast to the surrounding gloom. Then comes the judges' robing-room. It opens on to an apartment quite soberly furnished, where the substitutes come for a chat, while waiting their turn to go to the Council Chamber to explain the cases entrusted to them. This Council Chamber is a fairly large apartment, with a decayed look about it. In the middle is an oval table with a green cloth, round which are set seven arm-chairs for the counsellors, and the chair of the substitute. Were it not for a respectable row of stout volumes ranged in a sliding book-stand, one would say—may Themis pardon the blasphemy—that it was a table devoted to secret games of baccarat !

Round this table the six counsellors and their president meet twice a week, on Tuesdays and Fridays. But though badly housed they do not scamp their work. On the one hand they have to decide appeals brought from decisions of the judges of instruction relative to applica-tions for bail. On the other, they have to settle, in the case of all persons ac-cused of felony, whether they are to be sent for trial be-fore the Court of Assize, or whether they are entitled to the benefit of a find-ing of "no true bill." In this latter task they are en-lightened by the public prosecutors who come, in turn, to deliver their re-ports on all criminal cases before the Court. The coun-sellors deliberate, and one of them is

selected by the president to draw up their decision. This labour, portioned out among six counsellors, is no light one for each counsellor, since in the course of the year the Chamber delivers, under this head alone, from six to eight hundred judgments. But this is not all. The new Code of Criminal Instruction has operated with peculiar cruelty towards these magistrates by imposing on them the duty of pronouncing rehabilitations. From this time forward every person punished for a criminal offence can, at the end of three full years, have the record of his sentence struck out if he proves to have been of good behaviour during that period. This enactment was the first sign of a social movement to which we owe the recent Bérenger law. Before it took place, the number of rehabilitations *per annum* did not exceed seventy. Now they amount to more than eight hundred. But progress continues its work, day by day, even in the Palace of Justice.

A new habitation has been prepared for the Chamber of Indictments. At present it is occupied by the juries appointed to assess compensation for disturbance. For once, the civil law takes precedence of the criminal.

CHAPTER XIX

THE COURT OF ASSIZE

GENTLEMEN OF THE JURY

IN every canton of France an annual assembly, composed of mayors, justices of peace, and municipal councillors, selects a number of citizens of good repute for character and conduct to act as those judges of fact in important criminal cases who are styled "gentlemen of the jury." The names chosen are forwarded to the judicial authority, and a fresh selection is then made out of them by a commission which meets in the chief town of the department. The persons selected by this latter body form the general jury list ; and from this general list are drawn by lot—once a quarter in the provinces and once a fortnight in Paris—the names of those who are actually to serve on the juries at criminal sessions. The number required is thirty-six acting and four supplementary jurymen. All men over thirty years of age are bound by law to serve on juries. Nobody unless he is over seventy can refuse to take his part in the administration of justice, under a penalty of five hundred francs. All citizens thus enjoy the honour, though all do not equally appreciate it. A juryman receives a ridiculously inadequate allowance for travelling expenses; for his loss of time while engaged he receives no compensation at all. His business suffers from his absence, and his wife, during her husband's temporary administration of justice, does not always remain the model wife, content to stay at home and knit stockings. It is true that for the retired captain, living on his half-pay amidst the dulness of provincial towns, there is nothing irksome in this little trip to town. The veteran fastens a broad piece of ribbon to his buttonhole, brushes up his Sunday hat with vigorous elbow, and takes out the venerable frock coat which lies sleeping on a bed of pepper and camphor at the bottom of his chest of drawers; then, with waistband tightly buckled, clothes smartly arranged, and a suspicion of dye about the grizzled tips of his moustache, he alights at the Hôtel de France, determined to save society from danger and to show his contempt for droning counsel.

But it is very different with Jean Mathurin Besnard, the metayer.[1] When one evening in harvest he sees the parish constable arrive with a peremptory summons requiring him to serve on a jury, he knocks the ashes out of his pipe against his boot heel furiously, and, pointing in despair to the standing crops, curses the judicial system, the government, and the taxes; asks whether there are not shopkeepers enough in the town to make a jury without tearing him away from his land, the land he loves, the land he could clasp passionately in his arms like a sweetheart; and, bending down hastily to his interrupted task, he finishes in the dusk the work of a day which has gone only too fast.

See them all assembled in the hall of the Assize Court, the members of the jury. The sessions are about to begin. Unknown for the most part to each other, they watch one another closely, and insensibly fall into groups round those of their number who have decorations. There they are, all of them men of respectability come together to try the pariahs; the flourishing notary, with eye-glass and flowing whiskers, who knows his way about the place, and is looking out for some barrister of his acquaintance to get him excused on account of his profession; the elderly man of independent means, stern, silent, and self-conscious; then some Bohemian artist, with luxuriant hair and loose neckcloth, who will be too easily attracted by the improbable and the romantic to make a good juryman. . . . And, farther down, keeping modestly in the background, will be seen, on this judicial stage where a bourgeois' fate is sometimes decided, a notable member of the fourth estate in the person of some foreman, grave, attentive, almost contemplative; one who, in the uprightness of his intentions, would make a model judge were not his head stuffed with newspaper articles.

They are worthy men, all of them. . . . Individual failings, corrupt bargains, violent decisions are not to be dreaded when a

---

[1] A farmer with fixity of tenure, who divides the profits of the land equally with the landlord. The metayer system in France and Italy has been described by many writers, from Arthur Young to John Stuart Mill.

man is not sole judge. With his eleven companions by his side, a juryman will make it a point of conscience to appear upright, scrupulous, and disinterested; and it may be stated as a fact that, from the moral point of view, the collective is higher than the individual standard. On that point all thinkers are agreed. Worthy men, I repeat it, are these gentlemen of the jury. But with such a want of experience and decision! No! It is far from easy for a man to isolate himself so as to become absolutely impartial. Every opinion of a juryman is in its essence subjective. He will never condemn or acquit a prisoner on considerations of the public good, but solely for some reason drawn from his own experience. A man's guilt will make a greater or smaller impression upon him in proportion as he himself runs the risk of being a sufferer from the crime in question. It is a notorious fact that before a country jury girls guilty of infanticide are generally acquitted. A natural child! What would have become of the little creature? It would have been necessary to bring it up at the expense of the parish; and when it reached the age of fifteen it would have taken to burning hayricks! As to the man accused of arson, he knows what to expect. The peasant-farmer, exposed without protection to fire, will show him neither leniency nor mercy.

It is the same with indecent assaults on children; for villagers' children often remain by themselves at the farm while the father and mother are working in the fields. The coiner has no more pity to expect. A countryman will, as cases show, send a man to the galleys for passing a counterfeit half-franc. The severity of a Versailles jury has become traditional. Composed of market-gardeners, half-pay officers, and retired clerks, living in suburban cottages which are open day and night to the depredations of the Parisian scum, they punish without pity any malefactor hailing from the great city; the verdict asked for by the prosecution is always found, and sometimes a good deal more. A good instance of this happened a few years ago in the case of three young scoundrels who came from Paris to murder an old woman who kept a small inn at Argenteuil; the public prosecutor only asked for one head; the Versailles jury gave him all the three.

The Parisian jury is quite otherwise composed and more difficult to analyse. It will not give a caste verdict, because in Paris the various castes run into one another too much. But it is at the mercy of a good speaker. This will not be the counsel, who is rarely listened to, nor even the Advocate-General, whom the fault-finding Parisian condemns because he represents authority. No; it is from among their own body that the jury will choose this real leader, some reasoner with an abundant and easy flow of language; a man with a talent for seeing into millstones and round corners, who is the more dangerous to the good sense of his colleagues as he is more skilful in playing with paradoxes.

A Parisian jury is moreover under the spell of two mistresses: fashion and sensation.

During several years the appearance in the dock of heroines of the revolver and the vitriol flask was a mere matter of form. It had become a tradition to acquit in cases of crime caused by passion. The Ministry of Justice was compelled to take steps to do without a jury in the majority of these cases by a change in procedure; that is to say, ladies accused of causing wounds or injuries with vitriol were sent before a trusty " ninth Chamber," which did not neglect its duty.

Treated thus as an inferior jurisdiction and incapable of judging in certain cases, juries were put on their good behaviour. At the present day they return fairly reasonable verdicts in cases in which love has played a part. None the less, in these delicate matters, a Parisian jury remains a big baby which must be kept in leading strings and carefully looked after.

We were speaking just now of sensation. A Parisian jury is easily moved by the notoriety or celebrity attached to a case. Suppose there are two wretches who have committed similar crimes. If the first is lucky enough to have done the deed in the middle of a Ministerial crisis, on the day when the Grand Prize is run for, or during the annual demonstration on May Day; if, in one word, there was any chance of the murder passing unnoticed, the jury will be complaisant, and the culprit will easily obtain the benefit of extenuating circumstances. If on the other hand the crime has caused excitement, if the press has taken it up, if the newspapers have published portraits of the victims accompanied by appalling descriptions, the prisoner is certain to be condemned to death. Billoir, who deserved six months in gaol for having given an unlucky kick to his old mistress in the middle of a drunken quarrel, was condemned to death because the dismemberment of the body had excited universal horror; and, to crown all, Marshal MacMahon left him to the guillotine " on account of his

excellent antecedents," that is, because he was an ex-soldier and
had dishonoured the army.

THE TRIAL

Our good jurymen are now met in the Assize Court, feeling
rather out of their element in the midst of judicial parade. The
usher reads out the general list of names; excuses are made
on behalf of some because of illness, or because they must live by
daily labour. A few others are sent about their business because,

THE DOCK.

at the last moment, it is found that they have at some time been
convicted of a penal offence; so carelessly are the lists drawn
up. Occasionally a man who refuses to serve has to pay into the
treasury—or rather out of *his* treasury—a fine of 500 francs, and
his name is put back into the urn for next sessions. At last the
non-effectives being got rid of, and the panel made up by the
addition of supplementary jurymen, the jury for the sessions is
complete.

N

The president of the Court of Assize[1] then has the accused brought into the Council Chamber, whither he himself goes, followed by the thirty-six jurymen, and accompanied by the advocate-general and the counsel for the defence. "Prisoner," says he, "these gentlemen have been summoned to try you. I am going to put their thirty-six names in the urn ; you have the right to challenge any twelve of them ; the Public Prosecutor has a right to challenge an equal number. As soon as the names of twelve unchallenged jurymen shall have been drawn out of the urn the jury will be constituted." Then, pulling up the right sleeve of his scarlet robe, the president shakes the urn containing the ballots on which the names of the jurymen are inscribed, and calls them out, as they appear, in a loud voice.

"Present !" answers the juryman.

"Challenged !" thunders the advocate-general or yelps the prisoner's advocate.

Except the cunning rogues who get themselves challenged so as to escape serving, when they have the means of arranging matters, a juryman who has this "Begone" flung full in his face reddens violently; his eyes roll round like loto balls, and he opens his mouth as if for a protest which is stopped on his lips by the awe he feels for the majesty of justice. After all, there is nothing discreditable in being challenged. Although neither the Public Prosecutor nor the advocates engaged are accountable to any one for their challenge, it is always easy to guess its motives. The advocates for the defence will challenge a married juryman in a case connected with morality ; in a case of embezzlement by a clerk, he will challenge employers of labour; in a case of infanticide, young fathers of families.

In some cases, in political trials for example, and on occasions when the selection of the jury is made in public, as is usual in certain provincial courts, the right of challenge assumes a vital importance ; then the advocate-general and the counsel for the defence watch one another out of the corners of their eyes. They wait !. . . . Neither party being able to make more than a certain number of challenges, they each hope that the opposite side, acting on false information, may unwittingly deliver them from

---

[1] *I.e.* the presiding judge. Criminal cases at the Court of Assize are heard by three judges sitting together.

an enemy. There begins a curious duel, rich in comedy both as regards the gestures and the attitudes of the combatants. The name of a juryman suspected by both parties is drawn out of the urn : nobody says a word ; the juryman, full of dignity, moves majestically to his place ; he is just about to take his seat, he is already sitting down, when, at the last moment, a sharp and sudden cry of " Challenged ! " pulls him up on the very verge of his judicial functions.

The juryman starts, takes up, with sullen air, the hat he had just put down, and disappears, covered with confusion, in the mocking crowd of his colleagues. People have no idea of the minute investigations made by the prosecution and defence into " their " jurymen ; the political opinions of the husband, the religious profession of the wife, the family connections—the police inquires into everything as if it was a question of drawing up a report on the physical and moral condition of a contumacious prisoner. As a result, the Public Prosecutor and the counsel for the defence arrive at an astonishing degree of information.

A few years ago there appeared before the Assize Court of Corsica a young journalist belonging to the Bonapartist party, named Antoine Léandri. He had taken to the bush[1] with a little army of malcontents to protest against certain harassing administrative regulations. He was brought before a Corsican jury on a charge of stirring up civil war. The procureur-général Moras and the counsel for the defence, Maître de Montera, engaged in a Homeric battle over the selection of the jury. Each exercised his right of challenge with the most determined zeal. When at length their right came to an end, both of them reckoned up the jurymen who had survived the slaughter, and, after having gone through the names, the procureur-général Moras bent towards the counsel for the defence and remarked, with a smile, " Your man is acquitted by ten votes to two." " So he is ! " answered Maître de Montera, after having verified the numbers in his turn. And this is what actually happened, the trial making no change, and the eloquence of the two speakers not turning a single vote. Under the circumstances, the calculation was easy enough as the question involved was purely political. But the selection of the jury often demands a more subtle study of the human heart.

[1] *Prendre le maquis.*

Our readers may remember the case of Madame de Chicourt, the Toulon beauty, who with her lover, M. Fouroux, mayor of that town, appeared before a jury of the department of the Var in January, 1891, on a charge of procuring abortion. Those who saw and heard her in Court, with her languid Creole speech, her feline attitudes and her exquisite gracefulness, will never forget this charming prisoner, whose guilt was so small and whose punishment was so severe.

The bitterness of party disputes in the south of France is well known, and around the name of M. Fouroux, her accomplice, raged a terrific combat. As Fouroux was a radical, the Public Prosecutor challenged all the radicals; the advocate for the defence retaliated by throwing out all the opportunists he possibly could. In the end, the jury contained no man of any known character, but consisted of twelve peasants of the mountains, ill-clothed, sour, ruined by the vine disease, content to put up at the small inns of the outskirts to save a little money. These men cared little about the political opinions of the chief prisoner, but they were exasperated by having to listen for three whole days to stories of trips to Paris, perfumery, ladies' toilettes, and elegant suppers ; and they convicted the graceful and coquettish beauty because, to their eyes, she represented luxury, ease, and pleasure, an insult to their daily growing wretchedness.

"My child," said the grandmother of George Sand's *Valentine*, "take a lover of your own rank !"

"Prisoner at the bar," we should be disposed to say in our turn, "get yourself tried by jurymen of your own class !"

But we have found our way to the great hall of the Assize Court. A bell announces the entry of the jurymen, and here they are.

THE HALL.

It is now time to give a rough sketch of this Court of Assize for the department of the Seine, in which the fate of so many lives comes up for decision.

At one end, on a daïs, stand the three judicial arm-chairs ; the advocate-general is on the left, and the registrar[1] on the

---

[1] *Greffier.*

right. Then, facing one another, are two long galleries, filled with seats. On the side of the advocate-general, well placed both for seeing and hearing, is a bench for the twelve jurymen ; it is prolonged so as to accommodate those jurymen who have not been called upon to serve, but who want to be present at the proceedings as spectators.

Below the jury-box stands a plain desk for the usher. Opposite to this are two long enclosed spaces, the first for the prisoner, the second for the reporters. They are separated from one another by a movable partition, which allows the part reserved for the press to be increased or diminished, according to the number of prisoners in the dock. A strong light falls from the lofty windows in front, striking the prisoner full in the face, while the jury remain in the shade. Such is the rule observed in the building of law courts. Below the dock are the

A CORNER OF THE REPORTERS' BENCH.

seats allotted to advocates, and, on the right, immediately beneath the registrar's desk, are a little table and two chairs for the parties[1] to the prosecution, who, in accordance with tradition, are supposed to come and implore justice at the feet of the Judge. Right in front of the judicial daïs is another table, long in shape, and scratched all over with marks of nails. It is the table for articles produced in evidence.[2] What countless vials of vitriol, revolvers and knives, blood-stained garments, from satin dresses to workmen's blouses and ladies' corsets, have been piled up in this Morgue for things inanimate ! What a history of human crime and human passion a collector of these articles could have written ! A few labels affixed

---

[1] *La partie civile.*   [2] *Pièces à conviction.*

to the objects in this ghastly museum, a date, a name recalled, this would be enough and far more terrible than any lengthy narrative.

In front of the table for articles produced in evidence is the bar, where the witness will come presently to raise his right hand towards Bonnat's magnificent picture of Christ.

The Court have not yet entered, but the hall is already crowded. A few intruders are turned out of the reporters' box ; in the middle of the part railed off from the public, Léon, the apparitor of the Order of Advocates, scrutinises the advocates' benches, and gently ousts from them some profane person who will soon be brought before the *bâtonnier*, and not dismissed without a severe reprimand for ·illegally wearing the forensic gown. In the reserved inclosure, despite a recent circular,, may be seen dainty costumes and fashionable bonnets ; while tittering may be heard mingled with exclamations and little cries uttered by women who are being pinched. A little time ago was the heyday of reserved tickets ; large numbers were distributed to gay ladies ; and certain Court officials made great sums by selling them· In those days the Court looked like a theatre ; nothing was wanting, neither fans, opera-glasses, applause, trembling at the pathetic moment ; and, during the adjournment—I had almost said the *entr'acte*—the champagne corks popped gaily.

AN HABITUÉ.
(Sketch by P. Renouard.)

Meanwhile, standing up at the back of the Court, packed one against the other, like sardines in a box, crushed and flattened by the throng, may be seen the people who take their pleasure cheaply, the non-paying public ; an astonishing medley of colour, crumpled neckcloths and small caps, faded dresses and old jackets of which the original hues have quite disappeared. In the midst of the crowd may be seen, like a white post, the spotless cap of some confectioner's apprentice. The populace want their share of the fun, and push their way in by main force. It is not cards but blows that are exchanged between these impatient competitors. By dint of steady shoving, a young telegraph clerk has forced his way to the very front, and there he will remain, delighted if gasping, for the rest of the day.

The crowd is sharply divided ; in the reserved seats, delicate

laces ; in the back, blue handkerchiefs ; there, the scent of helio-
trope; here, the smell of sausage and garlic. But look at the faces
and attitudes.   Everywhere there is the same expression of eager,
feverish curiosity, the same thirst for strong emotions, the same
passion for this drama of real life.   In capital convictions, when
the president pronounces the word "death," the same thrill runs
through all veins alike, and the same exclamation of horror
escapes from every breast.   The cry of awe-
struck terror, which the hear-
ing of a

death sentence calls
forth, may be heard uttered at the
same pitch, and in the same tone,
in the Court at Paris and in the Courts of little provincial towns
in Flanders as well as in Gascony.   The human voice, that
marvellous instrument whose tones express the most minute differences of feeling, has here no variability, whether it be the liquid
utterance of the Parisienne, the grating chuckle of the tatterde-
malion, or the harsh accents of the peasant.

THE COURT

But, hush, here comes the Court !   Every one cries " Sit down,"
and every one stands up to get a view !   Every eye is turned towards
the little door by which the prisoner enters between his two guards.
There are a few final expulsions from the reporters' box ; a lady,
who offers the press-men to remain there to cut their pencils, finds
no favour.   A young barrister, with a military tuft, points out the

witnesses to a well-dressed friend.   Behind, on the left, the caps
and flowing sleeves of probationers who have come late may be
seen perched on the benches and ranged in rows along a dark
passage ; some of them climb on to the stove or the window-sills,
and watch for the moment when a fellow-student who has come
in better time will leave a vacant place for them in the middle of
the pretorium.

At last silence is obtained; the hubbub, passing through the
whole descending gamut of sound, dwindles to a hum, and from a
hum to a whisper, and the president now slowly utters the sacramental words, " The sitting is opened."   A few questions are then
put to the prisoner : his surname, Christian names, age, profession ;
then the twelve jurymen rise, and each of them proceeds to take
the customary oath :—

" *You swear and promise before God and man to examine with
the most scrupulous attention into the charges that will be brought
against N——, not to betray the interests of the prisoner nor those of
society which accuses him ; not to communicate with any one till after
your verdict ; to listen neither to hatred nor malice, fear nor affection,
to make your decision after duly weighing the charges and the
defence, according to your conscience and inmost conviction, with the
impartiality and firmness becoming to an honest man of independent
mind.*"

Each juryman raises his right hand and answers, "I swear
it !"

A few years ago there was a kind of fancy among jurymen
to refuse the oath because of the religious formula involved.   Some
worthy men, who were very indifferent in matters of faith, suddenly
discovered conscientious scruples of which they had till then been
quite unaware.   The oath stuck in their throat.   Some veteran of
1848 had started this kind of protest against clericalism, and, as
the juryman is by nature one of Panurge's sheep,[1] the noble army
of " non-juring jurymen " grew rapidly.   A few fines brought this
little faction to reason.   Jurymen learnt that it was silly to harass
one's life or lose a summer holiday by so feeble a sacrifice to philosophy.   Peace was restored ; the fashion has now passed away ;
and nobody refuses any longer this little harmless ceremony,

---

[1] See Rabelais, *Pantagruel*, bk. iv. c. 8.   Panurge, who is on board a ship carrying
a flock of sheep, purchases one and throws it overboard.   On this all the other sheep
leap after their comrade and are drowned.

although, as statistics show, there are as many free-thinking jury-men as there were before.

After the oath, outward manifestations on the part of the jury are at an end. They will generally listen to the pleadings without a word, unless some prater bethinks him of putting a question, in which case all his colleagues will believe themselves bound to do likewise. But this is an exception; and the jury-box will remain the most lifeless part of the Court, up to the moment of the verdict. It is now the president's turn to come on the scene.

THE PRESIDENT

In the hieratic days of the magistracy, which are not so very long ago, the president of the Court of Assize was not a simple man; he was a demi-god. Scarcely had he, a plain counsellor of the Court, been invested with these important functions than an aureole appeared round his brow. He no longer walked, he advanced; he no longer spoke, he pronounced; a kind of civil pontiff, he launched forth upon the vulgar, not the greater excommunication, but the thunders of discretionary power. True, some of the old presidents were gallant men, like M. de Saintes, who said with a smile to the Countess de Tilly, charged with throwing vitriol at a dressmaker, her rival, " Stand up, prisoner at the bar; for your ladyship knows that we are compelled to designate you by this term." But it also happened that the interrogatory was often reduced to a simple monologue, interrupted at long intervals by these two objurgations, " Prisoner, explain yourself," and the moment the prisoner opened his lips to answer, " Be silent!"

These were the halcyon days of that ineffable thing, the summing-up; in which the case for the prosecution was restated with such complacency, and the defence whittled away with the most utter disdain. The summing-up was abolished in 1880, when its abuses were exposed by Maître Lachaud, owing to the extremes to which they had been pushed by Judge Bachelier, a past-master in the art, during the trial of Mdlle. Marie Bière.

The majority of our readers are certain to remember this counsellor *à la* Louis XV., with his powdered wig, his bands that looked like a courtier's frill, and the little hands of which he took such exquisite care, dainty as those of a fashionable abbé of the old court. His summings-up were delightful, and in his flute-like voice he would say the most terrible things with such perfect grace that, excepting the prisoner, every one was forced to smile. Of this time also was the old counsellor F——(he is dead, trouble not his shade!) who only had three formulas for summing up the defence. It was "rather long," when the advocate was his friend ; "too long, as usual," when the advocate was unknown to him ; "as usual, too long and, moreover, badly put," when the advocate was a republican. Counsellor F——was an Orleanist.

The authors of this book, simple observers of the manners and

COUNSEL FOR THE DEFENCE.

customs of the law courts, wish to avoid the introduction of any political remark into these pages ; it is not for them to offer any opinion on the historical value of the change in the judicial service, which followed the decrees against the monastic corporations ; but it must be said that, if it deprived the bench of some of its dignified attributes, prisoners in particular and the cause of justice in general have most decidedly gained by it. We do not say that all presidents of the Courts of Assize have become models of impartiality and sweet reasonableness ; but, excepting when politics intrude, a man is no longer "finished off ; " he is tried ;

and the brutality of the old-fashioned *hanging* judge has been superseded by a more serious desire to investigate facts and motives. During the last few years the psychological side of criminal trials has undergone a remarkable development, and among our presidents of assize are to be found thinkers and analysts of the first order.

The ideal president ought to put all his logic and all his subtlety into the work of piercing the secrets of a tortuous mind : he should be able to unravel all the stratagems of woman, she being far better skilled than man in the art of self-defence ; and he should have the power of summing up a whole argument in three words. He should preside at a trial as if taking part in a conversation,

DURING THE SPEECH OF THE PUBLIC PROSECUTOR.
Sketch by P. Renouard.

without raising his voice, and without threatening ; but, when the male or female prisoner sits down after having been under examination for a quarter of an hour, they should have been turned inside out, and the jury should be in possession of all the facts.

M. Bérard des Glajeux, to-day one of the presidents in the Court of Appeal at Paris, realises in more than one respect the type of a perfect president. Equally out of the common was President Cartier, who died a few years ago. The reader can recall him with his bright red face, his long whiskers nearly white, his nose like that of Punch, and his large eyes, beaming with a wondrous comicality. He succeeded by assuming an air of familiarity, of "good fellowship," we had almost said by blarney ; a man besides of a tolerant spirit who did not expect his fellow-creatures to be saints.

But the best thing he ever did was his examination, conducted with the most marvellous irony, of the abbé Roussel. The latter prosecuted his ward, Mdlle. Annette Harchoux, for forging his name ; a charge the young lady paid back on her trial by reproaching the poor abbé for certain undue lengths to which he had been wont to carry his former solicitude.

These dialogues that take place at the assizes, when conducted by a master of the art, have a vividness that the theatre cannot give. There are in the former intonations, attitudes, retorts, shudders, that all the art of the most skilful dramatist is powerless to repro-

DURING THE SPEECH FOR THE DEFENCE.
By P. Renouard.

duce upon the stage. A prisoner before his judges never expresses his feelings by those noisy manifestation—cries, tears, exclamations —with which actors in a play think themselves bound to accompany their protestations of innocence. The drama of an Assize Court is much more sober in its setting, but much more interesting than what is enacted on the stage, and nothing ever strikes the spectator as out of tune, for it is the actual expression of nature itself.

THE ADVOCATE-GENERAL

By the side of the presiding judge may be seen the representative of the state, the Advocate-General ; " the advocate digger " as prisoners call him. In popular portraits he is represented with short whiskers, thin lips, frowning brows, and a malevolent expression. He is not always like this, nor does he necessarily impress his points on the Court in tones of thunder, accompanied by furious gesticulation. Advocate-General Bernard, at present a counsellor of the Supreme Court, who prosecuted in the trials of Madame Clovis Hugues, Pel, Marchandon, and so many other celebrated cases of the last few years, was on the contrary a most gentle speaker, so scrupulous and tender-hearted that sometimes he seemed to be acting for the defence. He spoke to the jury in a tone of resigned melancholy, knowing perfectly well how to win them by means of some fellow-feeling, to which he would give expression for their behoof. M. Bernard's very moderation was the greatest danger the prisoner's advocate had to guard against.

Advocate-General Sarrut, who was prosecutor in the case of Prado, is a very different man. His style is terse, incisive, pitiless. Immovable as a statue, he weaves his arguments so closely that the prisoner will not find one single mesh left open for his escape. There is in him no trace of indignation or anger, but at the same time there is none of tenderness nor mercy; there is no touch of feminine nature about him, if we may not say nothing human ; above all, nothing is sacrificed to ornament or grace. Such is a speech for the prosecution by Advocate-General Sarrut. It is a sermon. Those who in the foggy light of an autumn day heard this gaunt, melancholy, hollow-cheeked man, with his straight hair, and red beard cut to a point in the Huguenot fashion of Charles IX., ask for the head of Prado, must have looked upon him with a kind of terror as an inquisitor of old arisen from the grave.

M. SARRUT, ADVOCATE-GENERAL.

Very different again is the Procureur-Général, M. Quesnay de Beaurepaire : in the first place he is a man of letters, who loves form and grace of diction, with a subtle brain that disdains no refinement of sentiment. At the bar of the Assize Court, the author of *Le Forestier* shows his turn for descriptions, picturesque to the verge of being overdone, but painted with the richest colouring and the most powerful of brushes. He has a lazy, drawling accent; he wears his cap like a student, at the back of his head; in his gait there is something uncertain and irresolute. The man in fact, with his rough features, his prominent bones, his mocking and sarcastic eye, gives rather the impression of a Breton peasant than that of a Parisian Procureur-Général. But the alteration in him when he begins to address the Court is astonishing. After five minutes the spectators cease to think about his walk or his accent. An actor of incomparable skill, a speaker and thinker of unquestionable power, a remarkable man, in fact, stands before you. Under his searching and crushing analysis the prisoner has no secrets. The Procureur-Général attacks him in front directly, describing him by a gesture, piercing his very soul with a glance, weaving round him a net of suggestive phrases, while ever and anon he makes him start by some sudden and unexpected apostrophe. "I know your name," said M. Quesnay de Beaurepaire to the mysterious Campi, "I am going to tell it you! . . . ." And he seemed as if about to fall upon him, his finger stretched out as if pointing at the corpse. The prisoner waited all trembling while his adversary lengthened out his words, and prolonged his silence till the culprit began to think his secret known, and his real name on the point of being cast in his teeth. Then, with a disdainful smile, satisfied with the effect produced, M. de Beaurepaire finished his sentence in a tone of contemptuous irony: "I know your name, and I am going to tell it you; you are the murderer of the Rue du Regard!"

Eight years after the trial of Campi, M. de Beaurepaire crowned his career by his celebrated speech before the High Court of Justice against General Boulanger, and by the oration he delivered in the Gouffé case. On the latter occasion he showed much good sense and sound judgment in opposing that love for the marvellous which has reappeared in our day under the scientific name of hypnotism. In this combat the school of Nancy received a fatal blow.

THE BAR

We will now take a look round on the other side of the bar. Here are the advocates. Some of them are veterans, old stagers at the Court of Assize, who for forty years have sung the same old

SKETCHES IN THE COURT OF ASSIZE.
By P. Renouard.

song in the same confident tone. Some are young fellows, striplings fresh from the conference, nervous as at a first assignation, as fascinated ·by time-worn arguments as a rhetorician by the charms of some ripe beauty. There are some of them whose reputation is growing, whose career the press follows with interest, whose portraits will perhaps find a place in a future edition of this work.

At the present time the Parisian criminal bar is ruled by three great names, Lachaud, Maître Demange, and Maître Albert Danet. We say Lachaud, because he is a possession for all time. If the hero is dead, his memory and his tradition have survived him. Beethoven was not a musician, but music itself ; so Lachaud was not a defender, he was *the* defender of accused persons. An orator, if you like, and a great orator, skilled in all vocal harmonies, in all modulations of tone, with ten, nay twenty different voices at his command, according as he was called upon to convince or to

MAÎTRE LACHAUD.

persuade, to touch or to terrify ; but, before all, he was a tactician of the very highest rank, and a psychologist by whose side specialists of that name were mere stammering babes. Lachaud had often won a case before he began his speech ; he had won it by some adroit question addressed to the chief witness, by some sagacious preparation of his client, by a smile or a sarcastic interjection, with which he underscored the feeble arguments in the prosecutor's address. His knowledge of a jury was extraordinary. Lachaud would make twelve separate speeches if he had to deal with twelve jurymen of different conditions. He knew well that a consideration which moved a draper would make no impression on

a mining engineer.   With a marvellous intuition, he would find his
way into every man's heart, executing variations on the same
theme with incomparable vivacity, speaking to each juryman in
turn, fixing him with an eye which saw everything, never letting
him go till he was thoroughly convinced.   He had an exquisite
wit and a kindly and indulgent soul.   He was a good man to the
poor, he loved his art more than anything, he was the protector,
the friend of all those with power to think ; and, in troublous
times, he was the disinterested and generous defender of freedom of opinion.   Like Lenté, that other giant, he came, so to
speak, to die at the bar, already overcome by the numbness of
approaching death, but rousing himself to utter one last touching
address before judges whom his darkened eyes could no longer distinguish.   And he fell into the eternal sleep with his face turned to
that exquisite portrait of Madame Lafarge—a youthful figure with
soft hair, large lustrous eyes, and pale complexion, showing a white
rose in her bosom—a portrait which, painted for his chambers in
the Rue Bonaparte by Madame O'Connell, recalled to him the first
triumph of his youthful years.

His successor, Maître Demange, is, above all, an orator.   He
has the same variety of gesture as Lachaud, the same enthusiasm
and the same wealth of expression.   His voice is rich and ringing ;
his rhetoric is less persuasive than Lachaud's, but perhaps more
moving.   He has two favourite notes, one warlike as a clarion,
the other melodious and soothing, and there is occasionally too
quick a change from one to the other.   For the rest, Maître
Demange has all the external charm of Lachaud, an honest,
sympathetic face, bordered with whiskers that enjoy perpetual
youth, and a magnificent breadth of chest.   Since the case of
Prince Pierre Bonaparte, which established his reputation, and
that of Dr. Garrigue, for whom he obtained an acquittal at
Périgueux on a charge of poisoning his father, Maître Demange
has been engaged in nearly all the great trials of recent times.   He
appeared for Dr. Castelnau, for Fenayrou at Versailles, for Madame
Achet at Moulins, without speaking of sensational assize cases,
like that of Pranzini at Paris.

By the side of Maître Demange stands Maître Albert Danet,
honeyed, persuasive, irresistible, to whom a jury can refuse nothing.
If he failed in the case of Marchandon, it was because this wretch
was impossible of defence ; but he obtained an acquittal for Lucien

Fenayrou, and he had the skill to persuade M. Grévy that Abadie, the ferocious criminal for whom he appeared ten years ago, could be permitted to live, without risk to society.

IN SUPPORT OF THE PROSECUTION

In Lachaud, Demange, and Albert Danet we have seen three different types of counsel for the defence. Time was when it was hard to find a leading man among counsel for the prosecution, or advocates who support the indictment, and serve as auxiliaries to the Public Prosecutor. Accustomed to plead for the acquittal of prisoners, the great advocates of the assizes have no practice in sounding the charge or raising the war-cry for their condemnation. These two intellectual feats are impossible to one and the same mind. This year an ideal prosecuting counsel has at last appeared in Maître Waldeck - Rousseau, an ex-minister who has quitted the great things of the political world, and is on the way to take the first position among advocates retained in large cases at the law courts. We have seen Maître Waldeck-Rousseau measure himself with Maître Demange in the mysterious Chantelle case ; the former demanding justice in the name of the murdered notary's

MAÎTRE WALDECK-ROUSSEAU.

heirs, the latter defending Madame Achet. Tall, phlegmatic, rather English in his manner, perfectly self-possessed, speaking with unimpeachable authority, he dissects a criminal case as if he were analysing an account ; that is, so far as clearness is concerned ; but, that elegance may not be lacking, he sets forth his facts with a cold irony and · humour positively delicious. Maître Waldeck-Rousseau is the ally whom the Public Prosecutor has long been dreaming of, I had almost said dreading ; for when a man of this stamp has thrown a strong light on a case, nothing more remains to be said by others.

WITNESSES AND EXPERTS

We have delineated the principal actors in the drama: the presiding judge, the jury, the public prosecutor, the advocate ; and we have sketched the impressionable and noisy crowd of spectators. It would be beyond the scope of this volume to do more than outline the secondary characters :

The witness for the prosecution ; important, listened to, congratulated. The witness for the defence; hesitating, awkward, often snubbed and reprimanded by the presiding judge. The accountant not gifted with grace of style, but terribly conscientious. The expert in handwriting, " this character from farcical comedy " as Georges Laguerre so neatly called him, grave, solemn as an undertaker, and wearing a look that sends the irreverent reporters on their bench into a fit of laughter. Look at Doctor Brouardel, a marvel of precision and clearness, expounding his medical science so simply and gracefully as to be within the comprehension of his most ignorant hearer. Look at Doctor Motet, the great authority on insanity, with his choice and elegant phraseology, his mental pictures beautifully sketched in a few clever strokes, his analysis of mental states, which the psychologists already mentioned ought to come and hear with the humility of school boys.

DOCTOR BROUARDEL.

Look at the usher, stout, short of breath, full of business, pushing through the crowd, in perpetual search of his witnesses who have run off to get a drink. Then, modest, obliging, wholly unbiased and always able to foretell the verdict, comes the clerk of the Court, M. Wilmès ; he has succeeded the great Commerson, who now lives in retirement at Versailles, after half a century of official life, hale as at thirty, always jovial and good-tempered, the great Commerson, whose strong sense, as Lachaud wittily said, " survived fifty years of summings-up," and yet there is still some one whom we have forgotten. Who is it ? The prisoner.

THE PRISONERS

We need not linger over unimportant cases of injury to the person or commonplace infanticides. It is true that every case at the assizes, however ordinary its circumstances, could in itself

furnish matter for study and observation. There is much that is curious in the physiognomy of the little clerk driven to embezzlement by betting on horse-races. Curious too that of the waif of society who after twenty years of unsettled exist-

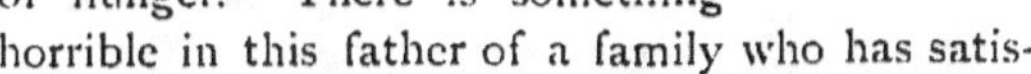

ence became a thief one night out of hunger. There is something horrible in this father of a family who has satis-fied a brutal passion on the person of his own daughter. It is very interesting to watch this Gobséck, extradited from Belgium, who holds forth on finance with an assurance that shows complete contempt for his judges. And heartrending

it is to hear this poor girl, dismissed from her situation because she was about to become a mother, who in an hour of desperation has left the child of ignorance and misery to perish. Let us touch

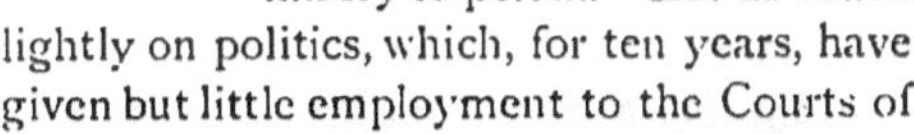

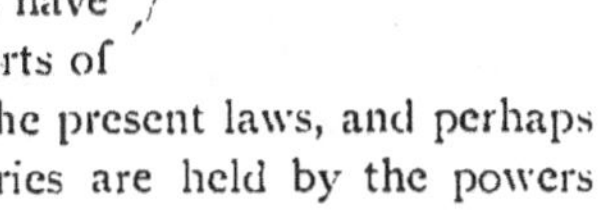

lightly on politics, which, for ten years, have given but little employment to the Courts of Assize, thanks to the liberal spirit of the present laws, and perhaps also to the just mistrust in which juries are held by the powers that be.

POLITICS IN THE ASSIZE COURT

To find a striking political trial, we must go back to the action brought in 1881 against M. Henri Rochefort by Consul Roustan, after the expedition to Tunis. Maitre Gatineau, a deputy for the department of Eure-et-Loir, was charged with the defence of the editor of the *Intransigeant*. The mere name of Gatineau is enough to produce a smile and banish dulness.   With his hair dyed green, his gold-rimmed glasses, his ruddy face, and his eyes that sparkled with bucolic archness, Gatineau, under this Rabelaisian exterior, was a stout fighter and a formidable opponent.   Sharp as a needle, he demolished the most pompous arguments of the public prosecutor by some stroke of irony delivered with an assumed rustic accent. This prosecution, entered upon with such solemnity, produced nothing but endless laughter.   M. Henri Rochefort and his counsel told the jury anecdotes of Moorish life and stories about the Kroumirs, and the jurymen, after spending a whole day in danger of splitting their sides, forgot all about the facts of the case, and gave a verdict for the newspaper with thanks, possibly not even thinking that they had at the same time passed censure on

one of the most important episodes in contemporary history. Since that date, except the trial of General Boulanger, which did not take place in the law courts, but before the Senate, we cannot mention any political case which has caused a sensation.

From time to time some obscure anarchist is brought before the Court of Assize for having distributed in barracks papers calling on the troops to mutiny in case of any disturbance.   He has refused the aid of an advocate ; but a *comrade* has asked leave to defend him, and for two or three hours, not without a certain vigour that occasionally impresses the hearers, the most furious revolutionary demands will be hurled in the faces of a middle-class jury.   In the end, there will be a verdict without extenuating circumstances, a sentence of two years' imprisonment, and a fierce cry of " Anarchy for ever ! " taken up in chorus by the prisoner's friends, who crowd the body of the Court.   Thus we see that at the Court of Assize politics form only an interlude ; let us return to its regular clients.

VICE AT THE ASSIZES—THE BEGINNERS

First of all come the juvenile criminals, whose numbers have increased terribly in these last few years.   Gilles and Abadie, those two ill-favoured street Arabs who shed so much blood in the suburbs of Paris ten or twelve years ago, were little more than sixteen. Gamahut, the murderer of Madame Ballerich, was leader of a band whose oldest member was twenty. Twenty was the

IN THE DOCK.

age of Corporal Géomay, executed in 1890 for the murder of a spirit-dealer on the Boulevard St. Germain ; and of the same age were Mécrant and Catelain, the accomplices of Sellier and Allorto, in the murder at Auteuil. Kaps, when he strangled an old man named Vinçard after a drink-ing bout, was only fourteen. A sort of fatality seems year by year to lower the age of the youngest murderer, " Nonsense," say these boy criminals ; " I am too young for the mowing machine," and, through a dream, they seem to see the mirage of New Caledonia. The dangerous clemency of M. Grévy kept them confident for a long time, and, in spite of the necessary reaction which has since taken place, the legend still survives in the world of rogues and bullies who are the plague of Paris.

HEROES OF THE CRIMINAL CALENDAR

No less than ten of these can be counted during the last five or six years, although it is perhaps improper to place an assassin like Marchandon, or a murderer of fallen women like Pranzini, on the same level with that master in crime, the mysterious Prado; a man of culture and of biting wit, whose appearance betokened ancient breeding, refined education, and a past crowded with adventure, travel, and brigandage.   Never will those who beheld him forget that man, who sat in the dock as if at home, directed the whole proceedings, and pursued with reproaches and satire his two mistresses, the fair-haired Eugénie Forestier and the bright and sparkling little woman from Bordeaux who called herself Mauricette Couronneau.

Another hero of crime also was that extraordinary creature Campi. He had murdered in the Rue du Regard an old gentleman, M. Ducros de Sixt, who lived a very retired life, completely given up to good works. " Your name ? "—" Campi." " Your age ? "—" Thirty-three." " Your profession ? "—" None." " Your home ? " —" None." The legal chronicler will always have before him the man whose very memory is a terror. In his bold and resolute glance could be read an expression of savage hate against

SKETCH BY P. RENOUARD.

society.   The presiding judge, M. Bérard des Glajeux, with all his art, could not extract from Campi the secret of his crime.   Campi was not a thief ; he had killed M. Ducros de Sixt to satisfy a feeling of revenge.   What was it ?   He never told, and he died nameless, casting a look of pity and disdain at the executioner.   Of his own accord he threw himself on the fatal plank, shrugging his shoulders and muttering, " It is only this ! "   In our memories of the Palace there still arises the face of the alchemist Pel, a watchmaker at Montreuil, accused of many poisonings, a would-be scientist who

had tried experiments with arsenic *in animâ vili*, doubtless thinking that the life of a few old female servants was of no use to the
world. With his great sunken eyes, his enormous spectacles, his

ghastly paleness, and his straggling beard of uncertain colour, this
solemn, silent man recalled some legend from the middle ages,
and looked as if he had just stepped out of the dungeons of some
feudal castle.

CRIMES CONNECTED WITH LOVE—VITRIOL AND REVOLVERS

Of the three great dramas of passion which during the last ten
years have excited public opinion, and provided material for the
novel and the theatre, two had their catastrophe outside Paris.
Henri Chambige was tried at Constantine; the brothers Peltzer were
tried at Brussels. Two marvellous cases, almost perfect, we might
well say, if it were not a blasphemy in such a connection. In the
Chambige case, a young man of high education, a dainty writer, a
sentimental delineator of the first rank, was brought little by little,
through self-analysis and morbid study of his own feelings, to desire
death in company with a young girl of irreproachable character,
without thinking, unhappy creature, of the orphans that this imitation of Werther would leave behind. In the Peltzer case, the
death of the husband, an advocate named Bernays, was decided
upon and arranged by the wife's lover; the crime is committed by
deputy at Brussels, while the principal criminal, Armand Peltzer,

shows himself at Antwerp ; the deed is due to gratitude, being undertaken by a brother whom Armand had formerly saved from bankruptcy, and who now comes back from America with made-up face, disguised, his skin stained with a composition of bistre and amber which gives him the appearance of a South American, so unrecognisable that he can present himself to Bernays, his former friend, as the agent of an Australian company, and strike him down in perfect safety, so as to set free the woman whom his brother coveted. But these two cases, celebrated as they are, lie beyond our scope. At Paris, the only great drama of human passion demanding our attention is the Fenayrou case. This, moreover, was heard at Versailles in the first place, and only sent before a Parisian jury after the first decision had been quashed. The lying in wait in the little house at Pecq, the lover decoyed by the wife into the husband's power, struck down without pity, the body forced into a piece of lead piping and thrown into the Seine ; the economy of Madame Fenayrou, a little tradesman's wife with an air of respectability, who, in going from Paris to Pecq, took a return ticket for herself and a single one for Aubert, because Aubert was not to return—all the dark story is still present to the minds of our readers, and a mere mention of its name is enough to revive the drama in all its details. At the time of the trial public opinion was divided between two opposing theories. Some declared that the husband had avenged himself ; others that he had killed Aubert because this young man had discovered some terrible secret, the secret of an abortion, perhaps a poisoning. The president, Bérard des Glajeux, alone understood that it was the woman who had taken revenge. " This is a woman's crime," said he to Gabrielle Fenayrou, in his rather cracked but incisive voice ; " Aubert had ceased to love you, he was going to be married, you had chosen the propitious moment for throwing yourself at your husband's feet, knowing that he would forgive you, and that he would satiate your hatred while believing that he was only carrying out his own revenge." This was the truth of the matter. Of the actors in the drama the husband died in New Caledonia ; the wife, sentenced to perpetual confinement, ever silent and impenetrable, continues at Clairvaux to drag out the existence of a prisoner for life.

Their story has not taken us long ; but this study of the Court of Assize and its passion dramas would not be complete without a few words on the use of vitriol and the revolver.

The reign of vitriol was inaugurated in 1877 by a gay lady, styled Madame de la Tour in the roll of honour of that profession, but in reality named Widow Gras. Old age was close upon her, her hair was already white, and she was on the point of being abandoned by a rich young lover, who was going to be married. She now conceived the infernal plan of making him unfit for marriage by disfigurement, in which event she intended to attach herself to her victim for life by assuming the part of a sister of mercy. The most interesting character in this intricate drama was a workman, the metal-worker Gaudry, a playmate of the Widow Gras when she was only a house-porter's little girl, and her con-

stant lover afterwards, whose fondness for her had been increased by her success, her elegance, and the high rank of her lovers. Widow Gras called Gaudry to her assistance, coaxed him, promised to marry him as soon as M. de R——, on whom she wished to wreak vengeance, said she, had been "vitriolised," and she put into his hands the bottle of sulphuric acid. She was condemned to fifteen years' penal servitude, and to-day she keeps a restaurant near the Rue de Maubeuge. From the date of her crime vitriol became the chosen

VITRIOL.
Sketch by P. Renouard.

weapon of deserted milliners, deceived wives, and sometimes of neglected fancy men. A few severe verdicts have put an end to the favour it enjoyed for some two years.

The most celebrated heroine of the revolver was Marie Bière, the sentimental singer, who, in 1880, shot her old lover, a well-known clubman, on the Place de l'Opéra. She was rather pretty, spoke in the sweetest of tones, and no woman ever born knew so well what attitude to assume before her judges. Lachaud got her acquitted amid a scene of indescribable enthusiasm. Marie Bière subsequently married in Roumania; but the school she founded has ever since enjoyed great prosperity. The revolver still continues to be the *ultima ratio* with nervous people of both sexes.

AN ACQUITTAL

Ten times, perhaps twenty times a year, and at Paris oftener than elsewhere, the regular frequenter of the Court will be present at a sight like this. . A little milliner or shop-girl is seated in the dock, sobbing, with her face thickly veiled, half fainting against the knees of the municipal guard who supports her gallantly. The public prosecutor, as a matter of form, has asked for a conviction which he does not expect, for juries can never bring themselves to send a pretty woman into solitary confinement for five years, and five years is the minimum sentence allowed by law. The lover, who appears in a more or less damaged condition at the bar, has been properly mauled, and the advocate for the defence has overwhelmed him with a storm of invective. The speeches come to an end, and the jury have retired to deliberate on their verdict. Then the excited and feverish Court becomes literally stifling. People have crept along all the corridors and slipped in at all the doors, the ladies have invaded the front seats, and their coloured dresses stand out in bright relief against the black gowns worn by the advocates.

Certain persons absolutely unconnected with the bench, though some of them have possibly appeared as defendants in the Eighth Chamber, have majestically taken up a position behind the president's chair. Close to the usher's little desk may be seen a regular frequenter of the Court of Assize, an old gentleman, with white whiskers, who has never missed a trial for twenty years; he has been dubbed "the thirteenth juryman," and may be heard declaring that the jury will not deliberate for more than ten minutes.

And, in fact, a bell placed over the door of the jury-room rings twice, with two sharp tinkles, which are forthwith repeated by a bell placed over the main entrance to the Court. The jury are returning, most of them well pleased and radiant; one or two only look a little doubtful and ask one another "what the newspapers will say about it." Slowly they regain their seats, while the judges, informed of their return, come back into Court by the little door opposite. "Sit down ! sit down !" is the cry on all sides. The usher calls out "Silence !" till he is hoarse, and the guards exert themselves to make ladies who have mounted on the benches get down again. At last the murmur dies away, and the president says in emphatic tones, " Whatever the verdict of the jury may be, I must insist on the public keeping strict silence. I shall not hesitate to have any one who presumes to applaud brought up before the Court." Then courteously turning to the right, he proceeds, " Mr. Foreman, be so good as to acquaint the Court with the result of your deliberations."

With his right hand on his heart, trembling slightly, and his voice a little quavering, the foreman of the jury begins to read, sheltering himself behind the large sheet of white paper which shakes in his hand. " On my honour and my conscience, before God and before man, the verdict of the jury is *Not guilty.*" It is an acquittal !

" Bring in the prisoner again," orders the president. All eyes are turned towards the little door which gives access to the dock ; fresh cries of " Sit down !" arise, men struggle for a sight of the prisoner, and the president raps on his desk with his paper knife : " Clerk of the Court, acquaint the prisoner with the verdict." " The jury have found a verdict of Not guilty," says the clerk in a clear voice, while the prisoner, with tearful eyes, leans forward to grasp her advocate's hand. The president then pronounces the acquittal in form. " We, president of the Court of Assize, in virtue of the powers with which we are invested by the law, having received the verdict of the jury to the effect that the prisoner at the bar is not guilty of the acts imputed to her, do now declare her acquitted of the charge laid against her ; and we order that she be forthwith released, if she be not required on another charge."

Then there bursts forth a storm not of enthusiasm, but of frenzy. Women rush towards the dock, cheering, crying " Bravo," trying their utmost to attract the heroine's attention. . . . Those farthest off wave their handkerchiefs, probationers in their excitement throw their caps in the air ; others, more bitter, remark " that if the prisoner has got off it is not her counsel's fault ; " the reporters, pressed for time, jump over the barriers and try to reach the nearest exit as quickly as possible. . . . Meanwhile, at the back of the Court, the crowd, like the chorus of a Greek play, takes up the dainty cries of the ladies in front till they swell into a

mighty roar. The latter, faithful to the freemasonry of the sex
celebrate their own victory in the triumph of another woman.
The former, the working women in white caps, cheer furiously,
till the guard clears the Court, the woman of the people who has
had revenge on a gentleman ! . . .

CHAPTER XX

PARIS escapes a scandal which disgraces most of the provincial
Assize Courts. It never sees the public removal of a prisoner to gaol
after conviction accompanied by the coarse jeers of an inquisitive
crowd. The Palace of Justice at Paris, in fact, provides lodgings
for its criminals. They are kept in one of its outlying buildings,
to wit, the Conciergerie prison, whence the guards bring them
straight into Court for trial by an inside staircase. Why, it may be
asked, the name "Conciergerie"? Possibly, says M. Pottet in his
book, because the existing prison, a barrack under the old kings of
France, was inhabited by a captain who bore the title of "Comte
des Cierges," or "Concierge," a person in the enjoyment of high
prerogatives, and very nearly as powerful as our contemporary
concierges or house-porters.

Before 1826 the entrance to this prison was in the Cour
d'Honneur, better known as the Cour de Mai, to the right and at
the foot of the grand staircase. The wicket-gate with its ironwork
grating which gave access to the prison still exists; it now forms
part of the Police Court buildings. Through this gate the great
men of the Revolution and the victims of the Terror passed on
their way to the tumbril which was to bear them to the guillotine.

This entrance to the Conciergerie was walled up in 1826. But
in walling it up the architect forgot that the prison kitchens were
situated on the other side of the wicket. The result is that at the
present time the prison cooks have to tramp right round the Palace
of Justice with a complicated apparatus of straps and buckets in
order to bring the prisoners their porridge. Always practical, these

architects! In order to make up for the closed gate on the Quai de l'Horloge, a new gate was then built between the two broad towers, the Tour César and the Tour d'Argent. Later on, in 1864, this new gate was walled up in its turn; and on the same quay, to the right and not far from the Tour César, a new gate was opened through which at present entrance may be obtained to the ancient prison. It was then that the Conciergerie was turned into a place of solitary confinement. For this purpose extensive works were carried out, the chief result of which was seen in the destruction of the ancient halls and dungeons in which so many historic characters have been imprisoned.

At the present day the Conciergerie may, for the purposes of a visit, be divided into two parts: the historical part, void of inhabitants but full of associations; and the part now used for solitary confinement. The first portion may be visited on Thursdays by special permission of the Prefect of Police. Let us enter. We pass through a heavy gate provided with an enormous lock, in which the warder's key sounds like an iron jaw breaking a stone. We then cross a little court, turn to the right, and there, before us, stands the pointed wicket-gate with the iron grating, above which may be read the words, *Maison de Justice*.

We go down a little stone staircase, and find ourselves in the old Salle des Gardes. It has been deprived of its ante-room and office, of its partitions and compartments, the sole remaining portion of the ancient decoration being its broad pillars, with capitals carved in a somewhat irreverent way; one of them representing with realistic fidelity a critical love passage between Abelard and Héloïse. In the embrasure of the window is a bench for the women to sit on who bring prisoners a dinner from outside.

In front of us is another wicket-gate with a peephole. This is the main entrance to the part used for the confinement of prisoners. A slight turn to the right brings us to a double staircase of stone with iron bannisters. That on the left hand leads to the hall of the Tour d'Argent, which, it is said, was once occupied by Queen Blanche and formed the prison of Damiens. The young Duke of Orleans was shut up there in 1889 before being taken to Clairvaux. That on the right leads to the hall of the Tour César, where Prince Pierre Bonaparte was imprisoned after the murder of Victor Noir in 1870 and Prince Napoleon after his manifesto of 1883.

THE SALLE DES GARDES.

The hall of the Tour César is now used as a private room by the governor of the Conciergerie. On the story below is the chamber once occupied by Ravaillac and Lacenaire.

The space beneath the Tour d'Argent contains the advocates' common room; and on the floor above is the private room where the presidents of the Assize Court come at the beginning of every session to examine prisoners.

Let us retrace our steps, recross the Salle des Gardes and look before us. In front we perceive a lofty gate of strong ironwork which leads into the dark gallery called the Rue de Paris. On the right is a little door, now walled up on the inside, from which there used to be a staircase leading to the Revolutionary Court. This tribunal was held in the room above, now occupied by the First Chamber of the Civil Court.[1] On the left is the hall of Saint Louis. Admission to this can only be obtained by special permission, but a view can be had of the interior through a grating by standing up on a stool in the Rue de Paris. It lies immediately below the Salle des Pas-Perdus.

The Rue de Paris is lighted by gas, even in the daytime. At the extreme end are new folding doors, giving admission to what

A KITCHEN CHIMNEY IN THE PALACE OF LOUIS.

From an old engraving.

remains of the old Conciergerie. The porter makes his keys grate in the locks, the doors open, and the visitor finds himself in an ugly, dark, white-washed passage, now divided into two parts. Here, in days gone by, were dungeons, as celebrated as those of the Bastille, with doors fast closed by thick bars and heavy bolts. These dungeons

---

[1] Established, for the trial of state-conspirators, March 10, 1793. Its powers were largely increased by Robespierre on June 10, 1794. It declined in importance after Robespierre's fall, July 27, 1794; and was suppressed May 31, 1795.

were occupied by Danton, Camille Desmoulins, General Hoche
Vergniaud and the young deputies of the Gironde, Marat, Couthon,
Saint Just, the German Adam Lux, " who died from the last glance
of Charlotte Corday," Hébert, Chaumette, and many other celebrities of the great Revolution. They, however, exist no longer ; the
works rendered necessary by the new prison installation have swept
away everything, even the subterranean dungeons, not unknown to
politicians and journalists of the First Empire, of the Restoration,
of the July Monarchy, and of the Coup d'État of December 2nd.

The corridor in which we now stand is furnished, on the left, with
new iron gratings of immense size. Behind it are the apartments
belonging to the old office of the prison and an exit, now walled up,
to the Cour de Mai. In front of us, through the barred windows
which give a dim light to the corridor, can be seen the women's
quarter and the cells which were tenanted by Madame Elisabeth,
Charlotte Corday, and others. Under the July Monarchy, these
different cells had for tenants well-known regicides and political
prisoners : Fieschi, Alibaud, Prince Louis Napoleon, the Duc de
Persigny, Doctor Conneau, &c.

THE DUNGEON OF MARIE ANTOINETTE

At the end of the corridor and on the right, facing a new door
which leads to the modern prison, is the famous dungeon of Queen
Marie Antoinette. It communicates with the cell of Robespierre,
the latter leading to the hall of the Girondins. All the other dungeons occupied by celebrated prisoners of the Revolution, and
before them by great historical characters, have disappeared. But
for a long time past, since the Restoration in fact, the dungeon of
Marie Antoinette has itself been deprived of its prison attributes
and turned into a chapel. Dr. Véron, in his *Mémoires d'un Bourgeois de Paris*, gives an amusing account of this change. In 1812,
M. Decazes, then a counsellor of the Imperial Court at Paris, paid
a visit to the Conciergerie as president of the Court of Assize.
While walking through the long corridors, he took a fancy to enter
the dungeon of Marie Antoinette. He there surprised one of the
junior warders engaged in a love idyll with a female prisoner with
whom he had made an assignation.

M. Decazes forthwith set to work to try and get this dungeon
turned into a chapel. He drew up a report on the subject, which

was approved by the Supreme Court at Paris, but Napoleon's Minister of Justice refused his sanction, and the transformation only took place when the Duc Decazes became Louis XVIII.'s minister, in 1816.

In 1793 there was no communication between the queen's dungeon and the little cell to which Robespierre was carried later on. The communicating door was walled up, like that which connected Robespierre's cell with the prison of the Girondins. The bed of Marie Antoinette was most probably placed against the door of communication. On the other side, in front, was the guard-room, through which visitors had to pass in order to enter the queen's dungeon. The door of communication has been again walled up, as can be ascertained by pushing aside a panel on which is painted a picture, unsigned, representing the queen taking the sacrament. Marie Antoinette is accompanied by two gendarmes, by a person said to be M. Magnin, and a lady who perhaps is intended for Mdlle. Fouché. This picture has a companion piece, representing the removal of Marie Antoinette from the Temple Prison to the Conciergerie. On the whole they are second-rate productions, whether by Drolling, as some say, or by Menjana, according to the opinion of others.

Of the articles used by the queen, there only now remain the little lamp hanging in the alcove and the crucifix that may be seen on the altar. As to the arm-chair in which Marie Antoinette used to sit, a former governor of the Conciergerie was obliged to have it removed to his office in order to save it from the horde of tourists of every nation, each of whom tried to carry off a memento in the shape of a nail, a tassel, or a piece of the woodwork. The large window, by which the altar stands, is fitted up with panes in stained glass of a most execrable style. "Turkish coffee-house windows" Victor Hugo called them. Above the altar is a Latin inscription due to Louis XVIII., and below this is a marble slab bearing an extract from the will of Marie Antoinette, quite illegible at the present day.

The dungeon of Robespierre, which stands close to that of the queen, is a very small apartment with white-washed walls and a window of blue and yellow panes, the bars of which have disappeared. At the back is a picture, possibly by Drolling, unless it be by Menjana, representing Marie Antoinette in her cell. She has a black veil on her head, and lies stretched on a truckle bed, close to the screen which separates her from the prying eyes of her warders.

THE HALL OF THE GIRONDINS

Opening out from and on a level with the dungeon of Robespierre, is the great hall which served as a prison for priests and royalists during the Terror.   Here, also, the Girondins passed their last night.   In modern times it has been turned into the chapel of the Conciergerie.   At about the height of the organ, the visitor will remark galleries fenced in with iron bars, which have a curious resemblance to the place in a bear-pit where the beasts are shut up when the keeper is about to clean their den.

The little door on the left opens on to the court where the September massacres took place.   The Girondins passed through it on their way to the scaffold.   In this celebrated hall Vergniaud and his friends took their last meal in the presence of the corpse of Valazé, after their condemnation to death, on the night of October 29th, 1793.   There is something curious in this little court with its monastic aspect, its white-washed walls, its stone table and its fountain.   Down to 1887 it was tenanted by cabmen sentenced to twenty-four hours' detention.   They are now sent to the Petite Roquette, and the court serves as an exercise ground for young girls under sixteen imprisoned for various reasons.   They make a pretty picture as they walk up and down this gloomy court, clad in heavy grey dresses and grey capes ; they have smiling faces in spite of the barred windows and the grim iron gate, in height equalling the wall which shuts them in ; and their careless, gay air shows no anticipation of the future which awaits them.

The three gates at the end of the chapel are now walled up, as well as the gate by which the Girondins returned from the Revolutionary Court singing the *Marseillaise*.

THE MODERN PRISON

We have just seen the historic Conciergerie.   We must retrace our steps to visit the prison now in use, which, as we have said, must be approached by the Salle des Gardes.

On entering we pass through a little room used for searching prisoners, and just on the right of this are the visiting rooms.[1]

---

[1] *Parloirs des parents.*

Imagine a couple of the compartments to be found in telephone offices narrowed down, and put side by side, but separated from one another by a network of stout wire ; imagine yourself shut up in one of these boxes without light or air, while in the other stands some prison friend of yours who is waiting to appear before a jury ; you will have some idea of what a visit to a prisoner is like. On the left are the cells, of which there are seventy-three. Every now and then a little telegraphic signal-arm placed before the door falls with a noise like a chopper. This means that a prisoner has called the warder for some urgent reason. Take a look into this cell through the little half-open wicket. You will see a darkish slip of a room, with three men lying brutishly on mattresses, their senses deadened by continual anxiety and never-ending reflection. They are all in a heap near one another—gloomy, spiritless, suffering, and pitiable. When they hear your steps they raise themselves on their arms, cast a glance of curiosity at you ; but when they see that you are only a passer-by and bring them neither orders nor news, they fall back again into their attitude of weary listlessness.

A little farther on a door opens on the separate exercising spaces, exactly like the cages to be seen in a zoological garden, where prisoners walk up and down in pairs, silently brooding. At the sound of steps they move hurriedly to the bars. They make the visitor think of an animal running up in hopes of a piece of bread. Tamed already by their imprisonment, on seeing your tall hat they make you a low bow, and remain in a respectful attitude till you have passed by.

Yet the exercise yard of the Conciergerie is less gloomy than that to be found in many other prisons. In the summer time three sickly little shrubs—two stunted lilacs and a half-dead spindle-tree—enliven the cold grey of the pavement and the harshness of the red brick wall with a soothing touch of green. "They do not live, you see, sir," says the warder, while we look at the three poor plants. "Here it is always too hot or too cold. Plants want air, sun, and liberty."

And what of men ?

The prisoners confined in the Conciergerie are those committed for trial before the Court of Assize, those who have appealed against a conviction by the Correctional Court of a Department within the appellate jurisdiction of the capital,[1] and those sentenced to death, during the three days' grace allowed them by the law for an appeal to the Court of Cassation.

[1] The jurisdiction of the Court of Appeal at Paris includes seven Departments: Yonne, Seine et Oise, Seine, Seine et Marne, Eure et Loir, Marne, Aube.

THE PRISON VAN.

CHAPTER XXI

THE DÉPÔT

ALL persons arrested in the department of the Seine and brought up for trial pass through the Dépôt. As its name imports, it is a place for depositing criminals of all sorts. To this place they are sent in crowds as they are taken up, and there they are divided into classes. On an average, the Dépôt receives 150 individuals a day.

Suppose that you are arrested by a policeman and taken to the station—the most respectable of us is liable to this accident—if no one comes to claim you from the commissary before the passing of "Black Maria,"[1] that handsome, sombre-hued carriage which resembles a mourning coach with the windows blocked up, you are shut up in this vehicle and sent on your way to the Dépôt.

But be of good cheer ; for, otherwise, your lot would have been far more pitiable : you would have had to march across Paris as one of a file of blackguards between two rows of armed soldiers. To-day you have escaped this ignominy by merely taking a quiet drive in a closed carriage.

The carriage stops on the Quai de l'Horloge, before one of the doors of the Court of Cassation reserved for judges only and opening on to the grand staircase. On each side of this door is an archway, the one leading to the office of the detective police, the other to the Dépôt. The carriage passes beneath that on the left and sets its burden down at the Permanence Office, which stands opposite to the Dispensaire, or head office for the supervision of public women. The Permanence is the ante-room of the Dépôt.

---

[1] *I.e.* the prison van, the French slang word for which is "panier à salade."

Whatever the hour of arrival, one in the afternoon, seven in the evening, or one in the morning, every one passes through it.

Two chief inspectors of the Prefecture of Police are charged with the duty of drawing up a brief statement as to the names, Christian names, ages, birth places, and professions of those who arrive ; and of entering the whole in the gaol book, the cause of the

THE COUR DU DÉPÔT.

arrest being duly set forth. ¶ This time you will not escape the ordeal of the march in Indian file between two rows of guards ; but the scene passes in a court-yard, where few people are present. The prisoners, without any distinction of sex, pass along a low pavilion which serves as the men's hospital of the Dépôt. They emerge into an open space, bounded by ruins on one side and a celebrated wall on the other, the wall of the Court of the Girondins.

Lastly they are brought without any ceremony through ordinary folding doors into the entrance hall of the Dépôt.

In front is a lodge with glass windows occupied by the commissary on duty and the warders dressed in a sort of exciseman's uniform. On the right is the men's quarter, on the left the women's quarter.

The commissary reads out the list of names. The prisoners take off their shoes, and place themselves in the embrasure of a door, close to the window, to undergo examination by the searcher. " Raise your trousers—undo your belt—lift your arms! " But all these precautions do not prevent the knowing ones from concealing some precious article.

The search ended, the prisoners are passed on to another official, who takes their measurement and registers their description and social rank. The description is supplemented, on the following morning, between eight and twelve o'clock, before M. Berbillon at the anthropometric department, which will be described later on.

After this last ceremony the prisoner is ready for oral examination before a judicial officer.

From this time onwards, the official reports concerning the prisoner will have been sent to the second office of the Prefecture of Police. In this place his " record " is drawn up, his antecedents examined, and, in certain cases, a preliminary investigation is made of the charge brought against him. The head of the above-mentioned office will have been able to examine him—a right rarely used —and even to set him at liberty, which is rarer still. This official has also the power to give tickets for the refuge at Nanterre to the infirm poor and to mendicants who have completed their term in prison.

The record thus drawn up is forwarded by the Prefecture to the Petit Parquet.

The Petit Parquet is an office occupied by two subordinates of the Procureur of the Republic. By a brief examination of the prisoners they find out the exact nature of the charges against them. They then send them, under the care of a municipal guard, to the Correctional Court for immediate trial where there is a *primâ facie* case, or they remand them for further investigation before a magistrate.

Attached to the Petit Parquet itself are several judges of instruction always ready to undertake this duty in easy cases ; and if an affair is very simple, the statements of the prisoner are quickly dealt with. In difficult cases, the record is sent to a judge of the Grand Parquet ; the accused has to change his abode, and leave the Dépôt definitely for Mazas or La Santé ; when required for the instruction or for his trial, he will be brought back to the Palace of Justice, but he will return the same evening to his new prison, by the Boulevârd Diderot or Rue de la Santé.

Heroes like Eyraud, Prado, and Pranzini alone have the privilege of being kept at the Dépôt, so that the detective officers may be better able to keep an eye on them.

YARDS FOR EXERCISE.
From a sketch by P. Renouard.

The rest are not supposed to remain there for more than three days, each room bearing a notice to this effect :

" Every accused person who has not been examined during the first three days of his detention at the Dépôt should address a complaint to the Director-in-Chief."

The Dépôt is thus only a place of passage. It was this peculiarity which suggested to an architect who had been twitted with the defects of the building the smart reply, " What does the bad arrangement of the Dépôt matter, as prisoners do not stay there long ? "

Nevertheless many improvements have been carried out, thanks to the Prisons Commission and to the present director-in-chief of the Dépôt, M. Meugé.

But there will always be one defect, and that is the want of air in the underground cells lying beneath that portion of the Palace which looks out on the Place Dauphine. They were built in 1864. Let us visit them, beginning with the men's quarter.

THE MEN'S QUARTER

A long two-storied gallery of cells like what may be seen in every prison : it forms a lofty, narrow nave, the walls of which are pierced for cells uniform in size and lighted by small opaque glass windows, and might be taken for the skeleton outline of a church as planned by some ascetic monk.

The cells are monastic in appearance, and are furnished with a table and chair ; at the back of each is a sanitary convenience.

At the end of the nave, looking like the choir of a church, is the common hall known as the Salle des Blouses, a vast barrack-room with large port-holes which open on to the façade of the Place Dauphine under the right hand staircase.

It is a fine place in the daytime when there is no one there, and visitors can amuse themselves by deciphering the golden book of Parisian criminal celebrities which adorns the wall.

Let us take a few of the inscriptions at random ; in the greater part the name of the hero is accompanied by the name of the quarter in which he lives as if it were a title of nobility :—*Le Zoulou de la Maubert ; Dédé de Charonne ; Bobèche—Tête de fer de Montmartre ; Lostrogaud de la Maubert*, 1890.

Some are enigmatic, as :—*Sénateur des Louis*, 491. *La grandeur et l'Ognon de l'Éden.* Others are melancholy, as :—*Adjutor de l'École dit adieu à ses amis.* And everywhere appears the constant refrain :—*Mort aux vaches.*[1]

The time to come and see the place is in the evening, after the last prison van has deposited its burden at the door. There is an elegant footbridge from which an excellent view may be obtained of the sweepings of street and hovel that swarm there, an ever-changing crowd of creatures always the same, heroes of Mazas or Poissy, hopeless drunkards or humble philosophers addicted to a free and easy life in the open air and content to depend for subsistence on windfalls of public charity.

Bed-time has come. The planks leaning up against the wall are pulled down and covered with mattresses to serve as camp beds. Old men in the first place, and then prisoners who during the day have acted as attendants find a place thereon. All the rest stretch themselves on the floor, on mattresses, in the proportion of four men to one mattress. And when the gas is lowered, a spectator of the scene would think of regimental life and of his first night as a conscript.

There is a special room set apart for prisoners possessed of clean linen and dressed in fairly respectable clothes. It has been christened the Salle des Habits Noirs. The " black coats " are not

---

[1] *Vache* is a well-known slang word for the police.

so very much better off than the " blouses." Their hall, which is
on the story above, scarcely receives any air or light, it is very small
and however little crowded, the inmates stifle together in the midst
of a horrible stench. On the days succeeding public holidays in
winter the crowd is much greater. The two halls overflow, and the
prisoners are put in the first available place. Then the scene gives
the spectator another impression ; in the shade, certain corners of
the Dépôt look like the 'tween-decks of a Transatlantic steamer
crowded with emigrants.

In the afternoon, the prisoners while away the time strolling up
and down in the exercise yards, which are placed in the two
interior courts of the prison, to the right and left of the principal
nave, like the two arms of the cross.

On the right is the corridor which furnishes the common
exercise yards. On the left, the corridor which contains those where
prisoners take solitary exercise.

The " solitary " yards of the Dépôt
are very like the wild beasts' cages in
the Jardin des Plantes ; but instead of
the open sky, they are surmounted by
a canopy of cast iron, supported by
pillars encircled with rings of steel
spikes like those of the Conciergerie,
but even more forbidding to look
at. There is no verdure to cheer the
eye of the imprisoned animal; nothing
but bare walls, more stifling, closer,
and more monotonous. The prisoner
finds the Dépôt more cheerless than
the Conciergerie. A network of iron
footbridges and staircases, like a cor-

A HELPER.

From a sketch by P. Renouard.

ner of the Eiffel Tower, overlooks the cages, which thus seem like
so many pits, and enable the warders to see into every one of them.

On one of the boundary walls the visitor remarks a small tower
with a little window which juts out. This tower contains the
strange spiral staircase which leads inside the Palace of Justice
from the Galerie de Harlay to the Court of Assize. We are in fact
in a sort of well, between the hall of the Assize Court and the hall
of the Correctional Court. The iron canopy is the corridor which

unites the two, and is also used as a waiting place for witnesses. The gallery full of cells which we saw a short time ago is exactly below the Court of Assize; the cells on the right hand have for ceiling the Galerie des Prisonniers, and the common exercise yard is shut in between this gallery and the buildings of the Court of Cassation. The common exercise yards differ slightly from the solitary ones. The common yards are not barred in like cages; they are rectangular stone inclosures, opening, by means of little wicket-gates, on to the same corridor, and forming little courts where the prisoners pace up and down like collegians. There is a separate yard for old men, another for those of middle age, another for youths of from seventeen to twenty, and another for the black coats. Another privilege for the well-dressed!

The children form the saddest sight of all: they do not play, but watch one another with furtive glances; they mostly consist of street Arabs who have run away from home and taken to thieving for a livelihood. If any one speaks to them, they eye him with the suspicious look of little wild animals which resent being tamed; the more impudent assume a hypocritical air; here

INTERIOR OF A YARD FOR EXERCISE.

and there may be seen heads of little cherubs. There is a collection of cells reserved for them in the adjoining building. But the space is so confined that there is rarely room for all. They have a school-room where one of the warders officiates as teacher, but they do not make much progress under his care.

At the entrance of the principal nave is a waiting-room, where the unfortunates who happen to be brought in at night are temporarily lodged. By its side is the hall where those destined for Mazas undergo the preliminary search; they are searched in a state of nudity; the men strip themselves to the skin in a kind of confessional box; the searcher looks through the clothes, examines the man, and then passes him on into another niche, where he is at liberty to resume his clothing; the open space between the two niches is hidden from the rest of the hall by a curtain.

THE WOMEN'S QUARTER

The women's quarter runs parallel to that of the men, but does not communicate with it; to enter it, the visitor must return to the main entrance of the Dépôt.

A FEMALE PRISONER.
By P. Renouard.

In organisation it resembles that of the men. In the centre is a long nave, located beneath the chamber of Correctional Appeals. At the entrance are the waiting-room and searching-room, a little pavilion with white curtains; women are never completely stripped to be searched. At the end, beneath the Harlay staircase, are the common rooms. They are two in number. One, reserved for women with babies, an agglomeration of rags or alternation of woe-begone faces and light curls; the other allotted to prostitutes arrested for breach of the regulations.

The second is well known from the picture by Béraud; but the painter has represented the scene in very rosy colours. In reality, the girls are all mean-looking, vicious, and debased. The crowd leaves an impression of pale flesh, red jerseys, red corsets, and red hair. Occasionally one of the young girls is pretty and has some remains of freshness; but the language is always foul and the gestures obscene. Even a judge of instruction, hardened as he is to filthy words, does not readily risk himself in this place. Yet on a little schoolmistress's chair at the back of the hall, immediately beneath the skylight, a nun of the order of Mary and Joseph keeps watch unmoved, as if unconscious of her surroundings, while the pranks of these jades and their vile remarks form an accompaniment to her prayers.

The women's quarter is not shaped like a cross. The central nave is only flanked by a narrow court, divided in two by a corridor on one side is the exercise ground for female prisoners, on the other the sisters' garden. This is the garden we viewed from above on our way to the part of the law courts allotted to the Order of Advocates; and now we can see the wooden gallery where we were formerly stationed from below.

Being closer, we can now distinguish the costume of these good, simple, loving sisters who may be found in every part of the Dépôt; the cap and white band showing beneath the triple veil in black, blue, and white, above the white wimple and the black dress. At the garden-gate is a little child. A sister has just dressed it and is watching it from the wicket below. The poor little things do not get much care at the Dépôt. There is no asylum for them. They may be seen with yellow tickets on their backs in every corridor, dragging weary steps behind the sisters or standing moodily alone; these children are foundlings, little creatures who have been lost or abandoned; they are marked like packages, so as to be known again; yet there is perhaps little chance of any inquiries being ever made about them. If the visitor passes by the chapel on the other side of the garden, he will come on another spec-

A CORRIDOR IN THE WOMEN'S QUARTER.

tacle equally fitted to arouse his pity. For here is the women's infirmary, here are the unhappy beings who are kept in padded rooms, fit homes of madness.

From the women's quarter there is a staircase leading to the corridor of the Souricière.[1] This is a new corridor which, starting from the men's quarter, brings the Dépôt into communication with every part of the Palace of Justice, and gives access by the way to the Petit Parquet and the Souricière itself.

____
[1] _I.e._, mouse-trap,

Q

THE CORRIDOR OF THE SOURICIÈRE

This is a corridor built in the form of a tunnel, low-vaulted, like a sewer. Its advantages are obvious. It enables accused persons to be conducted to either the Petit Parquet or the Correctional Court without taking them into the open air. But the loneliness of the situation must cause some alarm to the guard entrusted with this duty.

About half-way, some water and vapour baths are in process of construction. This is a new departure in the way of luxury; and

IN THE INFIRMARY. AN EPILEPTIC.
From a drawing by P. Renouard.

this Dépôt, so denounced, and so badly situated, will soon become a model establishment. A ray of golden light tries to pierce the gloom of this gray corridor; it is the staircase which comes from the Petit Parquet. Let us see it.

THE PETIT PARQUET

Those who knew the old Petit Parquet will be surprised. In place of the forbidding vestibule which looked like a damp and unhealthy cellar, in place of the dark corridors which led to wretched little offices reeking with vile odours, there are now lofty, airy, and well-lighted halls, opening out on to the Sainte-Chapelle. Below the new buildings of the Court of Appeal, there is now a vestibule more luxurious in appearance than the ante-chamber of a minister. Criminals taken in the act have been daintily provided for.

We now regain our tunnel-like corridor and follow it to the end, which brings us to the Souricière; it occupies the basement of the Correctional Court.

THE SOURICIÈRE

The Souricière is the waiting-room for prisoners from Mazas. They are brought thence for examination before the judges of instruction of the Grand Parquet, for trial before the Correctional Court, or for transportation to the house of correction at Nanterre.

Whence comes this name of Souricière? Possibly from some ancient dungeons, situated near the Sainte-Chapelle, and famed for the swarms of mice which they contained. Citizen Beauregard, who was imprisoned there, tells how he had to keep his face covered all night to save his nose and ears, and how his trousers were completely eaten away. Possibly from the very appearance of the cells, which with their doors chequered in little squares look exactly like mouse-traps. For this very reason the Souricière has also been styled the "Thirty-six squares." It is not a pleasant abode. The cells are very narrow; they are only lighted by the little square panes of opaque glass in the door; and they have no ventilation save through one of these thirty-six squares which is left open, Inside the stench is pestilential. And this is all. To leave men, with the terrors of an examination or a sentence hanging over them, in these boxes the whole day is a reprehensible and useless refinement of torture.

Some alterations have recently been made at the Souricière. The reader will naturally suppose that these have been in the way of sanitary improvement.

Nothing of the kind.

The authorities have merely built a number of new cells, as

cruel as the old ones, in order to unite the old Souricière to the
corridor leading from the Dépôt. And the reader should remember
that the guests of the Souricière arrive in the morning from nine to
eleven ; that they only depart between six and seven in the evening ; and that, in the meantime, they receive no refreshment. It
is a wonder how any of them survive. Accused persons who happen

"THE THIRTY-SIX SQUARES."

to be acquitted are compelled to return to Mazas, like their comrades,
to have their names formally erased from the gaol book, after which
they are at liberty to leave. But the prospect of liberty assuages
their troubles, and they do not much mind the final ride with the
others in " Black Maria."

Those amenable to the Court of Assize and the other prisoners
of the Conciergerie escape the horrors of the Souricière. They leave

the Conciergerie by an underground passage ; this runs behind the barred chamber of the vestibule and joins a spiral staircase which gives access to the Court of Assize. This same staircase leads to the Anthropometric Department.

CORRIDOR OF THE SOURICIÈRE.

CHAPTER XXII

THE ANTHROPOMETRIC DEPARTMENT

If you are an interested visitor, you must first mount an incalculable number of steps, the ascent lying through a kind of massive pigeon-house; then after taking five or six turns in different directions, you will arrive in a little waiting-room. It is plainly furnished with benches and rows of pegs. You now receive two commands: the first is to strip yourself, the second to hold your tongue.

But we can leave this staircase to those whom it may concern, and, if you like, take the road appropriated to free visitors, that is to say the new gallery, which extends from the Sainte-Chapelle to the vestibule of the Court of Assize. Almost in front of the stately hall where the counsellors of the First Chamber of the Court of Appeal will soon come for their diurnal slumbers, you see a plain-looking door, and then a stone staircase which you ascend, and, when you have reached the topmost steps, you can read, printed above another little door painted brown, the words:

SERVICE D'IDENTIFICATION

ANTHROPOMÉTRIE ET PHOTOGRAPHIE JUDICIAIRES

Let us enter this sanctuary.

The high priest is a young and kindly *savant*, M. Alphonse Bertillon, creator of the anthropometric service; the Government having, in return for his assistance, appointed him chief ruler of the department.

M. Bertillon was struck by the insufficiency of the methods hitherto employed to establish the identity of habitual criminals. It was obvious to him that the thing needed was not so much a law for dealing with habitual criminals as the power of applying it.

But how was the habitual criminal[1] to be discovered when he concealed his identity? The latter knows that, having already undergone a certain number of convictions, he will be liable, if convicted again, to transportation for life to a penal colony. His course is therefore clear; to try and pass himself off as some one else, to assume an imaginary civil status, and to get for himself a new and clean character under a false name—so true it is that some men will believe anything!

Then begins the struggle between justice and this unknown, who, out of malice will choose in preference a common name, very widely spread, such as Martin, Bernard, or Duval. But the criminal records, ranged in alphabetical order at the Prefecture of Police, possess under the names of Martin, Bernard, and Duval piles of notices five or six hundred yards in height; to find the exact details relative to the alleged Martin, Bernard, or Duval will be almost impossible, or at any rate extremely difficult.

Suppose that the man in question has suffered three or four convictions under his real name, then if he chose to take an *alias* there was no rapid or precise way of recognising him. The authorities groped their way in darkness.

At last Bertillon appeared.

Turning to account his scientific knowledge, he came to the conclusion that it was possible to find a criterion of identity, based on the principle of measurement of the body, it being an established fact that, out of 100,000 individuals, there was not one whose head and chief members were of the same dimensions.

The young anthropologist's attention was chiefly directed to the parts of the body least susceptible of variation during the period of full growth. He was led to take as his data the length of the head, measured from the concavity at the root of the nose to the occiput; its breadth, measured from one parietal to the other; the length of the left middle finger, that of the left foot (the members of the body on the right side being liable to exceptional development under the action of physical toil), the length of the ear, the length of the forearm, the measurement

[1] *Récidiviste.*

with the arms stretched out cross-wise, and lastly the colour of the eye.

These data taken, the point was to find some method of classi-fication for the pile of individual records which would encumber the pigeon-holes of the anthropometric department as soon as it began to act. For the efficacy of the system depended on its prompt applicability. Each person arrested for an offence at common law was to be passed under the measuring post and com-pass of the anthropometer. Their number can be readily imagined ; thieves, forgers, murderers, swindlers, and vagabonds innumerable cross the door of the Dépôt every day. What method was to be adopted to simplify inquiry? M. Bertillon, who is a man of essentially simple mind in the scientific sense of the word, re-solved to have recourse to a system of elimination, after having established three great general classes, each distinguished by the stature of the individuals measured, who were to be divided into *short*, *middle-sized*, and *tall*. Suppose that, at any given time, the anthropometric department possesses 90,000 records of individuals who have been measured, or, to coin a word, *Bertillonised*. These have been divided into three classes, each containing 30,000. The first comprises persons of short stature, measuring from 1 metre to 1 metre 60 mm. in height ;[1] the second comprises those of middle stature from 1 metre 61 mm. to 1 metre 70 mm. ; and the third comprises those of tall stature from 1 metre 71 mm. to 2 metres.

This is the first division.

Each of these three classes is subdivided—always by threes—into three groups of 10,000 according as the measure of the head—from the root of the nose to the occiput—is small, medium, or large.

With the third subdivision these 10,000 individuals are classed in three groups according to the length of the left middle finger : small, medium, or large.

The three classes in the next subdivision only comprise 1,000 subjects each, divided according to the length of the left foot.

The fifth subdivision is divided into three groups of 300, classed according to the dimensions of the forearm ; and we arrive at the last subdivision, which only comprises three sections of 100 subjects each, divided according to the length of the little finger.

Thus unity is reached at last.

---

[1] One French *mètre* = 3·281 English feet. A *centimètre* (indicated by " mm.") is the hundredth part of a *mètre*.

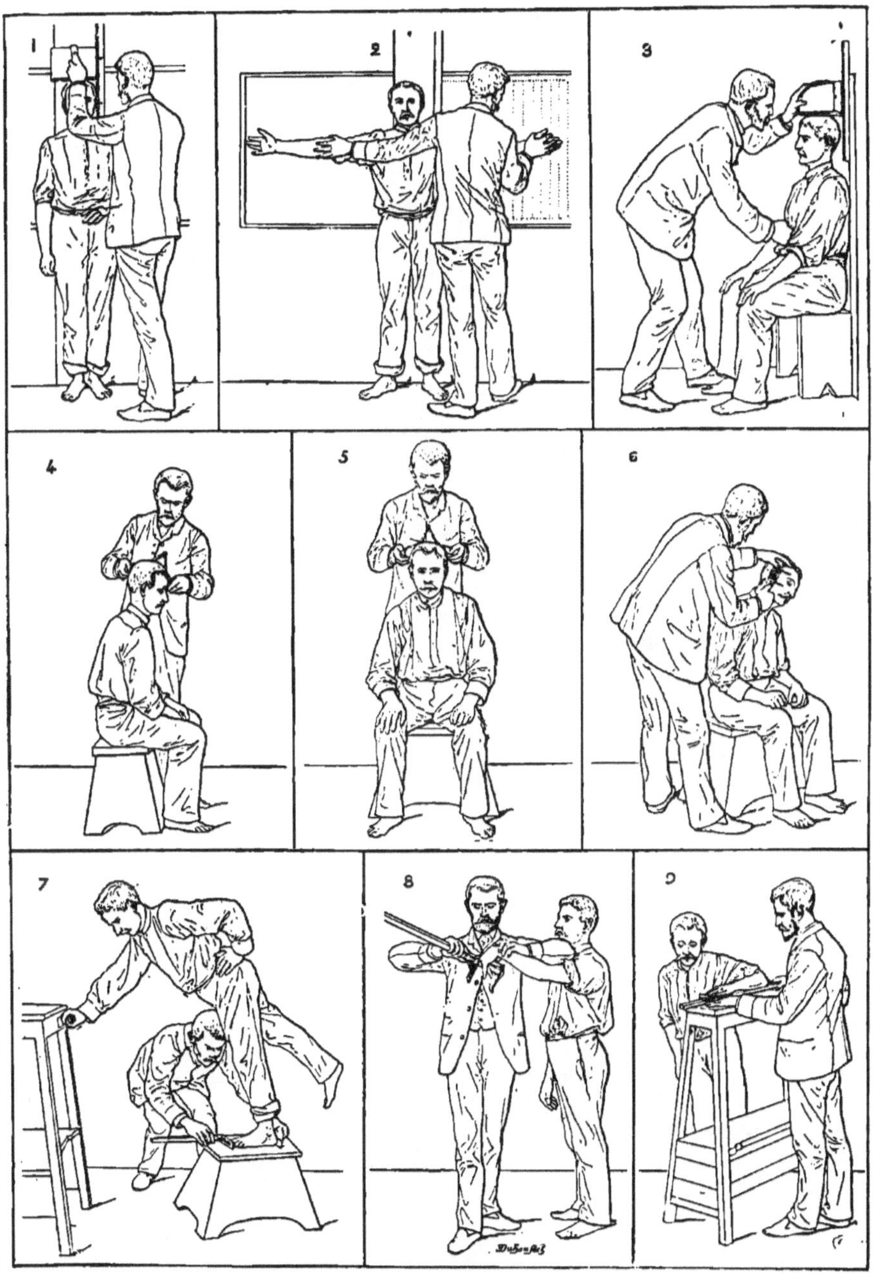

JUDICIAL MEASUREMENT.

1. Height. 2. Stretch of Arms. 3. Half-length. 4. Length of Head. 5. Width of Head. 6. Right Ear.
7. Left Foot. 8. Left Middle Finger. 9. Left Forearm.

Now, suppose that out of 90,000 individuals there happen to be two equal to one another in height, length of the head, of the left middle finger, of the left foot, the forearm and the little finger—a thing which happens once in 100,000 cases—here would still be 100,000 chances against one against these two individuals having an iris the same colour.

Consequently, when a subject, male or female, has been measured by the anthropometric department, and his description noted on a

ANTHROPOMETRIC SERVICE PHOTOGRAPHY.

separate record, it is enough, should he be arrested again, to again take his exact measurement in order to find his first description in a few minutes, and so his first record.

When it is remembered that, besides this careful record, two photographs are taken of every subject, it will be readily understood that any confusion is impossible.

Now that we know the mechanism of the anthropometric service, we may enter the apartments allotted to it.

The morning, especially from eight to eleven o'clock, is the time when they present most animation, as, after twelve o'clock, every person under arrest has to be ready for the judge of instruction.

But from the earliest hour the spectacle is full of interest. The waiting-room is crowded by ragged creatures, with stubbly hair and unshorn beards. It looks like the common dressing-room of a cheap bath-house or a general review of the beggars of·a district· There are eight municipal guards present to see that obedience is paid to the regulations: speed in the work of stripping and silence in the ranks. Do not, however, believe that justice, so careful in the search for truth, goes so far as to impose an official uniform on its ordinary clients; and when a stern voice bids subject No. 1 come forward, it is in a simple but suitable dress that he presents himself for measurement.

If he has already undergone the ordeal after a previous arrest, and is willing to speak the truth about his previous record, he is soon dismissed.

But there is nothing interesting here. The thing to note is the certainty with which the chief of the department is able in a few minutes to confound the imposture of this other ragged scoundrel with cadaverous face, and evil look, who, grinding his teeth, declares that his name is Dumont, that·he has never been convicted, and that he is the victim of an abominable error of the police.

He knows, nevertheless, that a year, or perhaps two years ago, he was brought before this very same machine, and that his head has been measured by the legs of this very same compass which the assistant is now applying to his forehead and temples. But he persists in denying this, being ignorant of the marvellous efficacy of the Bertillon system. "They measure such a lot here," says he to himself, "that they will never find me out."

Criminals have no idea, either, to what exactness of detail the classification of the department has been brought.

He is now measured lengthwise and crosswise. He passes under the movable peg so that his stature may be ascertained. He stands on the wooden stool to have his foot measured. Carefully made instruments take the dimensions of his ear, his finger, and his forearm. This completed, an official, after studying the results arrived at, goes to a little pigeon-hole, and takes therefrom a square of cardboard, on which is a record of fifteen characteristics, supported by the addition of a photograph. He returns with it, and standing before the so-called Dumont, says to him:

" You still declare that your name is Dumont ? "

" Most decidedly."

" That you were born . . . . . ? "

" At Marseilles, in 1854."

"That you have never been convicted ? "

" Never."

The official carefully scrutinises him. He assures himself, from a comparison with the photograph before his eyes, that there can be no doubt of the identity, and he then makes the following little speech :—

"You are a liar ! Your name is not Dumont. . . . . You are called Tavernier, Christian name Adolphe ; you were born at Pontoise on June 2nd, 1851 ; you have already suffered four convictions, two for theft and two for swindling."

The wretched man stands crushed and dumb-foundered.

The inquisitor adds : " Guards, raise this man's sleeve ; on his left arm he ought to have a figure tattooed in blue, representing a heart pierced by an arrow, and surmounted by a cap of liberty."

The guard lifts the sleeve, and the tattoo marks appear to the consternation of the culprit, who would like to bury himself in the ground.

The man's antecedents are forthwith noted on the police reports relative to the case in hand ; and with this full record before him the judge will know the character of the person with whom he has to deal.

The visitor will note the comfort and convenience which marks all the appointments of the anthropometric department ; it has been arranged with a method and order which are above praise.

On the top story are the rooms for photography. The manipulation of the lenses and plates is so quick that proofs can be taken in a moment, without interruption and without delay, the department having two ends in view ; simplicity and despatch.

Cases, however, arise when M. Bertillon's clients refuse to let the photographer take their portraits. To escape this decisive proof, they wriggle about, move backwards and forwards, refuse to approach the seat placed before the instrument. Stratagem has then to take the place of persuasion.

At each of the four corners of the studio is an instantaneous photographic apparatus, concealed behind little boxes which contain plates. A photographer takes up, as if by chance, the box which masks one of these instruments. He pretends to look for a proof in it, and cries out :

" But, by the by, we have your photograph here ! "

The trick always succeeds. These words make enough impression on the person interested to fix him to his place if only

ANTHROPOMETRIC SERVICE MEASUREMENT.

for one or two seconds ; and this is time enough for the hidden operator to do his work. And Justice possesses at once a portrait of the victim against his will.

And now, with all things marching to perfection, and science bringing the treasures it discovers nearer to us day by day can it be supposed that the police will not draw further profit from their inventions? The time will come, perhaps, when it will reproduce your words, your gestures, even your very thoughts. . . . , in which case it had better take for device the saying of Alphonse Bertillon himself, a truly " anthropometric " jest :

" We must remember to observe a *measure* in all things."

CHAPTER XXIII

THE DETECTIVE POLICE [1]

AT the end of a long, dark corridor, not far from the Advocates' Library, is the office of M. Goron, head of the Detective Police, whose duties are well known—the discovery and arrest of supposed evil-doers.

The creation of the Detective Police dates from 1832. Beginning with a staff of 31 men, its numbers were increased, in 1848, to 160. At the present day it includes more than 300 men, exclusive of the superior officers. The private soldier in this battalion holds the title of inspector; he has for superior officers the brigade inspector and the chief inspector.

The first head of the Detective Police was M. Allard. He held the office from November 15th, 1832, to December 15th, 1848. After him came Perrot, Canler, Balestrino, Collet, Tenaille, Claude, Jacob, Macé, who held his post from February 17th, 1879 to March 31st, 1884, when he retired on a pension.

M. Kuehn only remained for a short time at the head of this department. He was succeeded by M. Taylor, under whom the Prefect of Police appointed a deputy.

This deputy, M. Goron, formerly a commissary of police, was appointed head of the Detective Service on November 14th, 1887, in succession to M. Taylor, who is now public prosecutor at the Court of Simple Police.

M. Goron is a Knight of the Legion of Honour. He is about forty years old. It has not been left for us to sound his praises. The head of the Detective Police has friends everywhere, both at

---

[1] *La Police de Sûreté.*

the Prefecture of Police and at the Parquet, where he is held in
the very highest esteem.

M. Goron is a man of rare intelligence and keenness; in the
exercise of functions at once difficult and delicate he has shown
himself to be gifted with the most perfect tact; and to these
precious qualities he joins courage, loyalty, and courtesy.

Those who have the good luck to enter M. Goron's private
room will find it a veritable museum; by the side of a superb
collection of weapons is a large frame filled with the photographs
of a crowd of celebrated criminals.

M. GORON, HEAD OF THE DETECTIVE POLICE.

The members of the service employed at the offices are principally
occupied in receiving and registering notes and reports on matters
of justice (of which there are about 150 to 160 a day); in drawing
up and despatching statements required by the administrative
and judicial authorities; in making abstracts relative to the position
of all individuals sent to the Dépôt by the police commissaries of
Paris or the suburbs; lastly, they are in constant correspondence,
by letter or telegram, with the provinces or foreign countries.

The agents of the special brigade, composed of an inspector-
general, M. Jaume, four brigadiers, a sub-brigadier, and twenty

inspectors, undertake important missions of special delicacy or danger, both at home and abroad. The special brigade searches for and arrests great criminals, those who perpetrate vast financial or commercial frauds, &c.

The section for reports and warrants[1] comprises a chief inspector, a brigadier, and forty inspectors, whose attention is devoted to researches, inquiries, and investigations of every kind.

The brigade for warrants is more especially occupied in tracking out criminals with a view to their immediate apprehension; that for reports is chiefly engaged in providing information.

The latter body having to draw up long reports by which the judge of instruction is often induced to declare a person hitherto merely suspected as *primâ facie* liable on a criminal charge are chosen from among the better educated class. They collect the information required by the public prosecutor at twenty-four hours' notice in the case of offenders caught in the act, and brought before a criminal court for immediate trial.

A brigadier, who acts as cashier of the department, a clerk and ten inspectors form the section of requisitions. Their chief duty is to carry out the requisitions of the public prosecutor; to take in execution persons who have become State debtors from having to pay fine or costs, &c. This body of men brings into the State coffers every year some 70,000 or 80,000 francs which, without their aid, the Treasury would regard as bad debts.

The Mont-de-Piété brigade only consists of a sub-brigadier and three inspectors, charged with the supervision of pawn-shops.

One of the most important brigades is that of "the public streets." It consists of a brigadier, four sub-brigadiers, and thirty-four inspectors, commanded by Chief Inspectors Gaillarde and Rossignol. The members of this brigade, known as the *flying brigade*, have no special duty.

They stroll about on the chance of finding employment. It is, in fact, by walking up and down the most crowded streets, by visiting banks and churches, by keeping an eye on the starting-places of omnibuses and on race-courses, that they manage to run down and catch in the very act certain individuals whose movements have struck them as suspicious.

Their duty is exceedingly difficult, and to obtain success they need special aptitudes. These agents are the terror of pick-

---

[1] *La section des notes et mandats.*

pockets, *roulottiers, voleurs à l'Américaine, à la tire, au poivrier, cambrioleurs*,[1] in one word, of the numerous varieties of thieves whom they are instructed to look out for.

As to the "morals" police, consisting of thirty-two agents, it is well known that their duty is to carry out the public raids on women of improper character which have so often provoked the protests of the press, and to look after the houses licensed for prostitution.

Lastly the central or permanent section is the largest of all ; it comprises a chief inspector, a brigadier, seven sub-brigadiers, and 124 inspectors. Some of these agents have fixed posts in the offices, at the central administrative department ; others remain ready in case they should be required for urgent service by the police commissaries ; others are on duty in certain financial establishments, the Treasury, the Bank of France, the Stock Exchange, &c. Those who are not occupied as above remain at the detective office, ready for any emergency.

They have many functions ; they protect persons who are threatened with murder or violence ; they are charged with the duty of conducting prisoners into the town in order to confront them with different people, &c. Lastly they collect information in cases where it is urgently required by the Government or the public prosecutor.

---

[1] These are all slang words. A *roulottier* steals from vans or carts ; *voler à l'Américaine* is a general term for the confidence trick. *La tire* is a phrase for pocket picking : a *voleur au poivrier* robs drunken men (*poivriers*). A *cambrioleur* obtains entry into apartments and carries off the ornaments.

CHAPTER XXIV

JUDGES OF INSTRUCTION [1]

THE INSTRUCTION

LET us make a bow to the judge of instruction.

There is no business more difficult than his.

His functions and the sphere in which he exercises them are of the most extensive and unlimited description, the law having but loosely defined and regulated his powers. The judge of instruction should leave no stone unturned that may lead to a discovery of the truth ; he must prosecute the most careful researches ; he must pursue the most trifling clue ; he must verify every fact ; he must direct investigations and seizures ; order examinations by experts ; summon and hear witnesses ; interrogate persons accused of crime ; and make play with the whole arsenal of orders and warrants to appear, produce, impound, and arrest.

It is needful, therefore, not only that the judge of instruction should possess wide legal knowledge, but that he should also be endowed with accuracy, insight, decision, adroitness, patience, and good-temper. He should be astonished neither at the loftiest sentiments nor the most criminal ideas, neither at exhibitions of virtue nor subtleties of vice. Nothing ought to move, much less surprise him.

<hr>

[1] *See* Chapter I., p 4.

The judge of instruction ought to possess a well-tempered mind and an iron frame ; he should have moral force and physical health, a clear head, and a perfect digestion.

At night, in the midst of the deepest sleep, the judge of instruction is liable to be suddenly aroused by intelligence of an important arrest or an urgent interrogatory.   And when he enters his office, between one and two in the afternoon, he may either have to hurry away the next minute on some distant business, or be detained there till eleven o'clock at night.

At Paris the judges of instruction, to the number of twenty-eight, hold their sittings on the three upper stories of the Palace of Justice which lie directly above the three corridors of the Correctional Chambers, with the exception of two of these magistrates, who are stationed at the Petit Parquet.

To reach their offices, the visitor must ascend several pairs of stairs, and make his way into an enormous hall, of great length and rectangular shape, lighted by windows which open on to the court of the Sainte-Chapelle.

He will first have to state his business to an office clerk, in a dark blue uniform, the copper-gilt buttons of which are kept bright from constant rubbing against benches and wood-work.   This clerk is usually seated at a desk which looks like a stone washing-stand, on one of the sides of which a gas lamp, with a common-looking green shade, stands like a flag.

There, with a dignified air, more supercilious than that of the judge under whom he acts, the office clerk receives from the numerous witnesses cited the summonses which explain their attendance. Occasionally the subaltern identifies himself with his superior.

" In what case do you appear, sir ? "

" The Malthassin case."

" Very well, it won't take long ; you know *we* knock off *our* instructions pretty briskly."

Every day in the week an immense number of people of every class, beggars and millionaires, cobblers and members of the

Institute, cross and re-cross each other in the waiting-rooms. Here a cook in a white apron talks lovingly to a municipal guard ; there, with their arms folded in the attitude of blind men waiting for alms, the witnesses of some accident bide their time, leaning against the wall, and fixing their eyes on vacancy. One of them sighs and keeps looking at his watch with significant nods of his head ; another reads his newspaper through and through, from the date at the beginning to the printer's name at the end ; another, possessed by an irresistible desire for movement, walks up and down, counting his paces, and feverishly biting the points of his moustache.

Suddenly the electric bell rings, the clerk rushes off ; eyes are raised, and with neck stretched out towards the door by which the clerk is to return, each witness waits anxiously to hear what name will be called out.

The clerk reappears, and solemnly delivers his message.

" In the Malthassin case, the judge of instruction cannot hear any one more to-day; you will return to-morrow."

A deep stupefaction falls upon every one, and the hubbub of departure drowns the curses of the irritable and the grumblings of the discontented.

The accused alone does not wait.

Let us follow him along the side corridor with a municipal guard on either side of him.

A door opens before him, on the lintel of which appears a square copper plate engraved in large letters with the name of the judge whose office it is.

The room is small ; at the back, close to the windows, stand two mahogany desks side by side, one for the judge of instruction, the other for his registrar. On the left or the right is a second door opening into a smaller room used for receiving friends or confidential communications. By the judge's side is the button of an electric bell, connecting his office with the clerk's lobby, or with the guardroom of the Petit Parquet ; some offices are provided with speaking-tubes. Sometimes the examinations or the depositions are interrupted by a little knock at the door. It is a municipal guard with a note, or an advocate in his robes come to ask for leave to communicate with a prisoner, or a clerk with a visiting card.

At last the day's work is over, the prison van has carried its customers for the day to the various prisons of Paris; then, between four and five o'clock, the judges of instruction come forth, grave, sad, or smiling, according as they happen to have extracted confessions, failed to do so, or obtained some hope of eventual success.

Behind them, after having only waited to arrange the papers and turn out the gas, comes a train of very solemn personages.

Let us bow; these are the office clerks who are passing.

And now let us see the magistrate at work.

A crime has been committed and the perpetrator remains unknown.

The first question is to discover this criminal, who, more cunning than a beast of the chase, has doubled again and again, crossed his tracks, and baffled all the dogs of justice in his efforts to avoid capture.

The judge of instruction then investigates with the greatest possible care, with the most minute attention, everything which in the ordinary or exceptional habits of the quarry may furnish a clue. Papers, letters, trifling articles, be it only a pin found in some peculiar position, are examined with the most anxious precautions. Persons who have had relations with the victim are heard and their declarations tested.

The author of the crime, or rather the presumed author, is found; but he shuffles and denies; the proofs are not convincing enough to enable any one to affirm his guilt as certain. What is wanted is an admission. But how is the judge of instruction to obtain it? The public has heard many tales of the mysteries of instruction. Every day we are reminded of what has been called the *handcuff trick*, the "*Handcuff him, guards!*" which has become a legend at the Palace; of episodes like the telephone incident in the Wilson case;[1] then there is the celebrated blank sheet of paper which the magistrate holds in his hand, declaring it to contain depositions of the most damning kind, the statement that an accomplice has been arrested and confessed all; then, that no declaration has been made, &c., &c.

It would of course be foolish to deny that all these methods have been put in practice; but let us hasten to add that such a

---

[1] The world has not yet forgotten this extraordinary incident. M. Vigneau, in charge of the instruction in the decorations scandal, telephoned to a purchaser of the riband of the Legion of Honour, passing himself off as M. Wilson.

case is a great exception. Those who employ these methods are generally young judges of instruction, who are wanting in any deep knowledge of men and things. They are, in any case, severely denounced by old magistrates, who have grown gray in the harness. These latter insist on the most perfect good faith in the modes of action employed ; they object to trickery, which is more and more falling into disuse ; and they hold that, even in the most hardened, there is always a weak point, a defect in the brazen armour, which it is their duty to discover.

And thus it is to be regretted that the delicate work of preliminary investigation should be sometimes confided to deputy judges, who, despite the best intentions in the world, have not sufficient liberty of action, even if we leave out of sight the state of dependence in which they stand to the Ministry of Justice, and the small amount of experience they possess.

One of the formalities of instruction on which the public looks with much suspicion is the dictation of the depositions by the judge, who makes a summary of them, which is taken down by the registrar to form the record.

Often, in the course of a trial, a prisoner or a witness will be heard to say that what is put into his mouth by *le curieux*, as the judge of instruction is called in the slang of the criminal class, does not represent the statement really made.

But there is no real cause for objection ; on the one hand, credit for fairness and honourable feeling should be allowed to the judge, who in the vast majority of cases has nothing to gain by purposely distorting the facts ; on the other, there is the presence of the registrar, who also hears the depositions, and is thus able to check the correctness of the statement dictated to him.

All one can say is, that the judge of instruction, when persuaded of the guilt of the man before him, is liable sometimes to give a little too much colour to an admission. But this is rare, and too much stress should not be laid on it ; we have said " too much colour," let us say "too deep a shade" and we shall be nearer the truth.

The accused person or the witness, moreover, always has his deposition read over to him. If, therefore, he thinks that what he said has not been properly taken down, he can always refuse to sign the paper.

A FEW SPECIMENS

It is impossible to speak of the judge of instruction without devoting a short sketch to M. Guillot.

He is stout, short, and thick-set, with strong bristling eye-brows. His face is lit up by two lively little eyes that drill you through like a gimlet, and will gauge you any man in five minutes. Such is the magistrate who, on many accounts will be remembered as the type of the modern judge of instruction. He is a glutton for work, and has written a book, *Paris qui Souffre*, touching as a wail of pain and misery. He will probably retain his post for life, owing to the distinction with which he fills it, and his want of ambition for any other. And, with all this, M. Guillot devotes his few spare hours to philosophic studies which have opened to him the doors of the Institute.

Those whose idea of the judge of instruction is derived from penny periodicals will be astonished to hear that M. Guillot passes the greater part of his afternoons in examining children, poor little wretches abandoned by their parents, or guilty of some petty theft; in trying to awaken their slumbering conscience; and in doing his best to place them under charitable care, so that they may be preserved from the house of correction, the normal school of crime, as it has been called. To him, in fact, together with President Flandin and a young advocate, Maitre Rollet, known familiarly as the St. Vincent de Paul of the Law Courts, we owe the repeal of the old abominable laws relating to children; the brutal and hurried committal to prison, without any consideration of the child's circumstances, or appeal to feelings of compassion.

But very different appears M. Guillot when he finds himself face to face with a criminal of mark. The majority of our criminal heroes have passed long days in his room at the Palace: Campi, Prado, Pranzini, and many others. If they have not all left it unmasked, they have all come out subdued.

M. Guillot's plan is first of all to begin by analysing the character of the man who is brought before him. The study of the crime charged will only come in the second place, when the judge will be able to interpret the act in accordance with the nature of the individual, now thoroughly brought to light.

M. Guillot undertakes this work of analysis with extraordinary zest.   In vain does his subject shrink back and twist about ; vainly does he coil himself up like a cat who thinks she cannot be caught because she hides her ears ; in vain does he endeavour to weave together a logical skein of falsehood.   Fascinated by a searching tongue which plucks the truth from his heart, a day must eventually come when he will say to this man who divines everything : " Well, yes, you have discovered my secret ; " and he will drop his mask, like an amateur beaten in a fencing bout.

Sometimes when he does not feel himself sufficiently master of the situation, M. Guillot will call to his aid 'the witness—generally a woman—who alone has the power to extort a confession.

The reader will remember the case of Marchandon, who a few years ago murdered a widow lady in the Rue de Sèze.

Marchandon, who had been in service and committed a murder in Paris, was living at Compiègne as a man of small independent means with a mistress named Blin, whom he passed off as his wife. He cultivated an orchard, he was a candidate for office, and he had called on the municipal council to suppress a disorderly house, the neighbourhood of which shocked his virtue.   Brought before M. Guillot, after the assassination of Madame Cornet, Marchandon obstinately refused to make confession.   The judge saw that he could wring nothing from this wretch ; he summoned Jane Blin, and, calculating rightly on the indignation of the woman, who was furious at having, though without knowing it, lived with an assassin, he placed the pair face to face with one another.

Read over again the report of this meeting !   The fierce and selfish character of the woman comes out with an astonishing clearness.   Before her the man is shame-faced, crushed, and overcome by the love which he still feels for her.

JANE BLIN.—Wretch, it is on your account that I have been brought here.   You have deceived me ; without my knowing it you have involved me in your criminal existence.   It was you alone who murdered Madame Cornet.

MARCHANDON.—No, no.   It is Anatole !

JANE BLIN.—I saw you after the murder.   You were depressed.   You kept saying that you wished you were dead. You were looking out of the window all the time.   Come now, confess you are trying to pass your crime off on another.   You did it all.

MARCHANDON.—Well !   Yes, it is I alone !

JANE BLIN.—Tell the whole truth.

MARCHANDON.—Leave me alone ; make an end of this. Let them kill me at once !

JANE BLIN.—They will kill you soon enough. No fear of that. But you must tell all, so that people may know that I was your first victim. How did you kill this woman ?

MARCHANDON.—In her room.

JANE BLIN.—She was asleep ; you must have woke her up.

MARCHANDON (*despairingly*).—But, since it is Anatole (*an imaginary person invented by Marchandon*).

JANE BLIN.—And your braces, which were found by the side of the corpse ?

MARCHANDON.—It must be Anatole who put them there, so as to ruin me.

JANE BLIN.—Be quiet then ! This was the reason of your trips to Paris, here is the secret of the letters you used to receive from great ladies, whose lover you pretended to be. Repent, wretch ; repent. If I have lived with an assassin, let him at least ask pardon of God. Come now, how did it happen ?

MARCHANDON.—I had the kitchen key. I got in that way. I took a large knife which was lying on the dresser. I made my way into the room. Madame Cornet had taken off her clothes, put on her nightdress, and got into bed. Then I showed myself and she saw me. . . . she screamed with fright. . . . she rose up ! . . . she tried to escape. . . . I seized her. . . . I struck her.

JANE BLIN.—This is the truth ?

MARCHANDON.—Oh, yes !

JANE BLIN.—Swear it by the head of your mother.

MARCHANDON.—I swear it !

Three months later Marchandon was guillotined on the square of La Roquette.

Another judge of instruction, well known to every newspaper reader, is M. Laurent Atthalin. With his flowing hair brushed back from his forehead, his long and carefully trimmed beard, M. Laurent Atthalin is the model of a polite judge. He sends his man to the scaffold with all the formality of a gentleman of birth. Before him have passed Euphrasie Mercier, M. Wilson, the members of the Patriotic League, the Russian Nihilists, as well

as Turpin, Triponé, and the other persons involved in the recent
Mélinite scandal.

Lastly comes M. Doppfer, from Alsace. Patriotic and conscientious, he is honesty itself, and pursues his task without noise
or display, but at the same time with the steadiness of a pack-
horse, which moves slowly, but never stops to take rest on the
way.

Eyraud and Gabrielle Bompard learned something of this.

CHAPTER XXV

THE PROCUREUR AND HIS STAFF

THE judges of instruction take action at the call of the Parquet, and it is only in compliance with requisitions from the Parquet that they determine the fate of an accused person by a declaration that there is no ground for prosecution or an order sending his case before the competent jurisdiction.

What is the Parquet? A singular word, which in the sanctuary of justice makes one think of the Temple of Finance.[1]

The Parquet is simply the Procureur with his deputies. The Procureur dominates all this little world ; and he settles himself questions of some importance by directing prosecutions or casting a veil over certain disgraceful scandals.

At the moment at which we write the head of the Parquet in the Paris Courts of First Instance, is M. Banaston, who succeeded M. Bernard. He is a distinguished magistrate, who, when he was Advocate-General in the Assize Court, showed marked skill as a speaker, and is now esteemed for courtesy and tact in the exercise of his official duties.[2]

---

[1] The word *parquet* is regularly used to denote the chief meeting place of brokers in the Paris Stock Exchange. It is also used as equivalent to *Ministère Public*, explained above, Ch. I. p. 2 of this work.

[2] Since the above was written M. Banaston has died ; he has been succeeded in his office of Procureur at the Paris Courts of First Instance by M. Roulier

CHAPTER XXVI

ROUND ABOUT THE PALACE OF JUSTICE

THE PALACE DOCTOR

FOR many years, it might be said for many centuries, persons who came to the law courts on business, whether for themselves or others, and were suddenly taken ill there, persons who were seized with a fit in the overheated Courts, and would-be desperadoes who made classical attempts at suicide with the clerk's penknife in the presence of the judge of instruction, had nothing to keep them from departing this life but the insufficient attentions of the Court ushers, office clerks, and municipal guards on duty. No regular practitioner was attached to the judicial establishment as holding a "post of succour"; when necessary, a doctor from the neighbourhood, a stranger to the great judicial family, had to be called in.

There was something particularly shocking in this both for judges and advocates; it was impossible to die *en famille;* it was a stranger who came to give you the last consolations of medicine.

The Council-General for the department of the Seine saw the magnitude of this void, and resolved to fill it up. The office of "physician of the Palace" was created, and the present holder, the amiable Doctor Charles Floquet, was specially appointed to look

after the indispositions of the legal community. Dr. Floquet at
once understood what was wanted by the members of the great
family which he was entering.   What the Palace of Justice required
was not a doctor of the old school, solemn and long-worded, always
disposed to make silent examinations or formidable soundings,
always ready to write prescriptions stuffed with technical terms.
No, what was wanted was a man who, while fully qualified so
far as medical attainments went, should conceal his professional
characteristics under an affable exterior and should be completely
one of the *family*.

THE PALACE DOCTOR.

An advocate or a judge overcome by the heat of Court needed
a doctor who could make him smile ; the accused who made an
attempt at suicide needed a doctor who, while bandaging his wounds
with a light strip of gummed taffetas, would remind him that ink
erasers are made to scratch paper not human skin.

In a word, the Palace of Justice wanted a man who, in case of
need, would be able to revive a patient by cordial words, rather
than by a cordial without words.

Doctor Floquet has so well understood the importance of this part of his duties that he has employed his leisure time—people do not die in the law courts every day—in legal studies. He is a licentiate in law, if you please; and a violet riband, once rect-angular, but now grown round shaped, is fastened to his button-hole; he has an engaging manner and a pleasant voice. No one knows better than the Palace doctor how to soothe with a word the anxiety of lawyers troubled by coughs or colds. As he passes by he whispers a recommendation of some powder to be taken in hot milk without appearing to attach any importance to the case; the invalid is reassured and his ailment disappears.

The day, a distant one we may hope, will come when others will occupy the place now held by Doctor Floquet. But it will be no discredit to them if we declare that none will ever surpass him in the qualifications of his office, or find on their rounds more friendly hands held out to them. Doctor Floquet, for the due performance of his duties, has to be constantly on the move from one part of the Palace to another; certain people, seeing his room door nearly always shut, imagine his office to be a sinecure. To these we offer the following curious statistics of his services. In 1890 there were at the law courts :—

Medical Cases.

Cardiac affections	9
Cases of syncope and vertigo	42
Cases of hemorrhage	12
Affections of the respiratory organs (acute and chronic laryngitis, spasms of the glottis, &c.)	29
Affections of the digestive organs	21
Cases of cerebral congestion	9
Epilepsy	15
Hysteria	42
Catalepsy	1
Nervous attacks	11
Alcoholism	6
Mental affections	3
Total	200

Surgical Cases.

Contusions	34
Sprains	2
Luxation of the shoulder	1
Luxation of the elbow	1
Wound penetrating the chest (attempt at suicide)	1
Wounds and various accidents	16
Total	55

Altogether 255 cases . . . and not one death ! This is the bright side of this little account.

COMMANDANT LUNEL AND HIS GUARDS

The guard attached to the Palace of Justice reminds one of the National Guard. He has the air of a family man. One look at him is enough to tell you that he is not troubled by barrack regulations or constant parades ; and that the thin soup and sorry rations which the soldier of the line has to put up with are, for him, replaced by a substantial dinner looked after by an attentive housewife. From this doubtless comes the mingled look of solidity, complacency, and comfort which appears in the air of the Palace guard, his physiognomy, and his gait, the latter being as slow and solemn as a law-suit itself.

There is certainly a mysterious affinity between these pacific pretorians and the building in which they live. But let not the reader be deceived ; the Palace guard is in every way the reverse of the National Guard, who used to assume a war-like bearing in order to disguise his character ; the great majority of the Palace guards are old non-commissioned officers who can point to a record of numerous campaigns and excellent conduct during their time of service. Their very language is in keeping with their bearing. The Palace guard never swears, and always expresses himself in well-chosen terms.

Their uniform has retained a slightly archaic stamp. The Palace guard of the present day, together with the pupil of the École Polytechnique, is one of the last representatives of the cocked hat, which he wears, unlike the gendarme, with the point in front. He is clothed in a tunic and trousers of black cloth with large red stripes—the colours of the Civil Tribunal and the Assize Court.

The duties of the Palace guards consist in constant observance of the everlasting instruction, " Keep order."

Only, as order is already kept by their colleagues of the Republican Guard, who look after the malefactors, the judges, and the public, the only order remaining to be kept is reduced to a homœopathic dose. And so, after roll-call and a microscopic inspection which takes place every morning in the still deserted galleries of the Palace, the duties of the Palace guards are limited to distributing among the public moving in the corridors a few injunctions of which the most frequent may be reduced to three formulas.

1. " Sir, smoking in the corridors is strictly forbidden." And, if it is an advocate engaged in finishing a cigarette, " Maître (*with a smile*), you know that cigarettes in the corridors. . . ." When the culprit happens to be a judge, the guard looks another way.

2. " No, madam, I cannot let you go about the building with that dog."

THE COMMANDANT LUNEL.

3. On days when great criminal cases are on and all those whom the case does not concern want to get a sight of the assassin, "Useless to persist. No admission without the president's permission or a reporter's card."

And, as the visitor always does persist, the guard adds :

"Go and see the Commandant Lunel."

Commandant Lunel, chief of the Palace guards, has never, in the course of his campaigns, been called upon to sustain assaults like those he has to face on the days when Pranzini, Prado, Eyraud and their successors fill the Court to suffocation. We need not speak of male applicants. They are disposed of with a "Sorry, sir ; but it is quite impossible, the Court is overflowing." But would-be spectators of the fair sex—and there are some charming ones—are more obstinate. On those days the commandant has before him whole battalions of pretty women who, though they have no valid pretext for their importunity, are never at a loss for a plausible excuse.

The chief—a gallant man—is lost in regrets ; he falls back on superior orders, the crowded state of the Court ; and he contrives not to put the fair cohort out of temper, though all the time he only admits the authorised few.

Before becoming the amiable superintendent of the Palace guards, .Commandant Lunel was director of the riding school

at Caen.   The services which from his great experience and con-
summate skill he has been able to render to the organisation of
cavalry remounts are of inestimable value.

It is well known that Commandant Lunel is one of our best
riders.   Marshal Canrobert early remarked his abilities in this
direction, and during the Crimean campaign entrusted him with
the direction of the cavalry remount at Varna.   He has subsequently held the posts of director at the stud farm at Pin and the
remount at Versailles.   His service record is extremely brilliant.
Since 1841, when he entered the sixth Regiment of Lancers, there
has been no campaign in which he has not had a share.   He received the riband of the Legion of Honour after Solferino ; he
obtained the rank of colonel on February 10th, 1871, after having
taken part in the battles of Le Bourget, Le Raincy, and Buzenval ;
and he has held the military command at the Louvre.

He was appointed to the command of the Palace guards on
July 17th, 1874, and to that of the guards at the Tribunal of
Commerce in the year following.   He has introduced several
useful reforms into the internal arrangements of the Palace.

It must be added that he realises the ideal commandant who
is " father of his battalion," and that he enjoys the warm affection
not only of his guards, but of all at the law courts who ever come
into relations with him.

A last trait : he is not averse to comic songs, which he composes
and will sing to you, if you call upon him after dinner, in a way
which would force a smile from the most austere magistrate.

THE ADVOCATES' RESTAURANT

The Café Louis, called after its proprietor, is outside the Palace
of Justice, and a sort of annexe to it.   It stands in the little Rue
Mathieu-Molé, consisting only of four houses, which unites the Rue
de la Sainte-Chapelle to the Quai de la Seine ; the latter faces the
shed which has been built for the steam fire-engines near the fire-
men's barracks.

In order to get there unobserved, the people of the law courts,
who alone use the café, cross the courtyard of the Sainte-Chapelle,
and go out by a vaulted corridor, looking like a postern-gate, that
pierces the great building of the Correctional Courts.

The café has only one room, the arrangement of which has required much ingenuity. Every corner has been utilised down to the last fraction of an inch, and the chairs and tables look as if they were specially made to be folded up under one another at a moment's notice. The kitchen, formed by a glass partition, takes up one of the angles ; the counter stands half hidden in the place left free between this kitchen and a little staircase, under which, at the back, there is even a cupboard in reserve, used as a pantry. The rest is occupied by six marble tables, in front of which are benches cushioned in red plush ; in the middle of these is a centre table with eight chairs, and on the walls are mirrors.

Here, on every Court day, come in succession or all together crowds of twenty, thirty, or forty customers—advocates, solicitors, ushers, registrars—fresh from the Courts, almost all in official dress—who give the room the picturesque appearance of a conference of learned men, met together to drink a friendly glass.

Those who, engaged in cases which head the list, have had to come to the law courts at an early hour, arrive first for breakfast ; they are the advance-guard. But from half-past twelve, when the lists have been read through, a fresh set of faces appears ; many whose cases are fixed to be on in the course of the day, at one o'clock, two o'clock, or later, come to while away the interval, or the time when the sitting is suspended in the middle, by a game at cards or chess.

These are always the same people, divided into two sets, "the men of the woods" who are faithful to the queen and knight, and the men of cardboard, the devotees of whist. Sometimes a few timidly venture on a game of piquet or écarté, but the professors of high finesse cast a disdainful eye upon these inferior games.

All types of players may be seen there ; and they form a study the more curious and interesting because the peculiar character of each comes out under the fascination of the cards, just as in the public contests of open Court. Here may be seen the man of methodical and regular habits, who will not pass over a slip, acknowledging his own with sorrow, and pouncing without mercy on those of his partners, exactly as he does in Court ; the blunderer who throws his cards pell mell as he does the papers of his briefs ; the prig, who plays like an amateur, without interest, and loses his tricks one by one as indifferently as he does his clients' cases, in *dilettante* fashion ; the passionate man, who goes

THE ADVOCATES' RESTAURANT.   Drawn by P. Renouard.

into a rage, gives one look at his cards and if they don't please him, throws them on the table in his excitement, just as in Court he would hurl aggressive arguments at his opponent's head; the calm man, conscious of his strength, whose deep voice, more resounding than the trumpets of Jericho, seems to exact respect from fortune as much as it frightens those who contradict him; the retired judge, who is not afraid to interrupt the traditional silence of whist by comic stories, or even broad ones; the funny man, of over-flowing spirits, who has charming flashes of humour, but sometimes, alas! descends to a pun, the besetting sin of judges and advocates; lastly, the grumpy martinet, surly of face, who holds forth at length, lays down the law, expresses his contempt, and sends his neighbours to sleep from very boredom, as if he were still addressing the Court.   And countless others.

Chess engages the attention of strategists, of men of exact habits, of the fanciful, of the bold, of the prudent.   There they sit, in this war of wooden figures, looking like champions; and they wage the mimic fight with the same heat, the same earnestness, the same ambition for conquest, and the same exultation in victory that mark them when they struggle to save a client's .fortunes or rejoice over a client saved.

It is a pity that suitors cannot come in person and pick out the advocates they want in the midst of this revelation of feelings in undress and character laid bare.   They would then be able to discover the right temperament and the special aptitudes required for the conduct of their suits.   They would be able to make their choice with full knowledge of the man, which they can hardly do when everything is masked under the assumed formalities of the consulting-room.   But if a layman risks himself in this crowd of noisy, talking, singing, black-robed men, he feels that he is in the way.   He is an intruder; they scowl at him, and he beats a retreat.

After four o'clock on week-days, and during the whole of Sunday the place is a desert.

THE REPORTERS

At the Court of Assize, when a great case is being tried, a score of men may be noticed crowded, squeezed, wedged together in a compartment next to the prisoner's dock, writing on their knees or on wooden tablets placed before them.   On important days at the

Correctional Court they are in still worse plight ; stuffed into every corner, bending down in the most unnatural positions, standing up in the embrasures of the windows, seated on the steps of the daïs. Here they are engaged in scribbling on endless slips of paper, writing away from morning to night, as if indifferent to their surroundings, till by the time their work is over they find themselves, like the companions of Charlemagne, with "stiffness in the loins, cramp in the neck, blisters on the fingers."

These are the law court reporters. Their portraits cannot be reproduced here for obvious reasons, but a few facts about them must find a place in our book. Their corporation, in fact, is one of the original corners of legal life, and one of those least known even to regular frequenters of the Courts. The latter know that the reporters possess in common two little rooms, the way to which is well known to advocates and even to magistrates, but they know little more of the Association of Press Reporters at the Palace of Justice.

Many associations are well fitted to attain the end for which they have been formed, but are divided into cliques, and racked by petty jealousies and personal dislikes. Not so the present chroniclers of the Palace. No, the Association of Law Reporters is not of this kind. It is not a corporation; it is a body with several heads and a single heart. The members often have discussions among themselves ; but however numerous and diverse the opinions put forward, however lively the opposition they meet with, the ultimate decision always finds unanimous support. Formed into a syndicate, like all those who work for their living, the pressmen of the law courts have not turned their society into a league of comrades. They have done better, they have become friends, united like brothers by close bonds, closer than that of mere association, useful as that was in the first instance. Their excellent head, Alexandre Pothey, the regretted Rocher, Émile Corra their late syndic, Albert Bataille their present president, Davrillé des Essards, a member of the Municipal Council of Paris, so expert in all questions of co-operation, have leagued them together for the protection of their corporate interests, at cost of much trouble, and in spite of many obstacles.   Daily intercourse, difficulties overcome in common, kindred emotions, similar qualities of heart and head, and perhaps also similar weaknesses, have made them in some sort members of one family.

The two little rooms allotted to them by the authorities in a corner of the law courts have not the convenient but commonplace air of an ordinary newspaper office.   They are the meeting place of men who trust one another, and are bound together by the links of a deep, an intimate, and a matured affection.   They have different opinions and origins; in tastes and principles they may be opposed to one another; their views and sentiments are often in direct contradiction;   they will argue to the bitter end *de omni re scibili et quibusdam aliis;* but their union is superior to theories and doctrines ; and the most furious opponents will become reconciled if asked to render a service.

ALEX. POTHEY, DOYEN OF THE LAW REPORTERS.

They form a true *family;* the word has been degraded by abuse, but in this case the thing is present in all its force. It is a real family. It takes the young new-comer by the hand, guides his first steps through the Palace of Justice, and unfolds to him the secrets of legal life.   His education completed, it will not stop there ; it will do more than facilitate his work ; when absent, it will find him a substitute ; when calumniated, it will defend him ; when ill, it will care for him and assist him as far as its modest resources will allow.   It is easy thus to imagine the gratitude he will feel towards it, and the readiness with which he will in his turn do good to its other members.

But what need is there of words ?   Is not this book itself a sufficient proof of their *esprit de corps ?*

The authors have fixed on the subject of "the Paris Law Courts" because they could find no other which they were so well fitted to

treat ; because the law courts have been the source of their friend
ship, and the be-all and end-all of their lives.

As one of their oldest members, M. Fernand de Rodays, has
said, " Is not the Palace of Justice the most curious magic lantern
which man has ever devised ?" From January to December they
see it, they study it, they watch it. Almost in spite of themselves
they have learnt gradually to know it by heart. This mighty
edifice with its corridors, its turnings, its doors, its staircases, its
corners—they know it from its roof to its wonderful basements.

They are by profession the historiographers and critics of its
varied world of magistrates, advocates, criminals, and supernumer-
aries, having in the discharge of their duties to watch the events
which take place there. Of everything and everybody they have
personal experiences and documents collected day by day, for
their business enables them to penetrate every day into the most
secret corners of the world of the Courts.

So well acquainted are they with the people who move between
the Rue de Lutèce and the Place Dauphine that old or young,
conservative or radical, if you listen to them, their judgment is
always unanimous. In all we note the same objects of admiration,
the same objects of respect, and the same objects of contempt ;
the same scepticism and the same repugnances. Radicals and
moderates, in order to agree with one another, have only to make
a sacrifice of form ; the formulas differ, but the thought is
identical.

How, indeed, could it be otherwise ? How can they help being
tarred with the same brush ? Enforced pupils at this practical
school of psychology named " The Courts," they have acquired on
the same bench—this hard reporters' bench so often invaded by
the outside world—the special knowledge of which they treat in
due accordance with the rules of the law courts. They have all been
through the same experiences repeated a thousand times over, and
in consequence they have drawn from them identical conclusions.
No better proof of this can be offered than the very unity of the
present work.

CHAPTER XXVII

THE BUILDING OPPOSITE THE PALACE OF JUSTICE

THE TRIBUNAL OF COMMERCE

AT the corner of the Boulevard du Palais and the Quai de la Cité, fronting the Palace of Justice, rises a detached building, square in shape, and surmounted by a fine cupola ; this is the Tribunal of Commerce. The special system of jurisdiction for commercial matters originated with the numerous and important fairs of the Middle Ages.

The need for an expeditious and suitable tribunal to settle disputes between merchants determined King Charles IX. to issue, in 1563, and at the suggestion of Chancellor de l'Hospital, the first ordinance creating a commercial jurisdiction in Paris. The notables charged with the duty of administering justice in this Court were the *consuls of the corporation of merchants;* whence arose the terms *consular judges, consular jurisdiction* or *consular Courts*, still in use at the present day, to designate judges and tribunals of commerce.

The early system of commercial tribunals lasted till the Revolution without any great modifications; and the law of August 16th-24th, 1790, which reconstituted them, laid down for their guidance a code of regulations which largely obtains at the present day.

We need not enter into technical details, which indeed would be beyond the scope of this work. Suffice it to say that they are composed of judges elected from the commercial body in accordance with the forms prescribed by the law of December 8th,

1883. The functions of these magistrates are limited in duration, and they receive no payment. The jurisdiction of the Tribunals of Commerce extends over the whole *arrondissement* for which they are established, and is applicable to all disputes relative to com-

DOME OF THE TRIBUNAL OF COMMERCE.

mercial matters and to bankruptcies. Appeal lies from their decisions to the Court of Appeal for the district in which they happen to be located.

But in order to obtain a full knowledge of the importance and powers of a Tribunal of Commerce, we have only to enter the building which stands opposite to the Palace of Justice in Paris, as though to enter into competition with it and obtain the custom of its suitors.

On entering the vestibule, we are at once informed as to the history of the building. On our right, in fact, we find, engraved on a marble slab affixed to the wall, the following inscription :—

IN THE YEAR 1860
DURING THE REIGN OF
NAPOLEON III. EMPEROR OF THE FRENCH
THE COMMISSION FOR THE DEPARTMENT OF THE SEINE
VOTED THE ERECTION OF THIS EDIFICE
BARON HAUSSMANN, SENATOR
PREFECT OF THE DEPARTMENT OF THE SEINE
M. DUMAS, SENATOR
PRESIDENT OF THE COMMISSION FOR THE DEPARTMENT
M. DENIÈRE
PRESIDENT OF THE TRIBUNAL OF COMMERCE.

On the left is another inscription, forming a pendant to the first :—

IN THE YEAR 1865
DECEMBER 26TH
THEIR MAJESTIES NAPOLEON III. EMPEROR OF THE FRENCH
AND THE EMPRESS EUGÉNIE
VISITED THIS EDIFICE WHICH WAS THE SAME DAY MADE OVER
TO THE TRIBUNAL OF COMMERCE
AND THE COUNCILS OF PRUD'HOMMES
BARON HAUSSMANN, SENATOR
PREFECT OF THE DEPARTMENT OF THE SEINE
M. CHARLES BERTHIER,
PRESIDENT OF THE TRIBUNAL OF COMMERCE
MM. BIÉTRY, BRIQUET, DÉLICOURT, CHUNOT
PRESIDENTS OF THE FOUR COUNCILS OF PRUD'HOMMES.
A. N. BAILLY, ARCHITECT.

On the right is the hall of the Council of Prefecture. In the vestibule on the left, that which opens on the Court of the Cité, notices of matters affecting commerce are posted up on boards protected by wire. The public may there get information as to the names of stockbrokers and commercial brokers, with the dates of their entry on their employment and the names of their predecessors. Those who intend engaging in commercial transactions will do well to come here and read the lists of debtors who have obtained orders of discharge, of those against whom receiving orders have been made, of those who are subject to a committee of inspection, of insolvents and bankrupts. The names of all such are carefully posted up ; and if a trader, when the time comes for the settlement of his account, finds himself met with the plea that the debtor is insolvent, he has only himself and his own negligence to blame.

By the side of these lists are posted large placards bearing, in huge letters, the following exhortation to prudence, which, it would seem, is very necessary in this abode of justice : *The public are requested to be on their guard against touts*[1] (understand, agents of doubtful character), *and to entrust no business to them."*

This danger is less to be feared at the ordinary law courts, where "general agents" of this type cannot appear at the bar in the name of their clients. Besides this, they give the place a wide berth, doubtless because of its proximity to the office of the Public Prosecutor. Should you ever come across them in the corridors of the Temple of Themis, be sure that nine times out of ten they are there to give account to a judge of instruction or the Correctional Court of some act of swindling or breach of trust committed against a too confiding client.

Let us enter the tribunal.

Before mounting to the first floor, the visitor should stop and admire the magnificent double marble staircase which leads to it. At the bottom, two stone lions represent strength, while up above appear four majestic statues, personifying Commerce, Navigation, Mechanics, and Industrial Art.

The staircase abuts on the Salle des Pas-Perdus. In each of the four corners is a date to remind us of the chief epochs in the development of the commercial jurisdiction ; 1563—1673—1807—1865.

1563, as already stated, is the year in which Charles IX., his majority having been solemnly proclaimed on August 17th, in a

---

[1] *Racoleurs.*

THE GRAND STAIRCASE OF THE TRIBUNAL OF COMMERCE.

" bed of justice," signed the decree establishing the jurisdiction of the judge-consuls for the traders of Paris.

In 1673, Louis XIV. issued a most important decree, forming by itself a regular Commercial Code, which prevailed down to that of 1807, promulgated by Napoleon I., and still in force in our own day.

1865 is, as we have seen, the year in which the new building was thrown open.

In the Salle des Pas-Perdus our eyes are met by a notification of the fees payable to attorneys.[1] This reminds us that these attorneys are not considered officers of the Court like the solicitors and ushers at the Civil Tribunal. In spite of their ribbed cap and Venetian cloak, they are only private individuals, without any public status, whom the Court allows to represent parties, and recommends to the choice and confidence of suitors. Those employ them who like, and their ministry is not obligatory in any case.

At Paris, the number of *agréés* is fixed at fifteen. This is very little ; and it is a matter of astonishment to find so small a number in the first Commercial Tribunal of France. Reform in this particular is urgently needed ; for, overwhelmed as they are with work, the commercial attorneys find it a physical impossibility to give personal attention to all the cases entrusted to them. As a natural consequence, the small cases have to give place to the larger ones, and the attorney is compelled to hand them over to the direction of secretaries, whose experience and knowledge are not always an equivalent for the master's supervision.

The commercial attorneys, being simply agents employed by their clients, cannot represent them at the bar, except when furnished with special powers or accompanied into Court by the clients themselves.

In no case can they bring before the Court in which they practise[2] any demands for the recovery of costs from their clients. And there is a notice to this effect on the very door of the Court.

The whole building is covered with copies of a placard. But this introduces an innovation intended to accelerate the course of procedure. In fact, we find it stated here in black and white, that as soon as the parties present themselves at the bar, their case will

---

[1] *Agréés.*

[2] The French for this is *postuler ;* the *agréés* were formerly styled *postulants* or *procureurs aux consuls.*

be immediately heard by a judge. Whence it is to be inferred that judgment will be given with the shortest possible delay. There is only one drawback, the realisation of the promised reform has not yet found its way into practice. None the less the Tribunal of Commerce prides itself on the rapidity of its procedure. It is the principal merit to which this popular institution can lay claim, for it is generally very costly, and practically inaccessible to humble folks.

It is only sensational cases, such as company suits, or claims for forfeits against actresses which are really discussed. As for the rest, the cases in which unimportant people are concerned, the Tribunal has no time to go into them thoroughly in Court. It passes them on to be settled by an arbitrator, an expert or agent of some kind, an honest man no doubt, but not possessing all the qualifications of a judge. If the case requires no reference to an expert, the Court directs it to be set down for immediate hearing ; that is to say, it is submitted to a judge who, after summoning the parties and hearing their statements, draws up, to the best of his ability, a judgment, which the overworked section he belongs to will, generally speaking, adopt.

This is, in fact, the "one judge" system, which has been so constantly denounced, even in cases where the competence of the magistrate is beyond question.

As regards the formalities of the Court sittings, the uninitiated who set foot in the Tribunal are generally struck dumb with astonishment. Judges, attorneys, registrar, ushers, speak a barbarous tongue. The poor wretch who appears at the bar unsupported feels crushed before he opens his lips. He is not wanted, and they let him know it.

His opponent's attorney bullies and ridicules him.

"What is your claim ? " asks the president curtly.

" He owes me 250 francs ! "

" —Before some one," says the attorney on the other side contemptuously. The phrase "before some one" means that the attorney does not think it worth his while to argue the case and will have it referred to an arbitrator.

"Before whom ? " says the president ; "what's this about ? "

The attorney, overburdened with his heaps of papers, has completely forgotten the case. He refers to his notebook. " It is about pens," cries he boldly. " What kind of pens ? " returns the president.

"Steel pens," whispers his secretary.

Says the attorney with an air, "Steel pens."

The president turns over the leaves of a memorandum book, runs through the list of experts, and finds one who is an expert in pens ; so here is a case settled.

"But . . . . ," timidly objects the plaintiff.

The apparitor, a gentlemen of solemn air who wears the chain of a sacristan, removes him from the bar, and with a sweep of his arm motions him to be seated.   It must be said, in defence of the magistrates, that the staff of the Tribunal is absolutely insufficient. At the Civil Tribunal there are seven Chambers ; at the Tribunal of Commerce, with far more cases, there is only one sitting every day.   In the former there are a hundred and fifty solicitors, and in the building opposite but fifteen attorneys.   Add to the labour of the sittings the reports to be made in bankruptcies, the judicial liquidations, deliberations to be held, judgments to be drawn up, meetings of creditors and shareholders, and you will understand how urgent it is that the Tribunal of Commerce should be reformed by the establishment of divisional chambers and by increasing the number of attorneys, or, what would be best, by making the bar really accessible to all, without intermediaries of any sort.

Unless this is done in a few years time, the Tribunal of Commerce will lose much of its authority.   This would be unfortunate, for, with all its faults, it manages in great commercial disputes to render real services to the cause of justice.   Those who want a change are the lesser men ; imbued with the spirit of association, so strong nowadays, they will before long be driven to supersede it by syndical chambers, courts of arbitration conducted by experts : this, in fact, is the true judicial system of the future, a justice which will cost nothing, and will understand the questions it deals with. But this is not a polemical work!   Let us listen to what goes on in the Court.   Here by chance is a case which the attorneys have thought important enough to be argued.

These attorneys are curious beings to contemplate.   They wear black coats and white cravats ; and with a short surplice of plaited silk, rather like the robe worn on state occasions by Roman prelates, they look like bluebottle flies that go buzzing about full of importance.   They talk in stilted phrases, quite puffed up by a sense of their merits and of the importance of their duties.

The occasional presence of advocates does not make much impression on them, and they ungraciously leave to such a few little cases which are unworthy of their lordships ; while at the same time they lose no chance of playing their rivals all sorts of dirty tricks.   In days gone by they were even less obliging. So at least it would appear from the following little anecdote which is told in the corridors of the law courts. Each attorney has his particular desk before the bar of the Tribunal ; and, when he has to speak or be present at a sitting, he takes his place there. They were exceedingly jealous of this privilege, and would let no outsider use any of these fifteen desks. One day an advocate presented himself to plead before the Tribunal of Commerce, but was pitilessly refused the right of standing before any of the unoccupied desks.

"But no one is using this desk !" groaned the unhappy man, bending under the weight of his papers and looking for a place to lay them down in.

"Extremely sorry, my dear sir, to contradict you," answered an attorney in the mildest of tones, "but Maître X——will be coming shortly, and he particularly asked me to keep his place for him. Be sure that he also will be extremely sorry." And at every desk which the luckless advocate approached as if it was the promised land, he found himself repulsed on pretexts equally discourteous and frivolous.

The president of the Tribunal had at last to intervene to check these petty annoyances ; and in order to put a stop to them once for all, a sixteenth desk was erected, the monopoly of which the attorneys could have no right of claiming.

As soon as the attorneys have finished their arguments, the Court withdraws to its Council Chamber to deliberate on the terms of its judgment, and the suitors who are waiting for the decision, unless they prefer to watch one another's faces or become absorbed in their own reflections, may cast their eyes over the pictures which adorn the hall where the sittings are held. Only two of the required four have yet been finished. The first, which is to the left of the entrance, represents Charles IX. establishing the judge-consuls in 1563. The second commemorates the promulgation of the Commercial Edict of 1673. The third and fourth will represent episodes connected with the promulgation of the Commercial Code in 1807, and the opening of the present building.

Let us now leave the hall of audience, and, crossing an inner gallery, pay a visit to the side of the building opposite that just described.

We first notice two rooms, known as the bankruptcy department, and by their side are the syndics' offices, which are ornamented with a printed list of forthcoming sales.

In these rooms are held meetings of the creditors of an insolvent business; it is here that they learn with what sauce they are to be eaten. They are certain to be losers; it is only a question of more or less. " Are we in for 20, 40, or 60 per cent. ? " they ask each other anxiously, as they enter the dreaded chamber. And, according as the syndic's statements have been favourable or the reverse, you will see them come out and leave the Court with an expression of cheerfulness or dejection on their countenances.

Continuing our exploration of this side of the gallery, we pass by the private rooms of the reporting judges; next, in the other corner, we come upon the secretary's office and the private room of the president of the Tribunal, which is used for the Council Chamber. The second story is devoted to the clerical work of the Tribunal. It contains the registry offices, the records of bankruptcies and liquidations, the private room of the secretary-registrar and the pay office. Here are registered partnerships, marriages, separations, trade marks, trade names and other commercial matters.

Here also arbitrators bring, sealed up, the reports which they have been directed to make for the information of the judges, and the registrar's clerks draw up and make copies of judgments to be called for by the suitors. On the third story there is nothing interesting to notice; it is occupied throughout by the ushers of the Court. We will not enter, as these gentlemen dislike being disturbed.

THE PREFECTURE COUNCIL [1]

The building opposite the Palace of Justice also provides a home for the Council of the Prefecture of the department of the Seine. This branch of administrative jurisdiction is but poorly lodged. The only chamber for the sittings of the Council is on the ground floor. It is fairly large, but plain, cheerless, and rather

[1] See Ch. I. p. 7.

damp—no doubt to remind people that the Council was established in the month of *Pluviôse.*[1] It looks like the ordinary Court of a justice of peace with no spectators.

Outside the circle of persons interested, and apart from trials of disputes as to the validity of municipal elections, which attract more politicians than journalists, the sittings of the Council, which have been thrown open to the public since 1865, excite no curiosity. The reason is that the cases which are subject to the special jurisdiction of the Prefecture Council are from their very nature dull, and if they offer variety they are wanting in the picturesque.

The Council sits every day. It is divided into two sections, each directed by a vice-president. At Paris the prefect himself has no right to preside over the Prefecture Council; there is already a special president; it is even doubtful whether the prefect of the Seine himself has a right to a seat, like his colleagues in the provinces. This point of law has never been settled.

The State is in this Court represented by four Government commissaries, chosen as a rule from the auditors of the Council of State, their nominal chief being the secretary-general of the prefecture. One of the officials of the prefect's office acts as registrar, and is styled secretary-registrar.

A seat on the Prefecture Council in the department of the Seine is not obtained in the ordinary course of official promotion. Sometimes clerks in the civil service, who have already gained a good official position, seek and obtain the appointment; sometimes an ex-member of the Chamber of Deputies, under a temporary cloud with his constituents, canvasses for the post as a field for the employment of his energies. For a seat on the Prefecture Council, though much sought after, is very far from being a sinecure.

The members of this body are paid at the same rate as judges of the Court of First Instance; their duties are very absorbing, and for the due performance of them require a very extensive acquaintance with administrative law. On this account admission to the Council Board was for many years only accorded to men of ripe experience. Not till recently have young gentlemen fresh from the law schools and dreaming of future prefectureships been allowed to make it the first step in an administrative career. But young Frenchmen, if shrewd by nature or well-advised, who

---

[1] Literally "rainy." *Pluviôse* was a month in the Revolutionary Calendar of 1793. It corresponded to the period January 20th to February 19th.

look forward to a post of secretary-general or sub-prefect, are careful not to begin their career by a seat on the Prefecture Council. The latter might aptly be compared to a well or a prison. The difficulty is not to get in, but to get out of it.

The saying "When the house goes, everything goes" would seem to be especially applicable to the Prefecture Council of the Seine. Every structural alteration in the Paris streets brings it an increase of contentious business. In virtue of the great principle of the separation of powers—to which we bow—it has special cognisance of all disputes arising between public contractors and the administration ; also in all complaints made by private persons of damage arising to them from the acts of these contractors, but not, says the law, if caused by the act of the administration. For these last, complainants must apply at the building on the other corner of the quay.

Procedure before the Prefecture Council is of a summary kind. Notices of proceedings are given by the agents of the administrative authority, and in 1889 a law was passed giving statutory validity to the whole of the expeditious methods which had been introduced in course of time. This law has moreover established a new practice in cases of urgency, a kind of application by summons in chambers, which adds to the advantages already offered by a rapid and cheap mode of procedure. But—the inevitable *but* —owing to the special character of the suits which they have to decide, the Prefecture Councils very frequently resort to the assistance of experts. There is a regular list of accredited experts, public engineers, civil engineers, architects, who all covet a share in the honour and profit to be obtained from these judicial commissions, where the suitors pay the bill and bear the delay. And thus, nothing has been changed !

A ratepayer who wishes to obtain the reduction or discharge of an improper assessment must apply to the Prefecture Council. Under this head alone the Council for the department of the Seine pronounces on from fifteen to twenty thousand appeals every year, though, it is true, they have been first examined by the direct taxation authorities, to whom they are submitted.

If you have a watch-dog assessed as an article of luxury on the many-coloured papers which our tax-collectors distribute with a liberal hand, complain to the Council ; it will decide on the animal's character.

As to repressive jurisdiction, the Prefecture Council takes exclusive cognisance of offences against the law of public highways; with other roads it has no concern. Breaches of the regulations as to military service are also within its competence, and owing to the enormous compass of the fortifications at Paris it has plenty of work in this particular.

It would be impossible to enumerate in detail all the duties that constantly or occasionally devolve on the members of a Prefecture Council, for, in a thousand cases, the prefect has the right, when he thinks fit, to delegate his authority to one of the counsellors.

There are certain special cases when the Prefecture Council must be consulted. The Council gives leave to take legal proceedings against municipalities and public departments. The counsellors audit the accounts of tax-collectors, when their amount does not exceed the sum which brings these functionaries under the direct supervision of the Cour des Comptes.[1]

They preside over the acceptance of tenders for public contracts, and the number of commissions in which they take part is incalculable.

The member of a Prefecture Council is a true Jack-of-all-Trades; he renders more services than one can imagine; he is a functionary removable at will and badly paid. Yet to the great public, who are ignorant of the reason of his existence, he remains a mystery. In every session of Parliament some Deputy, a fanatic in the cause of retrenchment, springs up and demands his extinction, and every time he is saved by the Minister, who is well aware of his value.

However great our innate respect for the sacred principle of the separation of powers, it cannot be denied that a prefecture counsellor in many places does twice the work of an ordinary judge; but, unless a complete transformation takes place in our administrative system, it is difficult to see how so useful a member of the public service is to be suppressed.

THE COUNCIL OF PRUD'HOMMES

All round the great square hall, which was once called by a facetious attorney the "Central Hall," are to be found the offices of the Councils of Prud'hommes. They have been but recently lodged in the Tribunal of Commerce, and are little special

[1] See Ch. I. p. 7.

tribunals which determine disputes between workmen and their employers with cheapness, smoothness, and impartiality. There are four boards, each of which takes charge of some particular industry. There is the board for the metal trades, the board for chemical manufactures, that for various industries, and the last for textile fabrics. Each board holds four sittings a month, and is composed of three workmen and four employers one week, and of four workmen and three employers the following week. Every case before being brought to a hearing must first pass before the board of conciliation; this consists of two judges, who try, with admirable conscientiousness and patience, to effect an agreement between the two parties who wish to go to law. Not belonging to the class of those who merely administer justice, but also to that of those who pay for it, they know well that the cheapest justice is still heavy for the purse of humble folk, and feel that a bad compromise is better than a good lawsuit. Each tries hard to impress this maxim on the most determined litigant. So much earnestness and persuasion do they throw into their arguments that they manage to effect an amicable arrangement in a large number of cases, about half of those commenced being ended before them in this way. In other cases, they give the irreconcilable disputants a letter inviting them to appear that day week before the general board.

M. ALARY, WORKING PRINTER, PRESIDENT OF THE PRUD'HOMMES 1879-1890.

On the appointed day, the workman and his employer, each of them a good deal heated, are punctual in their attendance. The appearance of the Court is curious. There is neither solemnity nor splendour. Rooms with bare walls, and wooden benches for the public; for the prud'hommes there is a long desk, separated from the audience by a breast-high barrier. The only ornament consists of a bust of the Republic on a bracket. Authority is represented by a solitary policeman. But he, being entrusted with the duty of maintaining order which nothing disturbs, spends his time conscientiously in sleep. There are neither decorations nor gowns ; the seven members of the general board, like the two members of the conciliation board, have, for sole official mark, a silver medal suspended from the neck by a silk ribbon. There are no formalities, no formulas ; no oath and no pleadings. Every member of the board can speak or ask questions when he likes. At the bar all alike, both men and women, speak in their own defence ; the whole thing is settled in a sort of family meeting, among persons who know the value of time and of money, so hard to earn. Those on the bench do not preside but judge ; the parties do not plead, they explain ; and the cause of justice loses nothing.

Yet the spectacle, with all its simplicity, is not cheering to the reflective mind ; for what strikes one is the smallness, ridiculous were it not distressing, of the sums in dispute. The parties here are not struggling for lost savings or endangered capital ; it is their bread, earned by the sweat of their brow, for which they are contending at the bar with gleaming eyes and empty stomachs.

Just listen to some of the cases which come before the tribunal.

Here comes a workman from whom his employer withholds a few days' pay. The workman alleges that he was hired for ten days ; the employer replies that the time fixed was one week. And the difference between the two sums is nine francs three francs per day—and three francs a day in Paris !

Here are shoemakers who claim nineteen sous for making a pair of cloth-boots, usually sold for eight or nine francs in a shop.

Here are cabinetmakers who have been refused forty francs for making a piece of furniture in antique style, for which the purchaser will pay thirty louis!

Then come little sempstresses who claim twenty or twenty-five sous for a garment, which, by the confession even of the employers, has taken ten hours' work. There are makers of neckties who give their work-girls three or four francs for a *dozen* silk bows to be retailed at five francs a-piece! There are young apprentices of fifteen with drawn features, round shoulders, weary feet, broken down by long rounds and heavy burdens, to whom dressmakers or laundresses refuse payment of wages amounting to fifteen or twenty francs per month, and the long succession goes on in this way till evening. These cases are in themselves uninteresting. But what a mass of hidden suffering they suggest! They do not, like ordinary civil suits, reveal ruined families, deserted hearths, shipwrecked happiness. They show us the human being, who suffers in his body, who toils for something to eat, and has not wherewithal to satisfy his hunger. To sum up, a sad little Court is this Council of Prud'hommes. A tribunal reserved for poor suitors and petty suits, and where there is nothing to tempt curiosity. But, stop a moment. Before this humble board, which aims at making peace, the real struggle in progress is that between labour and capital, the same which perhaps to-morrow may convulse the world.

CHAPTER XXVIII

EVOLUTION AT THE PALACE OF JUSTICE

THE Palace of Justice and the Tribunal of Commerce having been visited, our tour of the law courts is now done. But we have an instinctive desire to survey the building as a whole, after having admired it in its details. The visitor, quitting it almost against his will, returns, as if to concentrate in one last glance upon the vast façade the spectacle of the marvels which he has seen within. He seeks unconsciously to compress his scattered memories into one final emotion, which may be the sum and substance of the whole. After our walk through chambers and galleries, halls and cells, we cannot leave the building we have traversed without giving it one final look as we retire.

The first thing that seems to strike our eye as we are looking back is a figure which eclipses all the others : that of *Justice*. The Palace is no longer anything but a frame ; its inmates become secondary characters, and, though we have nowhere painted it, the figure of Justice seems to start forth on every side. There she is in an actual portrait ; the painting bears its date of 1891. A strange presentment, startling in the discordance of its features without unity or harmony ; made of bric-à-brac, and attired in a harlequin's cloak. The allegorical figures on which our contemporary artists spend so much time have as a matter of fact nothing in common with Justice as she is. To be realistic, they should, instead of the classic vestments, clothe their model in motley borrowed from antiquity and touched up by a modern costumier. A dress of the first empire trimmed with polished jet bugles in the present fashion, beneath which the dress-improver of a year or two back should be apparent, would suit best. At her feet, close to the traditional balance, the place of the mirror of truth should be taken by a magnifying glass.

The man who undertakes to model a bizarre figure like this will have struck the true note. He will have faithfully reproduced the mixture of antiquities and novelties, the combination of superannuated usages and fresh ideas, among which Themis at the end of the nineteenth century divides her fancy. He will have shown her as she is ; not as an old goddess trying to become young again, but as an Immortal undergoing a slow but constant transformation.

Transformation ! It is the word of our transitional age. The law of Heraclitus, " All things move and become transformed," has never found a stronger application in the moral world than at the present day, when man no longer opposes any resistance to progress. But nowhere does the evolution of material things show itself so distinctly as at the Palace of Justice. Here the truth of the principle formulated by the old philosopher, and taken up again by the English school, stands forth in the building as in what goes on there. The mason and the advocate are both its agents, and, if the walls reveal it to you, the pleadings within confirm the first impression.

In this last chapter we shall sketch very briefly the evolution of legal life, so as to separate the ancient and the modern, which, in the building we have described, live side by side with one another in perfect harmony. For this purpose it will be enough to classify the documents, exhibited in our work in logical order, chronologically, and to group them according to their age or nature. Thus analysed into its various elements, the Palace of Justice will be seen to consist of four distinct Palaces : the ancient Palace, the Palace of yesterday, the Palace of to-morrow, and the Palace of the future.

THE ANCIENT PALACE

We first find the Palace of time long past, the Palace of royal ordinances, the Palace of *présidents à mortier*, the Palace of *gens du roy*. Let us view its antiquity with respect; it is contemporary with the Sainte-Chapelle and equally picturesque. A legacy from the judicial system of old days, it was overthrown by the Revolution, but it has arisen again and is still very far from dead. We have seen it in all its glory, at the beginning of the legal year, when the sceptical crowd of its inhabitants go as a body of formal worshippers to hear the *Veni Creator* of the Red Mass; and to perpetuate the Solemn Sitting, a tradition which only endures because it is a tradition. We have met with it again here and there during the course of the year. Quaint costumes and quaint usages, ratification of letters of pardon, sales by the "auction light," taking of the oath by probationers, meetings of columns, constitution of the Bar as a privileged corporation, with its prud'-hommes (masters with masters under them!)[1] with right to inflict punishment—all this belongs to the past. To it also belongs the curious cap and gown by which the French man of law of Edison's day is attired almost in the fashion of a doctor of the age of Molière. The doctor of to-day appears at the bar in ordinary dress; but the advocate who examines him still wears the robe of Master Pierre Pathelin. A little time ago the wearer of this robe was forbidden to cultivate a beard; the advocate had to shave his face clean, and the razor might be considered an instrument of the profession. The most curious thing is that the world of the Palace of Justice regards these little inconveniences as prerogatives, which it will never willingly renounce. A *bâtonnier* who would not dare to cross the Seine dressed up in his court robes would rather resign than plead in an ordinary coat. And yet the same man would look on an English barrister's wig as intensely comic!

THE PALACE OF YESTERDAY

All this side of the Palace is more than a hundred and fifty years behind the age; but, though it shows us justice under its most ancient

---

[1] The French is *maîtres sur maîtres*. It is needless to remind the reader that all French barristers are styled *maître*, not *monsieur*.

guise, it is not the sole representative of a past time to be found here. There is something besides ceremonies and costumes which belong to another epoch ; ideas, the ideas of certain magistrates especially, belong to another age, more near to ours, but none the less quite of the past. Is this the result of worship of the past, of education, or merely of temperament ? We will not inquire, but this is unquestionable ; on every step of the ladder may be found some judge who bears about him a strange air of being behind the times. He is as *provincial* in his life as a countryman who has lost his way on the boulevards. Like the Gascon who thought himself a Parisian because he had learnt the guide-book of the capital by heart, he imagines that the Code contains all the rules of modern life, nor does he take any count of present manners. The compromises which the world has made in many ways with strict morality fill him with astonishment and indignation.

Suppose, for instance, that a man keeps a mistress. In our present civilisation this is certainly an irregularity. The Church forbids it, and the Code, a defender of the family relation, has taken the ecclesiastical prohibition as a basis for its enactments. Nevertheless, it is common enough to see bachelors seek before marriage the happiness to which it is the mayor's special duty to give legal sanction. Many magistrates—when seated on the bench—choose to regard all these irregular marriages as highly reprehensible. When a bachelor of twenty-five appears before them, they do not fail to say to him in a severe tone : " The information we have received regarding you is not unfavourable ; but you often came home very late at night ; you *no doubt* keep a mistress ! " The reproach varies according to the case. If the accused has been surprised some evening when he was killing time in questionable society : " You were giving yourself up to debauchery ! " blurts out the president. If, on the contrary, the accused indulged in what Parisian slang has picturesquely styled *le vieux collage*, the judge cries out in scornful tones : " You were living with a concubine, the woman X——, and you passed her off as your own wife ! " Between the two formulas there is a whole ascending scale, the maximum of severity being always reserved for the man who lives in concubinage. This old-fashioned rigour is sometimes increased by an extraordinary ignorance of practical matters. Certain judges of the Court of Appeal have never got beyond the experience they acquired during their student

period (1845–1848). More especially, they do not seem to know
that money, since their youth, has lost three-fourths of its purchas-
ing power.   In connection with this, there is the sagacious remark
made by the president of the Paris Assize Court at a recent trial.
"You robbed your employer of 300 francs (£12); and with this you,
for a whole month, lived in luxury with a courtesan!"   And in the
same train of ideas is the remark of another president, who,
speaking of a fair leader of the gay world, said: "A woman
living alone at Paris could not spend 19,000 francs (£760) in the
course of the year."

Even magistrates who are younger, more intelligent and
altogether more sensible, occasionally let slip puerile reflections
of this nature. Witness, for instance, the advocate-general—one of
the most distinguished at the law courts—who one day put this
question to a celebrated murderer: "You tried to make your
victims believe that you were the owner of vast estates in the neighbourhood of Madrid!   You even sometimes presented yourself
before them in the dress of a Spanish grandee!"[1]

This simplicity is extraordinary.   It clashes with modern progress, and makes us say that the class of magistrates just described
forms yet another separate Palace, which is not that of the remote
past, nor that of to-day; it is the Palace of the generation before
last. Bound as it were in the trammels of a procedure which is
ridiculously slow for a generation that travels by rail and talks by
telephone, these judges, eminent as they may be, cannot realise the
fact that the society which moves before their eyes is not that of
1806 ; and that though the Code remains unchanged, the world's
ideas, its prejudices, its theories and its wants have undergone a
change.

So much for the magistrate who seems never to have lived at
all. We may pass over those who serve as links in a period of
transition and the few exceptional specimens described in the
preceding pages. Let us take a look at the ultra-modern type.
He is not the man to shave his chin in obedience to traditional
ideas. Tradition? He thinks of it as little as a man condemned
to death thinks of his loss of political rights. For precedents and
predecessors he cares not one single straw. One thing alone

---

[1] The French *château en Espagne* is a phrase meaning the same as the English
"castle in the air." This comic rascal's victims must therefore have been as guileless as
his judge.

occupies his thoughts : the effect produced outside by the sentence he pronounces, and, above all, by the smartness and vigour with which he rallies the unfortunates who stand before him.

A cunning master of fence in these contests of wit, he reminds one of a man taking pistol exercise at a cardboard target. He is well acquainted with all the prejudices of the moment; but if he is on his guard against them, he shows none of them. His sole object in life is to create a sensation ; only let people talk about him and his ambition is attained. He pretends to have a horror of the journalist, but if by chance he meets one in the galleries when leaving Court in the evening, he never fails to whisper a word in his ear to remind him of the exact spelling of his name, it being often mutilated by the printer. This kind of judge is happily not very common at the Palace of Justice. But we must draw his portrait if only to bring out more strongly the character of those to whom he presents a contrast. He represents neither the Palace of yesterday nor that of to-day, nor, we may hope, that of a day to come.

THE PALACE OF TO-DAY

Between these two varieties comes the representative of the modern world ; the man of 1891 who is trying to let in some of the outside air, to freshen up the stale atmosphere of the Courts, where every one is absorbed in the contemplation of ancient texts. It is the advocate who more especially plays this part of the *vir novus*. It is he who stands in the breach against the champions of outworn doctrines and musty sentiments. Not that he is a Revolutionary. Far from it ; but, in spite of himself, he cannot help yielding to the laws of evolution. He knows the people well, for he has been among them ; he has welcomed them to his chambers, that confessional where, though the light can enter, the secrets told remain honourably kept. He has listened to the complaints of his visitors, and seen their tears. He knows the sufferings of the poor and the sorrows of the middle class ; and he is able to make them known, and resolved to impress them on the judges who from the height of the bench look coldly down upon the level of things in general. At the Palace of Justice he represents naturalism as opposed to the idealism of the Advocate-General. The Public

Advocate invokes great principles, and speaks in the name of justice, the family, the rights of property and other commonplaces; it is for the advocate to uncover the sores of society, to show its scars, to tell the tale of its misery and its griefs.

Hence come the different styles of eloquence preferred by the Public Prosecutor and the counsel for the defence. The representative of the former still retains almost all the rhetorical and redundant forms of the old parliamentary harangues; he is invariably inflated and grandiose; the advocate (we are speaking of the new school) tries to be precise and clear, to secure attention by simplicity, and to awaken feeling by a plain picture of the truth. The new generation is on the way to create a new eloquence, of a mathematical type. Less ornate, but more solid than the old, it will in reality require more knowledge and greater talent. The orator will vociferate less, he will not gesticulate, but he will be more convincing. In ten years from now the transformation will be complete. One symptom proves it. Certain young representatives of the Ministry of Justice have also had recourse to these simpler oratorical methods, and their success has shown that the least pretentious eloquence is the most effective; that judges and jurymen are more easily moved by analysis of causes than by declamation; and that the report of an expert in medical jurisprudence carries more weight than the most magnificent peroration.

The day may come when this change will make itself felt universally. The two sides of the bar will abandon, the one its grandiloquent "opening speech," the other its thrilling "reply;" instead of these they will discuss the actual charges, examine them seriously and wisely with the careful attention of physicians who differ as to the proper remedy to apply. Justice will then have taken a great step forwards; instead of being a kind of "cult," with ceremonial and ritual, it will become a school for the study of moral diseases; the Palace of Justice instead of a temple will become the most imposing and the most august of our hospitals.

THE PALACE OF TO-MORROW

The time for this change is not yet, and the Palace of which we have just been dreaming belongs to the far future.

But what of this Palace of the future? For obvious reasons it

is difficult to be precise about it.   At the present day the air is full
of reforms.   In the Chamber of Deputies and the press, the most
various projects are being constantly brought forward.   No judicial
incident, however unimportant, takes place without giving rise to
a crop of suggestions.   But, as everybody knows, there's many
a slip 'twixt cup and lip ; between the idea of a reform,
however desirable, and its realisation.   It seems pretty certain,
however, that justice is tending to become more simple, less
slow, less showy, and consequently less picturesque, but more
practical.   The object of all innovations is to shorten delays
and to make justice more accessible to humble folk, that is
to those who most need its protection.   The jurisdiction of justices of peace is being extended, Boards of Conciliation are
being multiplied, attempts are being made to develop the
system of arbitration.   The farther we go the more marked
will be the change, the greater the modification in the outward
aspect of judicial life.

For example, it is highly probable that we shall see judges
appointed by election[1] and the robe abolished ; the right of
audience in Court no longer confined to advocates, or, in other
words, the exercise of the profession of advocate no longer
dependent on the will of a " Council of the Order ;" this last
change alone would be the beginning of a new system at the
Palace of Justice.

Without going so far as to speculate on the overthrow of all
" traditions," it is not rash to anticipate a whole mass of legislative
enactments which cannot fail to react on the relations between the
judges and the judged.   To this number belong the reform of the
Code of Civil Procedure and of the Code of Criminal Instruction, the
revision of certain chapters of the Civil Code, and the remodelling
of certain repressive laws.   The number of problems which present
themselves and call for solution is certainly beyond count.   Thus
many people look on the usher, whose popularity has never been
excessive, as a useless and a costly luxury, and in the vast majority
of cases the post might be abolished with advantage.   Others cannot
very well appreciate the division of labour between the advocate and

---

[1] The election of judges existed during the Revolutionary period.   As might have
been expected, it gave rise to the most scandalous judicial partisanship.   It was abolished
by Napoleon Bonaparte on his accession to the Consulate.

the solicitor.   Others would greatly like to see a jury in the Correctional Court; convinced that despite some inevitable mistakes, temporary magistrates are better fitted to judge their fellow-men than professional magistrates, who are insensibly impelled by the very habits of their life to see in the prisoner before them only a subject for a sentence.   Even the question of the advantages of *one* judge, with a jury in civil cases, has been canvassed, and the idea has given rise to many a debate.

The phrase "as few judges as possible" has become popular, just like the new political watch-word, "as little government as possible."   And some bold spirits have gone so far as to demand obligatory arbitration in civil disputes.   The latter acknowledge that the decisions of arbitrators may not be always in strict accordance with the letter of the law; but they are pretty certain to coincide with common sense, which is a sufficient consolation.

They also maintain that under a system of arbitration it will be possible, without much difficulty, to ensure competence, which they hold is more apparent than real under the present system, where it seems the judge is presumed to be omniscient.   The suitors, they say, will, in the natural course of things, be brought to choose those arbitrators who are best suited by profession or aptitude to settle the difference in hand.   Would it ever occur to two men of letters to submit their disputes to a tribunal of cobblers ?   Certain literary and artistic societies compel their members to submit all professional quarrels to the arbitration of the governing body of the society itself, or of a committee appointed by it.   Is not this a step towards arbitration obligatory by law ?

But these are theories of reform whose practical value might be debated till the end of time.   One of them alone has the happy privilege of obtaining the support of all who appear before the courts, and that is the endeavour to reduce the cost of justice.   Serious efforts have been made to bring about this reform.   But it is to be feared that many years must pass away before we can hope to see the famous principle of "justice for nothing" applied in all its strictness.   The dream of the future is the discovery of a judicial system which, together with absolutely free justice, will ensure the appointment of magistrates—permanent or temporary —possessed in their several stations of character, competence, knowledge, and conscientiousness.   When sitting in judgment on their fellow-men, they will have but one care, the discovery of the truth, and but one aim, the application of the law. They will regard the accused as innocent till the very moment when the verdict has been given against him. And, models of dignified and calm urbanity, they will make no partial distinction between the mighty and the weak.

But this ideal Palace belongs not to the immediate, nor to the far future. It is a Palace in the air.

THE END.

RICHARD CLAY AND SONS, LIMITED, LONDON AND BUNGAY